Praise for Ca
Just a Heartbeat Away

"An utterly satisfying and delicious read. One for the keeper shelf!"
—Jill Shalvis, *New York Times* bestselling author

"Gorgeous, brilliant, with characters so unique and real they leap right off the page. It's a master class in achy breaky yearning. Don't start this one late at night unless you don't need to do anything the next day except for pre-ordering the next one."
—Sarina Bowen, *USA TODAY* bestselling author of the True North series

"Emotionally intense and real, *Just a Heartbeat Away* touches the soft place in your soul. Cara Bastone's debut novel will warm you from the inside out and stay with you long after you finish the book."
—Christie Craig, *New York Times* bestselling author

CARA BASTONE

just a *heartbeat* away

ISBN-13: 978-1-335-04537-9

Just a Heartbeat Away

Recycling programs
for this product may
not exist in your area.

HQN
22 Adelaide St. West, 40th Floor
Toronto, Ontario M5H 4E3, Canada
www.Harlequin.com

Printed in U.S.A.

For Jon

just a
heartbeat
away

CHAPTER ONE

SEBASTIAN DORNER USED to be the kind of man who knew how to sit across a table from a woman. He used to know when to slant her a slice of white smile. He used to know when to unbutton the top button of one of his tailored suits. He used to know how to signal a waiter with two fingers and a slick nod toward an empty glass. He used to know how to lean across that table and brush soft hair back from softer skin.

But Cora's tank of an SUV had gotten hit by some drunk college kid's Camry, and she was gone. And Sebastian Dorner was gone, too. The car accident that had taken his wife's life had sliced neatly through a tether he hadn't realized he'd been leaning all his weight against. He was falling.

Had been falling for the last six months.

And now he wasn't even the kind of man who remembered how to comb his hair. He scraped a dry palm over the back of his head and, glancing down, realized his shirt was misbuttoned.

True, there was a woman sitting across the table from him. But they weren't in some swanky, dark bar. He couldn't even get his knees underneath the preschool-size worktable. The sickening smell of graham crackers went straight to his gut. He'd been here ten minutes, and he hadn't been able to raise his eyes to the woman's face, let alone to the happy patchwork of art dotting the walls.

What if one of those drawings was Matty's? He didn't

think he could bear to look at something Matty had created. The idea that his four-year-old son was living a life Sebastian knew nothing about was so brightly painful, he couldn't move his gaze past the crayoned-up tabletop.

"Mr. Dorner." Her soft, quiet voice was soothing, sure. But even silk sheets could scrape a sunburn. Sebastian was too raw for this. He was too nothing. Too nowhere. Too no one. "Thank you for coming today. I know… I know this is a really hard time for you and Matty."

He grunted.

There. That was almost human. Somebody get out the gold medals.

"I wanted to talk to you about some things I've been noticing with Matty."

That got Sebastian's attention. His eyes shot up to the preschool teacher's face.

"Is he all right?" Sebastian restrained his wince. What a dumb question. Of course the kid wasn't all right. His mom had just died.

"Actually," the woman—Miss Derossi? Miss Desposa? Something like that—said, "Matty is doing really well, academically. I'm sure you're well aware of how bright he is. And creative! He made me a bracelet out of old crayon wrappers the other week." She paused, like Sebastian might respond to that, but when there was nothing, she continued on. "And from a grieving perspective, he's doing very well."

Well? Was there any *good* way to grieve? He almost scoffed. "What do you mean?"

"I mean he's a healthy kid. He's not bottling anything up. He cries sometimes, gets mad sometimes, but more often than not, he's playing and happy. He'll talk to other kids, or me, about his mom. He's done a lot of drawings of her, too."

Sebastian grunted.

"But I've noticed a few things that have me worried." She cleared her throat. "About you."

Again, Sebastian scraped that dry palm over his unkempt hair. "Me?"

"Yes." She shifted in her chair. She didn't look uncomfortable or judgmental. That, more than anything, would soothe Sebastian when he would think about this conversation again and again in the months to come. "Mr. Dorner, Matty is showing some preliminary signs of neglect."

Neglect?

She could have reached across the table and smacked his stubbled face and she wouldn't have shocked him more. *Neglect.* The word was like a never-ending knife through his gut. Every time he thought it was done running him through, suddenly there was ten more feet of blade.

Neglect.

"I'm—I'm sorry?" He tried to clear the gruff out of his throat. "I don't understand."

Her dark eyes, the only thing he'd really remember about her appearance later, were calm and held his very steadily. "He hasn't been showing up to school dressed properly for the weather, and his clothes are often…unclean. It seems like he isn't bathing regularly, especially since he often shows up with yesterday's paint on his hands and arms. And though I got him on the school's lunch program, you haven't applied for the scholarship help. I could get in trouble for allowing an unregistered kid to have a free lunch every day."

Humiliation was a hot lick of flame from every side. It had been two months since Cora's parents had headed back to White Plains. And his friends Mary and Tyler were a huge help, but they had lives; they couldn't be there every single day.

How did I let this get so fucked?

There was nowhere to look. Nothing to say. All he could think about was his stupid fucking misbuttoned shirt. "He told me he always got lunch at school. I just thought…"

He trailed off because he had no idea what he'd thought. He'd trusted a four-year-old and never thought to double-check. Just like he'd trusted a four-year-old who'd said that Mommy let him wash himself and Mommy let him pick out his own clothes every day. He'd never double-checked any of it.

Neglect.

The word was out of the jar and it was so big, looming and leering, that he knew he'd never get it back in. That word was, apparently, his new asshole of a best friend. His life partner now.

And he fucking deserved it. He'd let his kid come to school with no lunch. Yesterday's clothes. Dirty hair just like his daddy.

"Fuck," he muttered into the dry hands that he'd dragged up to cover his horrified expression.

"I don't know what you're going through, Mr. Dorner, no one can. But I've lost people in my family, and… I know what it feels like to spin off into nothing."

He glanced up. Was that what he was doing? Spinning into nothing? God. Sure felt like it.

"There were some things that really helped me get my feet back on the ground, and I made one of them for you." She slid a piece of paper over to him and it was a shocking white to his stinging eyes. A bright block of accusation sitting there over top of the spirals of green and purple crayon on the tabletop.

Neglect.

It was a checklist. All the things he needed to do every day to take care of his son. A sharp gasp of shame had

Sebastian coughing into his elbow. "What's this?" He already knew.

"Just something to help you keep everything straight." She leaned over and tapped firmly at each bullet point. "Three square meals with a snack after school. There should be at least one fruit and one vegetable at each meal. Even breakfast. Which, you know, breakfast vegetables are tricky for everyone so don't worry about that so much. But definitely for lunch. He also needs a main course and a little side. Something to drink, too. I made a list of good options here, all things you can pick up at the grocery store. Or even have delivered. Now, do you use a laundromat? Or a washer and dryer at home?"

He just stared at her.

She plunged on. "Well, I included the number for a pickup/drop-off laundry service. I thought it would be a relief for a little while not to have to worry about it. They bring it back folded and everything. For bathing, these are some signs that your kid is ready to bathe by himself." She handed him a pamphlet. "Although I don't think Matty is quite there yet, so you should still be doing a lot of it for him."

He sat there, numb and dumb, while she went through each point. There really was a remarkable lack of judgment in her tone.

He steepled his hands over his nose and mouth and leaned his elbows forward on his knees, so awkwardly tall next to the small table. "I can't even imagine what you must think of me right now."

She sighed and leaned back. "Mr. Dorner, you want to know what I think? I think that life is hard. And even harder when you've just lost someone. I also think that sometimes it helps for somebody to tell you what to do next. And this—" she tapped the checklist "—is what you need to do next."

"Matty!" Sebastian called down the hallway. "Carrots or zucchini?"

"What?" His four-year-old mini-me appeared in the doorway of the kitchen.

"Do you want carrots or zucchini in your lunch today?" It had been two months since his meeting with Miss DeRosa—he'd checked with Matty on her name—and Sebastian was really hoping that the rusty, cranking feeling in his chest was a sign that the gears were starting to turn. He slapped a dishtowel over his shoulder, swigged lukewarm coffee, and ignored the rib-deep exhaustion that had weighted him to the bed for an extra fifteen minutes that morning.

"I think you have to cook zucchini, Daddy."

"Nah," Sebastian said as he eyeballed the vegetable sticks he'd shoved into a Ziploc. "It's like cucumber." He snapped a quick bite of one of the extra zucchini sticks he'd just sliced and immediately spat it into the sink. "Yup. You're right. Carrots it is."

He slid the final item into the green cloth lunchbox and turned to his son. Sebastian's brow furrowed.

"You're in shorts."

"So?" Matty puckered his blunt little face in a look that Sebastian recognized very well at this point.

"So, it's February in New York." He put the exact same expression on his own face.

"Fine. Pants." Matty turned but quickly jumped back around. "But no mittens. Nonnegotiable!"

From his little four-year-old mouth the word came out much closer to "nah-nuh-goshe-bo." Nonnegotiables were something that Sebastian and Matty had been talking a lot about over the last two months. It was a running list they kept. Things that they couldn't argue over, no matter what.

Sebastian admitted that maybe they weren't using the word completely right, but still, he liked the list.

– Daddy home for dinner, bath and bedtime. Non-
  negotiable.
– Matty eats one green thing every day. Non-
  negotiable.
– We don't talk about getting a dog again until
  Matty's birthday. Nonnegotiable.

It was a good list. And the first thing had been the
easiest to keep up with. Two months ago, Sebastian had
walked out of Matty's classroom and called his architecture firm. He was cashing in on the vacation he'd stored
up over the last decade. It would be all used up fairly
soon, and Sebastian wasn't completely sure what he was
going to do next, but for now, the only thing he was worrying about was Miss DeRosa's checklist.

It was taped to his fridge. There was a fingerprint of
tomato sauce in one corner, scribbled notes to himself all
over it, words crossed out and added. It had been a life-
line for him. Guided him more than he ever would have
expected.

It was a little cure-all. He wasn't sure what kinds of
things Matty should do after school? The checklist knew.

– Playdates (arrange with other parents at school)
– Children's museum (if he likes it, invest in a
  membership)
– The library (Matty can even get his own library
  card!)
– No more than half an hour of TV each day (anything on Netflix Kids acceptable)

And on and on. It was a single sheet of paper, but, to Sebastian, it was a roadmap that he never planned on deviat-
ing from.

Also taped on the fridge? The number for a grief counselor he'd seen for the first time last week. Sebastian's skin had shrunk two full sizes while he'd sat in the pastel waiting room. If he'd learned one thing from his meeting with Miss DeRosa, it was that he had no desire to be blindsided by another grown-up again. So, he'd rehearsed what he was going to say to Dr. Feldman. Rehearsed it. Like a play.

Feldman had seen through it in about four seconds and Sebastian had left the office with four inches of pamphlets, permission to hire the occasional babysitter, and the distinct feeling that Sebastian Dorner was currently trapped inside someone else's life.

Matty appeared back in the kitchen in jeans and a Captain America zip-up.

"Mittens can't be a nonnegotiable," Sebastian told his son. He chuckled at the immediate outrage that bloomed over Matty's face. That was new. The chuckling. It was too new to feel good yet. "But how about this? No mittens if it's more than forty degrees outside. That's reasonable."

"What's the temperature right now?" Matty asked suspiciously.

"Check for yourself." Sebastian nodded his head toward the window thermometer they kept. He knew Matty could read it. Kid was smart as a whip. "Hey, is Miss DeRosa still checking your lunch?"

"Sometimes. It's forty-two degrees!" Matty pumped one triumphant fist in the air and had his dad chuckling again.

"All right. Make sure she checks it today."

Sebastian scrawled a few words onto a torn piece of paper and tucked it against Matty's juice box.

That night, when Sebastian's shirt was wet across the chest from Matty's bath and his son was soundly snoozing in his room, Sebastian unpacked the lunchbox. He found the same crumpled piece of paper he'd sent that morning.

There was his own cramped chicken scratch writing: *How am I doing?*

And then there was a drawing that she'd done, this Miss DeRosa. It was of a stick figure hitting a ball out of a baseball park. The stick figure was labeled *you* and the ball was labeled *life*.

Sebastian's face pulled into a surprised laugh.

He was knocking life out of the park. Well. Imagine that.

Without thinking too much on it, he went ahead and taped that up on the fridge, too.

CHAPTER TWO

Two years later

SEBASTIAN COULD NOT believe he was scrolling through a dating app. What the hell was his life? He tossed the phone to the side and tipped his head back on one armrest of his new couch.

"Come on, you can't give up that easily," Tyler said as he sauntered back into the room. He handed Sebastian a beer and tossed his feet up on the coffee table as he plunked into the recliner.

Sebastian recalled the horrifying last hour of his life. Choosing a profile picture. Distilling his life into a handful of words and a—sweet Jesus—smattering of emojis. *You call that easy?*

Tyler and Sebastian had met in kindergarten and hadn't questioned a good thing. They still didn't. They disagreed more often than they agreed, but they'd drink poison for each other if it came to it. Hell, Tyler had even moved back to Brooklyn after Cora had died. He'd claimed that he was just done with LA, but Sebastian knew that his friend had come home for him and Matty.

That was the majority of the reason Sebastian had even downloaded the damn dating app in the first place. Tyler had *insisted* it was a good idea.

"Hand it over," Tyler demanded, holding his hand out for the phone.

Sebastian complied and chuckled as Crabby, their two-year-old poodle mix, immediately bolted over the second he saw Sebastian's hand moving. Crabby blinked up at his owner, poofy tail wagging furiously, like, *got any ear scratches you might wanna distribute?*

Sebastian obliged and scratched behind the dog's one white ear. "I really don't think this is the way I find somebody." He nodded toward the phone.

Tyler scoffed. "Seb, this is how *everybody* finds somebody. Here, what about her?" He flipped the phone around and showed a picture of a very pretty girl on a beach.

Sebastian lifted a dark eyebrow. "Tyler, I'm forty-two. With a kid. And enough gray hairs to prove both. I'm not dating some twenty-five-year-old cupcake in a thong bikini."

"You don't have to make a life with this woman. Just take her to some bar, buy her a drink and then let her remind you why God gave us opposable thumbs."

"You're a moron."

"Actually, I'm a genius. You're just too pedestrian to recognize my brilliance. How about her?"

He tossed the phone over and Sebastian flipped through the profile of a professional-looking woman with chin-length blond hair and a very white smile. Apparently, she was a wine connoisseur. Sebastian clicked the phone off and needled one corner of it into his brow.

"What if I'm just not ready for this? I mean, what if I get to some date with some woman and I'm just…lost? Or thinking about Cora."

Tyler swept a hand out. "Then you get there and you're lost and thinking about Cora, and you come home. And then I come over, and we have a beer."

"I used to be good at this."

"I remember. Used to steal chicks out from under me all the time. I was relieved when you got married."

Sebastian scoffed. Tyler had *not* been relieved when he'd gotten married. He'd actively lobbied against it. He'd never particularly gotten along with Cora. Cora was a perfectionist who had planned out every single second of her days; Tyler was a contrarian who enjoyed throwing everyone's rhythm off. Not exactly a match made in friendship heaven.

More than that, though, Tyler had never understood why Sebastian's response to Cora's unexpected pregnancy was *marriage*. In fact, he'd thought it was downright batshit. "Father and husband don't have to go hand in hand, Seb," he'd pleaded. "Come on, man. You'll be a good dad no matter what. Don't walk the plank!"

Sebastian hadn't seen another way. He figured life moved at a breakneck pace whether you were there for it or not. He was determined to be there for it. So, he and Cora had gotten hitched, barely knowing one another. Seb figured that they'd muddled their way through well enough.

Even if things between Ty and Cora were always relatively tense, it was definitely true that Tyler's luck with women had increased once Sebastian was off the market.

"I just don't want to go online shopping for a woman," Sebastian said as he clicked back into the app to scroll through a few more profiles. He tossed the phone back over to Tyler. "I just met Cora and liked her. And that was that. None of this swiping left or right bullshit."

"Seb, you gotta try something. You never leave your house long enough to meet anyone. You're either in your workshop or at Matty's school, or you're right here in your damn living room. Not exactly a swinging singles scene."

That was true. Unfortunately. He played his last card. "I like things just me and Matty. Why complicate it?"

"Because as much as I enjoy being your platonic life partner, I am a wolf, and you, my friend, are a swan."

Sebastian laughed, swinging his head to one side to eye his friend. "What the hell does that mean?"

"It means I prefer to operate alone, taking a mate on a seasonal basis. But you? You mate for life. Like a damn swan."

"And you really think I'm gonna find a lady swan on that hookup app?"

Tyler rolled his eyes. "No, I think you're gonna find a hookup on this hookup app. It'll just be a little dessert to tide you over while you wait for your lady swan."

Sebastian laughed and groaned at the same time. "Just delete it."

"Too late. I messaged the cupcake for you."

SEBASTIAN IGNORED THE vibration of the phone in his pocket. Cupcake wouldn't stop messaging him, and it was driving him up the wall. Fucking Tyler.

"Sit," he said sternly to Crabby, who hovered his booty about an inch off the ground while his front feet danced. It was the closest they could get to a real sit. Better than nothing.

Sebastian leaned forward over the crates of produce at the Grand Army Plaza farmers market and picked up two eggplants, comparing them. This was one of those times when he really lived by the old adage *fake it 'til you make it*. He had no idea what to look for in an eggplant, so he chose the purpler one and set the other back.

Now he just had to Google eggplant recipes. And then find some way to trick his son into eating it.

He chose some kale and lettuce, bypassed the bok choy and snatched up the last good bunch of carrots. He paid the vendor, pushed everything into the tote bag over his shoulder and checked his watch. He had approximately nine minutes before Matty's karate class was over. Just enough time to pick up a cup of coffee. Perfect. Sebastian clicked his tongue at Crabby and the dog sprang forward like he'd been born to prance through that farmers market.

Sebastian sidestepped a loudly arguing couple and tossed some change into a hardworking saxophonist's case. Traffic whizzed by on all sides of the plaza and it seemed like every driver was extra appreciative of their car horns and middle fingers today. *Ah, the soothing sounds of Brooklyn.*

He stopped at the coffee truck on the other side of the plaza and was grabbing his cup of coffee when a soft, familiar voice spoke from just over his shoulder.

"Oh, hi!"

Sebastian looked back and immediately bobbled his coffee. "Miss DeRosa! Damn. Hot. The coffee, I mean."

She pulled a napkin from her purse and handed it over so he could mop the coffee off his hand. "Via."

"Sorry?" He looked up at her and blinked.

"Via. You can call me Via, now that Matty's not in my class anymore."

"Oh right. Then you can, of course, call me Sebastian, Seb, whatever." *Brilliant, Sebastian, a real wordsmith.* He balled up the napkin and tossed it, thanking God when it banked into a trashcan. At least he didn't look like a complete doof. "Via's a pretty name."

"Short for Violetta." She crossed her arms and smiled down at the dog who was once again hovering his butt above the ground, his tail thumping with the regularity of a windmill. "And who's this?"

"This is Crabby."

She chuckled, flashing slightly crooked teeth at him. "Matty named him?"

Sebastian nodded. "He put his foot down, said it was either Crabby or Sebastian. I think I chose wisely."

That made her really laugh; her head tipped to one side, her hair dusting her shoulder. Had she been this pretty when Matty had been in her pre-K class? Her glossy, dark hair was shorter now. It was in a blunt cut just above her shoulders, still just as wavy, though. She wore a bit more makeup than she used to, making her look a touch older. Her dark eyes took up nearly half her face, and her small, slightly squished nose was just like he remembered. He hadn't remembered that mouth, though. Small and plump, her lips were a lovely mauve against her golden skin.

"Sounds like Matty. How's he doing? How're both of you doing?"

For a second, that day in her classroom lanced through Sebastian and he fought the urge to visibly wince. The white-hot shame of being told he was neglecting his son had never quite subsided. No matter how good a father he was now. But he swallowed hard and pushed the feeling down. She hadn't been judgmental then, and she didn't seem judgmental now.

"We're doing really well. Got our hands full with this guy." He nodded down at Crabby. "And we moved a few months ago, so we're still settling into the new place."

"Where are you living now?"

"Still in Bensonhurst. I didn't want him to have to change districts, so we found a spot not too far from our old place."

"Oh!" Her eyes lit up. "I'm in Bensonhurst now, too. I actually just got a job at an elementary school there. Matty would be going into second grade already?"

"Good memory. Yeah. I can't believe it, honestly. Second grade already. So, you're not in pre-K anymore?" His phone buzzed in his pocket, another message from Cupcake, he was sure. It reminded him how much he didn't want to do things that way. And here, right in front of him, was this pretty woman who'd helped him out of one of the darkest moments in his life. Plus, she was looking very cute in a summery dress and her perfect little sneakers.

This was the kind of woman he'd like to go out with. He didn't have to squint at a profile pic or read between the lines of the two-hundred-word description of her life. He could just absorb the heat of her sunshine on a perfectly good late summer Saturday. Live. In person. *Ask her. Just do it.*

"Pre-K was what paid the bills while I got my certificate, but I knew I wanted to be in the counseling department of an elementary school somewhere."

"So you won't lead a classroom?"

She shook her head.

Just do it.

"Via, you know I never really took the chance to truly thank you. For what you did for me and Matty. I'm not sure I know how to really express it… Ah, I was wondering if you'd let me buy you d—"

"Hey, babe, you wanted me to get olive oil and what else?"

Sebastian's attention focused immediately on the extremely good-looking man who'd just walked up to them. Like, stupid good-looking. He had a model's face and a swatch of long, carefully unruly black hair. This was Brooklyn, so of course the kid was way too hip for mankind. He wore suspenders over a flannel shirt. Seb tried hard not to raise his eyebrows.

"Oh, Evan, this is my friend Sebastian. Sebastian, this is my boyfriend, Evan."

Of *course* she had a boyfriend. She was pretty as heck, sweet and accomplished. Just *of course*.

Evan was a few inches shorter than Seb and leaner, like

a runner. Seb was built more like a tank. Barrel-chested and wide stanced. Both of them towered over the very slight Miss DeRosa.

"Nice to meet you." Sebastian made himself hold a hand out for a shake. The kid's grip was as limp as any twentysomething's hand Seb had ever shaken. With a small start, he realized that Via and Evan were probably the same age. His eyes tracked over to study her face again. He hadn't ever really thought about her age before. He'd just seen a pretty woman and thought, *Yes, okay, yes, please*. But now that he looked, he guessed she was in her midtwenties.

And he'd been about to ask her out.

Yikes. That put them at somewhere around a fifteen-year age gap. Not a huge deal, he supposed, but he got a quick, horrifying visual of himself with saggy skin and white hair, while Via still looked young and golden and gorgeous. Yeah. No way.

Bullet dodged. He was sure she hadn't come to this farmers market to get cruised by forty-two-year-old dads.

"Well, Via, it was really nice to see you again. But I've gotta get Matty from karate. And then we've got a date at the park with this maniac." He nodded down to Crabby who, not receiving enough attention, had rolled to his back and continued to wag.

"Okay. It was really nice to see you, too." She reached out and took one of his hands in both of hers. She gave a small squeeze.

A hand hug.

He liked that.

He waved to them both and was just stepping away when she reached out and grabbed his arm. "What school did you say Matty attends now?"

"PS 128."

That calm-bright, crooked-toothed smile broke out over her face again. "That's where I just got hired."

"You're kidding!" Now he was extra glad he hadn't asked her out. Although, she'd already seen him at his most humiliated. What was a little dollop of embarrassment to add to that?

"I'll be seeing you around then."

"Definitely. I'm actually technically on staff there as well."

"Really?"

He nodded proudly. "Lunch monitor." He ignored Evan's surprised snort. *Dads can be lunch monitors, too, dumbass.* "Plus, I coach the soccer team for Matty's year."

"Well, I'm glad I'll know at least one person on the first day of school."

She looked genuinely relieved, with just a hint of nervousness, and it surprised Sebastian. He'd had the impression that she was completely put together, professional and prepared.

He opened his mouth to say something, tracked his eyes over to Evan and clapped his mouth back closed. "Well, ah, can't be late for Matty." He tossed a thumb over his shoulder.

"See you on the first day of school," she called, and Sebastian waved over his shoulder.

He didn't look back as he strolled across the plaza.

She was way too pretty for him to do anything but walk away.

CHAPTER THREE

"YOU'RE OUT OF soy milk."

Via jumped about a foot in the air and banged her elbow into the side of her fridge as she whirled around to see who the intruder in her kitchen was. "God. Fin. You just about scared me into my next life."

Serafine St. Romain, Via's foster sister and best friend for the last decade, sat with her feet up on Via's breakfast table, a bowl of cereal in her hands.

"No, sister. I've seen your next life. It's not for a long time." Serafine was from Louisiana and had spent the first thirteen years of her life in the bayou, surrounded by a little bit of voodoo, hoodoo and everything in between. She wasn't magic, per se. But she was occasionally spookily right about the comings and goings of the world. Her messy dark hair tumbled over her pale shoulders and her eyes were way too alert for 6:00 a.m. "Did you hear me about the soy milk?"

"Yeah, I was gonna go grocery shopping tonight after work anyways." Via's stomach flipped. *Work. Oh Lordy.* Was there anything more nerve-racking than the first day of school? "Are you still up from last night?"

Serafine wasn't a good sleeper. "Yeah. Weird vibes floating around Brooklyn last night. Just couldn't drift off."

"Oh, I'm sorry, Fin." Via waggled the coffeepot toward her friend and got a nod. Via poured two cups, tossed some cinnamon in one of them for Serafine and pulled up a chair next to her. "Just coming by to eat my cereal?"

They'd lived together up until four months ago when Via had finally saved up enough to live on her own. A personal dream of hers ever since she'd been shuffled into the foster system at age twelve. She loved her new little one-bedroom in Bensonhurst. It had peeling paint, sure, but good light and a real kitchen. And if she was lonely now and again, she figured that was just her body's way of getting used to a new normal. *Nothing to see here, folks.*

Besides, Serafine stopped by a few times a week anyhow.

"I came to wish you luck, sister. On your very first day in a real public elementary." Fin's eyes took in Via's outfit in a critical yet not judgmental way. "You look good."

Via suspected she was a little dressier than she had to be in her emerald tailored pants and her ivory silk blouse, but she'd wanted to look a little older this morning. She'd wanted to look put-together in every possible way. God, she couldn't wait until she hit thirty. She was twenty-seven and sick of it. Maybe it was her small stature or her young face, but she felt like she'd spent her entire life just shy of being taken seriously. She'd left her hair kissing her shoulders and added some small gold earrings that she'd splurged on when she'd been hired.

She teased at one of the earrings. She still couldn't believe she could afford things like this. Shiny things. Superfluous things. Extras. *Frosting*, Jetty, her foster mother and Serafine's aunt, had used to call things like that. Frosting on the cake of life. Well, Via had spent pretty much all of her twenties baking the cake, and now she was learning how to add a little frosting.

"Thanks." She looked up at Serafine and told the truth,

the way they always did with one another. "God, I'm nervous."

Serafine nodded once. Then set her cereal aside and held up three fingers one at a time. "You're qualified. You're hardworking. You're naturally gifted at working with children."

Via nodded, too. "Thanks. I know you're right." She rose and grabbed a protein bar from her fridge and poured her coffee into a travel cup for the walk to school. "And you're getting crumbs on my kitchen floor."

"Adds character," Serafine insisted through a mouthful of dry cereal.

Via chuckled and kissed her friend on the top of the head. A puff of lavender and bergamot came off of Serafine's wild hair. Via grabbed her keys off the hook and took a deep breath.

"Wait!" Serafine called, pulling her feet off the table and setting her bowl aside. "I brought something for you."

"Oh, Fin." Via's whole face warmed as she saw the pendant swinging from Serafine's fingers. "It's stunning. Did you make it?"

"Of course. Special for you. Cleansed the crystal myself. It's garnet. For career success."

It was a rough-hewn stone of deep red, small and interesting. It rolled across the small gold swatch of Via's chest and settled perfectly on her breastbone. Though Via had always been a little skeptical of tarot cards and tea leaves, something in her had always bought in to Serafine's crystal work. The woman prescribed crystals the way other people did ibuprofen, chicken soup, a pint of rocky road and a rom-com. Via felt like she could almost feel it working already, bringing her success even as it warmed against her chest. And it was gorgeous to boot.

"Frosting." Serafine smiled.

Via's hand automatically went to the pendant. "I was just thinking about that."

"Well, I wanted you to have some first-day juju, and I know how much you love shiny things."

Via laughed, blushing a little. "Well, it's gorgeous." She gave Fin a hug, a real one.

Via took a fortifying breath and headed out the door. She had her witchy sister in her corner, a magic necklace and a master's degree. *Bring it on, Brooklyn Public Schools.*

TURNED OUT THAT lots of people had first-day-of-school jitters. Via was comforted by the teachers rushing the hallways with school supplies in one hand and coffee in the other, waving harried hellos and lining up at the Xerox machine. She was even more comforted by the wave of loud, chirping, summer-fresh children that poured into the school around 8:15.

Right, she reminded herself. She could do this. This was the easy part. As the new third–fifth grade student counselor, Via wouldn't see any kids on her first day, but she did have an insane number of files to read over. She'd come in the week before to set up her office, and now she smiled as the sun shifted overhead and caught the three clear crystals that spun in her window with the breeze.

She ate lunch by herself, at her wooden desk. At 4:15, she took a deep breath and checked her makeup in the bathroom on the way to the staff meeting in the library. The weeklong orientation she'd gone through last month had been with all the new staff in the district, but unfortunately, none of them had been from PS 128. And she hadn't gotten a chance to meet hardly anyone when she'd come in to set up her office, though a few people had popped their heads in to say hi.

She stepped into the back of the library and put a small, professional smile on her face. She could do this. How many new schools had she been punted into as a foster kid? How many mandatory after-school programs and group therapy sessions had she had to step into and find a place for herself? The answer was a lot. The answer was also that it never seemed to get much easier. The main difference here was that this room, right here, was Via's choice. This was a step she *wanted* to be taking in her life. She took a deep breath.

Teachers were milling around, greeting each other, finding their seats. Via was just about to walk up to a group of older, chatting teachers and introduce herself when Principal Grim tapped one of her very large rings against a water glass.

The sound tinkled through the room, and Via felt like she was at a wedding. Not that she'd ever actually been to a wedding. But, you know, goals.

"Shall we?" the mildly eccentric but very competent older woman called to her staff.

Via slipped into one of the chairs set up toward the edge of the room and watched everyone settle in around her. Principal Grim was just standing up when something caught Via's eye.

She looked across the room and there was Mr. Dorner— Sebastian—giving her a half smile and a wave. Right. He'd said he was on staff, but it was still a surprise to see him at the staff meeting.

Via felt herself light up like a birthday candle as she waved back. It was really nice to see a familiar face. Even if his face wasn't *so* familiar to her. He looked very different from when she'd had Matty in her pre-K class. His hair, somewhere between brown and gold, was shorter and trimmed, long on the top, tight on the sides. He had more of a beard now, but it was neat and intentional. Not the five-day-old scruff he'd sported for most of that entire year. And he wore a casual button-down and dark jeans. It definitely had a different effect than the rumpled suit he'd worn every day for most of Matty's pre-K year.

Sebastian turned back to the front of the room, but Via surreptitiously studied his face for just a moment longer. He'd looked like some of the other dads at the farmers market, maybe a little taller and fitter, but he'd looked like he belonged there. But in this elementary school library surrounded by women in colorful dresses and alphabet earrings? It made his blunt features somehow blunter. His shoulders wider. It was like spotting a lion among a flock of flamingos.

A lion who was chatting easily with a few of those flamingos, chuckling and sharing gum.

Hmm.

"All right, you brilliant people!" Principal Grim stood up, her dyed black hair almost maroon under the fluorescent lights. "It's time. You know what time. Get those hands up."

Via looked around in confusion and saw that almost the entire staff already had their hands in the air.

"Let's get those spirit fingers working and give it up for another fantastic school year!" All the teachers shook and waved their fingers furiously. Smiling to herself at the absurdity, Via did the same.

A KNOCK ON the frame of her office door had Via glancing up. "Sebastian!"

"Hi." He practically filled the doorway shoulder to shoulder. "How was the big first day?"

She took a deep breath and finished slipping some

files into her shoulder bag for the walk home. "Hungry. I didn't bring enough snacks."

He chuckled. "Well, you can always come down to the cafeteria at lunchtime. I've got the hookup on all the extra carrot sticks and tahini dip you could ever want."

She laughed. "That's really what they're serving in the cafeteria?"

He nodded, scraping a wide paw over his beard. The scratching sound carried across her small office. "Oh yeah. Principal Grim got us onto this healthy eating pilot program through the city. We're getting Whole Foods's day-old goods or something like that."

"You're kidding."

He shrugged, a little half smile on his face, and Via couldn't tell if he *was* kidding.

"So, what'd you think of the first staff meeting?"

Via blinked at him. She made a point to always tell the truth. But it was her first day here and she had no idea who might be passing by in the hallway. She went with the most evasive version of the truth her conscience would allow her to tell. "I, uh, wasn't expecting quite that much dancing."

Sebastian outright laughed. At one point, Principal Grim had had the entire staff in a circle with their hands waving and their hips circling. "Yeah, she has sort of a freewheeling leadership style. And she believes wholeheartedly in the body's expression of the inner mind." He looked down, apparently saw his sleeves were different lengths and started peeling one of them back to even them. "It didn't scare you off, did it?"

Via shook her head, throwing her bag over her shoulder. "No way. My best friend is basically a psychic, so the more mystic juju there is, the more comfortable I am."

"Like, a crystal ball type of psychic?" He looked intrigued, finishing his sleeve.

Via shook her head. "She's never practiced with a crystal ball before. At least not with her clients. But she does use other kinds of crystal." She pointed to the ones dancing lightly in the breeze at the window.

"And that, too?" He nodded toward the pendant at her chest.

"Oh. Yup. She gave this to me this morning. For luck." She automatically started playing with it.

"Well." Sebastian squinted at the clock on the wall. "I think I've given Matty enough time to scream his brains out on the playground. I should probably get going."

"He's in the after-school program?"

"Only when we have a staff meeting. I swear it's his favorite day of the week, though. A real hit to the ego that he'd rather play on the same jungle gym he did at recess than go to the library with his old dad."

She laughed again. "Well, you gotta keep it fresh. It's like a long-term relationship. You can't just go to dinner and a movie on every date."

He blinked at her, scraping that same paw over that stubble again. "Yeah. I guess you're right."

"See you tomorrow?"

"You got it."

And then he was gone and Via walked home on her own.

HER FIRST WEEK of school passed in a blur of new students and names and more paperwork than Via had thought humanly possible. When the dismissal bell rang on Friday, she flopped gratefully back into her swivel chair and eyed the ceiling of her office.

She felt like she'd just run a marathon. Three marathons. Back to back.

"Hey," a voice spoke from the doorway of the office and Via looked up to see one of the first-grade teachers. Sadie Carroll. Young and pretty, she always looked very stylish. They'd sat next to each other at the staff meeting but hadn't crossed paths the rest of the week. "You survive your first week?"

Via sat up. "Define *survive*."

Sadie laughed. "Sounds about right. First year's the hardest. Although, this is my third, and I'm still waiting for the easy part."

Via nodded and started packing up her bag.

"So listen, some of us do this happy hour thing on Friday afternoons. Any chance you'd wanna join?"

Via's heart leaped and she couldn't help but feel like that middle school foster kid again. Equal parts eager and terrified at any invitation. She swallowed, keeping her seesaw of emotions off her face. "That sounds great."

"Oh good!" Sadie clapped her ringed fingers together and shook back her chin-length red hair. "We just walk to that bar one avenue over, Cider. You know it?"

"Sure, it's got the steel pumpkin on the sign."

"Right. They keep a table for us on Fridays."

"Do they have food? I was just considering gnawing off the corner of my desk."

Sadie laughed, although Via had barely been making a joke. Former foster kids took snacks very seriously. "They've got a turkey sandwich that'll get you face-to-face with your maker."

"Is that a good or bad thing?"

Sadie laughed again. "Come and find out."

"Can significant others join?" Via asked as she slung

her bag over her shoulder and followed Sadie out of the office.

"Oh, you've got a person?"

Via nodded. "Evan."

"Man Evan or woman Evan? If I can ask."

"He's a man." Via cocked her head to one side, intrigued by the question.

"I thought I'd check because my girlfriend's name is Rae, and everybody gets confused. Well, anyways, Evan is definitely invited. Everybody's been so curious about you, I'm sure they'd love to meet your SO."

Via ignored the way that piece of information made her stomach clench. She hated being the source of any gossip or in the spotlight. Her first few years in the foster system had been spent scrupulously attempting to camouflage herself in all possible ways. Drama of any kind meant getting shuffled into a different home, a different situation. After three different homes, Via learned that keeping her head down and blending in meant that she got to stay put. Even a decade and a half later, Via found herself shying away from *anything* that might make her a target for drama or gossip.

But she told herself it was natural for her coworkers to be curious about the new girl. And it wasn't like Evan was some salacious secret. He was her boyfriend of almost two years. It was normal—*NORMAL!*—that he'd meet her coworkers.

She and Sadie chatted on the walk over to the bar and Via realized that they were some of the last people to arrive. She and Sadie slid into the last two available seats. The bar was funky and dark. It had the typical Brooklyn gimmick to make it memorable and patently Instagramable. In this case, the gimmick was an entire wall filled with slowly creaking gears. Mumford & Sons played over the speakers and a waiter in an old-timey cap completed the look.

Via was mildly surprised to see who'd shown up. Sadie had said *happy hour*, and Via had automatically pictured all the younger members of the staff. But Shelly, the middle-aged librarian, was there; Becky, the older fifth-grade teacher; and Jim, one of the older fourth-grade teachers was there as well.

On Via's other side was one of the second-grade teachers Via didn't know very well.

"Cat Foster," the woman reintroduced herself. She was probably midthirties, had some gray in her curly brown hair and wore a large, artsy wedding band on her left hand. "How was your first week?"

Almost everyone had asked that same question. "Good. Busy. Lots of things to get in order before I can run the position the way I want to, but, you know, good."

"The last person in your position wasn't exactly…organized."

"I noticed," Via said dryly. She bit her lip for a second. That hadn't been the most professional thing to say, but the woman had left her about two hundred disorderly files, some of which were on students who didn't even attend the school anymore.

Cat laughed. "Well, that's public school for you. You've got the people who join up to make a difference—" she tipped her beer toward Sadie "—and you've got the people who join up in order to do the least amount of work possible while still getting the health insurance." She tipped her beer back, as if into the past, to indicate the person who'd had Via's job before her.

"How's your class this year?" Sadie leaned around Via to ask Cat.

Cat dropped her head back and made the sound of angels singing in a chorus. "A-ma-zing. It helps that there's only twenty-two of them. Last year I had twenty-eight," she told Via as an aside. "But they're also just a really good group."

"I'm so jealous that you have Joy and Matty. Those two are the best. I almost considered moving up with that class, just so I could have them another year."

Via's ears perked up. "Matty Dorner?"

"Yup," Cat answered. "And Joy Choi is his best friend. They're the cutest. Utterly inseparable and so sweet with each other." She placed a hand over her heart and rolled her eyes backward. "I love them."

"I had Matty in pre-K. He's such a great kid. So creative and smart. Always making little presents for everybody."

Suddenly, Via was very aware of Sadie's and Cat's eyes on her like laser beams. She tried not to shift uncomfortably.

"So then," Sadie replied, "you're familiar with the fabulous Mr. Dorner."

"Oh sure. I had Matty for a year, so we knew each other a bit." A very little bit. Via had watched him go from disheveled, barely aware, grief-stricken dad to vaguely aware, semi-put-together, grief-stricken dad. She couldn't exactly wax poetic on the man. Via studied the giddy energy coming off the two women.

"So, what's his deal?" Cat asked, leaning closer, her elbow on the table and her temple leaning on one fist.

Oh. The pieces clicked into place. They were interested in Mr. Dorner gossip. She looked back and forth between Cat and Sadie. The flush in both of their cheeks and their wide eyes. Yet another piece clicked into place. They were attracted to him.

Huh.

He wasn't Via's type at all, so she hadn't particularly noticed. She liked tall and lean. Dark hair and dark eyes. Like Evan. She was attracted to pretty men. And Sebastian was definitely…not pretty. His features were blunt and wide, almost plain, except for those light gray eyes. Even with his short, trimmed hair, he looked vaguely mountain mannish.

She looked back at the flushed faces of her colleagues. Well. To each their own.

"I don't know much about him, really. Just that he's a good dad." She'd seen plenty of proof of that, especially toward the end of the year when he'd started to get his act together. She couldn't imagine how hard that must have been after losing his wife. She'd gotten the impression that he'd been learning fatherhood from scratch. And he'd done well, in her opinion. Better than a lot of dads she'd had in the class. Of course, Via didn't say a word of that out loud to Sadie and Cat.

"Does he date?" Cat asked, leaning forward a little more.

"Cat!" Sadie laughed. "What do you care? You've been married for a decade."

"Morbid curiosity. And no curiosity-killed-the-cat jokes." She pointed between them. "Just because I can't buy doesn't mean I can't window-shop."

"I honestly have no idea if he dates or not. I didn't know him very well back then, and I've only run into him a time or two since."

"Damn." Sadie leaned back. "I really want some deets on that guy. I could never crack the egg when Matty was in my class."

"And what do you care?" Cat leaned over and asked. "You're engaged yourself."

Via caught sight of a pretty engagement ring on Sadie's hand that she hadn't noticed before.

"I might be engaged, but I'm not dead. A Thor look-alike has universal appeal."

Via laughed along with the women. Maybe this job wasn't going to be *quite* as professional as she'd thought. And honestly, she didn't mind one bit.

CHAPTER FOUR

SEBASTIAN TRUDGED UP the stairs of his front porch, swinging his house keys on one finger and sighing deeply. He'd done it. He'd gone on a date, and he'd kissed a woman who wasn't his wife.

It had been…fine. Emma was pretty and smart, and it wasn't her fault if Seb's rhythm had been off the entire night. Majorly off. Like, laughing-at-everything-she-said-because-he-couldn't-tell-what-was-a-joke kind of off. Honestly, he'd been pretty surprised when she'd kissed him outside the subway entrance. He would have preferred to take her all the way home, but in New York City dating language, getting on the train with someone was the same as inviting yourself upstairs for a cup of coffee. He'd tried to get a cab for her, but she'd insisted she was a big girl who could ride the train at 9:00 at night.

He wondered if that had been her subtle way of telling him the date was ending too early.

He let himself into his house and locked the door quietly, immediately crouching to pat Crabby's sleepily wagging behind. He clicked his tongue and had the dog at his heels as he grabbed a beer from his fridge. Sebastian cocked his head and followed the noise of his television.

"What the hell?" Tyler gaped at him from one end of the couch. "Dude, it's like 9:25. I didn't tank my Saturday night to babysit for a date where you don't even score."

"How do you know I didn't score?" Seb raised an eyebrow as he plunked down on the couch. Crabby hopped up beside him and curled into a little doggy doughnut. Seb kicked off his shoes and stripped off one sock and then the other, stuffing them in his sneakers. He leaned his head back and rolled it to look over at Tyler.

"Because you're as well ironed now as you were when you left, and you've only been gone for like an hour and a half. And even Seb ten years ago needed more time than that to close the deal."

Seb laughed into his palm as he scraped it over his face. "I got a good-night kiss outside the F train. Does that count?"

"Depends." Ty weighed his head back and forth. "Tongue?"

Seb raised both eyebrows and didn't answer.

Tyler lowered the volume on the TV and eyed his best friend. "You all right, man?"

"Yeah. It was just weird was all. Being with her was fine. But kissing her was weird."

"Because of Cora?"

"Sort of. I mean, Emma's the first person I've kissed since Cora. But it really just felt weird to kiss someone I had no interest in. Pointless, I guess." Seb started peeling the label off his beer bottle. "The whole night I couldn't shake the feeling that I was in the wrong place at the wrong time. I don't know. Like the person she messaged for a date and the guy who actually showed up were two different people." He laughed humorlessly. "I felt like my own imposter."

Tyler recrossed his feet on the coffee table. "You mean like right after Cora died?" Seb could hear the very careful tone in his friend's voice.

Seb didn't have to ask what he meant. Tyler had been there. Seb hadn't just felt debilitating grief, he'd felt like everything in his life was…off. Greens weren't the same green. His regular coffee cup was heavier and wider. Old familiar songs had new, unexpected lyrics. Even his body had felt different. He'd looked in the mirror and seen someone else, a sad, shell-shocked brother, maybe. Sebastian hadn't felt like he was in the right life, or the right body, for a year after Cora had died. It had taken that long.

"No, not like that." He glanced up at Tyler and finished peeling the label off his beer. "You don't have to worry about me going back to that place. Really. It wasn't like that." He gathered his thoughts. "The whole time I just felt like I was an actor in a play or something. She'd be like, 'tell me about yourself, Sebastian,' and I'd look into the wings like, 'line.' You know?"

"No, I don't really know. I'm always effortlessly charming and perfectly self-assured on dates." Tyler grinned when Seb blew a farting noise. "Was she boring or something?"

"No." *Yes, a little.* "She was totally fine. I just don't know about this whole dating-for-the-sake-of-dating thing."

"Trust me, dude. It's good for you."

"Daddy?" Matty was in the doorway, knuckling one eye and looking like someone had run a vacuum cleaner over his hair.

"Hey, buddy." Seb set his beer down and opened his arms to his son. "What's up?"

Matty climbed into Seb's lap and rested his head on his shoulder. Seb relished it. Only when Matty was very, very tired was he this snuggly anymore. His kid was growing up. Losing those chubby cheeks. Seb knew that *Daddy* was on its last legs. He was only ever *Dad* when Matty was around friends. It plucked a bittersweet chord in his heart. Of course he wanted his kid to grow up. And of course he wanted his kid to stay a baby forever.

"I'm thirsty." Matty reached down and tangled one hand in Crabby's fur.

"Why didn't you drink the water in your water bottle?" Seb always left water there for him. He had somehow ended up with the thirstiest child on the planet.

"I wanted some of your water." Matty's sleepy words were mostly just hot kid-breath into Seb's face, and he couldn't help but chuckle. Matty always insisted that whatever water Seb was drinking tasted better than any other water. So, for Matty's entire life, Seb had been drinking water with kid backwash in it.

Planting one arm around his son, Seb leaned toward one of the side tables and grabbed a glass from earlier in the day. "Here you go." He turned to Tyler. "You can head out if you want."

"Nah, I'll stay for the game." Ty nodded toward the baseball game he'd been watching.

"Can I watch some of the game, too?" Matty asked, blinking those sleepy gray-green eyes up at his dad. His sucker dad.

"Sure." Matty would be asleep again in about three minutes anyways. With his kid on his chest, his dog snoring into his thigh and his best friend across the room, Seb didn't feel alone. He let his mind drift back to the date. The pretty woman and the warm good-night kiss.

He sighed. It might be strange, but he preferred the second half of his night to the first.

Sebastian plunked down next to Shelly and Grace, two of his favorite staff members at the school. They were straight shooters. And both of them had lost their husbands so when they'd found out he was a widower, they'd sort of adopted him into their group of two. He sat with them at most of the staff meetings.

"And that hair!" Shelly was whispering to Grace. "My God, silkier than a woman's!"

"I was too busy trying to pry my eyes off his face," Grace whispered back.

"What're we discussing?" Seb asked as he handed each of them a stick of gum, their usual routine before one of these meetings.

"The new counselor, Via DeRosa, brought her boyfriend to the end of our happy hour on Friday."

"Oh." Seb was surprised. Usually Grace and Shelly were gossiping about someone they'd seen on *The Voice* or *Dancing with the Stars*. Not an actual person.

"And let me tell you," Shelly continued, "that boy could be on television with that hair."

"I've met him, actually. At the farmers market at Grand Army Plaza a few weeks ago."

"So you agree then?" Grace asked.

"Oh sure. Totally. Great hair." He grinned at his two friends and leaned back, letting them continue gossiping without him.

His eyes wandered around the room and he did a double take when he realized that Via was looking at him. Studying him, actually. She jumped a little when he caught her eye. He sent her a little salute and instantly rolled his eyes at himself.

A salute? *What the hell was that?*

She apparently *didn't* think it was the dumbest thing a man had ever done in the history of the world, though, because she sent a wave back his way.

The meeting was more of the same. Updates and policy reminders and handouts and the prerequisite get-up-and-jiggle-around as a full staff. This time, Seb found himself catching Via's eye and grinning when Principal Grim had them bending forward into a shoulder shimmy, apparently to gear them up for the week. Via just grinned right back.

After the meeting, Seb picked up Matty from the after-school program and started digging through his backpack the second they hit the sidewalk. "You didn't eat a single one of these apples I cut for you?"

"I tried one!"

Seb identified a single green apple slice with approximately three tooth marks in it. "Right. Well, it doesn't count as your green thing for the day if you don't actually eat it."

"I'll have my green thing at dinner." Matty let his dad strap his backpack onto him as he leaned forward. "Wait! Is that Miss DeRosa?"

Seb looked up and sure enough, Via was walking half a block ahead of them. "Yeah. Didn't I tell you she works at your school now?"

"No way?! Can I run and say hi?"

"Sure."

Seb crunched into the apples his son hadn't eaten as he watched him sprint up the block to Via, his backpack bouncing wildly with each step.

"Miss DeRosa! Miss DeRosa!"

Via turned and, when she saw it was Matty, smiled so brightly that Seb coughed on the apple he was swallowing. *Damn.* Packed a punch.

Right. *A twenty-four-year-old punch*, he reminded himself.

He swallowed his apple and sauntered up to them as she finally unhanded Matty from the hug she'd wrapped him up into.

"It's so good to see you, Matty. I heard that you're in Mrs. Foster's class this year?"

"Yup. And I just got bumped from the red reading group to the blue one."

"Wow! Matty, that's so great."

"Really?" Seb butted in. It was news to him. "Knuckles, my dude."

Matty absently knocked fists with his dad, something they often did when one of them had a small victory, before he turned back to Miss DeRosa. "Yeah, the books were easier in the red group, but Joy is in the blue group."

Via smiled at Seb before she looked back down at Matty. "Is Joy your friend?"

"*Best* friend." Matty frowned. "But she's never allowed to come over."

"But you get to play with her at the park all the time." Seb reminded Matty, brushing a hand over his son's hair. The Chois had moved from South Korea to Brooklyn about three years ago, and the language barrier had made it hard to make playdates with them. But through clumsy charades, lots of smiles and mutual unspoken agreement, they usually met at the park at 4:00 on Sundays and Wednesdays to give Matty and Joy time to hang out together.

"Right. Do you walk home from school, too?" Matty asked, tugging gently on Via's hand.

"Yup. I'm only a few blocks that way."

"Us, too! Right, Dad?"

Seb smiled at his son. He was a brilliant reader and could already draw a respectable self-portrait, but Seb feared directional skills were not his son's forte. "Sort of. We're more in that direction."

"You're looking limber after our staff meeting today," Via said as the three of them fell into step together.

"Oh yeah." Seb grinned at her. "Principal Grim likes those shoulders to stay loose." He glanced at the necklace on her golden-skinned chest, his eyes ricocheting away. "What's the blue one for?"

"I'm sorry?" Her brow furrowed in confusion and a little line appeared between her eyebrows. Seb told himself that the little line wasn't cute.

"You said your red necklace was for luck. What's the blue one for?"

She looked down at the light blue crystal on her chest, her fingers absently twirling it. "Oh. Apparently it's for, uh, making friends. Fin thinks I need help in that department."

"Your best friend thinks you need more friends?"

"She's more like my sister than my friend." Via shrugged. "We grew up in the same foster home. Though my foster mom was her aunt."

"Ah," Sebastian said as a memory swirled through his brain.

I don't know what you're going through, Mr. Dorner, no one can. But I've lost people in my family and... I know what it feels like to spin off into nothing.

She'd grown up in a foster home. Had she lost her parents? Seb swallowed through the worst of the humiliation that came whenever he remembered that day.

Neglect.

He ran his hand over his son's clean hair and took a bite of one of those apple slices in his hand, all to remind himself that he wasn't neglecting his boy. He was doing the checklist. More than the checklist, in fact.

He cleared his throat. "I heard you went to the staff happy hour, though. That's pretty social."

She nodded. "Very social. Those ladies know how to cut loose."

He laughed. "Yeah, I tried my hand at a few and then decided I preferred my rear end to remain un-pinched by my colleagues."

Via laughed but her mouth opened in horror. "No! They didn't!"

"Oh yes, they very much did." He shrugged. "I didn't really mind. It was kind of like an initiation onto the staff. They all loosened up around me after that. I think before that there was kind of a fox in the henhouse vibe."

"Lion among the flamingos."

"What's that?"

"Oh." Via waved her hand through the air as her slashing cheekbones washed over with a light pink blush. "Nothing. It's just what I thought at that very first staff meeting."

"That I looked like a lion surrounded by a bunch of flamingos?"

She blushed harder and switched her bag to the other shoulder.

"Daddy, can Miss DeRosa come over for dinner?"

He pulled his eyes away from the pleasantly pink Miss Via DeRosa and looked down at his son, who was grinning like he did when he wanted an extra half hour of TV.

"Ah…" He glanced back at Via.

"Oh, I can't tonight, Matty."

Matty's face fell as he looked up to his dad for the assist.

"You really are invited, Via, if you wanted. And I know Matty wants you to come. He only pulls out the 'Daddy' big guns when he really wants something."

She smiled but her eyes skittered away. "I've got plans with Evan. You remember? My boyfriend."

"Okay. Maybe another time then."

Another time? The poor woman had already said no

twice. Why the hell was he setting himself up for her to say no a third? AND she'd just taken the opportunity to remind him that she had a boyfriend.

She nodded in a noncommittal way.

They walked in silence for three sidewalk squares before Seb broke the silence again. "You and Evan live together?"

What? Abort! Seb, you dumbass. Quit asking personal questions about her boyfriend!

She shook her head but didn't say more.

He knew when it was time for a quick exit. "All right, well, this is where the Dorner family turns off. We've got lima bean soup and broccoli pie waiting for us at home."

Matty looked up at him with exactly the horrified and disgusted expression that Seb had expected. It made Via laugh. Just like Seb had been hoping it would.

"Well, you fellas have a good night."

"Bye, Miss DeRosa."

"Bye, Matty. You can come see me in my office whenever you want. It's next to the art room."

"On the third floor?"

She nodded.

"Okay! I will."

She waved and walked on, and Seb tugged Matty on down the block.

"Dad, we're not actually eating that for dinner, are we?"

CHAPTER FIVE

"ARE YOU SURE?" Via asked for the fourth time. She knew that what she was doing could probably be classified as nagging, but she couldn't stop herself. This was a really big decision that Evan was making. And considering how serious they were about one another, it was going to inevitably affect her as well. The thought had her fingers trembling where she pressed them into her lap.

"I'm sure, babe. One hundred percent. I hate my boss. I can't stand to look at him for another fucking second. I gotta get out of there."

They sat at Via's small breakfast table. They spent most of their time at her place these days. He shared with two roommates, and none of them ever did the dishes. It turned Via off.

She leaned over and fiddled with the small bouquet of purple flowers at one end of the table. Evan had brought them as a way to soften the news he'd also brought.

"Okay, I get that you hate your job. And they definitely haven't treated you very well recently." It seemed like every day Evan had some story about how unfair his job as a paralegal was. "But quitting is a really extreme way of dealing with it."

She couldn't believe that *anyone* would prefer the potential drama of an unexpected quitting to the infinitely more respectful two weeks' notice.

Though he'd still been doing a lot of visual art when

they'd first met, Evan's job as a paralegal was one of the first things that had attracted Via to him. Still a student at the time, she had admired the nine-to-five dependability of his schedule and his paycheck. She'd thrilled at what she'd seen as his work ethic. It had seemed so grown-up to her. So reliable.

As a twelve-year-old foster kid, grieving her parents and lost in a whirlpool of a new life she didn't want, Via had just been getting comfortable at her first foster home when she'd been unceremoniously ousted. The couple's birth daughter, Megan, hadn't liked Via for one reason or another, and just like that, Via was tossed into another home. A group home that time. She'd slept on a metal bunk bed in a room with a glowing red exit sign over the door that kept her awake at night. Even at thirteen, she'd found that painfully ironic. Because there was no exit from this life she'd found herself in.

She'd gotten booted from that home when two of the other girls became convinced that she was stealing from them. She hadn't been, but it hadn't mattered. Within months of arriving, she'd been on the doorstep of a new foster home, her permanent one at that point. Jetty's home. Fin's home. But she'd learned her lesson.

Blend in. No waves. No drama.

In her mind, life was a car, speeding down the highway with a blindfolded driver. Everyone crashed at some point. Whether you survived or not just depended on what kind of car you had.

She'd spent every minute since she left Jetty's house making sure she had the safest model of car she could find. A good education. A good job. A little money in the bank. A lease on a nice apartment. Every day that she worked hard was like one more seat belt over her chest, keeping her safe.

The idea of Evan quitting his job was essentially inconceivable to Via. Like unbuckling his seat belt on the highway.

"You want me to just stay there? Where there's no respect for my time or my skills?"

Via rose to clear their dinner dishes. "No, of course not. But if you quit, that's it. Kaput. No more paychecks."

"That's the general idea."

She bit back on her frustration. She was trying her absolute hardest to understand this from his perspective. Just because it was a good job, with good benefits, didn't mean he had to stay there. Especially not if it made him miserable. "I'm just saying that if you give two weeks' notice, which is standard, you can leave guilt-free, get paid for another two weeks and possibly find something else in the meantime."

"Yeah, and I'd have to *work there* for another two weeks, which you're conveniently glossing over."

"I'm not—" She broke off and pinched the bridge of her nose as she leaned over the sink. She loved Evan, she really did, but conversations like this often spiraled off into arguments. And even more so lately, since she'd become busy with her new job. Evan didn't quite understand how stressful life transitions were for Via. How much she needed her focus to be in one place right now. Not to mention the fact that a public quitting scene, like the one Evan was dead-set on, made Via's chest tighten with anxiety.

She knew she couldn't out-and-out tell him he shouldn't do it. He took any disagreement very personally. Via could do this. She was a trained counselor, for God's sake. She changed tack. "It scares me to think of you without a job, Evan. You know how sink or swim New York is."

He knows it theoretically, a small voice said in her mind. Via, on the other hand, knew it quite personally.

"Well, good thing I have a damned good flotation device for a girlfriend."

She turned to him, and he was smiling at her up from under his hair in that way that made her knees weak. He gestured her over, and she went to him. He pulled her in between his legs and took her hands.

"I'm not asking for money or anything, V. I'm just asking for your support. I need to quit this job."

She nodded. She'd been waiting her whole life to be stable enough to offer support to someone else. After all, it was just Via on Via's team. She had Serafine, of course, but in terms of a financial safety net, Via only had what was currently sitting in her bank account. She asked herself one question: *Do I love Evan?* And that was all the answer she needed. When you loved someone, you did everything you could to support them.

"Okay. Do what you need to do, babe." She leaned down into his kiss and let him sweep her away.

Later, when she slid out of her bed to get a glass of water, trying not to wake up Evan as she did so, Via let the panic flood her. She sat in her dark kitchen, staring at a black window that threw her reflection right back at her. The words *flotation device* circled in her head like ravens.

IT WAS FOUR weeks into school and Via had joyfully settled into her new schedule. She saw students in the morning and did paperwork in the afternoons. She had regular appointments with a few different students once a week, but most of her time was spent putting out fires with students who'd been flagged by their teachers.

Billy Oaks showed up at school with a black eye? Send him to Miss DeRosa.

Kendra Dobbs's parents are getting a divorce? Send her to Miss DeRosa.

Jessica Rodriguez hauled off and punched a third grader? Send her to Miss DeRosa.

Miss DeRosa, for the record, was loving it. This was the only reason she'd taken on so many student loans. Why she'd spent so much time in school when she could have been working. Because working with kids who needed her? Truly needed her? There was just nothing that beat it.

Serafine was convinced that Via was in the middle of some cosmic death match with Karma. That because Via hadn't slipped through the cracks of the system and had eventually been filtered into a loving foster home, she felt that she owed it to other kids to make the system work for them. But Via didn't really care what the reasons were. All she knew was that at the end of the school day on her fourth Monday at PS 128, she felt like spiking her dang messenger bag.

She'd really, really done her job well. She'd straight-up conquered some problems for some kids. She'd had four appointments that morning, all of which had ended up on a positive note, and she'd finished her paperwork. That staff meeting was lucky she didn't moonwalk her way right in.

Without thinking, letting her adrenaline rush lead the way, Via found herself plunking down right next to Sebastian Dorner. She hadn't been avoiding him, but she'd been mindful of just how much all the other ladies at the school enjoyed gossiping about the fabulous Mr. Dorner.

"Hi!" he said in something like surprise. "Wow. You're, like, glowing. Did you get engaged or something?"

Her mind stuttered. Engaged? *Yeah. No.* "No. I just had a really, really good day at work."

He raised his eyebrows and nodded, offering her a piece of gum that she accepted. "That makes one of us.

I had a decidedly bad day at work." He held up one bandaged arm.

"Oh my God!" Via leaned forward, as if she might be able to see through the bandage. "What happened?"

"Lost a fight with a band saw."

"I…thought you were an architect?" She racked her memory for all the things she knew about Sebastian Dorner: Thor look-alike, widower, architect, father. She could admit to herself that it wasn't a very comprehensive list.

"I was. But I quit after, ah, when Matty was in your class, actually. I'm a furniture maker now." He lifted his ass off the library chair and pulled his phone out of his back pocket. He quickly exited out of some messages and then handed his phone over to Via.

Her mouth dropped open when she took in his webpage. "Sebastian, you *made* all this?"

She was floored, utterly floored. There were coffee tables and side tables and dinner tables. Chairs and bookcases and bed sets. All the wood he used was buttery and glowing, rich in tone and cut into interesting shapes. Every piece had some natural feature, like a knot or a live edge. He'd also integrated some sort of copper or steel into each piece in some way. It was utterly stunning.

When she looked up, he was grinning, with just a bit of color staining his cheeks. "Yup, I made all that."

"You're an artist." She stared at his profile as she handed his phone back over. She thought of his rumpled suits from two years ago. For some reason, she'd never thought that he would have a creative side.

He lifted his hips to put his phone away, and the movement pressed his shoulder firmly into Via's. "I try."

"Do you have a studio?"

"Yeah. It's in our backyard, actually. It was part of the

reason we moved. I was sick of schlepping over to Red Hook to work in a rented space twice a day."

"Why would you go twice a day?"

"Well, I'm a lunch monitor, so I always come back here at lunchtime."

A light clicked on. "Oh, I see, so you take a break in the middle of your day to come do lunch monitor duty."

He nodded. "And I run the second-grade soccer program on Tuesdays and Thursdays after school."

By her calculations, that meant that Sebastian was with his kid in the mornings, lunchtime and immediately after school. "Matty's lucky to have his dad around so much."

He blinked, those light eyes squinting as if he were trying to translate what she'd just said into a different language.

"All right, brilliant people! Palms up for positivity!" The staff meeting started, and thirty minutes later, Via found herself shoulder-to-shoulder with Sebastian, swinging their arms to and fro while Principal Grim led them all in a tight little cha-cha. She couldn't help but grin up at him, and he grinned right back.

Principal Grim was just about to end the meeting when Sebastian stepped forward, jamming his hands in his pockets in a way that instantly brought Matty to Via's mind.

"Principal Grim, I was wondering if I could make a quick request?"

"The floor is yours, Mr. Dorner."

Every eye in the room switched to Sebastian. Via watched in amazement as most of those eyes, young and old, cruised lazily from his face to his body and back again. He was seriously a big-ticket item at this school.

"I'm having a bit of trouble with the second-grade soccer group."

Via looked up at him in surprise.

"It's a bigger group than last year and rowdier. I have a few other parent volunteers, but honestly none of us know what the hell we're doing with the higher-needs kids. So, I was wondering if one of you brilliant, selfless, awe-inspiring trained educators wouldn't mind observing for a few practices? Maybe teach me some strategies to maintain order?"

For the second time in less than an hour, Via was utterly floored by Sebastian Dorner. He seemed like such a he-man. But here he was, asking for help, like it was no big deal. He was admitting that he'd been struggling, that he wanted to do better, to learn. She looked up at him standing there, such a huge, competent presence. And for the first time, she noticed the gray at his temples and smattered through his dark head of hair. A thought struck her. *This is a grown man.*

"I'll help, Sebastian," Sadie called out from across the room, tossing her chin-length red hair back. A few other ladies scowled, obviously having wanted to help the fabulous Mr. Dorner themselves. "I had most of those kids in my class last year anyway."

"Great!" His smile transformed his face, squint lines and all those white teeth.

Via shifted in her seat and cleared her throat.

The room emptied, and Sadie came up. Via was still gathering her thoughts about what she'd just seen. She wasn't sure why it had surprised her so much to see him ask for help like that. But it had moved something. She just wasn't sure what.

"I'm warning you, though," Sadie said, her engagement ring sparkling as she adjusted her bag on her shoulder. "I don't know squat about soccer."

Sebastian laughed. "Well, that pretty much makes two of us."

"But you're the coach," Via said, buttoning her light fall jacket.

"Yeah, but only because I wanted to be involved in whatever sport Matty wanted to play. I was a football player as a kid, but honestly, I was relieved that he didn't have any interest. Dorners have thick skulls—" he knocked on his own "—but I wasn't ready to watch my boy become a stain on the field."

Via blinked at him. She'd really, really stereotyped him. She'd thought, from his size and presence, that he was some machismo-filled gorilla. But here he was, an artist, unashamed to ask for help when he needed it and steering his son away from football because of brain injuries?

"Well, I guess I'll just Wikipedia soccer later tonight. Practice starts at 3:45 tomorrow?" Sadie said.

He nodded. "Seriously though, thank you, Sadie. I can't tell you how much I appreciate it. I think these last few weeks of soccer practice have given me even more gray hairs."

He scraped a hand over his head and smiled down at the two women who were smiling up at him. His squint lines deepened, and Via realized that she was letting her eyes wander all over his face. Via cleared her throat and took a step back.

Time to go.

"DO YOU THINK I'm judgy?" Via asked Serafine as the two of them lounged on the balcony of Fin's apartment the next night. She had a partial view of Prospect Park, and both of them liked the glimpse of the newly changing leaves.

This was the same place that they'd lived together up until last year, but Fin had made it completely hers since

Via had moved out. Crystals and sage, the walls painted in deep jewel tones and hung with mosaics and local art. An old Victorian-looking sofa sat in one corner, and she'd separated the large living room into two rooms with nothing more than three gilded hanging mirrors.

"You?" Fin's dark brows slashed across her pale forehead as she raised them up to her hairline. "God, no. You're the least judgmental person I know."

Via humphed and took a sip of the cheap red wine that neither of them minded drinking out of juice glasses. They'd just gorged on Indian food, and the cool early fall breeze was heaven on Earth as they sat with their feet up on the rail.

"I've been feeling judgy lately, and I don't like it. First with Evan and then with this guy at work, Sebastian."

"You mean because Evan quit his job with no notice and no backup plan? I think that one deserved to be judged, sister." Serafine set her wine aside to braid her wavy black hair, her many rings catching the light from a streetlamp and giving the illusion that she was sort of sparkling with energy.

Via frowned at her tone. "I don't know. He really wasn't being treated well there."

"Most people don't like their job, Violetta." She used Via's full name only when she was trying to infuse some love into whatever bitter medicine she was about to spoon over. "But most people aren't comfortable with hitting up their parents for money when they're willingly unemployed."

Via frowned into her wine. She was about to defend something that she kind of didn't want to defend. But he was her boyfriend, and they loved each other. "It's not his fault his parents have money. And why shouldn't he take it if they want to give it?"

Serafine sighed and tipped her head back toward the sky. When she spoke again, her Louisiana accent was syrupy smooth and threaded out into the night like smoke from the end of a cigarette. "There's nothing wrong with that, Via, really. I'm not judging him for having a different kind of family than we had. I'm just saying that quitting his job with very little thought and then relying on his parents to fill in the gaps isn't something that I thought you'd ever be attracted to."

Via froze. She blinked and saw barely any of the view in front of her. Leave it to Fin to hit the nail on the head. The very same nail that Via had been scrupulously avoiding. "I don't have to be attracted to every single part of him to want to be with him. He doesn't have to have every part of his life figured out to be a good partner."

Serafine sighed again, and this time, she laid a hand on Via's arm. "I'm not trying to shit on your boyfriend, Via. I'm just trying to put words to something that's been confusing me. And you're right, you don't have to love every single thing Evan does or says. But stability and independence are so, SO important to you. I never thought I'd see you with someone who didn't really value either."

CHAPTER SIX

SEBASTIAN WONDERED IF he was coming down with something. His head was spinning and he felt all clammy as he parked his truck on Court Street, a few blocks away from where he was heading.

Tell the truth, Seb, he told himself as he drummed his knuckles against his forehead. He wasn't coming down with something.

He just felt weird as hell because he'd slept with someone for the first time in almost three years.

Matty was spending a nice fall weekend upstate with his grandparents on Cora's side, so Sebastian hadn't had any reason to turn down the brunch date from Valerie. He'd let Emma down easy the week before, and he'd caught coffee with Valerie last weekend while Matty was in karate. He'd liked her enough to go on a second date with her. And he'd apparently liked her enough to sleep with her.

A brunch date. Seb hadn't even known that was a thing. But eggs Florentine had turned into a walk through Prospect Park had turned into checking out her apartment had turned into a sunny afternoon tour of her bed and her body.

He stepped out of his truck and jammed his hands in his pockets as he walked to the store where he was headed. It had felt good, he had to admit, to get some release after all these years. And it had been interesting to sleep with someone new. He'd missed sex. He'd definitely missed sex.

But the conversation directly afterward had knocked him for a real loop.

The bell above the door of the home goods shop jingled as he stepped through. The blond-haired woman behind the counter grinned at him.

"Would you date me?" Seb asked without preamble.

"Oh, uh, Seb," his good friend Mary stuttered, color flushing her pretty cheeks. "You know I just got out of that whole mess with Doug and—"

"No, no." He waved a hand through the air as he made his way through the empty store. "You misunderstand. I didn't say *will* you date me, I said *would* you date me."

"Oh." Understanding lit her eyes. "You're asking if you're datable?"

He nodded.

"Totally!" she chirped, scratching a small note to herself in a ledger. She tossed her long blond hair back. "You're a catch."

"But the kid thing, the widower thing, that throws a woman off, right?"

She raised an eyebrow at him. "Not the right woman."

"Hmm."

She leaned forward over the counter. "Shall I wager a guess that you may have had a run-in with not-the-right-woman?"

"Yeah. I got dumped this afternoon."

"Oh, Seb!" She sounded oddly excited by the news. "I didn't know you were dating! Oh, and jeez. Sorry. Getting dumped sucks. I should know."

"I guess I'm dating." He leaned his elbows on the counter and fiddled with some of the knickknacks she had for sale. "And I'm being dramatic. I wasn't dumped.

But I was definitely downgraded from relationship potential to a booty call."

Mary greeted a customer who'd just wandered into the store and lowered her voice to keep their conversation private. "What happened?"

"Well, this was our second date. I kinda liked her. She's cute. Runs a dog-walking business. Valerie."

"And?"

"And one thing led to another today and we…"

"Hid the salami?"

"Mary!" Seb blushed to the roots of his hair as he laughed.

Mary hid her pretty face behind her hands. "Sorry, it just slipped out."

"That's what she said."

"Oh my God."

The two of them were laughing like idiots as the bell over the door jingled again.

Mary wiped her eyes, chuckling to herself. "We just scared away my only real customer of the morning."

Seb looked around the shop. "Biz is that slow?"

She waved a hand. "It's always slow between Labor Day and Halloween. It picks up considerably after that. Oh! I have your check for you." She ran into the back room and pulled out Seb's cut of the dining room table she'd sold for him the other week. Clients typically commissioned pieces from him, but every once in a while, he'd make something just for the hell of it, and Mary would take a crack at selling it in her store.

"Thanks." He folded the check into the front pocket of his jeans.

"Finish your story about Valerie the dog walker."

"Well, afterward, I'm trying to make a plan to see her

again, and she says that it's best if we just leave it up in the air."

"What the hell does that mean?"

"Beats me." He shrugged. "But then she went on about how she didn't want to start anything up with someone whose life was so focused around kid stuff. Because it makes dating a lot more serious right from the jump. But that she'd had a good time and wouldn't mind hooking up again."

Mary's eyebrows were in her hairline. "Well. At least Valerie the dog walker is honest."

"Painfully so." He scraped a hand over his hair. "It just bothered me. The idea that I'm not datable because of Matty. That kid is the best part of me. All the good parts are because of him."

"Seb." Mary narrowed her eyes a little. "You know I love Matty. But he's not the only good thing about you." Her eyes narrowed farther. "I'm worried you don't realize that."

Seb waved a hand through the air. "Nah, I mean, I know I can be charming and fun to be around and all that. But when I started to really be a good dad? That's when the really good stuff kicked in. The patience, reliability, my ability to pay attention. I never really had that stuff before Matty." *Just ask Cora.*

She leaned back, crossing her arms over her chest. Her sweet face pinched into a mutinous expression. "It's not like you to be self-deprecating. Did you really like this chick or something? You're heartbroken?"

Seb laughed at the unexpected word. "No. God, no. I mean, she was nice. And cute. And it would have been cool to date somebody. But no. It wasn't a love connection. I just… Do you think that women see Matty and think, no-go?"

"Some of them, sure."

"Do you think widowed dads are undatable?"

"No. Of course not. It might be a different process than dating without kids, but you can make it be whatever you want it to be."

Seb was quiet.

"Are you sure you're all right? Is there something else?"

Seb slowly shook his head. "Nah. I mean, who knows? After your wife dies, there's always something else. It was just one of those days that felt off. Like I'm not me. I'm not the man I was before her or with her. And I don't know who I'm supposed to be after her."

"It's good you're trying, Seb."

He looked up at Mary. "Do you think Cora would have wanted me to try?"

Mary and Cora had gone to college together, although Seb hadn't really gotten to know Mary until after Cora died. She'd moved to Brooklyn just before the funeral, and they'd started a friendship from there. Sad beginnings, but they had a good thing going. Mary had been one of the first people to tell Seb that his furniture could sell. And that, in fact, he could sell it in her store if he wanted to.

"In theory, yes," Mary said slowly. "In practice? I think she would have scratched another woman's eyes out."

Seb laughed. It was very true that Cora had been protective over him. "But it's time, right? It's time for me to be out there trying to figure this part of my life out?"

"I don't know," Mary answered. "But if it's any consolation, it doesn't seem like you've screwed up anything so far."

Seb laughed into his palm. "Pretty low bar, Mary."

She shrugged, plopping her chin on one hand. "Gotta start somewhere, my friend."

"Jesus Criminy," Sadie groaned as she collapsed on the grass of the soccer field. Two of the parent volunteers escorted the grass-stained kids to the parking lot for pickup. Matty and Crabby chased a soccer ball on the other end of the field, and Seb grinned as his kid took a huge tumble, hopped up and kept running. Their maniac of a dog galloped alongside with his tongue flopping out and hearts in his eyes for Matty.

"I told you these kids were insane."

"Yeah, I mean they were hard in the classroom. But put 'em outside and suddenly they reveal their true roots as Lucifer's offspring."

He chuckled and started packing the extra equipment into a big gym bag. "That's why I called in a professional."

Sadie sat up on her palms. "I have had no professional training on how to keep a kid from shoving a soccer ball in another kid's pants."

"Yeah. That was really something. Casey took it on the chin, though."

"Actually, he took it right in the soccer shorts."

They both laughed at that one, and Sadie shaded her eyes as she squinted across the field.

"If it isn't my blushing bride!" Sadie called.

A very short black-haired woman with light brown skin strolled up, her hands in her pockets. Seb held out a hand.

"Sebastian Dorner."

"Rae Malek." They shook hands. "I'm Sadie's fiancée."

"Congratulations. Great girl you've got there." Seb tossed his head toward the redhead still sitting on the ground and then paused. He wondered for a second if he shouldn't have said girl. Maybe that was condescending.

"Couldn't agree more." Rae tugged Sadie up from the ground and pressed a quick kiss to her lips. "Ready?"

"Yes. Except for one thing." Sadie turned to Sebastian with her hands clenched in front of her face and huge doe eyes.

"Oh boy." Sebastian grinned at her. "I know that look."

"What look?" Sadie asked, batting her eyelashes.

"It's the I-just-did-a-huge-favor-for-Sebastian-so-now-I-get-to-ask-a-favor look."

Sadie and Rae both laughed.

"Any chance you're free on Saturday around 4:00 p.m.?"

"Sure," Seb answered. "Matty gets done with karate at one, and then we're free as a couple of birds."

"Well, we're part of a softball league and a few members of our team just moved to Weehawken."

"Ah."

"And according to league rules we have to forfeit if we don't have a certain number."

"Ah, well…"

"And, in particular, a certain number of men. It's a coed team and we're technically running a touch low."

"A touch?" he mused.

"Just a skosh." Sadie grinned at him, holding up two fingers in front of her eye. "A smidge."

"We have fifteen women and two men. We need one more or else we have to forfeit." Apparently, Rae was a straight shooter.

Sebastian could respect that.

"I'm not exactly a softball player."

"Hey." Sadie lifted both hands. "No judgment here about what you can or can't do with your bat and balls."

"Sadie!"

Rae looked horrified but Sebastian just laughed, tossing his soccer duffel over his shoulder. "I'm beginning to realize that you held back a lot when Matty was in your class."

"I try to keep it profesh."

He laughed again and allowed it to devolve into a groan. "I'll only say yes if I can bring my kid."

"Of course! I love Matty. Oh my gosh!" Sadie jumped and clapped her hands. "This is perfect!"

Sebastian said good night and whistled across the field for his dog and his kid. They tripped over one another and landed in a big hysterical pile. Sebastian smiled to himself as he untangled grass-stained kid from muddy dog.

CHAPTER SEVEN

"IS THAT THE PSYCHIC?" a low voice muttered from beside Via.

She turned and blinked in surprise when she saw Sebastian squinting toward the stands of the softball field. She hadn't realized he was on the team, as he hadn't been at any of the other games. And sure enough, he was looking right at Fin with her long black braid and purple pants. She was patting Sebastian's dog on the head and sharing a snack with Matty. Seemed they'd already made friends in the forty-five seconds that they'd shared a bench.

"How'd you know?" Via asked, amazed that he'd guessed.

Sebastian shrugged. "She's just got a, you know…" He waggled his fingers and widened his eyes. "Spooky vibe."

Via laughed and cocked her head to one side, her hair kissing her shoulder and reminding her that she needed to pull it up into a ponytail for the game. "I see what you mean. I think it's all the silver jewelry."

"What's the psychic's name, again?"

Via wondered for one vibrating second if he was interested in her friend. "Serafine St. Romain."

"Wow."

"Fin, to her friends."

"That's a lot of name."

Via raised an eyebrow. "You're one to talk."

"Hey! Sebastian is a classic name." She felt him eye her as she put one foot up on the bench to tie her running shoe. "So, you play softball?"

She tied a crisp little knot and moved on to the other shoe. "High school. And then a little in college."

"Oh. Wow. Now I'm nervous."

"You're not good?" Via squinted up at him; he was standing right in the sun. He moved a few inches to one side, and she dropped her shading hand.

"Eh. I can run. But I was wooed here."

Via looked around at the other members of the softball team, stretching and organizing equipment. Sadie was kissing Rae at the other end of the dugout. "Well, even if you're not stellar, nobody cares. It's a good group."

Seb knocked some dirt out of the treads of his shoe with the fat end of a softball bat. "You've been playing with them all season?"

"Just the last three weeks. Sadie talked me into it that first happy hour."

"Hey!" Sebastian called over to Sadie. "You didn't even get me drunk before you smooth-talked me. I feel cheated."

"I pulled a soccer ball out of Casey Dane's soccer shorts for you. You owed me," Sadie called back, and Sebastian immediately burst out laughing.

"Do I even want to know?" Via asked, waving at Matty and Fin in the stands when they caught her eye.

"She's been helping out with soccer practice, and it's occasionally a little…unruly. Seriously, pump 'em full of Capri Sun, and those kids go rabid." His eyes were on her as she tied her hair back into a ponytail. A frown line appeared between his eyebrows. She glanced up at that plain, wide-featured face, those light eyes so still and so bright, like they were backlit. Her dark gaze skittered away when he spoke again. "So, you're sporty, huh?"

"I'm lots of things," Via responded before she jogged out toward where the team was gathering around Sadie.

SEBASTIAN COULDN'T HELP but grin as he gripped the chain-link fence. He was surprised she hadn't broken the bat with that last hit. The ball was going, going, gone. And so was Miss Via DeRosa as she rounded first, gunning for second.

He tried to wipe the smile from his face—he was sure it was bordering on dopey—but he found it wouldn't quit. It was a joy to watch her play softball. She was powerful and light all at once. Actually, she made the rest of them look like they had their shoes tied together. Also, it didn't hurt that she looked so damn good with that cap pulled low over her eyes and those leggings that showed two perfectly hollowed ankles.

She was cute. It wasn't a crime to think she was cute, he reminded himself. It wasn't like he was going to do anything about it. This game had been all the reminder he'd needed of his age. His knees were already sore from the triple he'd managed to hit last inning. He could only imagine how they'd feel in the morning.

And there she was, bulleting around each base like a little midtwenties hummingbird. He knew she didn't worry about *her* knees. She was probably gonna swipe on some lipstick and go dancing with her hair model boyfriend tonight. She was young enough she probably still smoked cigarettes and didn't worry about the cost. She probably drank sweet drinks out of fancy glasses and showed up hungover to yoga the next morning.

Sebastian, on the other hand, was going to ice his knees while his kid fell asleep during *Turbo*.

Well, at least he'd had sex in the last ten days.

That was new for him.

"Dad!" Matty yanked on the pocket of Seb's athletic pants.

"Matty!" Seb parroted.

"I wanna throw the ball for Crabby." Matty's big gray-green eyes squinted, his lips pursing like he already knew what the answer was gonna be.

"I have concerns."

Matty's face scrunched further. Apparently, his dad's concerns were tiresome. "I can do it on my own!"

Seb raised one eyebrow.

Matty was already anticipating. "It won't be like last time. I swear. I won't throw the ball very far, and I'll stay where you can see me. Plus, I'm not wearing my nice clothes like before so it doesn't matter if Crabby gets me all dirty."

Matty held his arms out to show off his worn T-shirt and ratty jeans. His smile was growing bigger and bigger, knowing he was inching closer to getting what he wanted. He shook his little butt for good measure, knowing it always made his dad smile.

"All right. But right over there, okay? And if he starts running away, shout for me right away. Don't try to get him yourself. That's how we ended up in Prospect Park at 11:45 at night last month."

"Yes!" Matty did one more butt wiggle, this time because he was happy. "Thanks, Dad!"

And boy and dog were off, jostling each other as they sprinted to the other side of the field.

"I like the way you are with him," a slightly out-of-breath Via said as she came to stand beside him in the dugout.

"Wow, I didn't even realize you'd tagged in!" Seb

gazed down at her, the sheen of sweat on her face turning her skin a darker gold. *Stop saying wow, for fuck's sake, Seb.*

She nodded. "Homer."

"Second of the night. Impressive." Seb curled his fingers farther into the chain-link fence to keep himself from doing something dumb, like bumping her shoulder with his.

"Thanks."

"And thanks to you, too. For the parenting compliment."

"You deserve it. It seems like you and Matty have a good relationship."

Seb searched her face for judgment. Was she comparing him now to the way he'd been back then? Was she thinking of that day? Mismatched buttons and dirty hair and a slob of a father?

He didn't see that there, on her face. Her eyes were calm and wide, filling up half her dang face, her plush little mouth was tipped up at the sides, and she wrinkled her squished nose against a bead of sweat that traced down from her forehead.

"Well, I've worked to get us there. Being a good dad was something I had to practice."

"All good things take practice." She shrugged and looked out toward the softball game. "At least in my experience."

"Hey, would you wanna—" Seb cut himself off in horror. Holy God. He'd been about to ask her out again. Just like that. She looked up at him, sweaty and sweet, and the words dang near popped right out. Boyfriend be damned. Age gap and creaky knees be damned. He stalled.

She was still looking at him. He needed to say something. "Uh, would you want a ride home? I know we're in the same neighborhood. And, uh, Matty and I drove here so that we could bring the Pup McGruff, and I just thought I'd offer."

Pup McGruff.

He'd just looked into a beautiful woman's face, mumbled, stuttered and referred to his dog as Pup McGruff. Yeah. Any cool points he might have gained for recently having had sex were officially moot now.

"Oh, well, I'd never say no to that. I wasn't looking forward to the sweaty train ride home. Can Fin come, too?"

"Yeah, of course. Of course. Totally. I might have to move some of our camping gear to the truck bed but sure. Of course."

And that's how Sebastian found himself with a psychic in the front seat of his truck. Matty and Via sat strapped into the back seat, Matty in a booster, of course, and Crabby passed out, belly-up, on the floor. He put the truck in Reverse, then slammed it back into Park when he saw a guy struggling with a stroller in the parking lot. "Be right back."

Sebastian recognized him as one of the two other guys on the team. He jogged over.

"Hey, man. You're Giles, right?"

The slightly skinny man looked up from where he crouched, his eyes catching on Seb's face for a second. "That's right. And you're Sebastian?"

He was British, apparently, something that Seb hadn't noticed in their first introduction earlier that morning.

"Yeah. Can I give you a hand with the stroller? I used to have the same one for my son."

Giles rose up and nodded, stepping away. "My husband took our daughter to the bathroom, and my job was to get the stroller into the car. It's a little emasculating to fail so epically at the *easier* task."

Seb scoffed. "Trust me. There's nothing easy about this monstrosity. Here, you put your foot here and really jam down at the same time you rip back on this handle. I think of it like I'm starting a chainsaw. You try."

"Ahhhh," Giles muttered as he followed Seb's directions and the stroller folded down. "Brilliant."

"When in doubt, just kick the hell out of it. Or buy a new stroller."

Giles chuffed out a laugh. "Ah, here's my husband. Look, hon, I folded the stroller!"

Seb grinned at the satisfied look on his new friend's face. Giles's husband strolled up, a little girl, maybe two years old, on his hip. She glared out from under a mop of red hair, much like the hair of the man who held her.

"Sebastian, this is my husband, Benjamin."

"Sebastian Dorner." Seb shook hands with Benjamin and leaned in just a little to the sulky little girl. "And what's your name, beautiful?"

The little girl said nothing, choosing instead to pull an even more sour face in Seb's direction.

"Her name is Clara. And contrary to popular belief, she does speak. Are you Sebastian Dorner, the furniture maker?" Benjamin asked.

Seb looked up in surprise. "Yeah."

"Oh my gosh! I'm thrilled to meet you. I've been lusting after your website for months. You made a bookcase for some friends of ours. The Littlefields."

"Oh sure." Sebastian nodded. "They're nice people. Fun to work with."

"Are you taking on clients right now?"

"Always." Seb reached for his wallet and then remembered he was wearing athletic pants. "Let me grab you a business card from the truck."

"No worries, I'll reach out to you through your website."

"Great. Look, I've gotta run, but I'll see you next week?" The words were out of Sebastian's mouth before he thought twice about it. Somehow, between watching Via round the bases like a cheetah and chatting with these nice people in the parking lot, Seb had decided to come back.

"Sounds good, nice to meet you!"

Seb toggled his fingers at Clara, earning an imperious, affronted look from the little girl, and grinned at the two dads. He turned and jogged back to the car.

"Everything all right?" Via asked from the back seat. Seb saw that Matty had talked one of the two ladies into unwrapping a granola bar and handing him his water bottle.

"Yup, I just feel an obligation to pass on hard-won stroller knowledge to other dads. Plus, I think I landed myself an interested client."

"Knuckles, Daddy."

Sebastian grinned as he reached back and pounded fists with his six-year-old.

"Via tells me you're an artist," Serafine said from the front seat. They'd met briefly outside his truck, and Sebastian felt a little skip of his heart when she spoke to him now. She definitely had some strange energy coming off of her. Maybe it was her ethereal river of dark hair or those eerie eyes. Or maybe it was the fact that she was painfully gorgeous, fierce and beautiful like a goddess, or a pirate queen. But either way, Seb was having trouble looking her in the face for any length of time.

"Furniture maker."

Seb reversed the car and headed toward the BQE.

"He's an artist. You should see the furniture he makes.

It's stunning," Via chimed in from the back seat. Seb watched in the rearview mirror while she recapped Matty's bottle of water for him.

Seb tried not to shift under Serafine's sparking gaze. He wondered just how psychic she really was.

"Is that right? Via, you should buy something then, sister." She turned to Sebastian. "Her place is depressing. Where IKEA furniture goes to die."

"Fin!"

"It's true." Serafine shrugged, a touch of humor in her voice.

"You need some furniture?" Sebastian asked through the rearview mirror.

"No! I—yes. I do. I just moved, and I'm still getting everything settled. I was thinking of asking you anyway, before my very rude friend stuck her nose in my beeswax."

Matty laughed. "Hey, Dad."

"What's up?" Seb flipped his blinker on and exited onto Shore Parkway.

"Knock knock."

Sebastian grinned. "Who's there?"

"Nunya."

He grinned harder.

"Nunya who?"

"Nunya beeswax."

The three adults laughed, and Matty cheesed like he'd just won a gold medal.

CHAPTER EIGHT

"HO-LY MARY, MOTHER of God, sister."

Via knew exactly what Fin was going to say. She shook her head as she poured two glasses of cheap red wine and twisted open a big jar of pretzels. "All right, let's get this over with."

"That man is hotter than July. Like, a serious *hunk*." She laughed at herself. "Wow, sometimes I sound just like Jetty, don't I?"

Via laughed and nodded in agreement. But apparently Fin wasn't done.

"Like, you could roast a marshmallow on that man's hotness." Serafine accepted the glass of wine, the bangles on her wrists clinking together as she stretched out her legs onto the coffee table. Via didn't need to ask for clarification about who they were talking about.

"Yeah. I never really saw it before, but I gotta say, he looked good in those workout clothes." She'd been a little surprised at how handsome he'd been, all casual and Saturday rumpled. "All the ladies at school are always going on about how hot he is, but I didn't really get it until he hit that triple in the sixth inning."

"I know." Serafine licked wine off her lip and closed her eyes, like she was replaying the memory in her mind. "And the way he runs. Like a grizzly bear."

"Because he's so big. Yeah. He looks like he could smash through a brick wall if he wanted to."

"Hulk smash, sister. Hulk smash."

They both laughed, but Via was the first to sober. She cleared her throat. "Evan has a job interview tomorrow."

Serafine raised an eyebrow but didn't comment on the abrupt topic change.

"For a software company," Via continued, swirling the wine in her glass.

"That's great."

"Yeah. It is." The conversation stalled a bit, the way it always did when Via brought up Evan. She knew that Serafine was waiting for Via to ask her why. And that's exactly why Via didn't ask. It bothered her that her best friend didn't try harder to like Evan. And it especially bothered her that Serafine was usually, uncannily, right about these kinds of things. Via stubbornly ignored that. "So, how did the date go with the dentist?"

Safer to change the subject.

It was only because of how well they knew one another that Via caught the look of discomfort on Fin's face. Though Fin wasn't a stranger to the occasional hookup, dating was new for her and uncomfortable for reasons she had yet to explain to Via. "Ah, not meant to be. He took one look at my jewelry, heard that I make my living working with people's auras and he couldn't hail a cab fast enough."

"His loss."

"Exactly. His aura was all wonky anyways. You know I don't do well with the red ones."

Via nodded, having had this conversation many times. "Too practical. But what were you expecting, really, from a dentist?"

Serafine nodded her head from one side to the other. "People can surprise you. But maybe you're right. Maybe I need to start looking for an artist to date. Someone with a nice, yummy green aura."

Via gulped down some wine, her stomach tightening when she swallowed too fast. "I assume we're talking about Sebastian."

"His aura was deliciously green. With just a touch of purple around the center."

"And what does that indicate?"

"That he's open, willing to change, to be amazed. That he's on a journey toward connecting his heart and mind. And there's a little kiss of orange in there as well. That indicates a lot of passion." She raised a dark eyebrow. "Of a very specific variety."

"All right, all right." Via raised a hand. "He's my work colleague, I don't need to hear any more about his passion." She paused. "You want me to give him your number?"

Serafine hesitated infinitesimally, then abruptly nodded. "If it doesn't bother you, sister. I think that would be a good idea."

Via gulped her wine again. "Of course it doesn't bother me! Why would it? You're single, he's single… I think. I'll definitely pass it along." She continued to stare at her swirling wine. "Fin? My aura? Is it the same as it was before? Just blue?"

Serafine sighed. "Oh, Violetta. You know it is."

Blue wasn't a bad aura to have at all. It indicated peace, authority, a sense of calm. But it also indicated a deep loneliness. Via twiddled the wineglass between her fingers. She'd never asked what Evan's aura was. And she wasn't about to now.

"YOU'RE GETTING OLD." Sebastian grinned at Tyler as the man limped back from the play structure, one hand on his lower back.

Tyler plopped onto the park bench, shoving Crabby

to the side as the dog's tongue lolled out one side of his mouth. "Fuck you. I'm three months younger than you are. And besides, no one over the age of fifteen should be expected to do the monkey bars."

"You're just salty because Joy beat you." Seb recrossed his legs and watched as Matty and Joy took turns trying to scale a pole, fireman style.

"Joy always beats me. The kid is like an Olympic athlete already."

Sebastian's eyes wandered over to Joy's parents, both of them sitting on a bench on the other side of the playground, quietly chatting to one another. He used to sit next to them, but he realized pretty quick that they sat in silence if he was around. He didn't want to be the third wheel on their park dates.

"Hey." Seb turned to Tyler. "How're things going with Kylie?"

Tyler leaned forward and picked up one perfectly red Japanese maple leaf. He twirled it in his fingers and sat back, uncharacteristically quiet as he gathered his thoughts. Seb's stomach dropped. If he was reacting this way, then it was definitely bad news.

"She's…all right, I think. But it's not like she tells me much. You know, a fourteen-year-old kid isn't exactly wild about chatting with her forty-two-year-old brother on the phone. Sometimes she texts, and I can usually get her to open up a little more. But we're still getting used to it, you know? It's only been two years since we knew the other existed." Tyler tossed the maple leaf back to the ground. "Doesn't help that her mom hits on me every chance she gets. Gives me the willies."

"Well, you're not related to Kylie's mom."

"Yeah, but she had a kid with my father. There's some

lines a man doesn't cross. And double-dipping with your dad is one of them."

"Oh God." Sebastian grimaced.

"Exactly. Anyways, I've been trying to talk my way into visiting them in Ohio without having to see Kylie's mom too much. But I don't know, I don't want to push. I know that it's hard for Kylie to be around me. That I remind her of our dad." His face drew tight, and for a second, he looked a lot older. "And that's pretty much the last thing I'd ever want to do."

Seb winced as Matty lost his grip on the monkey bars and plummeted to the ground. The kid bounced up half a second later.

"Ay caramba!" he shouted toward Joy, who laughed her head off at her goofy friend.

"It's not your fault your dad didn't tell them about you before he died. That's on him, Ty. Him and him alone."

"Yeah, but I'm the one who's dealing with it, while that bastard gets to rest peacefully."

They both eyed each other for a second before they burst out laughing.

"Yeah, Ty, something tells me that Arthur Leshuski is not 'resting peacefully' wherever he is right now."

"Fair enough." Tyler grinned and carded a hand through his hair, like he was wiping away the thoughts of his dad. "Regardless, he gets to, I don't know, shovel coal for an eternity while I'm here dealing with his grumpy teenage daughter and horny ex-wife." He coughed into his elbow, an old tell that he'd had since childhood. "Let's talk about something else."

"I have a crush on a woman in her midtwenties."

Tyler's jaw dropped as he rotated around and gave Seb his full attention. "Do tell? You have my complete and undivided attention."

Seb waved his hand through the air, embarrassed that he'd said anything. "It's nothing. Really. This woman that works at Matty's school. She's cute. Too young. Has a boyfriend. The works. It's nothing."

"It's not nothing. It's a crush! Your first since Cora. That's big news, Seb. Big fuckin' news."

"She has a boyfriend," he repeated.

"So?" Tyler shrugged and kicked some dirt off his shoe. "He's probably her age, too, right?"

"Seems like it. He dresses in clothes two sizes too small and has a ponytail."

"Hipster? Please. Seb, you've got this in the bag. You're the mysterious older man."

"Much older. I played softball yesterday and I woke up feeling like Father fucking Time. Trust me. She's not interested in this. It just feels good to crush on somebody is all. It's not a big deal."

"Is she cute?"

"Sofuckingcute." The words came out in a rush. Sebastian hadn't even realized he'd been holding them in. "She has this squished nose, and she's all tiny."

"Blonde?"

"Brunette."

"Really? That's not your usual type."

Cora had been five-ten and platinum blond. Yeah, Via was definitely not his usual cup of tea.

"Mr. Sebastian?"

No matter how many times he went over it with her, Seb hadn't been able to convince Joy that it was okay to just call him Sebastian.

"What's up, Joy?"

"Matty's stuck in the tunnel."

"What?" Sebastian was up like a shot. This was one of the better maintained playgrounds, but still, this was

Brooklyn and he'd instructed Matty not to go in any of the structure tunnels. He had nightmares about syringes and used condoms, piles of dirty clothes that ended up having a person sleeping inside. "Show me where."

Joy raced forward, her braided black hair bouncing along her back. "Just over here! In the red tunnel."

Sebastian swung himself up onto the structure and ducked his head down to look in the red plastic tunnel that connected one end of the playground to another. There was his son, smiling sheepishly and trying to keep his chin from wobbling in front of Joy.

"Hey, Daddy."

"Hey yourself, little dude." Seb crawled halfway in to the tunnel. "What did I tell you about playing in these tunnels?"

"That it's not safe. But you never said I might get stuck!"

Seb sighed, yanking Matty's foot from his shoe and then the shoe from the crack in the tunnel. "I didn't know you might get stuck."

"Me neither!" Matty's face oscillated between humor and embarrassment, with just a touch of panic thrown in. Nobody liked getting trapped in a play structure tunnel. Especially when you knew you weren't supposed to be in there in the first place.

"All right." Seb scooted out of the tunnel after Matty and crouched next to him, jamming his son's foot back in his shoe. "We'll talk about it later, okay?" Sebastian was very aware that Joy and Uncle Tyler were standing just behind him; he didn't want to embarrass the kid.

Matty nodded solemnly, relief in every line of his blunt little face. He rose up, then knelt back down to talk right into Seb's face, the way he used to do when he was a toddler. "I get it, Daddy. About the tunnels. I get it now."

Seb lifted Matty down toward Joy and they chased each other over toward the jankity old seesaw. Yet another dangerous part of this playground. But, what were you gonna do? Not come to the playground with your kid on a Sunday afternoon?

"It's crazy how well-adjusted your kid is." Tyler shook his head, his hands in his pockets.

"What the fuck does that mean?" Seb's hackles rose, in the way that they only ever did with Tyler.

"Put your guns away. I just meant that the kid has been through so much the last few years, and you've really done a good job keeping him on an even keel."

Seb's anger pinpricked away. "Yeah. Well. When you're the only thing your kid's got, you figure it out."

"Don't diminish it, dude," Tyler said, his voice suddenly hard and his eyes sharp. "You stepped up to the fucking plate. And you did it because you're a good person. And a good dad. Don't act like just anybody could have done what you did, all right?"

It was with those words in Seb's brain later that night that he took out his phone. Matty was scrubbed from head to toe, still pink from his bath, and swinging his feet from the barstool at the kitchen counter. He was leafing through a picture book and picking at the smallest bowl of ice cream known to man.

Seb clicked around until he found his most recent message from Valerie the dog walker.

Hey, Sebastian! Wanna meet up this week?

It was topped off with the kissing lips emoji, in case he didn't understand that it would be strictly physical if and when they met up.

He was flattered. And part of him, the younger part

of him, couldn't flipping believe he was about to throw away a pipeline to some instant tail. But he looked up at his barefoot son clanking his spoon in his bowl and milking every second of the evening before bedtime.

Hi Valerie. Had a great time with you last week, and I like you a lot. But we want different things. Good luck with everything—Sebastian

He felt like a dinosaur signing a text with his name at the end, but come on, you couldn't sever ties with someone through a text message and not even have the courtesy to sign your own name.

He sighed and turned the phone over on the counter. He swooped in on his son, ripping him up off the barstool and tossing him straight in the air.

"Gah! Dad! What the heck! I didn't finish my book or my ice cream!" But he was giggling like a madman when Seb scraped his five o'clock shadow on the kid's exposed belly.

"Well, grab your stuff then. You can finish it in bed. It's past 8:30." He held his son upside down so that Matty could grab the book and bowl of ice cream. Which he did with a blinding grin on his face.

Seb hauled them down the hall and straight into his son's room, where he got to experience the acute joy of having his kid read a book to him. And he didn't even think about the phone he'd left in the kitchen.

CHAPTER NINE

"Hey!" Via almost winced at how chipper her voice sounded as Sebastian slid into the seat next to her at the staff meeting. *Tone it down, Violetta.* She sounded like a fourth grader. And she would know. She spent pretty much her entire day with fourth graders.

"Hey." He winced as he stretched his legs out in front of him.

"You all right?" She frowned down at his legs. His very long legs. How had she never noticed how crazy long his legs were before?

"Yeah." He paused and greeted Shelly and Grace, who were sitting in the seats in front of them. He passed around his usual gum, peeling his own slice and popping it into his mouth. He turned back to Via. "I'm still sore from the game on Saturday."

"Really?" She furrowed her brow. "Did you not stretch or something?"

"Oh, I stretched. There's just this delightful little thing called age. It starts to bite you in the ass around thirty-five and, you know what? I won't spoil the surprise for you."

She grinned at him, her head tilted. "You know, I've heard of it. Have you ever tried yoga? It helps with aches and pains."

"Oh Lord, I knew you'd be a yoga person." He shook his head.

Via laughed again and straightened the cuff of her blue

silk shirt. Blue like her boring, lonely aura. She swallowed down her frown. "Are you one of those men who insist that yoga is only for women?"

He looked affronted. "Definitely not. I just think yoga is for…bendy people. And trust me, I'm not one of the blessed."

"You might surprise yourself. I go to this great community yoga class in Crown Heights. There's plenty of… un-bendy men. You might like it."

"Are you inviting me?" His blunt face looked more confused than intrigued, and Via found her stomach was suddenly trying to lurch in two different directions.

"Oh. Well, it's open to the public of course." She turned back awkwardly to face front.

"You know, I'm kind of surprised that Principal Grim has never had us do yoga before."

Her shoulders loosened just a touch when she realized that he wasn't weirded out by her basket-case quasi-invite. "Actually, that's a really good idea."

"Wait! No." He looked utterly horrified. His mouth dropped open and his hands rose in front of him. "That's not what I was saying. Not at all. I definitely don't want to do yoga at these meetings. I was just saying—"

"Don't be modest, Sebastian," she teased. "That was a great idea. I can't wait to run it past Principal Grim. I'll bet she'll have us wear yoga clothes to the next meeting."

"What the hell are yoga clothes?" If possible, he looked even more horrified.

She bit the inside of her cheek. "You know, leggings, tank tops, that sort of thing."

He lowered his chin and pinned her with a stare. Via realized, with a tight little tap to her heart, that his light eyes were somewhere between gray and green. She hadn't noticed before. "You're telling me that you want me to wear leggings and a tank top to a staff meeting at the school my child attends?"

"You'd have a problem with that?" she deadpanned.

He broke first, chuckling. "Me? No. Although I think some of these ladies would have to burn out their retinas to get rid of the image of me downward dogging in a pair of leggings."

Via laughed again. "Seb, I think some of these ladies *dream* about you downward dogging in a pair of leggings."

His eyebrows shot up at the same time as her cheeks caught on fire.

She had not just said that. Nope. No, she didn't. That was someone else. Some passing idiot who was on her way to move to Alaska and stick her head in a snowdrift for the rest of her life.

She was flirting with him, she realized with something close to shock rocking through her. She couldn't remember the last man she'd flirted with, besides Evan of course. It was…not the right path to walk down. In fact, her eyes danced around the room quickly, trying to see if anyone was looking at them. Had anyone noticed the pink she was sure was in her cheeks? The breathy way she'd just been laughing? Oh God. She was at a staff meeting populated with women *panting* for Mr. Dorner gossip. She needed to ice-bucket this moment. Stat. And she knew the perfect way to do it. She straightened in her seat and pulled her phone out of her pocket.

"Before I forget, Serafine wanted me to give this to you." She held out her phone with Serafine's contact info pulled up.

"Oh." Sebastian's brow furrowed as he realized what Via was handing him. "Ah. She wants me to reach out about furniture making?"

Via cocked her head to the side, back on even footing. He was flustered. "No, I think she wanted you to have it for social reasons. A date? It's okay if you don't want to take it."

"Right." He stared down at the phone, just a touch of color in his cheeks. "Mind if I ask you how, uh, old she is?"

Via cocked her head to one side. "She's thirty."

"Right," Sebastian repeated and seemed to be weighing something in his mind. He cleared his throat and waggled the phone. "You mind if I text the info to myself?"

"Sure, that's fine." *That way I'll have your number, too.* She didn't say it out loud, of course. She paused and tried very hard not to ask. "You think you'll call her? Just curious." She shrugged and hoped it looked casual.

"I don't know," Sebastian replied as he handed the phone back. "How does she feel about kids?"

"What do you mean?" It was cute that that was the first thing he thought of when considering calling up a woman. Very cute.

"I just mean that I've recently had some…miscommunications with women about Matty. And I'm not really interested in connecting with somebody if they aren't cool with his place in my life."

"Ah." Via frowned. Who the hell were the women he was dating if they disapproved of Matty? Matty, the sweetest kid of all time. And anyone with eyes could see how important he was to Sebastian. "Fin would never hold that against you. If that's what you mean. We both grew up in nontraditional homes, so she definitely understands the importance of family in a kid's life."

"Cool." He shrugged and looked forward. Suddenly a small blush rose up out of the collar of his worn green button-down. He shifted. "Uh. You mind if I ask just how psychic she really is?"

Via laughed in delight. Jeez. He really was cute. All masculine and nervous at the same time. *He and Fin would make a cute couple*, she told herself. "Not as much as you're probably imagining. She can't touch your hand and know your bank pin or something. More, she's just intuitive. And she's usually right about everything. Annoyingly so."

He chuckled, but he still seemed a little nervous. "All right." He cleared his throat and suddenly looked very, very uncomfortable. "She doesn't talk to the dead, does she?"

Oh.

The air turned to ice in Via's lungs. She understood what he was really getting at now. His wife. Of course. She was sure he'd come to have certain beliefs about the afterlife after his wife had died. Most people did. It was a coping mechanism. But it had only been two and a half years or so, by her calculations. She was sure that he wasn't completely over it. And he certainly wouldn't want some spooky psychic attempting to make contact with his deceased wife over a Friday night date.

"No," Via answered resolutely. "She doesn't do that."

"Cool," he repeated, then turned his attention to the front of the room where Principal Grim was clinking her ring against her water glass.

Via missed the first ten minutes of the meeting. She couldn't explain it. Her mind was just elsewhere.

HER MIND WAS still elsewhere, when, later that night, she pulled a lasagna out of her oven and set it, steaming, on the table just under Evan's nose.

"Damn," he murmured. "That smells great, babe."

He finished slicing the bread he'd brought over from his house and slid it into a bread basket. Next, he gave the salad he'd made one more fluff with the tongs and then he gestured outward with his hands like a magician.

"Dinner is served."

Via laughed and brought over silverware and plates and slid into the seat across from him. One of the things that she'd first loved about Evan was how willing he always was to help cook. She'd given him a breadmaker for Christmas last year and had been pleased to see that he actually used it.

She served herself some salad while he sliced up the lasagna, trying to wipe the frown from her face before he looked up and saw it.

"What's wrong?" he asked, already sounding a little exasperated. But that might have just been her imagination.

"Nothing!" she said brightly. She felt it would be petty, after he'd made the bread and assembled the salad, to remind him that she really didn't care for raw onion in her salad. She'd told him before that she felt the strong flavor ruined the entire salad, but either he kept forgetting or he simply didn't care. She held in a sigh. She'd just eat around it.

He served her some lasagna, took a mondo bite of his own and dropped his head back. "Holy God, V. That is pretty much the best thing I've ever tasted."

Her annoyance with him waned just a little. "I'm glad."

"So, how was your day at work?"

Pleased that he'd asked, Via opened her mouth to answer but closed it again immediately when it wasn't her students' faces who flashed through her mind's eye, but Sebastian's. More specifically, it was the concerned look on his face he'd had when he'd asked about Serafine's psychic abilities. She frowned down at her plate.

"That bad?" Evan asked in surprise, attempting to interpret her expression.

"What? No." She looked up at him, chewing too much food in his mouth, his movie star hair falling across his forehead, and a strangely familiar feeling opened up in her chest. It was like a cold draft against a window that wasn't sitting correctly in its jamb. The feeling disconcerted her. She hadn't had it in years, but it had been happening a lot lately. Somewhere around the beginning of the school year, the feeling had been making itself at home again.

Why in God's name would she be feeling this chilly, drafty feeling right now? She used to have it when she was younger and completely alone and spinning from one untethered situation to the next. There was no reason for her to be having it *now*. She loved Evan. He'd helped her make dinner, he was asking about her day and looking so handsome it hurt, with his dark eyes and angular face.

She watched him reach out for seconds of the lasagna as he waited for her to gather her thoughts. She frowned. She knew from experience that in his second serving, he'd take too much, wouldn't be able to finish it and would throw the remaining bites into the trash. She literally had to turn away when he did it. Even the sound of that much food falling heavily into the trash made her wince.

"My day was actually pretty good," she said after a minute. "I made some progress with that boy Agwe I was telling you about."

"The Haitian one?"

She nodded. "Yup. He and his dad arrived in Brooklyn about three days before school started. I think it helps our relationship that I'm as new at that school as he is."

Evan pushed his plate away from him, still half full with lasagna he wouldn't eat but would claim was too unsanitary to put away now that it had been on his plate and touched by his fork. "What's wrong then? I can tell something is wrong."

That drafty feeling whistled through her chest again and Via almost made herself ignore it. But she remembered something that a social worker had once told her. That bad feelings were like monsters in the closet at night. If you got a friend, opened the closet and shined a light in there, the monster would up and disappear, nowhere to be found. The point being that bad feelings often subsided if you told someone about them. It was a tenet that Via had tried to live her life by, and it was a testament to how tumultuous her childhood had been that she could no longer even remember the face of the social worker who'd let her in on that particular secret.

"I… I guess I've just been thinking about my foster homes a lot over the last few weeks. Something is reminding me of my experiences there and I'm not sure what."

"Oh. Really?" Evan cleared his throat and reached for another slice of bread. He had a polite look affixed to his face. The one he always wore when she talked about her experience in the system, or even about her parents. At the beginning, when they'd first been falling in love, she'd sensed his genuine interest in her childhood. But when it had started to become clear that the stories were not very Oliver Twist, he'd sort of stopped asking about it. "Are there any foster kids that you're working with at school?"

"Two, actually. But I don't think that's what…" she trailed off in frustration. She wished she hadn't brought it up. She felt like she'd walked into a hallway only to find the far door was locked, and now she'd doubled back to find the original door was locked as well. *Shine a light on the feeling*, she urged herself. "I think it's just that I'm kind of having this feeling I used to have when I was a kid. And I don't know why I'm having it."

"What feeling?"

She couldn't name it. "It's, well, it's kind of like that feeling when there's a storm outside and all the lights flicker out. You know?"

He squinted one beautiful eye at her and shrugged. "I mean, yeah, that's happened to me before."

"Well," she soldiered on. "When that happens, everything goes quiet and dark. And you realize just how much noise your life usually makes. Like, with the refrigerator humming and the buzz of an old lamp, that kind of thing. And for a second, you just sit in the dark and the quiet, and listen to the storm outside and think, this is what life is *actually* like. And the lamp and the refrigerator, all they do is just cover it up."

The other eye was now squinting at her as well. "That's how you felt as a foster kid?" he asked slowly.

"I guess I just felt like I realized that the world was a naturally lonely place, only I hadn't known because I had my parents there to protect me. But when they were gone, I realized the natural state of things."

Evan's eyes had stopped squinting but now, much worse, they were wide and filled with what she was certain was pity. "Oh, babe, loneliness isn't the natural state of things." He paused and the pity in his eyes intensified. She could practically hear him thinking the words *poor little orphan girl.* "You just need to make friends at school is all. You'll feel less lonely then."

She bristled. And she wasn't sure if it was because this very affluent man with his entire family intact was telling her a thing or two about the world, or if it was because he was accusing her of not having made friends yet. Either way, she felt hot pokers of irritation rise out of her skin like the spines of a hedgehog.

"That's not what I'm saying," she insisted bullishly. "I'm not saying I'm lonely." Or at least she wasn't admitting it. "I'm just trying to describe this feeling I used to have that I've been having again. Like déjà vu. It's a cold feeling. Drafty—"

She cut off when his warm hands slid across the table and laced fingers with hers. "If you're cold, V, I'll warm you up. I promise."

She looked down at their linked hands. She had to admit that being held by this beautiful man, even just holding hands, did infuse a bit of warmth back into her body.

She looked at the lasagna on his plate and considered all the words she hadn't been able to say just now. It was ridiculous and unfair to think that Evan would know some magic words that would cure her of this feeling. The warmth between their palms, the bread in the basket, the sunny little salad, a person to share lasagna with, those were all things to be grateful for. Evan certainly didn't demand for her to be perfect. It would be the height of hypocrisy if she demanded that of him. She took a deep breath and tuned out everything but the feel of their hands pressed together.

And as for that drafty feeling? Well, it was her fault if she let herself sulk around and listen to the wind whipping through her.

"YOU DIDN'T."

Sebastian's large hand slapped a flyer down on Via's very tidy desk. She slid the flyer out from his paw and read it, her grin widening with each word she read. "I see that Principal Grim took my suggestion for a mandatory yoga session for the staff. At—would you look at that—next week's staff meeting."

"Traitor."

"It'll be good for you." She waved her hand through the air, and he snatched the flyer back, glaring at it.

"It wasn't enough for you to smoke me in softball, you have to rub my nose in your yoga prowess as well, huh?"

"Yoga isn't about comparing yourself to another. It's about your own practice. Pushing yourself."

"Well, I'm gonna be practicing myself straight to the emergency room next Monday." He scowled at her.

Via laughed. "You'll like it. I swear."

"And if I don't?"

"Then I'll do something that you're good at, and you can show me up." Via bit her tongue and hoped the heat on her cheeks wasn't visible. That had sounded suspiciously like she was asking him out on a date. *Yikes. Yikes squared.*

But Sebastian wasn't looking at her, he was studying the flyer, a frown on his face. "At least the leggings aren't mandatory."

"I'm sure you can wear whatever you want. But just keep in mind, if you wear shorts, that sometimes you go upside down."

"Dang. I was hoping to go commando that day."

She blushed even further and so did he.

"Sorry," he muttered, dragging a hand over his face. "I really wish I hadn't said that in the middle of a public school."

"On a workday," she added, biting her lip to keep her smile inside.

"To my son's former preschool teacher."

"And soon-to-be guidance counselor."

He groaned and took a step backward. "On that note, I think I'll quit while I'm way, horrifyingly behind."

"Have a good weekend, Sebastian."

"I'll see you tomorrow at the game, though, right?"

"Oh." The papers in her hands crumpled a little and she smoothed them out. "Great."

THE DRAFTY FEELING had subsided a bit as the week went on, though Via couldn't help but feel as if that were just a coincidence. Her life was almost too busy these days to indulge in the melancholy. Especially since she was attending a yoga class every day, before or after school, to prepare for leading the yoga lesson at next Monday's staff meeting.

Regardless of why the feeling was subsiding, Via was just glad that it was.

Her conversation with Evan, however, was not subsiding. It bothered her that he thought she didn't have friends at school. She'd joined softball! She was going to happy hours! She joked around at the Xerox machine with Cat! She'd started eating lunch in the teacher's lounge a few times a week. She'd even recently shared a sandwich with Grace, who'd forgotten her lunch at home. That was a big deal for Via, sharing food with someone. See! She had friends!

But why would Evan's words haunt her so much if they were patently false? She couldn't help but wonder if, at least partly, he was right. If, on some level, this internal checklist she'd been working her way down wasn't actually producing real friends, but some polite facsimile of friends. Like in a sci-fi movie with robots who looked just like people. What did they call those? Androids.

Via was starting to worry that Evan was right. She hadn't made any friends at school, she'd just made herself join in on a lot of activities and instead of cultivating real relationships, she'd made herself into a friend-droid.

Determined to rectify this as quickly as possible, Via invited Sadie to go see a movie on Sunday afternoon. Sadie had enthusiastically agreed, easing some of Via's worries.

The two of them suffered through an Oscar contender at the Cobble Hill theater. Via enjoyed the movie theater itself—with its tiny screens and red velvet seating—considerably more than the actual movie. She was glad to hear that Sadie felt the same.

"I'm so glad we spent an afternoon getting an inside look at that very famous and already well-documented historical figure's private life," Sadie said sarcastically.

"And I'm very glad we got to see the very famous, very rich actor who played him try his hardest to win an Oscar."

Sadie laughed and then fixed her face into a sage expression. "Yes, I think we're better for it." She rolled her eyes. "We should have seen a chick flick."

"Definitely," Via agreed.

"Next time we won't try to impress each other with our good taste and we'll go see a movie we actually want to see." Sadie winked at Via. "Ooh! I love the burgers at this place. You hungry?"

Via blinked for a moment. They'd been strolling casually down Court Street, the chic clothing shops with their linen pants and delicate gold jewelry sort of blending into one long window of fashion. They hadn't made plans past the movie and Via had been unsure if Sadie was ready to go home or what, but there she was, holding open the door to a burger joint, a huge grin on her face, her red hair tousling in the wind. *Want a burger? Let's eat!* Easy as pie.

"Oh! Yes. Sure!" Via wasn't hungry due to compulsive popcorn eating, but she was not about to pass up this opportunity.

Moments later they were seated in a booth and Sadie was dazzling their twentysomething waiter with her smile and a flirty flip of her hair.

"Sunday afternoon beer?" she asked Via.

"Sure." That was very uncommon for Via, but it kind of sounded fun.

The women ordered and chatted idly about school. Via hoped Sadie was having a good time. A few minutes later, when Sadie came back from the bathroom, her face was contorted into a mask of horror as she slid back into the booth.

"Is that a Christmas song playing over the radio? How dare they! The leaves are barely turning yet!"

Via smiled at Sadie's outrage. "Not a Christmas fan?"

Sadie shrugged. "Rae is Muslim and I don't celebrate anything really. My family was never big on Christmas. We're more of a Thanksgiving group of folks."

Via laughed at the snarl on Sadie's face. "I can see from your expression just how much you love the holidays."

Sadie waved her hand through the air and then almost gave the waiter a heart attack with that smile of hers when he set down their food in front of them. "I used to love Thanksgiving, but ever since I came out of the closet, it's just become the one day a year where my extended family either completely ignores who I am or they try to pretend that they're totally cool with it by talking to me about *Will & Grace*. Either way, it gets old."

"Is your immediate family like that, too?"

"No. Not really. I'm lucky in that way. My mom says she always knew and, honestly, I think my dad was kind of relieved that I wouldn't be dating men. Not that that means it didn't take them a long time to truly get on board with my life and choices and what it actually means for me to be gay. In practice, not just in theory. But they did well enough." Sadie took a gigantic bite of her four-inch-tall burger and crossed her eyes in ecstasy. "What are the holidays like in your family?"

Via's much more modest bite of her much more modest burger froze in her mouth. She made herself chew and swallow, reminding herself that this didn't have to be a big deal. "It's very small. But nice. My foster sister and I have some traditions we try to keep up every year."

She let that word *foster* out of its cage and watched it do its magic. It was a special word, one that Via knew meant different things to different people. Over the years, she'd learned to let it do the explaining for her. She'd also learned that she could find out a lot about a person based on their reaction to it.

"Oh." Sadie cocked her head to one side, her mouth still filled with burger. "I didn't realize that your family was nontraditional." She rolled her eyes at herself. "Stupid assumption, I guess."

Via nodded. Something about Sadie's reaction disarmed her a little bit. There was curiosity there, but not judgment. "Yeah. My parents passed when I was young and I went into the foster system. My sister and I are on our own now ever since her aunt, Jetty, passed away. She was my foster mom and Fin's guardian."

"Wow." Sadie was quiet for a minute and swallowed down her bite before she spoke again. "You've had a lot of loss in your life."

That drafty feeling opened up inside of Via with such a swiftness that it nearly took her breath away. It was like too much wind was rushing up to greet her and there was nowhere for her exhale to go. She'd thought it was important to share this with Sadie because that's what friends did, real friends. They shared things about their lives, even the hard, messy stuff. And Sadie had made it look so easy, talking about coming out to her family with humor and honesty. Via didn't want to be the closed-off weirdo who was fine being a friend-droid. She wanted friends! Real ones! Was that too much to ask?

But now there was pity on Sadie's face and Via could choose between obviously changing the subject and showing how uncomfortable she was, or she could dive in further to settle Sadie's curiosity. The thought made her feel sick.

"I'll be right back," Via said in what she hoped was a bright, unaffected voice. She went to the bathroom and tried to settle herself. She pulled her phone out of her pocket and considered calling Evan. But the drafty feeling was full force and she shivered against it, putting her phone back in her pocket. She took a deep breath and headed back to the table.

"I'm so sorry!" Sadie immediately blurted out the second Via sat down.

"You're sorry? For what?"

Sadie's cheeks were red and she looked more uncomfortable than Via had ever seen her. "I feel like I reacted in a really shitty way to you telling me about your family. I obviously made you uncomfortable. I just… I want you to know that it surprised me and it made me sad but that I don't pity you at all. And I'm really, really sorry if it seemed like I pitied you."

Via gaped at Sadie. And for what felt like the hundredth time that afternoon, Via attempted to learn something from her outgoing, loquacious friend. "You…really just say whatever you're feeling, don't you?"

"It's a blessing and a curse," Sadie said with a wince. "But I hope not a fatal flaw?"

Via smiled and shook her head. "Not a fatal flaw. I admire it. And, Sadie, no apology necessary. You reacted just fine. It's a hard thing to learn about people's pasts. I'm going through kind of a weird time right now. It's not you. Really."

"If you're sure…"

"I'm sure."

Sadie watched her closely for another beat before the worried expression gave way to her usual good-natured one. "All right. Well, if you have time, want to help me find a birthday gift for Rae? It's in a couple of days and I've been striking out."

Via let the pleasure of the invitation fill her up. Telling Sadie hadn't been perfect, but it hadn't ruined everything either. It was one more thing that Via told herself to remember about that afternoon.

SEBASTIAN MADE HIMSELF useful by dragging the tables and chairs to one side of the library. It was the day of the dreaded yoga staff meeting and his pits were already sweaty. Great. Just great.

As far as he could tell from chatting with his colleagues that day, the staff was split in two. Those who were already good at yoga and were thus pretty excited about it. And those who were terrible at yoga and were thus completely dreading it.

Sebastian's dread was twofold. One, he didn't want to slip a disc in the middle of a sun salutation (yeah, he'd Googled it), and two, he'd asked Tyler about yoga clothes and learned a great deal. All he knew was that he really, really didn't want to see Via DeRosa in some skin-tights.

It had been bad enough on Saturday watching her sprint around the bases in a baggy T-shirt and a baseball cap.

But how the heck was he supposed to keep his eyes in his head if she was bending over in yoga pants? The task was superhuman. Herculean, even.

He took his frustration out on the tables, stacking them together neatly. He was glad he'd already changed into his T-shirt and basketball shorts (with athletic briefs underneath, of course) because he was already too sweaty for work clothes.

When he turned back around he paused, a little jolted by the group of ten or so of his female colleagues who'd apparently been watching him move the tables around. The second his eyes landed on them, they scattered, like they'd been caught watching porn.

Pushing those thoughts as far from his mind as he possibly could, Sebastian found Grace and Shelly across the room, tittering into their hands.

"Looking mighty fine, Mr. Dorner."

"Oh, Shelly, not you, too," Sebastian groaned. "I'm embarrassed enough as it is." His eyes zeroed in on the yoga mats in their arms, looking like humongous, multicolored cannoli. "Oh crap. Was I supposed to bring my own? Great."

Something soft and cool touched his elbow and Seb turned, looking down into Via's dark, warm eyes. Crap. He'd told himself that he wouldn't look at her. His entire plan was to not look at her. And here he was, staring right at her. With her hair in a ponytail and looking as young as he'd ever seen her.

Too young.

And way too hot.

Damn. She wore a tight, long-sleeve T-shirt and yoga pants that had some sort of sheer cutouts on the side, making her look a little more naked than she actually was. Lovely. That was just exactly what he needed in a moment like this. A sheer strip of skin from her calf to her thigh, looking for all the world like a roadmap to heaven.

She looked young and energetic and athletic. Sebastian felt like an old dad with creaky knees, half a second away from a beer gut. Which, he supposed, he probably was. In fifteen years, she'd be his age right now. In fifteen years, he'd be Principal Grim's age. God. If that wasn't a visual that would snap him out of the puppy-dog eyes he hoped he wasn't giving her, well, nothing would.

"I brought a spare." She held out a baby blue yoga mat. "I figured you might not have one."

Was that guilt on her face? Did she, perhaps, feel a little remorse at subjecting Sebastian to this fresh-baked hell?

"Thanks." He sighed. "Let's get this over with."

"You're right. We should get started." Via walked to the front of the classroom. "Thanks for coming, everybody! Let's roll our mats out and get a jump on it!"

Sebastian repressed a groan. Of course she was leading the class. Because the universe wanted him to suffer. In fact, the universe wanted him to have to fight to repress a boner in front of his colleagues for the next hour. Because the universe was just that kind of asshole.

As PAINFUL AS some of that had been to watch, Via had to admit that the group seemed infinitely more relaxed after the yoga class was done. But maybe that was just because they were out of the danger zone.

"Call 911," Sadie murmured from her puddle on the floor. "Better yet, just call the morgue."

"Oh, come on." Via laughed. "That was a beginner's

class! We laid on our backs and meditated for the last fifteen minutes!"

"Well, it was the forty-five minutes that preceded the meditation that I hope you go to hell for," Sadie grumbled, making Via laugh again. "I need a drink. Anyone else want a drink?"

"I'm there," Grace called across the room, nudging Shelly, who nodded in agreement.

"Me, too!" Cat, Matty's teacher, called from the other side of the room, tying back her silvery brown hair.

"I'll come," Via agreed, surprising herself. She'd had tentative plans with Evan tonight, but he often canceled on her, so she didn't think he'd care if she canceled on him.

"Sebastian?" Sadie called across the room, rolling up her yoga mat.

Via busied herself gathering up her things. She didn't look over at him. In fact, she'd been studiously attempting to ignore his existence for the last hour. Sebastian was as bad at yoga as he'd previously advertised. But there was no ignoring his athleticism. The man had good lines. And muscles out the wazoo.

As she'd led the class, she'd looked pretty much everywhere else that she possibly could have. And even now, she felt strangely repelled from him. Like they were two magnets of the same charge.

"Well, actually," Sebastian's deep voice rumbled over her. "I wasn't sure how long this was going to last this evening, so I got a babysitter for Matty."

Via, still not looking at Sebastian, watched all the other ladies' faces light right up.

"Perfect!" Sadie clapped her hands together like it was a done deal.

"Lemme give him a call and see if it's all right."

"Your babysitter is a boy?" Cat asked.

"Well, yeah. My friend Ty. But I meant that I wanted to call Matty and see if that was cool with him for me to be out longer."

He turned and pulled out his phone, striding to the back of the library. He missed the nuclear explosion of gooey eyes that followed him.

"Oh my gawd. He's calling his son to let him know he'll be out longer than he thought?" Cat clutched her hands in front of her chest. "How in Jesus's left ass cheek is that man still single?"

"Beats me," Grace said, shaking her head. "If I were thirty years younger and forty pounds lighter…"

"Oh please." Shelly patted her own hair and her friend's shoulder at the same time. "You don't need to lose weight, Grace. None at all. But I have to admit, I'd count some calories to have a crack at a man like Sebastian Dorner."

"Where should we go for drinks?" Via asked in a desperate attempt to change the topic.

"Cider." Sadie shrugged. "They should be able to seat us, even without a rezzi. There's only six of us, seven if— hey, Rachel, you wanna join us?"

One of the quieter fifth-grade teachers blushed and nodded shyly, stepping over to join the group. "I wasn't sure if I was invited, but it sounds fun."

Via couldn't help but admire Sadie. Always shouting out her thoughts and inviting people to do things. She wore bright, mismatched clothes, and chewed gum the second the kids were out the door. She just always looked like she was having fun. Via thought back to their lunch together, the ease with which Sadie had talked about the holidays and coming out to her family. Via would have bet a lot of money that Sadie's aura wasn't lonely, boring blue.

A few moments later, Sebastian came striding back over, a bright smile on his face. Via looked up for just a second, but her eyes skated away before she could stop them. He slung his bag over his shoulder. "Where are we going?"

THE WALK OVER to the bar, just a few blocks, was boisterous and loose. Honestly, the yoga had relaxed the teachers way more than the Friday night happy hours ever did. Via walked in the front of the group with Grace and Shelly. She oohed and aahed over the grandkid pictures that Shelly was showing.

She liked the two of them. Shelly was sweet and a little shy. Grace was much more outgoing and could be crass. They had a good friendship going and Via liked being around them.

None of them had changed out of their workout clothes, despite the early October chill, and the bartender did a double take when the group filed in to the bar. It wasn't too busy for a Brooklyn bar on a Monday night, but they had to squeeze to fit into the last table.

A bolt of inspiration hit Via. Something she'd never done before but always wanted to. "First round's on me," she told the group.

A series of little cheers and hoots greeted her as each person told her their order. Mostly beers and wine; Grace requested sherry.

Via leaned against the bar, trying to get the bartender's attention and smiling to herself. She'd never had expendable money before. Not that she really did right now either, but she had enough in her fun fund to drop a hundred bucks at the bar for her friends. It filled her up to be able to do it. She wished, as she so often did, that she could take a snapshot of this moment and message it back through time to the twelve-year-old foster kid who she'd been. She just wanted to tell little Via that she was headed for good things. Adulthood. Stability. The ability to throw a little money around every once in a while.

Via's phone chirped in her pocket, and she opened up the text from Evan. Her smile instantly dimmed. He was irritated that she'd made other plans. And his job interview this morning had not gone well. The bubbling happiness that had been rising through Via just a second before was hardening, forming into a dull lump in her chest.

What was she thinking? She'd totally forgotten about Evan. She didn't have the money to buy these drinks now that Evan was unemployed. He hadn't had to rely on her for anything yet, but they were building a life together, and she should be thinking for two. It shamed her that she'd forgotten his money situation and the potential hard times he was going through when she agreed to go out with her friends. She'd ditched him tonight. In more ways than one.

"What can I get you, beautiful?" the bartender asked, leaning over the bar toward her. He was older, maybe forty-five, and very handsome. He had silver in his hair and tattoos on the backs of his hands.

Via blushed at the endearment, even though she was pretty certain that it was the kind of thing bartenders said to women all the time.

She placed her order and his eyes widened. "Wow, hard day, huh?"

She laughed. "It's not all for me. I swear."

He tapped the bar with the flat of his hand. "You got it, gorgeous. I'll be right back." A moment later he tossed a tray onto the bar and started loading drinks onto it. "You a yoga teacher?"

She looked down at her apparel. "Nope. I just led a class for my colleagues. We're teachers at PS 128."

"No shit? I thought y'all usually came in on Fridays. We'd have held a table for you if we'd known."

"We got a table just fine. And after the yoga, apparently they all needed a drink."

"After the yoga, I needed an IV and about a week of vacation," Sebastian's voice came from over her shoulder. Via and the bartender laughed.

"I hear that—I used to date a yoga teacher. Went to a class thinking I could impress her. Damn. Big mistake. It was one of them hot yoga classes? I saw spots for a week."

Via grinned at the bartender, noticing his eyes dancing between her and Sebastian. She took a step toward the bar and signed the bill he passed over to her.

"I'll carry that for you." Sebastian batted her hands away from the tray and grabbed the drinks. "It's why I came over."

The bartender handed over her copy of the bill and she smiled at him, trailing after Sebastian. The women cheered when he slid the drinks to the middle of the table, and Via found the two of them sliding into the last available seats, right next to one another. Well, fine. That was just fine. She couldn't avoid him forever just because he looked like a Greek flipping god when he chaturanga-ed.

Via looked down at the receipt in her hand, about to fold it into her pocket. "Oh."

"He charge you for something wrong?" Sebastian asked beside her, looking over her shoulder.

"No, he, uh, never mind."

"Ohhhh." Sebastian grinned at her, leaning over to read the receipt. "Christian the bartender left you his number."

She pursed her lips and shoved the receipt into her pocket, a little mortified.

"You're blushing, Via."

"Well…" She glanced over her shoulder where the bartender was busy filling drinks and chatting with regulars. "He's very handsome. I'm allowed to blush when a handsome man gives me his number."

Sebastian took a sip of his beer and tipped his chair back onto two legs. He squinted over at the bartender. "Really? You think that guy is handsome?"

Via glanced back over her shoulder. "Are you kidding? He looks like Dermot Mulroney."

"I have no idea who that is. But don't you think he's a little old for you?"

She laughed in surprise. "He's not old. He's probably like forty-five or something."

"And you're, what…twenty-three?"

She forcefully pulled her face into a scowl even though it was fighting upstream against a smile. "I'm twenty-seven, thank you very much. About to be twenty-eight."

Sebastian blinked at her for a moment, seemed to be turning something over in his mind. But then he shrugged. "Regardless, you're a baby. Spring chicken. And way too young for Father Time slinging drinks over there."

Via rolled her eyes. "Age ain't nothing but a number."

He let out a surprised laugh as he took another drink of beer. "Was that an Aaliyah reference? I wouldn't have thought you were old enough to remember her."

"Actually, that was an Andre 3000 reference." For some reason she was blushing. "And I'm old enough to have listened to both of them. Though I admit the Aaliyah album was a few years old by the time it made its way to my Discman." Her eyes got a little distant. "My parents were so thrilled to buy me that CD. They thought it was so delightfully American."

"They weren't from the States?"

She shook her head. "They came over from Italy after they got married. They didn't have much family left there, and my dad got hired as a professor at Brooklyn College. It tickled them to no end that their kid was into the GAP and rollerblading and *NSYNC." She looked down at the dark beer she was slowly rolling between her two palms. She so rarely talked to anyone about them. "They hated American food, though. I got grounded once when I came home with Doritos in my backpack."

Sebastian smiled, a complicated depth behind his eyes. She knew he understood what it felt like to speak of the dead, quasi-casually, in a bar. She was sure he knew how rarely she mentioned her parents. That he could feel just how rusty the hinges were on that particular door. And for some reason, maybe because of the kindness in his eyes, or simply because she knew he'd lost someone special as well, she wasn't embarrassed by the moment. She leaned into it.

"So you're Brooklyn born and raised?"

She nodded. "Bensonhurst, actually. It used to be a lot more Italian. I moved away after my parents died, to a foster home in Carroll Gardens. Then there was a group home in Bed Stuy. And then I landed in Brighton Beach. With Fin and Jetty. Now I'm back in Bensonhurst."

"Jetty was your foster mom? And Fin's aunt?"

Via nodded, stiffening immediately. She didn't want to talk about this anymore. It disturbed her that she didn't like him talking about Fin. She didn't know if they'd been texting or talking, or if they'd gone out yet. She didn't think they had, or else Fin probably would have mentioned it. But there was a strange feeling creeping over her.

She thought that he'd been getting to know her just then, but what if he'd just been fishing for details about Fin? That was fine, of course. It was a free country. But for some reason, it stung.

CHAPTER TEN

"SHIT! CRABBY!" SEBASTIAN stared down in horror at his phone. His waggling, attention-whore of a mutt had just bumped his hand and made him send the text he'd been debating sending for the last hour.

Actually, he'd already decided not to send it. It was a Friday night. That was a bad time to start texting with someone. First of all, it made him look like a loser for not having plans on a Friday night already. And second, it probably made it sound like a booty call text.

And third, he was currently texting a psychic, so she was probably going to read straight through any subtext right to the heart of what he was saying.

Hey, Serafine. Sebastian Dorner here. Via gave me your number. Would you want to get together for a cup of coffee sometime?

Translation: *I have a major crush on your friend, and my reasons for reaching out to you are so fucking cobwebbed in my brain that I probably should never have sent this text.*

Sebastian tossed his phone aside like he'd just discovered it was made of acid. Those things were freaking dangerous. He resolved, for the forty millionth time, that Matty was not going to get a cell phone until he was at least eighteen. A cell phone needed to be handled with even more caution than a car did.

He grabbed the remote and turned on the Yanks to try to get his mind off the text. Crabby inched just a bit farther into his lap, blinking up at him with big, innocent eyes.

It was a badbadbad idea to go on a date with Fin. If she even said yes. Sure, she was gorgeous. She was model pretty and had all that wild black hair and the mystical thing down pat. But that was most likely just going to fluster the hell out of him. He was sure he was going to accidentally talk about Via too much. And his crush would be even more obvious than it probably already was.

He let his mind circle back around to one very interesting piece of information he'd recently learned. Via DeRosa was twenty-seven. Not twenty-four, like he'd been assuming. Did that matter? It was only a three-year difference, so it shouldn't really matter. But here Sebastian was, texting a thirty-year-old woman for a date, and that was only three years' difference from twenty-seven. Ugh. His math didn't make sense. He knew that. He knew he was highlighting certain rules and crossing out others. But it didn't have to be airtight logic, he reminded himself. The simple fact was that Via was too young for him. Completely different stage of life.

Sebastian took a swig of his fairly warm beer and grimaced. His life had been a hell of a lot simpler before Tyler had forced him to start dating again. Well, he amended, he was going to have run into Via DeRosa again regardless of Tyler's pushiness. He was probably always going to have ended up with this crush.

Seb started pulling the label off his beer bottle, careful not to leave any glue behind. He wondered if he would have had a crush on Via even if Cora was still alive. He'd first met Via in the weeks after Cora's death. He couldn't even remember it. Most of those early weeks were a complete blur. He was pretty sure that Matty's grandparents, the Sullivans, had brought him to and from pre-K for the first few months, though Seb had very little memory of that time. He'd continued to go to work at the architecture firm. He'd barely eaten. Barely showered. Barely spoken.

He was grateful that Matty didn't really remember that time. He didn't want Matty to think of him that way. But he realized, with a twisting pang in his gut, that if Matty didn't remember that time, then he wouldn't remember his mother either. And Seb desperately wanted Matty to remember Cora.

Cora's parents were rigid people, good with Matty, but hardly the kind of people who wanted to reminisce about their daughter. Sebastian's parents were nostalgic people, but they were snowbirds who basically disappeared from Seb's and Matty's lives for everything but the summer months. Tyler brought Cora up every now and then, and so did Mary, but honestly, Seb often felt like Cora existed only within the confines of his own memories. And that terrified him, because she'd been such a force when she was alive. She'd changed every room she walked into. Injected every space with a sour-bright burst of energy and command and intensity. Cora had always reminded Sebastian of a Warheads candy. So sour it hurt, but still you wanted more.

She hadn't been easy to be married to. Neither had he. They'd been making it work. He could see now, though, that he and Cora had been sprinting to keep up with their lives, with each other. He, more than anyone, knew that you could only sprint for so long before you gave out. Seb wondered, painfully, if he and Cora would have figured out how to jog. Long haul.

He couldn't picture her at anything but breakneck pace. He'd been shocked at how quickly her flavor had seeped out of his and Matty's life. She was such a strong presence and then suddenly, terribly, she'd been gone. And there was so little of her left.

Seb wiped his eyes with the back of his hand. He didn't allow himself to wonder if Cora would think he was doing a good job with Matty. He knew for a fact that she would be surprised. Because when she was alive, he'd been a subpar father. Often absent. Around for the fun parts and gone for the troublesome parts. And then right after she'd died, he'd been a *terrible* father.

Neglect.

He was lucky. So fucking lucky that Via hadn't gotten the authorities involved. She'd given him a kick in the ass and set him on his way toward becoming a better father. Looking back, he could see now that the checklist she'd given him, the talking-to, it had been small. A sweet little nudge in the right direction. But at the time, it had saved his life. And Matty's.

His phone dinged from the other end of the couch, and Seb jolted like he'd accidentally sat on a beehive. Crabby sprang to his feet on the couch, letting out a surprised yelp, staring in one direction and then the other.

"It's all right, you sweet little dummy," Sebastian murmured, pressing his face into Crabby's fur as he reached past the wagging behind for his phone.

Seb took a deep breath and ripped off the Band-Aid. He opened the text from Fin's number.

Like a date?

Seb groaned and dropped his head backward. She wasn't making this easy on him. Why did he feel like this was a test? He hated texting. He sucked at it. There was too much subtext. Too much room for error. Not enough honesty. If he'd been sitting next to her, he would have known if she'd cocked her head to one side, blushed, bit her lip. Or if she'd recoiled or dropped her mouth open in horror. Instead he just had three words and a question mark and not a clue as to whether or not she wanted it to be a date.

She asked for your number, Seb.

He took a deep breath and opted for the truth.

Like a friend date where we decide if we like each other enough to go on a real date?

He let out a long, slow breath and resisted the urge to toss his phone away again. He was a grown man. He wasn't a teenage girl squealing into a pillow at a sleepover. He could wait for a reply like a normal—

His phone dinged, and he pounced on it.

Good answer. Sunday morning? Matty can come too if you want.

Sebastian pursed his lips in surprise. That was sweet of her. And considerate. And it was an infinite relief to him to know that Matty could be his wingman on a date he was pretty sure he didn't want to go on. Then he pictured his energetic son sitting in a café listening to two adults talk. He grimaced.

Better make it a coffee date at the park then?

They made arrangements to meet at the Ninth Street playground at 10:00 a.m. Matty would be thrilled to go to the playground twice in one day. Once in the morning with Fin and once in the afternoon with Joy.

Cool. That was great. Low pressure. No pressure at all. Just two adults getting to know one another.

Sebastian groaned and scraped his hands over his face. This was so dumb. He didn't want to go on a date with Fin. He just wanted to get over his crush on her friend.

"This is all your fault," he muttered to Crabby. The dog's only response was to roll onto his back. He happily received the belly scratch.

VIA WAS IN a very bad mood when she arrived at softball the next afternoon. First of all, it had been a bad day at school yesterday. A regular of Via's, Sarah Tate, had had a panic attack during their appointment. Sarah was a little slip of a fourth grader, always jumping a foot in the air at the smallest noise, wilting at anything that even slightly resembled criticism. Sarah had panicked because she had a scheduled visiting time with her father coming up. And honestly, she was just plain scared of him. Via hated the feeling that there was nothing she could do. She'd stayed late brainstorming with Principal Grim, was late for happy hour because of it, and then was late to see Evan.

Which brought her to the second reason for her wildly foul mood. Evan had wanted to come watch her play, but she'd really wanted him to get a jump on his job search instead and it had turned into a very long, very messy argument. Maybe she'd pushed too far; she knew that she'd been both pushing against him and pushing against the drafty feeling in her chest. And maybe it wasn't fair to bring that baggage into the argument and not explain it to him.

But really. It had been a few weeks of him fruitlessly

job-searching, and her skin got all itchy when she thought about it. She had no idea how he could possibly stand to be unemployed in a city this ready to spit you out. She would have taken a job at Crown Fried Chicken by now. Anything to pay the bills she knew he had rolling in.

He was so blasé about it that she was sure he'd ended up taking that money from his parents. It must be nice to have a safety net. And she'd never, ever begrudge somebody utilizing it. But Evan didn't *need* to be using his parents' money. He hadn't been laid off. He'd quit. And he hadn't found another job because he wasn't really looking for another job.

It wasn't that she didn't want him to come to the game. It was just that she wanted him to prioritize. She'd said about half of what she'd wanted to, and he'd stormed out of her apartment. She'd gotten ready for softball, second-guessing every word she'd said.

Via looked around the softball fields. They were still green, even with the yellow leaves blustering along each side. She supposed it was chilly, because she could see Giles's husband and their darling little redheaded girl dressed up like they were headed to the Arctic on the bleachers. But she'd worn a layer of Under Armour workout clothes. Plus, her temper was probably warming her from the inside out. At least Evan was good for something right now.

My very own rage furnace.

Via was both relieved and bummed that Fin wasn't here to watch the game today. On one hand, she'd be able to see through her in a second, and Via wondered if she could handle that kind of clarity right now. She kind of felt like the only thing that was holding her together was the sticky cloud of nasty feelings. If somebody parted the curtain for her, she might just fly into a million pieces. On the other hand, Fin was good with millions of pieces. She was patient and funny and had good witchy medicine that always seemed to stitch Via right back up.

The team was stretching on the field, Giles and Sadie tossing a ball back and forth. At first, she didn't see Sebastian, but then she noticed him sitting in the dugout, arms crossed, leaning over to hear something that Rachel Donahue, the fifth-grade teacher who'd joined them for drinks after yoga, was saying. Apparently, Sadie had talked Rachel into joining the team, too. Which wouldn't normally have bothered Via. But she was in such a shit mood to start with. And here Rachel was, flirting when she should have been stretching. They didn't need another member of the Sebastian Dorner fan club on this team; they needed a second baseman with sticky hands, for God's sake!

Via tossed her softball bag on the ground and unzipped it so fast she almost took a finger off. She jammed her hat low on her head.

"Hi, Miss DeRosa."

Via looked up to see Matty leaning against the chain-link fence, his fingers twisted high above his head and his feet lifting off the ground while he held himself up.

"Hi, Matty." She smiled, feeling the top layer of her foul mood lift off like suds in the breeze. "How are ya?"

"Good," he answered absently, his feet dancing over the dirt and his head lolling to one side. She looked closer; his eyes looked a little glassy.

"Are you sure?"

"Well, no. I'm mad."

"Why?" She pulled out her mitt and a bottle of water.

"Because I wanted to bring Crabby, and Dad said no."

"Why did he say no?"

"Because there's a parade so he didn't want to drive and Crabby hates the train."

"That sounds pretty reasonable to me. You wouldn't want to make Crabby do something he doesn't like to do, right?"

Matty shrugged. "But now I have to do something I don't want to do."

Via cocked her head to one side. "You mean be at this game without Crabby?"

He nodded, sidling over to her and peeking into her bag with the curiosity of a bored kid.

"Well, did you bring something to do? A book or a game or something?"

Matty crouched and peered even farther into her bag. "Dad made me leave before I could get anything to do."

"Actually, you pouted in your room for twenty minutes without choosing something to do. So when it was time to leave, you didn't have anything to bring," Sebastian corrected from over Via's shoulder.

She jumped a little bit; she hadn't realized that he was right there. The man was quiet as a cat.

Matty scowled up at his dad and Seb scowled right back. Via chuckled at how incredibly similar they looked. "Well, it's a good thing you didn't bring anything to do."

"What?" Matty looked up at her.

"Yes." She nodded solemnly. "I wouldn't want anything to distract you from your mission."

She could feel Seb's gray-green eyes on the side of her face but she ignored them.

"What mission?"

"Do you remember my friend Fin? You sat with her a few weeks ago?"

"The pretty lady with the loud jewelry?"

Via laughed. "Exactly." She crouched low and brought

her voice down an octave. Matty leaned in to hear her better. "Don't tell anyone. But Fin is a little bit magic. Just a little bit."

"What do you mean? Magic isn't real. Right?"

"Well…" Via weighed her head back and forth. "There's lots of kinds of magic, and lots of them aren't real. But some of them are. And Fin's magic is real. She can't turn you into a toad or something like that, but she can do spells."

"What kind of spells?"

"Like, good luck spells and get well spells. She can do spells to help people who are sad or lonely or scared. That kind of thing. It's kind of like medicine, but you have to believe it for it to work."

Matty's blunt little face was open and very still as he listened. There was no trace of a pout anywhere on his little mug.

"So," Via continued. "Fin asked me if I could help her with some spells she's working on, but I have to play this dumb softball game. Can you help me? Can you take over my mission for me?"

Matty pursed his lips but there was no confusing the look of intense interest in his eyes. "What would I have to do?"

"You'd have to collect some ingredients for one of her spells. Here." Via dug through her bag and came up with a small towel. She pulled out her practice bat and tied the four corners of the towel to the end of the bat. She showed Matty how he could carry it over his shoulder like an old-timey drifter. "You can put everything you collect in here. You need to find two yellow leaves and two red leaves from the trees. A flower. Something shiny. And…" She racked her brain, trying to think of something that would take a long time. "Some rocks from the gravel area over there. I want you to find one rock of every color."

"But those rocks are all gray!"

"No. Not if you look closely. Lots of those rocks have little flecks of other colors in them. You'll see." Then she gave him a skeptical look and held the towel carrier away from him. "Unless you don't think you can help. Then I'll just tell Fin that I'll do it on my own tomorrow."

"I can do it!" Matty insisted, reaching forward and propping the bat on his shoulder. "It might take me all day," he grumbled a little, not wanting to seem too eager.

"Well, do the best you can. I'm sure Fin will understand if you can't find everything."

Matty marched away toward the tree line at the edge of the softball field and Seb let out a low whistle behind her.

"I think *you're* the one who's magic. I thought that kid was going to pout himself into an early bedtime."

"He's having a bad day?" She turned to Seb.

"I guess." He squinted his eyes as he watched his son inspect a few fallen leaves, discarding them. "He's usually not quite so ornery. Maybe he's having a growth spurt. Anyways, thanks for distracting him. That was incredible. They don't teach stuff like that at parenting classes."

"You take parenting classes?" Via asked, grabbing her bag and noticing that Rachel was watching the two of them talk from across the dugout.

Sebastian nodded. "Yeah. My grief counselor recommended it after Cora died. Just something to help prop me up a little bit. Some structure to lean on. But I really liked them. And they helped. Every time I think I'm an expert, he goes and grows up a little more, and then I'm lost again." Sebastian sighed, but it was more happy than sad.

"Hi, Rachel," Via called when the staring started to become annoying.

"Hi, Via!" Rachel called back, her eyes still bouncing between Sebastian and Via. Rachel's brown hair was up in a high bun, and she'd chosen one of the team shirts that was just a touch too small. Maybe there'd been a shortage in sizes this late in the season. She was shy and usually pretty sweet. Via generally liked her. She couldn't exactly say why Rachel was bothering the crap out of her right now.

"All right, people. Huddle up!" Sadie called, gesturing to everyone around her.

The game started, and their team gained a firm lead, mostly thanks to Via's three-run triple in the bottom of the fourth. Mindful of Rachel's watchful eyes, Via had avoided Sebastian, choosing instead to chat with Sadie and Rae. She noticed that Rachel took that opportunity to sit next to Sebastian. The two of them chatted and laughed for the majority of the game.

They were just sending their players out to the bases a few minutes later when Matty appeared on the other side of the short fence that lined one side of the field.

"Daddy," he called in a tear-filled voice, his face white as milk. Via took a few stumbling steps toward Matty the second she realized that he had vomit on his shirt.

Sebastian whipped around just as Matty's head lolled to the side and he hit the ground like a bag of rocks. His dad sprinted across the field and, again, Via thought of a lion. He was glinting and primal, his brown hair streaked through with gold in the sunlight. He took the fence in a graceful, one-handed hop and if Via hadn't been so worried about Matty, she might have sucked in a breath at the competence of it. Within seconds, he had his son gathered up in his arms.

"Matty. Matty, buddy. Wake up, Matty."

Via was at their side a second later, just in time to see

Matty's eyes clench closed; he wouldn't open them. "I'm cold, Daddy," he whispered and it was music to every adult's ears in the vicinity. He wasn't unconscious.

"There's an urgent care three blocks over from here," Sadie huffed out as she hurried up. "They take walk-ins."

"Right, I know where it is," Sebastian said faintly, cradling his shivering little boy in his arms.

"I'll get your softball stuff and bring it to school, okay?" Sadie continued. "Just go."

"Right."

And then he was striding away, toward the street. He shifted Matty in his arms so that he could do that two-fingered whistle that quite literally stopped traffic. A cab pulled up to the curb. Via was at his elbow, brushing the hair off Matty's forehead and surreptitiously taking his temperature. The poor kid was burning up. "Do you want me to go with you?"

She felt like she was asking Matty as much as she was asking Sebastian, but it was the father who replied. "No, we're fine."

He kicked open the door of the cab and told the cabbie the intersection of the urgent care. He barely glanced back at Via. "We're fine just the two of us."

He pulled the door closed and the cab drove away.

TYLER TURNED FROM the fridge and thrust a beer into Seb's hand. "I'm resisting the urge to give you a real crisp slap across the face right now, my dude."

Seb chuckled humorlessly and took a long swallow of beer. "Because you think I'm overreacting?"

Tyler pulled out a barstool and sat down. "Because Matty is fine. And because you did EVERYTHING you were supposed to do. You were a great dad. You're taking great care of him and still you're beating yourself up."

"I know. I think I'm having flashbacks to when Cora died or something. Blink of an eye, you know? I keep replaying the moment he fainted. He's never fainted before. I keep thinking how big he looks these days, but he was so fucking small when I picked him up." Seb squeezed his eyes closed, as if he could keep out the memory. He scraped the back of his hand against his wet eyes.

"Is he out for the night, you think?"

"You never can quite tell with a sick kid, but he's sleeping soundly."

"All right. Let's watch a movie or something."

"You don't have to stay, Ty."

"Shuddup. Matty's sick. You look like you stuck your finger in an electrical socket. I'm staying."

Sebastian laughed. "You know, this is why we became friends in kindergarten."

Tyler looked up from his phone. "Because of my loyalty? Sense of right and wrong? You sensed my future devotion to your big-ass kid?"

"Because you just wouldn't leave."

Tyler rolled his eyes and laughed. "Hey, overstaying your welcome is actually a very tried-and-true strategy. Pretty soon, you don't have to wait for a welcome anymore."

They chose one of the endless iterations of the Jason Bourne franchise but ten minutes in, Seb's mind was already miles away. He took out his phone and scrolled through his text messages. He found one, a number he hadn't programmed into his phone yet. It was the text that had sent him Fin's contact info. Via's number. He didn't think too hard on it.

Just an FYI, Matty's all right. Took him to urgent care and then his general practitioner. It's just strep. He's on medicine and sleeping.

He didn't sign the text or tell her who he was. He wasn't about to participate in whatever fancy footwork was required for texting a twenty-seven-year-old crush on a Saturday night when she was probably out clubbing with her model boyfriend. He didn't have the energy. If his text was dumb or stilted or weird, so be it. He just wanted her to have the information. It was less than thirty seconds later that he got a reply.

I'm so relieved. Strep is no fun, but I'm sure he'll be feeling better when he wakes up.

Seb was just contemplating a reply when the thought bubbles popped up and he whipped his thumbs off the keyboard. She was typing. He pictured her in a bar, that bartender from Cider slinging an arm around her. Even though he knew that Via would never let a man put his arm around her when she had a boyfriend. His phone made that swooping sound, and her text popped up.

How are you, though? That was really scary.

He chuffed a little laugh. Scary was understating it. Heart-stopping was what it was. He looked up and saw Tyler's eyes on him. Tyler gave a pointed look at his cell phone and raised his hands up, like, *don't mind me*. Seb didn't think Tyler would be quite so gung ho about this if he knew Seb was texting someone who had absolutely no interest in him.

My hair's gone completely white. You'll barely recognize me the next time you see me. I look almost as old as your hot bartender.

He smiled at his phone as he sent the text and turned back to the movie. He watched a gunfight, barely even seeing it as he replayed his own words back in his head. The smile melted off his face. Shit. That had been way too flirty. See? This was why he was supposed to fling his phone across the room when engaged in a texting conversation with a beautiful woman. He always, always ended up putting his foot in his mouth.

"I'm such a fucking idiot," he told Tyler.

Tyler turned the volume down on the movie. "Yes. Absolutely. What are we talking about?"

Seb wagged his phone through the air. "You should just take this away from me. I'm so not good at digital crap with women. I swear. Me texting is the same thing as your skinny jeans phase. You're just like, dude, *no*. Can't pull it off."

Tyler laughed. "To be fair, I think I could have rocked the skinny jeans if they hadn't been quite so…skinny."

"Pretty sure you're missing the point."

They both laughed again and Tyler rolled his head to look at Seb. "Are you texting or sexting?"

"Sexting?" Seb tried to pick his jaw up off the floor. "You think I'd sit next to you on the couch and sext some woman, you perv?"

Tyler shrugged. "I've sexted a woman while I was sitting next to you before. It's only weird if you make it weird."

"Oh for fuck's sake. That's ALWAYS weird, Ty." He side-eyed his friend. "No, I'm not sexting. I'm just texting. But I accidentally made it flirty when it shouldn't be."

"Accidentally?" Now Tyler was side-eyeing him right back. "There is no accidental flirting. It might not have been in the plan. But if you're flirting, it's because you want to be."

"Bah." Seb glared at his phone and considered turning it off completely. "All this shit is just way too complicated. I'm just going to turn it off—ohchristshetextedback."

Seb ignored Tyler's laughter and opened up her text. He stared at it for a hot second before he let out a very surprised chuckle. She'd sent back a GIF of a ninety-year-old man doing quite a seductive striptease. He had a white beard down to his belt, and he helicoptered his shirt around his head.

He showed Tyler, and both men laughed again at the GIF. "If you don't want it to be flirty," Tyler told him, "just text her whatever you'd text me if I sent you that."

It was good advice. Seb thought for a second and typed out his response.

Well played.

Damn. Still seemed kind of flirty.

VIA HUMMED TO herself as she cut up fruit for a fruit salad. The coffee was taking forever to brew this morning, but it didn't matter. She was in a good mood. Energized, even.

She jumped a foot in the air when Fin's phone vibrated on the countertop next to her. Jeez. Maybe she should have half a cup instead of her usual full. She was a little on edge.

"Fin! Your phone's blowing up!"

"Who is it?" Fin called back from the bathroom.

Via flipped over the phone and checked the display. She blinked and set it down, taking a step away. Her hand felt tingly where she'd touched the phone. For some reason, her stomach was clenching. "It's a text from Sebastian Dorner."

Apparently, he'd made use of the contact information

Via had forked over. She glared at the coffeepot. Seriously, what the hell was taking it so long? She contemplated leaving her coffee maker on the curb and going to buy some ridiculously expensive chrome contraption from Sur La Table.

Yeah right. Via had had to psych herself up for three solid weeks to buy herself a pair of fifty-dollar gold studs. There was no way she was blowing half a G on a coffee maker. She talked herself off the ledge.

"So, you've been texting each other?" Via called, slicing the melon on her cutting board just a tiny bit more forcefully than she usually did.

"A little. Will you read it out loud?" Fin called back.

Via sighed. "Can't you take a bath at your place?"

At least twice a week, Via woke up in the morning to find her best friend luxuriating in her tub.

"You know my bathtub leaks. Read the text!"

Via gritted her teeth and unlocked Fin's phone, her heart softening. Fin used the same pin code as she did. 1885. Their address at Jetty's house. It wasn't fair to be snippy with Fin just because she was getting texts from Sebastian. There was absolutely no reason to get weird.

"He says, 'Serafine, I'm so, so sorry to text this close to when we're supposed to meet, but my son came down with strep yesterday. I'm not comfortable leaving him until he's feeling better. Can we reschedule?'" Via set the phone down and kept carefully cutting melon. So, apparently they'd made breakfast plans together. "That's true, by the way. He had to race Matty to the doctor straight from softball yesterday."

"Text back, 'Feel like company? Via and I could bring by some breakfast for you.'"

"I'm not texting that!" Via slid the melon into the bowl and started dicing mango.

"Why?" Fin shouted back, her voice echoing from the bathroom and down the hall. Via's neighbors probably hated when Fin came over for bath time.

"It's pushy. I'm sure he doesn't want guests over right now, and I wasn't invited along on your...date in the first place. It would be so weird for me to show up."

"Look, Violetta, either we can take the long way, and I can slowly convince you that it's fine, or you can just trust your *psychic* friend that this is all going to be just fine, okay? Text him."

Via didn't respond, but she did send the text. Fin could be a pain in the ass, but she was usually right about these things.

It was less than a minute before Fin's phone vibrated again. Via picked it up and cleared her throat. "He says, 'Actually, that would be great. I have two friends over to see Matty, and neither of the bums thought to bring anything to eat. Is that too many people to feed?'"

"Text back, 'Be there in forty-five minutes with breakfast in hand. Feel free to kick us out whenever you want.'"

Via chuckled and sent the text and then picked up her own phone, just as a new text from Evan popped up. She clicked out of the message without reading it and went into her text strand with Seb from last night. She smiled at it. He was funny.

Hey, Fin tells me we're coming over. Does Matty need anything in particular that we could pick up on the way?

She clicked back and read the text from Evan. He was visiting his parents upstate and obviously very bored. Just got a new high score on QuizUp! She could think of exactly zero things to say back to that.

Seb texted back, and she immediately read it.

His royal highness has requested a Nintendo DS because he's 'sick and deserves one anyways.' Do not get him that. I repeat. Do not come here with a Nintendo DS. Some tissues would be nice.

Sounds like he's feeling better ;)

Modern medicine, am I right?

Her fingers paused over the keys before she exited out of the text strand and instead called Evan. He answered on her first ring.

"Hey, baby."

She smiled at his smooth baritone. So familiar. "Hey." She regretted fighting with him yesterday.

"Whatcha up to?"

She cleared her throat. "Fin and I are visiting a friend from school for breakfast. That guy you met at the farmers market? Sebastian? Well, his kid got sick, so we're gonna go visit."

"That's nice. You knew him from before, right? You had Matty in pre-K?"

She felt a burst of love for Evan. He'd always been a good listener. She had so many students and so many different stories about them. It really was kind of remarkable that he could keep track of all of them.

"Yes. Right before I met you, actually."

"I remember how worried you were about the kid. His mom had just died?"

"Yeah." Sadness crept into her voice. "What are you up to this morning?"

She could hear some clicks and pings in the background that indicated he was probably still playing QuizUp while they were talking.

"I'm just hanging out until noon, and then I have a meeting with my dad's friend from work. Remember, I told you about that?"

"Right!" How could she have forgotten? She'd been wanting to help prepare him for this meeting. It was really important that he got it right. "He's going to try to pull some strings to get you hired on as a paralegal in BK, right?"

"I guess."

His noncommittal tone had her stomach sinking. He could come across as very aloof if he wasn't interested in something. She didn't want his dad's friend to think he wasn't serious about getting a job. "Do you have your résumé with you?"

"Yeah. Look, babe, I really have to jet. You wanna talk more later?"

"Sure, there was just one thing I wanted to say. I just wanted to tell you that I'm sorry we fought yesterday."

"Apology accepted," he replied without any hesitation whatsoever.

Via paused. "That wasn't exactly what I meant."

"Right. Look, let's talk about it tonight, okay? Love you."

"Love you," she answered faintly as the call clicked off.

She heard Fin pad, barefoot, into the kitchen. But she didn't turn around. She didn't want to see the expression that she knew was going to line her friend's face. Via caught sight of herself in the shiny toaster. She only had to look at herself to see it in full force.

CHAPTER ELEVEN

SEBASTIAN DIDN'T ANSWER the door to his little brick two-story house. The most beautiful woman that Via had ever seen answered the door. Maybe thirty-five years old with a symmetrically perfect face and rivers of long blond hair, she grinned at Via and Fin and waved them inside.

"Hi, I'm Mary, Seb's friend. He's with Matty right now." The woman stepped aside in the small foyer, her rust-colored sweater dress and high-heeled boots look-ing so cool that Via almost winced. "And this is Tyler."

Mary pointed through the doorway into the homey little living room toward a man who was setting aside his phone and rising from a plush armchair. He had an easy smile on his face that completely froze in place as he looked up and saw Via and Fin.

All three women waited for Tyler to say something. Anything. But he didn't. He just continued to stare straight at Fin.

"Uh…" Mary started.

"Whoa," Sebastian said, as he stepped into the living room from the kitchen entryway, drying his hands on a paper towel. "Weird vibe in here."

He tossed the paper towel back into the kitchen, and Via saw that it banked perfectly into his trashcan.

"Hi, Via, Fin. Welcome." He stepped over and in turn, took each woman by an elbow, leaned down to kiss her cheek. Via felt the rough scrape of his stubble, the brief press of his mouth, and she froze as stiff as that Tyler guy. She couldn't remember if any man had ever casually kissed her cheek like that before. It was strangely old-world. And charming.

"This is Tyler Leshuski and Mary Trace, two of my closest friends. Did everybody get introduced?"

"Yes. Yeah. Uh, sort of." Tyler came unfrozen and stepped toward the women, his hand held out. He was cute, if a little preppy, in his khaki pants and polo shirt. His blond hair sat high up off his tan forehead and his eyes were so blue they could give you a toothache. He also had the strangest, slightly stunned expression on his face. He took Via's hand first. "You must be Via DeRosa? I've heard so much about you from Matty."

She nodded. "Nice to meet you. And you, too, Mary."

Via turned back just in time to see Tyler holding his hand out toward Fin, almost tentatively, almost like he wasn't sure if he wanted to touch her or not. "And you are…"

"Serafine St. Romain," Fin answered, one eyebrow halfway up her forehead in an expression that only someone who'd known her as long as Via had would interpret as delight. She'd flustered Tyler somehow. And it was tickling her. She eyed his hand for a second longer than necessary before she pressed her elegant, ringed fingers into his.

Tyler jolted, and looked for a second like he wasn't sure if he wanted to yank her forward or push her away.

"Let me help with your bags," Mary said, breaking the tension and giving the fairly awkward group a task.

Breakfast. Time to set up breakfast. Thank God.

"How's Matty?" Via asked as she stood hip-to-hip with Seb, unloading groceries onto his kitchen counter.

"He's all right, slept through the night. I can tell the antibiotics are already doing their thing. Weirdly, he's not complaining about his throat being sore. It's the aches and chills and stuff that are bothering him. Wow. You brought a lot of food."

Via grinned up at him and Seb ignored the zinging flare up his elbow when her shoulder brushed him there. "I'm Italian. We bring food. Lots of food."

He laughed. "It's a good philosophy. It'll make you friends."

Via shrugged, her smile dimming just a little, and Seb wondered if she had many friends. People at school really liked her, so he didn't think it was a matter of being prickly. But she definitely had a lonely kind of vibe coming off her.

They filled their plates with bagels and spreads, fruit salad and pastries galore. They sat at Seb's dining room table, and he cracked the windows, letting the crisp fall breeze filter over them as he poured everyone a cup of coffee.

"So," Serafine began as she tore her bagel up into little pieces and dipped them in the nearest tub of cream cheese. "How do you all know one another?"

Sebastian had been about to sit at one end of the table, between Mary and Via, but he realized, with a little jolt, that this was supposed to be a sort-of date with Serafine. It felt a little strange to sit down next to her, at the head of his table. Public and a little declarative. But whatever. He wasn't going to be an asshole and pretend like he hadn't made a coffee date with her. Seb glanced around the table as he settled himself in his chair and saw Mary's curious gaze, Via's eyes steadfastly on her plate, and strangely enough, his gaze clashed with Tyler's. His best friend since childhood had an expression on his face that Seb had never seen before. What the hell was wrong with him? Sure, Fin was pretty, gorgeous even. But Tyler was acting like Cleopatra herself was gracing them with her presence.

"What's that? Oh." Seb tried to focus himself to answer the question. "Ty and I met in kindergarten. We've been best friends ever since. And Mary..." *Was best friends with my wife? Was Cora's friend from college? Helped scrape me off the sidewalk after my wife died?* "...and I became close a few years ago when she moved to Brooklyn."

"I own a little shop in Cobble Hill called Fresh. It's a home goods store. Furniture and kitchenware and things like that. Design-y stuff."

"Oh! I love that shop!" Via's eyes lit up, and Seb had to hope that this was the point when this breakfast hang became a little less awkward. Everybody besides Serafine was acting like they were here against their will. "You had a window display there a few months ago that I lusted after."

"With no shame," Fin added in that deep Southern lilt of hers. It was musical, like a slow-moving river descending into waterfall. "She was a real home goods hussy for a while."

Mary and Seb laughed.

"Which window display was it?" Mary asked.

"You'd set up the front room like a little living room. With that lavender suede couch and the metallic pillows. Oh! And the—"

"Peacock-green copper-based lamp. Oh, I remember. I had trouble parting with that set. Everybody wanted to buy it, but I wanted it for myself."

"As I recall," Seb cut in, "you ended up keeping that lamp for yourself."

"Not true!" Mary was outraged, gesturing toward him with the melon at the end of her fork. "I just had you make me another one exactly like the first."

"You made that lamp?" Via's eyes were wide and amazed. "I thought you only did furniture."

"I made the base." Seb waved his hand through the air. "Mary chose the shade. I've made a few lamps and chandeliers. But I don't love all the electrical components. Shocked the shit out of myself a few times while I was working on the wiring."

"Can I—we—see your workshop after breakfast?"

"Oh. Sure. It's not much to look at, but yeah."

Mary was opening her mouth, probably to smoothly introduce another line of conversation—bless her—when a bell tinkled from the other side of the house.

Seb dropped his head in his hand and grinned. "I knew I never should have given the kid a bell. I feel like a butler."

But Via was the one who was pushing out of her chair. "Can I go? I wanted to say hi."

"Are you sure you don't mind? I wouldn't want you to get sick."

She shook her head. "I wanna see him."

"All right. Down the hall, first door on your left."

Seb resolved not to watch her go. Instead he looked up at the remaining three people. Particularly at his typically gregarious best friend, who was avoiding eye contact and staring down at his food like it was his last meal. Mary and Fin struck up a conversation, but Seb kind of tuned them out.

He heard Via's low voice and then her light laugh. A minute later she was back.

"He says he wants some of his dad's water?" She looked confused.

Seb made wide, exasperated eyes at Tyler and finally, the man cracked, laughing.

"That kid, I swear." Tyler chuckled, affection in his eyes.

Seb sighed as he rose from the table and joined Via where she stood at the threshold of the kitchen.

"Here." He filled a big blue glass from the sink and handed it to her. "Tell him it's mine."

Via laughed. "Simple as that?"

Seb shrugged. "I should probably try to start breaking him of the habit of only drinking my water. Like, it's gotta be a control thing, right? But the truth is, I think it's kind of cute. And someday he's not even gonna wanna be seen with me. So whatever, the kid wants to share water? That's cool with me."

Via's cheeks were pink and her eyes wide and dark at the same time. She wore no makeup today, and it made Seb realize that she must usually wear some to school because she looked just a little different. Around the eyes. Her brown hair was up in a messy bun and she wore two gold studs in her ears. He thought she looked casual and, honestly, a little stunning, in her white shirt and jeans. He found it both the easiest and the hardest thing to keep looking at her. His eyes vibrated with the tension of holding her gaze.

And when she smiled and left the kitchen, taking the water to Matty, Seb felt like he'd been released from some sort of invisible force field.

When he returned to the dining room, he was amazed to see Tyler with a flush creeping up from his collar. Serafine was talking to him, and it seemed he was a little flustered. He'd never seen his friend thrown so far off his game before.

Via returned, telling Seb that Matty was asking for

him, and he was back in his son's room in a flash. The lamplight was dim in the *Cars*-themed room; red sports cars smiled down from the wallpaper runner on every side. Seb glanced up and was relieved that Via had seen it mostly tidy. The drawers on Matty's dresser were closed and the books on his shelves were mostly lined up. His stuffed animals and craft table were another story, but he was a kid. Seb couldn't bring himself to care.

"Hey, buster. How are you feeling?" Seb crouched at the edge of Matty's bed, adjusting the ancient Charlie Brown sheets that had been Seb's as a kid. A wiggling lump under the covers by Matty's feet told Seb exactly where Crabby had chosen to take a nap. He scratched at Crabby's back through the blanket and watched as the misshapen lump obviously rolled onto his back, belly in the air, even under the covers.

Both Seb and Matty laughed, but Matty's chuckle was subdued. "I don't feel good, Daddy."

"I know, buddy." Seb scraped a hand across Matty's forehead, feeling for a fever, even though he'd never had any idea what a fever really felt like. The kid had a naturally hot forehead anyway. But his hair and the collar of his pajamas weren't sweaty, so he figured that was a good thing.

"I'm sleepy but I can't sleep. My body won't let me."

"What do you mean?"

"I try to sleep but I keep shaking, and it wakes me up."

"Yeah. Those are the chills from your fever." Seb's heart broke a little as he reached into the closet and pulled out another blanket to tuck around his son. When he turned back around, Matty had his hands tucked under his chin and a tear was leaking from the corner of his eye. Matty had always had teary eyes. Just like his daddy. But Seb knew, instinctively, that this was a real tear.

He crouched next to the bed and slung a heavy arm over his son, holding him close for a second. Matty's familiar scent washed over him. His kid had always smelled like dinner rolls. Weird but true.

"What's wrong?"

"I wish Grandma was here."

"Grandma Sullivan?" Seb tried not to sound quite so astonished. Muriel was competent and confident and... harsh as hell. She was the last person on Earth that Seb would have wanted around while he was sick. She wasn't nurturing in the least, and it surprised the heck out of him that Matty would want her right now.

But then the reason sifted down and gently landed on Seb. It started out light and became heavier and heavier as it settled over him. Muriel was exactly like her daughter. Matty didn't want Muriel. Not really. He wanted Cora. He was sick and wanted his mommy.

Fuck. Seb squeezed his eyes shut and pressed his forehead against Matty's shoulder. Pain, acute and old at the same time, washed right through him. Right after Cora had died, he'd naively waited for the day that he wouldn't feel this excruciating sadness over the loss of her. It was far less frequent, but he knew now that it would never be gone. Not really.

"I'm gonna send my friends home, and you and me will watch a movie, okay?" He paused. "And I'll call Grandma Sullivan and see if she wants to come stay for a day or two this week."

"No, Daddy. Don't send them home. I like having them here. One of them is a witch. They can stay. But can I watch a movie still?"

Seb laughed a little at his breathless little boy. At everything the kid wanted. His yo-yo of emotions. He planted a kiss on Matty's hair, smelling like familiar shampoo and sick kid. "Of course."

He set up the movie, and by the time he got back out to the main room, they'd mostly cleared up breakfast. The group sat with their coffee cups in the living room, and Seb was relieved to see that they looked a bit more relaxed.

"Seb," Mary called. "Via wanted to see your workshop, remember?"

"Oh right. Now?" He wondered if he should ask if Fin also wanted a tour, but she seemed comfortable where she was.

"Sure." Via rose and took her coffee cup with her as he led her out the back door and through the postage stamp–size backyard.

He caught Via smiling at the swing set he'd installed for Matty. "It's nice that you have an actual house. For Matty to grow up in, I mean."

"Yeah. We were both done living in an apartment building. Here we are."

They strolled up to a converted garage with an old elm tree shooting yellow sprays of color from every branch and grass a month past a necessary trim. Sebastian bent and unlocked a padlock before rolling up the aluminum garage door and flicking on a few lamps in various corners.

"Sebastian!" Via gasped as she walked into the garage and turned a slow circle on the spot. "Good Lord! How many pieces are you working on at one time?"

He couldn't tell if she was impressed or put off by the organized chaos that bore down on them from every side. He chuckled and scraped a worn palm over his beard, as much in need of a trim as the grass in his yard. When you were a single father, you had to learn to let some things slide. The noise of his stubble against his dry skin was loud in the sudden quiet. He chuckled to himself, because he was seeing the garage workshop from her eyes and because he was nervous. Good and nervous. Like a damned teenager.

"Yeah, I swear there's a method to my madness."

"Oh, I wasn't accusing you of being messy. It's just a lot more…stuff than I imagined."

She wasn't wrong. There were shelves and shelves of slabs of wood that he'd benched for the time being. There were copper pipes lashed together in the corner, and barrels of more copper scraps and fittings that he usually melted down for ornamentation. There were wood scraps and castoffs of all shapes and sizes organized loosely by imagined project. And along one wall were his projects, all in various stages of completeness. In the middle of the garage were his huge, dinosaur-like machines. His band saw and table saw. His router and drill press. The last wall was covered in tools of every shape and size, some of them shiny and new and others looking damn near ancient. A thin layer of sawdust covered everything. But it was just that—thin. He might be a little messy, but he kept a clean shop.

"Well, once I start a project, I usually see it straight through to the end. But I've been a little harebrained lately. And my deadlines aren't so rigid. So I've been alternating a few projects, working on whatever strikes my fancy that day. That dining room set is my favorite. With the Shaker chairs and the table with the beveled edge. But I like that coffee table, too. The mirror over there is giving me gray hairs. Everything has to be so exact with it."

She had wandered over and was examining each item as he listed it. She was very quiet. So quiet he struggled not to clear his throat.

"The mirror isn't exactly your style, is it? The metalwork is so industrial and the angles of the wood are so exacting. Most of your other stuff has a more organic, freeform style to it."

She turned to him, a thoughtful look on her face, one hand tucked under her chin and the light catching on one of her small earrings. But as soon as she saw him, her expression morphed. Something in his face had her blushing.

"Or am I just dead wrong?"

He laughed. "No, no. You're dead right. That piece was contracted by a very particular client. One who I will not be working with again. But I'm not exactly gonna turn away a paying customer. I just don't like his taste. I agree. It's too architectural for me. There are no surprises." He walked over and whisked a hand over the top and side of the mirror, almost dismissively. "It looks exactly like the drawings I made up for him. It's boring."

"Surprises?" she asked as she walked over to the table with the beveled edge. "You mean like the way you sanded this beveled edge into the cut of the live edge?"

Sebastian raised his eyebrows. He was surprised she caught that. Most people wouldn't have noticed the detail, they just would have sensed the overall tamed wildness of the piece.

"Exactly. The whole thing was supposed to be live edge. But the damn thing snapped off at the grain when I was planing it. I was devastated at first. And angry. But then I realized I could just do something a little bit different than I usually do. Give the table two sides. A polite side." He pointed toward the side with the smooth beveled edge. "And the go-fuck-yourself side." He pointed at the wild, knotty side.

To his delight, Via grinned at his choice of words, her dark eyes sparking and her hands jamming in her pockets. "Do you have a client in mind for that one? I feel like it would have to be a very special person who could handle all that…personality in one piece of furniture."

He shrugged. "It was commissioned by an old friend of mine, but once the wood cracked, I knew he wouldn't want it. I'll work on something else for him. I think this one is meant for my house."

He slicked a hand over the top of the table, like it was a prized stallion. It was far from finished, rough and blond in places.

"Well, it suits you. The two sides of it, I mean."

"Lion among flamingos?" he teased her, straightening up and dusting his hands off.

She blushed, but this time there was less joy in it. She changed the subject. "I always like seeing an artist's studio."

"Have you seen a lot of them?"

She nodded. "Evan is an artist. Or…was. I guess I'm not sure anymore. He says he's done with it, but he had so much talent. And a lot of passion."

Seb picked up a stray chisel and hung it in its place on the wall, straightened a can of tung oil and tossed some dirty rags in the hamper he kept in the corner. "Oh? What kind of work does he do?"

"Mixed media. But mostly painting. Occasionally photography. He used to share a studio with a bunch of other artist friends. I spent a lot of time there and was always fascinated at how artists choose to organize their spaces. It says a lot about a person."

He watched as she sidled around the garage, peeking in a small set of drawers, lightly touching a loose screw on the countertop, squinting at the labels on all the different glues he kept.

Sebastian followed after her, tossing the screw into its bowl, closing the drawers and chucking out one of the glue bottles that he saw was empty. "You think so? The studio says something about the artist?"

"Oh, definitely." She nodded resolutely. "It's almost more interesting to me than the art itself. No, no way. I take that back. But I think it sheds light on the art. I like a little window into the artist's process." She turned and took her lip between her teeth, her dark eyes staring at the ceiling of the garage, searching for the words. "I've been to MOMA, to the Met, places like that, but I've never really responded as much to art when it's perfectly curated. You know, the right lighting with the right blurb, all of it lined up in perfect sequential order."

"No?" He was intrigued. "How do you like it then?"

"Well." She squinted, the toes of one shoe resting on the tops of the other. "My foster mother, Jetty, she had such an eye for art. And she could talk about it for days. She had a Picasso."

"You're kidding."

"I'm not. A real Picasso. It was a sketch on newsprint paper. Not a painting or anything. Just two messy figures and a haphazard sun all done in orange crayon. She had it framed, of course, but she never hung it."

"You're *kidding*."

"I'm not," she repeated. "She said it was a gift from an old, rich boyfriend, and she never liked it that much. It sat on the floor, leaning against the wall in the guest bedroom for years. And yet, she had three different O'Keeffe prints carefully framed and displayed in the kitchen. She had a Picasso *original* that no one ever saw and she could talk your ear off about Georgia O'Keeffe. I don't know." Via shrugged and seemed to come back from her memories. Back into the here and now. "It taught me something about art, I think. Not to have reverence for something that doesn't move you."

She strolled to the other side of the workshop and looked at one of the lamps he'd flicked on. It was the beta version of the one she claimed to have admired at Mary's shop.

"I guess that I just like art that fits into somebody's life, you know? I've seen Georgia O'Keeffe exhibitions before, but I still prefer the way those paintings looked on the old peeling wallpaper of Jetty's kitchen."

She turned back and caught his eye. After a second, those dark eyes of hers dropped and she shrugged her slim shoulders.

"I feel exactly the same way."

Her eyes swooped back up to him and she stopped shifting around on her feet. "Yeah?"

"Definitely. When I finish a piece, it's in the best shape it will ever be in. Sanded, polished to a nice glow, the works. But as soon as I send it home with somebody, I know it's only a matter of time before there's fingerprints on the copper, scratches on the wood, crayon or a hot coffee cup ring or whatever it is. This is art, sure, for me. The process of it is creative. And I love that. But in the end, I want people to *use* this furniture, you know?"

She nodded and turned away. "You can never come over to my place."

"I'm sorry?" He pushed his meaty hands into his pockets and froze. Had he said something offensive? Or— God—could she tell that he was one second away from blushing like a schoolboy just being alone with her? That would be humiliating.

"I think we're becoming friends, but I'm pretty sure you'd drop me like a hot potato if you saw the furniture in my house." She was grinning at him and it soothed his worry at the same time it made his stomach turn over. She had quite the smile, this Miss DeRosa. White, white teeth, that crooked one in the front catching the light.

When she lit up like that, lines beside those dark eyes fanned out and made her look a little older. In a good way. Too good of a way.

She's twenty-seven years old.

What was he doing? This was utterly ridiculous. This woman was in a completely different stage of life than Seb was. She was just starting out. She was living in her first apartment without a roommate, for God's sake. Seb was shooting himself in the foot spending time alone with her.

He should have insisted Fin join them for the tour. All he was doing was wasting time on someone who was just not right for him. Sure, she was cute as hell and her personality made his heart race, but honestly, he was just torturing himself. He needed to politely send her packing. Via and her pretty friend, who was practically just as young as Via was. What had he been thinking of? Sure, intergenerational friendships existed. And sure, they could be great. But he shouldn't have agreed to a date with Fin, and he sure shouldn't have invited them over.

Joking around with her at school was one thing. But listening to her tuck in a sick Matty? *Sebastian meet cliff, cliff meet Sebastian. Don't worry, I sprinkled glass bottles at the bottom just in case the fall doesn't kill you.*

Maybe Valerie the dog walker had been a little bit of a dick, but Seb realized that she hadn't been completely wrong. Dating a widower with a kid was just *different* than dating a regular single guy. There was no way that Seb wanted to put that kind of pressure on any woman who wasn't completely ready for it. Especially not one who was barely out of undergrad. Her age had nothing to do with it, Seb told himself. Her *life* was too young for his. And his life was too old for hers.

And, duh, boyfriend yada yada.

Seb started clicking lights off as he responded, showing her that the tour was over. "I wouldn't feel bad about having IKEA furniture; most kids do in their first places. You're young. You've still got time to get your space the way you want it."

He clicked off the last light and braced a hand under the garage door as she ducked under it. He could feel her eyes on the side of his face, but he didn't look up as he padlocked his shop.

"GOOD GOD," FIN muttered once they were far enough away from the house not to be heard. "That was one of the most intense energies of any room I've ever been in."

"I know," Via groaned. "So weird."

"Sexual tension sundae topped off with politeness whipped cream."

"Totally! I've never seen something like that before. I'm exhausted just from watching it. Did you get his number?"

Fin's brow furrowed and she switched the half-full grocery bag from one hand to the other. "Whose number?"

"Tyler's." Now Via was confused, too.

"Oh." Fin cleared her throat as she took an uncharacteristic amount of time to answer the question. "Right. Me and Tyler. No, I didn't get his number."

"Why not?" Via looked supremely confused. "That man looked like he would have kissed the ground you walked on. How could you have left without his number?"

Fin waved a hand through the air. "Ah, you know how I feel about red auras."

Via shrugged. "All right. You know best. But what I just saw? That was really special."

"I agree."

Via got the strange feeling that they weren't exactly talking about the same thing.

"HOLY GUA-CA-MO-LE," MARY SQUEALED as she danced across the room and grabbed Seb into her arms. "She is SO cute, you lucky dog! Seb, I'm so excited for you!"

"Oh. Yeah. Totally. Although I wouldn't really describe her as cute." Seb thought of Fin's fall of long, black hair, her spooky eyes and her loads of intricate jewelry.

"Are you kidding? She's cute as a button. I just wanted to put her in my pocket. When she read Matty that story, I almost died."

"Wait." Seb was putting the pieces together. "Are you talking about Via?"

Tyler stopped typing on his phone across the room.

"Of course." Mary looked confused. "The one you were supposed to go on a date with."

"No, Mary, I was supposed to be on a date with Serafine this morning."

Mary's face scrunched down in even more confusion. Her eyes flicked to Tyler for a second. "Hold on. The one who you obviously have a major crush on was NOT the woman who you had a date with? And the woman whose mere presence gave Tyler a lust-induced brain aneurysm—"

"Hey now!"

"—was the one you were *actually* supposed to be feeling things out with?"

Neither Seb nor Tyler said anything.

It wasn't uncommon for Mary to be this honest. But damn.

"I didn't have a lust-induced brain aneurysm," Tyler insisted sulkily.

"Then what the hell would you call it, Ty?" Mary asked, completely comfortable holding her friend's feet to the fire. She and Tyler had become close after Cora died. There was nothing like dragging a friend out of the wreckage of his life to bond two people. And they'd been equally present in Matty and Seb's life ever since.

"I was just surprised was all. She's really hot."

"She's too young for you," Seb snapped, falling back onto the couch and scraping his hand over his face. Mary and Ty looked at one another in surprise. Seb's temper rarely reared its head. Even in his darkest place, after Cora had died, he never snapped. "They both are. They're too young for us."

Seb lifted his head and stared Tyler in the eye as if challenging him to say different.

Tyler didn't disappoint. He tossed his phone on the coffee table and crossed one ankle over the other. Mary settled in on the far side of the couch, looking like she was wishing for popcorn.

"Maybe they're too young for you, old man. But not for me."

"We're the same fucking age."

"Apparently not."

"What's that supposed to mean?"

"It means that just because you have a kid you act like you're over the fucking hill. You're forty-two years old, Seb, not exactly about to join the AARP, okay?"

Mary snorted, her laugh bubbling out of her, and Sebastian fought to keep a good grip on his temper. He wanted to fight, goddammit, he didn't want to laugh right now. But Mary just had one of those laughs. Once she got started, you had no choice but to join in.

"You don't understand, Ty. Whatever, sure, forty-two isn't geriatric. And maybe if I'd met her at a bar somewhere, we could've left together." He didn't explain which *her* he was thinking of and neither of his friends asked him to. It was already written all over his face. "But the fact of the matter is, we're in completely different stages of life. THAT'S what the age difference means. I'm a father. Of a kid who is old enough to ask questions. A kid who deserves stability. I was *married.* I've buried a wife, for fuck's sake. I can't be running around with a woman who has to Google 'how to pay my taxes.' A woman who is young enough to—" He cut himself off and grabbed at a hank of his hair. "She's going to have a dozen more boyfriends before she finds the person she's supposed to settle down with. And I'm not up for that kind of carnival ride, you know?" The air was leaving his balloon, and in its place, was nothing but deflation. He wasn't mad. He was just bummed. Really fucking bummed. "I can't be. I'm too old, and I have way too much at stake."

Sebastian sat back and finally looked up at his two closest friends. He thought he'd see sympathy there, pursed lips and sad eyes. Instead he saw annoyance in one of them and frustration in the other; both of them had a fire burning. Mary leaned forward, Tyler opened his mouth—

"Daddy!"

A bell rang furiously down the hall and whatever his two friends were going to say to him had to wait. On perfect cue, his life interrupted.

CHAPTER TWELVE

SHE WASN'T PARTICULARLY paying attention or anything, but it didn't escape Via's notice that neither Sebastian nor Matty came to school on Monday or Tuesday. She wasn't surprised, figuring that Matty was still under the weather and Sebastian would obviously choose to stay at home with him. But Wednesday rolled around, and it was Tyler who brought Matty to school.

Via noticed as she jogged through the school parking lot toward the front entrance, but she was so late for a classroom observation session that she hadn't had time to do more than wave. She certainly didn't have time to go over there and ask him where Sebastian was.

Via was racing from one appointment to the next all morning, two of which were about Sarah Tate and her father, and it wasn't until the last fifteen minutes of her lunch break that she even got a second to think about the fact that Sebastian was MIA for the third day in a row.

She unlocked her cell phone and entered into a text strand before she exited out and called Evan instead.

He answered on the third ring.

"Hey."

"Hi. Just eating lunch, thought I'd call."

"Cool. I'm eating, too."

"Still think you'll be home on Sunday?"

There was a pause, where she heard him open a can of

soda and scrape a chair across the floor. "No, I'm thinking I'll drive back down on Saturday instead. I miss you."

She furrowed her brow. "You're gonna rent a car to drive home? Isn't it just an hour on the train?"

"Crap. I spoiled the surprise. I wanted to tell you in person."

Via set down her sandwich and rubbed her sweaty palm against her gray pencil slacks. "What is it?"

"Well, I got a car."

"What?"

The weight of car insurance and parking tickets and repairs instantly tumbled down over Via, so fast she felt like she couldn't have stood up if she'd tried.

"It's great, you're gonna love it. A silver Lexus. Four-door. Parking will be a bitch on my block, but I can keep it parked by your house, that'll probably be easier. I spend so much time at your house anyway."

"Ev, a car is an enormous expense. How did you afford it?"

"My parents gave it to me."

"Your parents bought you a car," she repeated blankly.

"No." He was irritated now. He'd obviously wanted her to be more excited than she was. "They didn't *buy* it for me. So save the judgment. They gave it to me. My mom just got a new one, and they gave me hers. It's used."

She said nothing and he barreled on. "And don't get up my ass about all the expenses. They said they're gonna keep it under her name, and they just added me to her insurance. They said they have no problem paying for it until I'm back on my feet."

"Back on your feet." Again, the words were lifeless coming out of her mouth. She was basically parroting them back to him.

"Yeah. That's why they gave it to me. Because I explained how fricking hard it is to get around the city on public transportation. They thought it would help me to make it to all my job interviews."

"Job interviews?" she asked weakly.

"Yeah, my dad's friend lined up two paralegal interviews for me for next week. They're downtown. Near Federal Hall."

Instead of elation and relief that Evan had two legit job interviews coming up, the only thing that was going through Via's head was how easy it was to get to Federal Hall from almost anywhere in the city.

Evan and his parents had decided that he needed a car for that?

To spare him from two twenty-minute train rides at a whopping $2.75 apiece? In her opinion, driving would be significantly *harder*. He'd have to fight traffic and find parking.

But, she realized as she dropped her forehead into her hand, that wasn't the point. The point was that Evan had wanted a car and, snap your fingers, he got a car. Like a toddler whining for a juice box.

He was saying something in that deep, familiar voice of his, the one that usually made her toes curl, but she couldn't even make out the words.

Via felt half of herself grip the edge of a door buried deep inside her. She wanted to slam it closed. With some attitude. She wanted the door to shake on its damn hinges. But the other half of her had two palms on that door, holding it open with all her strength.

She still wasn't listening to him. How could she? She was just. so. tired.

The landline on her desk rang, jolting her straight up and making her realize how far down she'd slouched.

"Ev? I have to call you back. My lunch hour is up."

She said goodbye and hung up with him.

"Via DeRosa," she answered her phone, her voice sounding strangely wooden.

"Via! Hi! I hope it's all right I called you at work."

"Ah, who am I speaking with?"

"Oh!" A bright, bubbling laugh came through the line. "Sorry. This is Mary Trace. Sebastian's friend? We met this weekend?"

"Of course, sure. Hi, Mary. What can I do for you?"

"Well, actually, I was calling to ask a favor."

"Oh?" Via had really liked Mary when she met her. The woman was friendly and sweet and obviously wanted to get to know Via and Fin. But that didn't mean she wasn't a little surprised to be getting a phone call from her in the middle of the workday.

"So Seb is home sick—he got what Matty had, did you hear that?"

"Oh shoot. No. I mean, I suspected when he wasn't in school but that sucks. Strep is terrible."

"I know. And I was supposed to pick up Matty and bring him home today, but my shop assistant is a no-show, and I really don't want to close down this afternoon."

"You want me to walk Matty home?"

"Would you? I'd owe you a million favors. Or maybe just the friends and family discount at my store?"

"I would have done it for free, but now that you've offered it, I'm holding you to that. I've been eyeing those brass-and-marble coasters for damn near a year."

Mary laughed that bubbly laugh again. "They're yours."

"I'll grab him after class and take him straight home."

"You're a lifesaver. I'll text Seb and let him know the change in plans."

"Tell him that Sadie will be with us, too," Via added

impulsively. She had no plans with Sadie that afternoon, but suddenly, walking Matty home from school and checking on a sick Sebastian felt really intimate. She didn't need a chaperone per se. But yeah. The thought of one of her colleagues seeing her walk Matty home by herself and assuming something... It made her stomach flip uncomfortably.

"Sure. Thanks again."

Matty was apparently overjoyed to be the kid who got walked home from school by not one, but two teachers.

"You're strutting like a rock star." Via smiled down at him.

"Am not!" Matty insisted, then screwed his face up into a little twist. "Which rock star?"

Via and Sadie laughed as Via straightened his backpack on his shoulders.

"Maybe Prince?" Via supplied.

"Definitely Prince," Sadie agreed. She had a huge smile on her face. "Just look at those little hips."

"My dad really likes Prince," Matty said, absently reaching up and lacing his fingers with Via's. "Sometimes on Sunday mornings we have raspberry pancakes and listen to 'Raspberry Beret.'"

Sadie and Via both threw their heads back and laughed. Hard. The image of huge, barrel-chested Sebastian making fruit pancakes and dancing to Prince with his son was too much for Via. She got that strange door open/closed feeling again, and it had her catching her breath.

"So he's pretty sick, huh?" Via asked, ignoring the tight feeling inside of her.

"Yup." Matty dipped the toe of his sneaker into a shoe print that had been pressed into the wet concrete decades ago. "I got him sick. But he says it's okay because it was an accident. And that dads understand that sometimes they get sick when their boys get sick."

Sadie made a little gasping noise and pressed her hand to her heart. Via understood perfectly.

"He should be better in no time," Sadie reassured Matty. "He only had to miss a few days."

"That's true," Matty said thoughtfully. "But it's not quite fair because when I got sick, I only had to miss school, but he had to miss fun stuff."

"Like what?" Sadie asked.

"Well, he had to miss nachos day in the cafeteria today, which is his favorite. And also he had to cancel two dates."

Via missed a step when her toe caught on a crack in the sidewalk, but Sadie didn't even notice. The redhead's eyes were narrowed in on Matty's face, an insane light in her eyes. She was finally getting a little Fabulous Mr. Dorner gossip, and she apparently didn't give a rat's ass about the integrity of the source.

"Your dad goes on dates?" Sadie asked innocently, shamelessly.

"Sadie!" Via hissed. It was so inappropriate to ask Matty this that she felt heat all the way to the roots of her hair.

Matty didn't seem to notice or understand the impropriety of the question. The six-year-old played with the toggle on his backpack strap and nodded fervently, almost viciously. "Yeah. Moms and dads can go on dates!" His face was knit with both certainty and confusion. Via got the distinct impression that he'd had this same argument with a classmate. "Well, I don't really know about moms. But dads can. My dad goes on dates all the time."

Sadie inhaled, swallowing wrong in her excitement

and coughing out her next words. "Really? He tells you about it?"

Matty nodded, like the answer was so obvious he was surprised he even had to explain it. "He always tells me where he's going and who he's going to be with. He says it's fair because I have to do that for him. But he goes on dates with ladies, and I go on playdates."

"Ladies?" Sadie asked, prying for more Mr. Dorner gossip. "Like lots of different women?"

Via was mortified, utterly mortified. They were prying into this man's private life. And for nothing more than gossip.

"Sadie," she murmured. She was going to take the first opportunity that they were alone to make sure Sadie knew that none of this could be shared with a single other soul.

But apparently Matty didn't care. "Yeah. Lots. But he says he hasn't met his match." Matty kicked a stone down the sidewalk in front of them and the movement had him tugging down on Via's hand. Sadie didn't even have to fish for more information; the kid was on a roll. "Daddy says that a lady can't be a match for him if she doesn't want to be a mommy. But that I shouldn't hope too much because that's really hard to find." Matty squinted up at the two women walking him home. "But I don't get it because there are tons of mommies. So I don't understand why he can't find one."

Sadie's expression instantly became chagrined. She'd been pushing in a fun way, but it was so clear that this wasn't a silly, salacious matter. This was Sebastian's life. Matty's life. This was a man who was trying to tread carefully enough that his son wouldn't get caught in the crosshairs.

"Well, you know," Via started. She was gonna give this her best shot. And then she was going to tell Sebastian everything, so that he could decide if more explanation was warranted. She owed him that. This wasn't a game. The man was a parent. And Matty was a person with feelings. "Finding the right person isn't easy. Because people meet each other all the time, but they don't always fall in love. Falling in love is a little bit magic. And you know how rare magic is."

"What do you mean, it's magic? Magic like Serafine's magic?"

Via weighed her head side to side. "Maybe. Honestly, I don't know. It's still a little bit of a mystery to me. But I guess what I'm saying is that the best thing you can do is just be happy you have a daddy who loves you so much that he wants to find the perfect person to fit in with your lives."

"Okay," Matty said, his eyes squinting across the street at a lady walking her poodle. He'd reached capacity for adult conversation. "You think that dog is Crabby's mom? Because Crabby is half poodle, but we didn't know who his parents were 'cuz we never met them."

"Could be." Via gave his sweaty little hand a squeeze.

"Who is Crabby?" Sadie asked, putting enough attitude in her question that Matty laughed.

"My dog!" Matty let go of Via's hand and sprinted up the last half a block, apparently very excited to get home.

He was banging on the front door and bouncing on his heels when Via and Sadie caught up. The two women stayed down on the sidewalk as they looked up to the front porch.

The locks slid and the door swung open to reveal a very tousled, very pale Sebastian yanking a T-shirt into place.

"Dad!" Matty lunged forward and hugged Sebastian around one thigh before he dropped to his knees and let himself get completely tackled by Crabby. The ecstatic dog trounced the kid, covering him all over in licks and face rubs. Sebastian weakly smiled at the boy's wild yelps of delight and sagged against the doorjamb as he looked down at the two ladies.

"Hi."

"You look awful," Sadie said candidly, taking a step backward like she could catch germs from ten feet away.

"I feel awful. I just took another round of medicine. I can't believe this was how Matty was feeling. I give him a lot of credit."

Sebastian's eyes found Via's and she found herself stepping up the stairs to the porch. His eyes were bloodshot, his face pale, there was a sheen of sweat covering all the skin she could see. He really did look awful.

"Seb, maybe I should take Matty out for dinner. Give you a few more hours on your own to rest?"

Matty looked up. "But it's my cheese night! I wanna go but only if I can get mac and cheese and a grilled cheese and a cheese stick like I would have here."

Sebastian groaned and leaned his clammy forehead against the door. "Matty, you're not supposed to tell people about cheese night." He looked up with one cracked eye, his hair sticking up in a hundred directions. "I swear we eat vegetables on every other night."

Via couldn't help but laugh. But her mirth dissolved when Sebastian wiped the sweat off his forehead with one shoulder and looked exhausted at the simple motion.

"No judgment about cheese night. But, Matty, I make a mean grilled cheese. I really think I should help."

Sebastian looked like he was going to argue, and Via took another step up the stairs.

"Come on, Seb. It's no trouble. And don't act like Mary

wasn't going to stick around and help for a few hours. Let me fill in for her, okay?"

"Looks like you guys have it covered!" Sadie called from twenty feet away. Apparently, she'd been slowly backing away from the house of plague this entire time. "I'm gonna hit the road but, Via, just call me if you need something, okay? See you tomorrow, Matty! Feel better, Sebastian!"

With a brisk wave and a backward skip or two, Sadie was jetting down the sidewalk toward the school.

Sebastian lifted his eyebrows and gave a little chuffing laugh. "I look that bad, huh?"

"You've looked better," Via observed dryly. "Come on, Seb. Let me help."

He gave a deep sigh and stepped backward, letting her come in. "You're right. I need a hand. Matty, you wanna show Via your puzzle collection? I'll be right back out."

He closed the door behind Via and she hung her bag and coat on the hooks in the front hall. She noticed they were his copper-and-wood signature style. Sebastian disappeared down the hall, and she took the opportunity to really look around.

The last time she was in his house she'd been so tightly strung. Nervous and off-kilter. She hadn't expected Mary to be so pretty; she hadn't wanted to butt in on his quasi-date with Serafine. She'd been worried about Matty. She just hadn't gotten comfortable at all. But now, with Sebastian in the other room and nobody around but Matty, Via let her eyes take it all in.

It was a very warm space. Every wall was painted, all slate grays and a few accent walls of royal blue. There were countless picture frames, photos of Matty at every age, Seb in a few places. And a gorgeous blond woman who Via could only guess was Matty's mom. Via made her way down the hallway toward the living room and paused to grin at a picture of a very young Seb and Tyler, not older than Matty, missing teeth and dirty, arms around each other's shoulders.

The living room, with its plush couch and armchairs, had a big, colorful rug and a spray of toys that Matty had already hauled out of a big tin chest in the corner.

"You have a puzzle collection?"

"Yeah! I love puzzles. No, Crabby!" Matty attempted to box out his dog who was boisterously nuzzling at the boy's hands. "Dad says I have to do them at the dinner table, though, or else the pieces end up mysteriously lost."

Via grinned and took Crabby by the collar so that Matty could pass by unhindered. "Do you want a snack before dinner?"

It was only 4:30. She figured she had an hour before she had to start making dinner.

"Yeah."

"Run that back, kid." Sebastian's voice came from over her shoulder and Matty froze in place, turning back to Via with a sheepish look on his face.

"Um. Yes, please, Miss DeRosa."

She hid her smile. "You got it. Why don't you get started on your puzzle and I'll bring it to you, okay?"

He scampered into the dining room to start the puzzle, and she turned to Sebastian. Something went smooth and soft in her belly. He'd changed into jeans and a fresh T-shirt, and his face and hairline were damp from where he'd splashed water over them. He still looked like microwaved death, though.

"Sebastian, why don't you go lie down?"

"I'm sick of my bedroom." He took on an ornery, stubborn expression that was especially prevalent in elementary schools.

For the second time in as many minutes, Via hid her smile from a Dorner boy. "All right, well at least go and lie down on the living room couch."

He looked for a second like he might argue with her, but it wasn't long before he ambled into the other room.

Via kept an eye on Matty in the dining room as she slapped together some peanut butter crackers and a handful of grapes. "Matty," she said in a warning tone, "does your dad let you climb all the way onto the table when you do your puzzles?"

"Sometimes!" he insisted with the defiance of a kid who got caught in wrongdoing. His neck went a little red and he slid back into his chair, eyeing the plate that Via set down. "Can I have water, too?"

Via grabbed him some and then went back into the kitchen, checking to make sure that they had everything she needed to make dinner for Matty. She noticed a few other things in the fridge and pulled them out.

She found a pot and the rest of the ingredients she needed and started chopping vegetables. It wasn't twenty minutes before she had the soup on the stove and she washed her hands. Via and Matty got a good jump on the puzzle, working on it for half an hour before she had him washing his hands and helping her make his dinner. He carefully buttered the bread and laid out the cheese slices for the grilled cheese. And then he studiously stirred the cheese mixture for the mac and cheese.

She grinned at his solemn little face as he cooked. Like it was a science experiment that might explode out of the beaker if he put in one drop too much milk. She wondered if Sebastian ever had Matty cook with him.

"Do you cook very often?"

"No." He shook his head. "Only sometimes with Grandma Sullivan."

"I used to cook all the time when I was your age."

"Really?"

"Yup. My parents were from Italy, and cooking and eating is a really big deal in their country. So even when I was a kid, I already knew how to make marinara sauce and pasta from scratch. All sorts of things. Stew and bread, all kinds of pastries."

"Do you still cook?"

"Every day," she told him. "I love it. It calms me down. I like to cook the way you like to do puzzles."

"Yeah, but you can't eat puzzles." Matty cracked up at his own joke.

"And you can't spread out macaroni and cheese all over your dining room table."

He laughed harder. "Well, you *could*. But then Dad would get really frustrated and make me clean it up."

She checked on Sebastian, who was snoozing on the couch, curled on his side with a blanket up to his shoulders.

She and Matty carefully shoved the jigsaw puzzle down to one end of the table and she sat with him while he ate. He really was a very competent conversationalist. He always had been, even when he was in her pre-K class, but it was easy to forget that he was just six years old. After dinner he brought his plate to the dishwasher, but he needed reminding to wash his hands and face.

"It's not bedtime yet," he told Via, just in case she got any crazy ideas.

She nodded solemnly. "Of course not. It's only 6:30. But I think we should go easy on your dad. Do you ever play outside after dinner?"

"Yeah. Lots of times. But not really when it's dark out." He peered out the sliding porch doors and grimaced at the glowing blue twilight creeping over the trees.

"You can play a video game, buddy!" Sebastian called from the other room with a voice that sounded like he'd swallowed some rough grit sandpaper.

Matty was in the living room like a shot, and Via followed after. Sebastian was just pulling himself up to a sit and clicking on the lamp next to the couch.

"Can I use volume, Daddy?"

"Only if you wear the headphones."

Matty was busy pressing buttons and plugging in jacks and putting disks in slots. He was a whir of digital-age action until he popped the giant headphones on, grabbed up the controller and plunked his butt down in front of the TV. Via was relieved to see that he was playing a soccer video game, not a fighting one.

"I can't thank you enough," Sebastian said, still lying partway down, his gray eyes squinting.

"I'm happy to do it." She lingered in the doorway. She knew it was probably time to go home, but she found herself wanting to stay until Matty's bedtime so that Seb wouldn't have to worry about it.

"What smells so good?"

"I made you some Italian cabbage soup. My mother always made it when I was sick. It'll keep for a few days so you can eat it whenever you want."

Sebastian pushed off the blanket and moved to stand.

"Oh! You want some now?" she asked. "I'll get it."

"You don't have to do that, Via."

"No, no!" She waved her hands in the air and was already darting out of the living room toward the kitchen. "Let me! Please, it's half the fun of making food for someone."

She served him a bowl and filled up a tall glass of ice water. She figured he'd feel awkward if she didn't take some for herself as well, so she put an identical serving on a tray and carried the whole thing out to the living room.

Sebastian's eyes were closed when she stepped toward the couch but as soon as she set the food down, he was sitting back straight, scraping a hand over his face.

"Are you sure you're up for eating?"

"Honestly, my throat is killing me, but I'm starving. I haven't eaten since yesterday."

She tsked and nudged his bowl forward. "I hope you don't mind that I raided your kitchen to make all this."

"Mind? Please. I'd been side-eyeing that cabbage since the weekend, trying to figure out what the hell I was going to do with it."

She laughed. "You bought it without a recipe in mind?"

Sebastian shrugged, taking a bite of soup and wincing. "My throat," he told her when he caught her eye. "Tastes so good, though. Yeah, I always try to buy a bunch of vegetables and then figure out what the heck to do with them. Cora used to do all the cooking, so I was pretty lost for a while after she passed. But I can make a fair stir-fry. Smoothies in the morning. Pancakes. Frittata. Tacos. Toward the end of the week, I'll make a huge kitchen sink omelette and just toss in everything we have left."

For some reason, that made Via smile around her soup-spoon. "Smart."

He shrugged again, and she could see how sick he really was, purple under his eyes and his face lined.

She glanced at Matty. "Can he hear us?"

Sebastian shook his head. "He's dead to the world right now. Freaks me out sometimes. Like, I could get murdered by aliens and he wouldn't even know."

Via laughed and set her soup aside. Her stomach flipped. Hard.

"Everything all right?" he asked, his voice a little less gritty after the hot soup had loosened up his throat.

"Well, I just wanted to tell you something." She plunged right in, even though she felt terribly awkward. "While Sadie and I were walking home, Matty told us about, ah, your dating life a bit." She could feel her color rising. "And he mentioned that he didn't understand why you couldn't find someone who wanted to be a mother. And I told him that finding the right person was harder than it sounded and required a little magic. And I just wanted you to know that that was how I handled it, in case you want to talk to him more later. I just didn't want him to tell you what I said and then feel super weird."

She was sure her face was bright red by now as Sebastian stared at her, his spoon in the air. After a second, he took another bite of soup.

"As an education professional," he asked carefully, "did you get the impression that he was talking about it because he feels confused and needed to run it past you?"

"Ah." Via went even redder. "No. I think he's pretty clear on most of it."

"Then why was he talking about it?"

Oh God. Thanks, Sadie, you nosy ass! "Well, Sadie might have been fishing for some details on the Fabulous Mr. Dorner."

He face-palmed. "Oh, for the love of God, tell me that nobody actually calls me that."

"You can't blame the flamingos for being curious about the lion."

He laughed and then winced, bringing his hand to his throat. He set his soup aside and took a few grateful swigs of ice water. "Can I ask what Matty said?"

Via cleared her throat. "Just that you were always honest with him about your dates, where you were going and

who you were going to see. And that you'd had to cancel
a few dates because you were sick."

Sebastian nodded and she wondered if it was the lighting or if his cheeks had gone a little pink. "Yeah." He
traced a hand over his hair. "I'm trying to get back out
there."

She started to tell him that he didn't need to feel ob-
ligated to explain anything but then he just kept right
on talking.

"It's hard, you know? Being a single dad and, ah, a
widower. Both things can kind of be conversation stop-
pers on a first date. I guess I'm sort of casting a wide net
these days."

Via knitted her brow and took a big gulp of her water.
It made her so sad to think that Sebastian was spending
time with women who pulled away from him because of
who he was, his situation. What a bummer. She didn't
like the thought of him looking so hard for companion-
ship and just getting lonelier in the process.

"No promising prospects?" she asked in a friendly
way, although her voice sounded weirdly gruff to her
own ears.

He shrugged and then looked up quickly. "I hope you
don't feel weird that Serafine and I aren't a love match.
We texted yesterday and both agreed."

"Oh really?" Via felt a strange tug in her stomach. She
had been worried about Fin and Sebastian dating, sure,
but at least she'd known that Fin would be sweet to him.
And that he would be respectful of Fin.

"Yeah. She's lovely. And beautiful. But in the end,
she's just too young for me."

Sebastian's eyes were on the video game when he said
it, and Via was glad, because his words jolted her. Too
young? It had honestly not occurred to her that Sebas-

tian would think of himself as significantly older than she and Fin. Sure, he was obviously very mature and in a very settled stage of his life. But just looking at him, he didn't seem that old. Sure, he had some gray hairs, and no hint of boyishness at all.

Evan had wide shoulders but slim hips and always kept his face shaved smooth. Sebastian had the more gruff, substantial look of a man who was done growing. He was simply…adding. Muscle, mass, beard.

She thought he was probably in his late thirties. Or maybe early forties. She considered asking, but the words wouldn't come. She took another gulp of ice water and let her eyes drift to the photos on the wall.

There was a series of photos of baby Matty squishing his cheek against the face of that same stunning woman in most of the other pictures. She looked like a Swedish princess. Long blond hair and sky blue eyes.

"What was your wife like?"

The question was a surprise to both of them. But Via asked it with the candor and matter-of-fact-ness that could only come from having lost people close to her as well. She knew what it was like to have people cringe away from your grief, your loss, and it had meant that she'd kept it bottled up for years longer than she should have. She hadn't planned on asking him the question, but she didn't particularly regret it once she had.

Sebastian cocked his head to one side and pulled the blanket back over his lap. Via tossed him a pillow and he jammed it behind his head as he shimmied down to a half sit. The soup had given him a little color back but she could still see the fatigue in his eyes.

"Cora was…very intense. Very particular. The only one like her. She had this feeling about her. Like licking a battery." He sort of laughed to himself. "She was loud and crass and people had very specific reactions to her. You were either laughing the second she came into the room or groaning. For instance, Ty never really warmed to her. She stressed him out. But Mary and she were best friends. Mary thought she was the funniest person alive."

Sebastian stretched out on the couch, and his feet came within six inches of Via's leg. He stared at the ceiling as he talked. "To Cora, the world was very A plus B. She liked things to fall in an order. A line. She liked controlling whatever she could control. Especially for Matty and for me. I hated that part when she was alive and missed it so bad when she was gone."

He brushed the back of his hand over his eyes and something came wildly loose inside of Via when she realized that he was crying.

"But she was also really fun," he continued. "It was like she spent so much time inside the lines that like once every two months she just had to cut loose and lose her mind. She'd party hard, not drinking, but like, at a water park or bowling or wherever. A one-woman party." He wiped his eyes again. "She loved peanuts."

Via felt something inside of her fold over, once and then twice. She kept waiting for him to describe Cora physically. She'd obviously been so gorgeous. But he didn't. He spoke about her as a person. A mother. A wife. And it touched Via. She felt tender, both with affection for Sebastian and, surprisingly, sadness that she hadn't known this woman.

"She was such a good mom. Honestly, it kind of surprised me. Because she was such a harsh lady. She didn't suffer any fools. She didn't bother with whiners of any kind. But she was so sweet with Matty. Rigid. Lots of rules. But so sweet. They had such a good thing going. He was lucky to have her. Some people go their entire lives without getting loved that hard. And he had it for the first three and a half years of his life."

"She died in a car accident?" Via asked, though she already knew it was the case. Just like her parents. She wondered for a second if Seb hated the phrase *car accident* as much as she did. Something about the word *accident* made it all seem so *whoopsy daisy*. Like they weren't people alive and well with lives and kids one second and then dead on the blacktop the next second.

She felt so small there on the couch with a hand-knit afghan over her lap. Like a child snuggled in for a scary story. She wanted to be able to comfort this man who was sitting there, looking so tired. So dreadfully sick. So sad he couldn't quite control the words coming out of his mouth.

"Yeah. Drunk driver. A college kid. He was all right, but his life was over, too. I met him once. Last year. He's doing time for manslaughter. I visited him in prison and wished I hadn't. He lost everything that day. Matty and I? We still have each other. But that kid's life is just over."

"Daddy, can I play one more?" Matty was turning around and pulling the giant headphones to one side. He looked like Princess Leia.

"No, it's time to start getting ready for bed."

Matty looked for a second like he was going to argue but he glanced over at Via, all tucked in on the couch, and he obviously scented an opportunity. "Can Miss DeRosa put me to bed tonight? Since you're sick, Daddy?" The second half of his statement proved just how much of a smooth talker this kid was.

"I'm sure Miss DeRosa has places to be," Sebastian said.

"Of course I can," Via said at the same time. She turned to Sebastian. "Really. I'd love to. You rest."

She didn't mind a bedtime story with a sweet, sleepy kid, but she was also very appreciative of a moment to gather her wits. That thing that had folded inside her stomach wasn't unfolding. If anything it was stubbornly pulling denser and denser. Watching him talk about Cora had been a moment filled with motion and transition. It was almost as if he knew she had put him in a certain box and he'd stubbornly picked himself up and plunked right down into another.

The lamp lighting his face from one side. The stubborn tears that he'd wiped at first and then just let glint in the green-and-blue light from the television. Christ. The look in his eye as he'd just said whatever had come to mind next.

It had been honest. More honest than she was used to from almost anyone. She thought that probably Fin was the only other person who would have told so much truth.

"Miss DeRosa, are you cold?" Matty asked as she ran the bath for him, readying his shampoo and a washcloth.

"No, why?"

"Your hands are shaking," the little boy observed.

And so they were. Actually, all of her was shaking as that thing inside her just kept folding down tighter and tighter. Soon it would be microscopic, and dense as the entire world smashed into the head of a pin. Tiny as it was, there was no room for this inside her. There was no room for this in her life.

"I'm all right." It was a bald-faced lie. "Sometimes that just happens."

She held out a hand to Matty, and naked and shameless, he climbed into the tub. "I can be by myself in here as long as you check me."

She nodded, handing him his soap, and went into his bedroom to turn down the covers on his bed and choose a few books to read together. She took a deep breath. She needed to hold it together for another hour, and then she could go home. She could go home and call Fin and figure out what the hell had lodged itself somewhere between her lungs. Every time she breathed, her heart rubbed against this dense, sharp little intruder.

Via picked some pajamas from the drawer and headed back to the bathroom. She couldn't help but smile at Matty's beard of bubbles and the matchbox car he was racing down the highway of his own shin bone. She slicked electric blue toothpaste onto his red *Cars* toothbrush and grabbed his Kermit towel off the hook.

"I assume this is yours and not your dad's?" she asked, knowing it would make him laugh.

"Daddy's is the blue one. You can tell because it's Daddy-size." He smacked his hand to his chin and made the bubble beard explode in every which way.

Via ignored the way that knot between her lungs did a little pulse at the mention of Sebastian's size and held the towel out like a cape for a prince. "Your Majesty."

Matty pinched his nose between two fingers and collapsed backward underwater, rinsing himself clean. He rose from the tub and Via wrapped him up like a little boy burrito. She handed him the toothbrush, and he brushed while a tiny lake formed at his feet.

"Are you feeling all the way better from being sick or just most of the way better?"

"All the way. Except right now I feel a little sick."

"Really?" She automatically reached out and felt his forehead with the back of her hand. He was hot, but he was also medium roasted from a hot bath.

"Yeah. In my eyes. They're scratchy."

"Ah." He was just tired then. That quelled her worry. "Get your jammies on, and then we can read a few books."

His eyes lit up and he spit toothpaste into the sink,

tapping the toothbrush on the side to get the residue off in a way that made Via smile. She could imagine Sebastian and Matty brushing their teeth side by side, the son imitating the father.

Via handed over the pajamas and it was just a few minutes later that Matty came scampering back from saying good night to his dad.

"Miss DeRosa?"

"Hmm?" Via sat across Matty's bed and leaned against the wall.

"Do you think my dad will be better tomorrow?"

"I hope so. But it might be the next day."

"Okay." Matty inserted himself between her and the book with enough force to make her say "oof."

"Oh!" Matty was back up like a shot and rifling through one drawer of his craft table. "I almost forgot, but I made this for you. Because you visited me when I was sick." He held out a lanyard with all sorts of colored beads on it. He'd even carefully braided part of it. "It's a key chain."

"I love it," she told him, completely honestly. "I'll put it on my keys right away. Thank you!"

"Welcome," he told her and snuggled back in to her side.

She'd chosen three books, but she folded and read him a fourth and by the last page, his eyes were glassy and blinking with all the speed of a tortoise crossing a highway.

She wished him good night and didn't get much of a response as she pulled the covers up to his chin. He immediately kicked his legs out one side of the covers and pillowed his hands under one cheek. Via closed the door halfway and headed back out to the living room.

Sebastian's eyes were closed, his breaths even and

deep. She quietly picked up the dishes and started carrying them out of the room. It was his voice, low and so heartbreakingly serious, that stopped her. She turned back around to him. Set down the dishes.

"We wouldn't have made it," he said hoarsely. His eyes were fevered slits. She wondered if he even knew what he was saying right now. "Me and Cora. I know I'm dumping this on you and that it's probably not fair, but you're the only one who has asked about her in almost two years. Everyone I talk to about her knew her already. They saw us married. They think of her as my wife. Even saying that now, I feel like such a—"

He cut off, almost violently.

Sebastian leaned forward and she saw that he'd sweat through his T-shirt. His hair was sticking up and he'd tossed the afghan over the back of the couch. He was feverish. She could basically feel his heat from three feet away. He was leaning forward on his knees. His eyes bright and dark at the same time. A look on his face told her he'd been trying, so hard, for years, but right now, he just needed to be broken.

"What do you mean?" she asked softly, knowing that he just needed to know that she was listening still. That it was okay to talk right now. To say everything he needed to get out.

"I mean that we weren't gonna make it as a husband and wife, I don't think. As a couple. If she were alive, I don't think she'd still be my wife." His face somehow tightened and crumbled at the same time. Via knew when someone was saying something out loud for the very first time. When the words were so raw they were almost a prayer. When a feeling that had been curling and spiking and growing inside you finally, finally found its way to the outside. To the world.

"There wasn't enough love there," he admitted, tracing a hand through his sweaty hair. He grimaced when he swallowed. "There was respect, but no affection. We got married when she got pregnant. We'd only known each other a few months. Because there's just no other way. For me. I had to marry the mother of my kid. I was so scared of being a dad. I guess I thought getting married, having a wife, living with my kid day in and day out would somehow make fatherhood a little easier. A little more paint by numbers and less white-knuckling the steering wheel." Sebastian laughed at a joke only he got. "But it wasn't. Being a dad was just as scary as I'd thought it would be and marrying Cora only made it worse because she carried my weight. We both knew I was shitty at it. Only there for the good shit, gone in a flash for the hard shit. She carried me. I let her."

Sebastian's head lolled to one side, his cheeks flushed and the dark sweat on the back of his shirt blooming. Via fished for his ice water that he'd set on the floor beside the couch and handed it over to him. He gratefully swigged it back and sucked an ice cube.

"Seb, you might not want to hear this, but you're an incredible father. Devoted, hardworking, loving, firm. It's your business whether or not you congratulate yourself, but you have to admit, empirically, you're a good father."

He nodded, but she wasn't convinced he really believed her. Or if he was even able to hear her words through the haze of his fever. He rested sideways on the arm of the couch. He slowly lifted his feet up, and when they caught on the big cushion, Via reached down and hefted them right up onto the couch beside her. "Sometimes I think that makes it worse. That I learned how to do it only after she was gone. I wish she could have seen the kind of father I am now. It would have made her proud of me.

I loved it when she was proud of me. And it didn't happen very often in those last few years."

His eyes pinched closed and he pressed his fingers into his eye sockets, obviously fighting a headache.

"Where's your medicine?"

"Kitchen cabinet next to the sink."

Via rose and brought the dishes into the kitchen. She selected some Motrin and one of his antibiotics, just in case it was time. She quickly chucked the dishes into the dishwasher so that he wouldn't wake up to a dirty kitchen. While she performed the task, she thought of the very first version of Sebastian that she had met. Disheveled, lost, terse, destroyed. He'd loved Matty, that had always been palpable, but he hadn't known right from left.

She'd thought at the time that it was just the shock of the loss he was enduring. But she realized now that perhaps he'd been just that clueless as well, when it came to taking care of his kid. She'd been witness to all manner of parenting styles. Often there was a primary parent and a secondary parent. That worked for some families. It wasn't necessarily something that he needed to be feeling epic shame over.

She filled a fresh glass of ice water, rooted around in the freezer for an ice pack and grabbed the medicine. "Is it time for your antibiotic as well?"

He cracked an eye and nodded, gratefully accepting the pills and the ice water. He hissed when she slid the ice pack between the couch pillow and the back of his neck, but he didn't move it.

"Via," he started, and she knew he was about to apologize for everything he'd just said. She didn't want him to.

"When my parents died," she cut him off, knowing exactly what she was risking—that drafty space opening up inside her, but for Seb, for this moment, she would risk it,

"I was lost, Seb. Gone. I've never found that part of me again. She's gone. I came out the other side a different kid. It changes you. The event changes you, of course. I'll never forget that day. But the grief changes you, too. The long, awful, up-mountain trek of grief, it changes who you are. I don't know that you should feel shame for being a different person after you endured the loss of Matty's mom."

He nodded and kept his eyes closed as he knuckled one eye and then the other. His face was lined and exhausted. He should be sleeping. She almost rose, to leave him in peace, when he rolled to one side and stretched out his legs. His feet slid over her lap and all the way to the other end of the couch. The heavy weight of his calves penned her in. He groaned just a little bit and cast a forearm over his eyes. If she could have reached the lamp, she would have dimmed it.

"Yeah, but what do you do, as a person, when grief changes you for the *better*? God, I feel so much shame for it. She died and I became a *better man*. It makes me sick with myself. I'm such a bastard. Why did it take that for me to be who I am now? Why couldn't I have done that when she was here?"

His arm was heavy over his eyes and his mouth was tightly clamped shut, his jaw square and dusted with more errant stubble than she'd ever seen him with before. His T-shirt was fully soaked through. If so many things were different, she'd go get him a fresh one, throw the sweaty one in the wash.

But as it was, all she could do was ignore the microscopic needle between her lungs and say the thing she'd wished someone had said to her. She had to keep going. For the first time, she wanted to keep going. The drafty feeling was absent, maybe because there was something else occupying her chest right now. Or maybe because that drafty wind couldn't blow her away when she was being pinned in place by that hot needle inside of her.

"What do you do when grief changes you for the better? Seb, you say thank-you to the world for being the world."

His forearm lifted off his eyes at her tone. He'd probably never heard her speak with such authority before, but she was an expert on this subject. The metamorphosis of grief. And he was her friend. And she was going to drag him out of the swamp if it was the last thing she did.

"You be grateful," she continued. "Grateful that you're *here*. That your little boy has a good, loving, competent father. A father who leaps a fence to sprint him to the ER and makes Raspberry Beret pancakes and tells him the truth about the dates he goes on." Somehow one of her hands landed on his calf and she gripped the warm jeans there, as if she could pin him down and make him listen. Make him hear her.

His eyes flashed to her hand but then back to her face like he was being nailed in place by a cosmic hammer.

"And you stop doing this math equation that's killing you. In one hand you have your wife's death, and in the other hand you have all the progress you've made over the years. But, Seb, A plus B doesn't equal *shit* in this case. You can't add or subtract those two things. They're a completely different language. And holding yourself hostage with your wife's death is false math that's *designed* to punish yourself. That's a way of turning your grief back in on you, to keep it trapped and circling."

He made a sound. Just a quick grunt, like she was pulling stitches out of a mostly healed wound.

"So, just stop doing that." She laughed at herself, at how bossy she sounded. "I know it's not easy, but you have to let it out. You're a good man who is grieving because his wife died. And no one, no one, no one ever feels *simple* after someone they love dies. Everyone feels complicated as hell, all loose strings and sloppy endings and regrets. That's life. That's the world. The same world where you get to make furniture and tuck your son in at night and walk him to school. You can't get one part without the other. It's just not the way it works."

This time, Sebastian didn't squeeze his eyes closed. He looked her square in the face while two feverish, determined rivers carved their way down his face.

A tight, tense feeling rose up in Via's throat, and her lips pursed at the same second a track of tears spilled out of her own eyes. They just stared at one another, dim gold in the lamplight, two people who'd been broken and were learning to live all patched up.

She knew that he might look at her and realize, terribly, that it never ended, the patching yourself up after you get so viscerally destroyed. But she also hoped that he'd look at her and realize that it was worth it. Every dirty, ugly, scraping step forward was worth it.

CHAPTER THIRTEEN

"Well, are you going to tell me what's wrong, or are you going to continue making everyone in this house ten minutes late for everything?"

Seb had to close his eyes and laugh at his mother-in-law's question. Muriel Sullivan, the least nurturing woman on Earth. And yet? She was still asking. She could have been ignoring his long stares out the kitchen window, his deep, unfortunate sighs, his losing track of his car keys four times in a row.

Seb had been that way since last week. Since Via had come over when he'd been sick. He'd been feverish and dozy and emotional, and she'd drawn his pain out of him like a long, thin splinter that he wasn't sure he'd even known was there. He'd felt like shit that night. Delirious and hot. He wasn't even positive what time she'd left, he'd passed out on the couch so hard. He'd woken up the next morning with his fever broken and a Post-it note on the coffee table with instructions to call her if he needed help getting Matty to school.

He'd lain there on the couch, stinking of sickness and broken fever, the afghan kicked off onto the floor, his face pressed into his arm. He'd waited for the wave of shame and humiliation to drag him down to the bottom of the ocean. Because, *oh God*, all that truth he'd told the night before. Just bomb after bomb. He'd said things out loud that he hadn't even let himself think in the privacy of his own mind. And of course, the person he'd chosen to tell it all to was someone he'd told himself he was going to STOP growing closer to.

He could blame it on the fever. Sure, he'd been loopy and hot and his vision had been all wobbly. He was lucky he hadn't confessed feelings for her.

He'd felt chagrin that he'd unloaded so unexpectedly and so fully. But the humiliation and shame never quite showed their faces. As he'd gotten up to shower and rouse Matty for school, Sebastian had slowly realized that as intense as the experience had been, he really felt like she understood what he'd been saying. Sometimes she seemed so delicate, with her sweet face and quiet voice, that tiny little stature, but she'd been strong and unfazed the night before. He'd slowly realized that not only did he not regret that conversation, getting it off his chest made him feel weightless, free, relieved.

He'd been well enough to walk Matty to school that morning, but not well enough to work in his shop. So he'd cleaned the house instead, taking a few rest breaks and a nap after lunch. It had been a day for the record books. He'd been weirdly energized, stripping his house of any remnants of sickness. He'd scrubbed every surface, and as he got used to this ethereal, cosmic lightness in his soul, he felt as if he were scrubbing away the last poisonous dregs of his unresolved grief over Cora's death.

He knew he wouldn't stop mourning her—that would probably never end—but he was prepared for it, it felt healthy. The twisted, shameful grief he'd kept hidden deep in his gut had been extracted from him the night before, removed with the precision of a surgeon.

It was only toward the end of that day, when he knew he'd have to head over to the school to get Matty, that Seb allowed himself to think, really think, about the woman who'd performed this emotional exorcism on him. He felt his floating lightness toss down a rope. And another. And another. Soon, he was tethered to the ground again and slowly lowering.

He knew he should be simply grateful that she'd taken care of his son. Made dinner. Provided one hell of a therapy session. But instead he'd felt the leaden weight of disappointment slowly descend over him from head to toe. She was such a wildly incredible person. So competent and kind and fierce and sweet.

And she couldn't be his.

He wanted so badly to feel only friendship for her. To just call her up, the way he would Tyler or Mary. Say, *Thanks, buddy. I really needed that talk last night.*

He knew he wouldn't call her. There was too much risk of saying, *Hey, come over again. Sit with me on my back porch after my boy goes to sleep. Let me kiss your shoulder and untangle your hair from your earring. I'll make mediocre dinner, and you can sit on my lap the whole time.*

He'd never risk that. And so he found himself coming to the exact same conclusion he'd come to when he'd shown her his workshop. She was cute as hell and was his perfect match in another world. But in this world, she was too young, attached to someone else, and someone that Seb needed to start distancing himself from.

He'd walked to pick up Matty, every other step filled with hope and relief and the others weighed down by disappointment and what-ifs. It was with this strange accordion of feelings, sandwiched somewhere between catharsis and fresh hurt, that he'd gotten to school five minutes early. He'd strode purposefully toward her office, popped his head in. He was just going to say thank-you. A quick, heartfelt thanks, and then he was going to grab Matty and head home.

But she wasn't there. Even the lights were out.

She hadn't been there the next day, Friday, either. Seb hadn't asked anyone where she was. He also didn't ask when she didn't show up for softball either. Between Via's absence and Seb's recovery mode, they'd barely scraped by with a tie game, and Seb and Matty had gone home grumpy and exhausted.

That's when he'd called his in-laws. Would they like to come down for a few days? And in typical Sullivan fashion, as if the invitation wasn't out of the blue or a secret delight to them, Muriel had emailed him their brisk, businesslike itinerary about four minutes after he hung up the phone.

Art and Muriel Sullivan had arrived Sunday morning and the following Wednesday they were still there. Both of them inserted themselves into the house without fear of being told to butt out. Seb was as grateful as he was annoyed. When his own parents visited—which was for about two solid months every summer—they were true houseguests, all the way down to dishes left in the sink and casual reminders that he needed to pick up more toilet paper. The Sullivans arrived, set their bags down and started running every aspect of the house with military precision. It was, and had always been, as relieving as it was condescending.

He didn't *need* the help. But it sure was nice.

Now, Wednesday late afternoon, after he'd picked up Matty from school, Seb sat at the kitchen counter, rocking his barstool back on two legs while he attempted to pay a few bills on his laptop. Muriel was putting the finishing touches on dinner and disinfecting his toaster, of all things.

He smiled at her question, which was somehow rude and kind all at once. *Well, are you going to tell me what's wrong, or are you going to continue making everyone in this house ten minutes late for everything?*

"You know, Muriel, sometimes you remind me so much of Cora it makes my chest ache."

Her head snapped up with the speed and intensity of a sniper finding a target in the scope of a rifle. Her rubber-gloved hand stilled for just a second before she resumed denuding the toaster with a round of steel wool. She ignored the compliment. "So, that's why you're sighing and leaving your keys every place but your pocket? Because of Cora?"

There wasn't censure in her voice, exactly, but Muriel was the queen of compartmentalization. And she'd never understood that Seb hadn't been able to put Cora's death in a box where it had belonged.

Seb typed a few keystrokes and paid Con Ed, then navigated to his National Grid bill. "No. Maybe. I don't know."

"No, maybe, I don't know," Muriel repeated, pursing her lips. "How eloquent."

Seb chuckled so that he wouldn't roll his eyes at his mother-in-law. "I mean, it's not for the same reasons as it used to be. But every time I make progress and move on a little more, I get so sad."

He could feel Muriel's eyes on his face and a familiar feeling of dissection gripped him. Cora had been able to do this, too. Just look at him and peel back the skin from muscle, the muscle from bone. Cora had said it was easy with Seb because he was such a big, innocent target. His dumb, blunt face showed every emotion. He stopped pretending to go line by line through the bill on the screen of his laptop and looked up at Muriel. The second their eyes clashed, she was back concentrating on the toaster.

"I don't know why that should make you sad. You're supposed to move on after someone dies."

She was being obstinate. But if she hadn't been, Seb would probably have plunked her in the car and raced her to a neurologist. "Right. But sometimes moving on feels like leaving her behind. For a long time, grief felt like my only connection to her. And…" he swallowed hard "…a part of me doesn't want to lose that, too."

Muriel's back was ramrod-straight as she attacked the toaster with fresh vengeance. Seb read through her lines, a skill that had been extremely hard-won, and realized that she understood what he meant, even if she'd never admit it. Muriel looked up at the backyard through the window over the sink and suddenly banged on it so hard the glass shook in its boots.

"Art!" she hollered at her husband through the glass. He and Matty were playing in the backyard. "Put down the newspaper and untangle your grandson's pants from the fence!"

Whether Art heard her through the glass or not, Seb wasn't sure, but he watched Muriel eye the backyard for another few seconds before she resumed her scrubbing. "Just another pair of pants to mend along with the khakis he ripped the pocket off of," she muttered to herself.

Seb sighed, turning back to his laptop. Conversation over, he supposed.

Muriel finished with the toaster and set it back on the counter, snapping off the rubber gloves and rinsing them, laying them out to dry. She immediately checked the roast in the oven and started dismantling the fridge for salad fixings. "Well, that's just silly," she said into the vegetable drawer.

Seb's hand froze over the keyboard. "I'm sorry?"

"Feeling regret that your grief is receding is silly. And a waste of time. You should be grateful."

"Well—"

"And of course your grief isn't your only connection to Cora. You have your son. And you have all of your memories of her." She slapped a bag of romaine on the counter and didn't turn around. "And of course you have Art and me."

Seb was momentarily stunned into silence. The Sullivans had been an amazing support after Cora had passed, taking charge with Matty on so many occasions. But Seb had never exactly *bonded* with them. He'd always felt like a presence they'd tolerated in order to have access to their grandchild. When Cora had been alive, he'd barely exchanged more than pleasantries with them on either ends of their visits.

Yet, here she was, referring to herself as a connection.

"Do you…" he almost didn't ask "…think of me that way? As a connection to Cora?"

"No," she answered so firmly that Seb felt immediate tears of reaction tighten behind his eyes. Damn, the woman was harsh. "But you remind me so much of Matty, and Matty reminds me so much of Cora, that, well, I guess it's all just one thing a part of the next."

She was describing…family. Seb blinked at her rigid back, the perfectly knotted apron and the dyed blond hair, white at the root and tucked into a crisp French twist. She thought of him as family?

"Muriel," he started, testing the waters. "If I remarried, would you keep coming here?"

"If I were invited," she answered stiffly. He couldn't see her face but he could hear her lip curling.

"Of course you'd be invited."

She said nothing. Not for a long time. Seb had already gotten sucked into a few work-related emails when she spoke up again.

"So, that's what it is then. You're conflicted because you have a woman in your life."

"Oh—"

"Well, that's silly, too. Of course you should have a woman in your life. Matty needs a mother figure."

Again, Seb was stunned. He wished to heck that she'd just turn around already but he knew that was never going to happen. "You'd be all right with me finding someone?"

"Of course," she scoffed, like it was a waste of breath even to ask. "If she were a worthwhile person. Had a firm hand with Matty. If she wasn't dreadful, naturally I'd be all right. I don't expect you to be a widower forever, Sebastian."

"Well…" He cast around for what to say next. It was a conversation that had about forty different threads he could follow. "It's not imminent. I—she's not available. And she doesn't even know I have feelings. It's just something I need to get over. I'm sorry I've been moping."

She was quiet again for a while. All while she dressed the salad and brought the roast out of the oven. She was slicing bread when she spoke again.

"Maybe she'd become available if she knew you had feelings. I can't imagine this other fellow can compare."

Seb coughed. Hard. "That sounded suspiciously like a compliment."

She rolled her eyes at him. "Don't be so melodramatic, Sebastian. I give you plenty of compliments."

"Name one other."

She glared at him, then went back to arranging the slices of bread in the bowl. "I've stopped folding your laundry, haven't I? I don't call the school to check in on

Matty anymore. I don't insist on picking him up from school or buying his clothes. What would you call all of that?"

"Oh." Seb furrowed his brow. It simply hadn't occurred to him. "You've been handing back the reins to me because you…trust me."

"Obviously I do. You're a good father. Don't make me hit you over the head with it."

He blinked at her. "But you've never liked me." Maybe it was a stupid thing to say, but it was a piece of evidence he'd clung to for years. It had allowed Muriel's disappointment in him to keep from sinking in too deeply. All the cutting comments and sideways glances, all the insinuations that he was incompetent, he'd been able to ignore to a certain extent, because she'd never liked him. There wasn't even the chance of being good enough. It was just a personality thing.

"Oh, don't be ridiculous." She filled a tureen with ice water to set on the table for dinner. He knew she'd fill a small pitcher next, with milk for Matty. And last would be the little carafe of red wine that she'd put out but frown when anyone partook. "I like you just fine. Now."

He couldn't help but laugh at her candor. "But before…" he prompted.

She just pursed her lips.

"Oh, come on, Muriel. We're this far in. Might as well go the whole way."

"Fine. Yes, before, I didn't like you. You got my daughter pregnant after a few months of knowing her, and you were an absent father."

She let that little gem sit between them, blooming noxiously like a plume of bloodred ink in the ocean.

"But I would have to be intentionally blind to ignore all the ways you've grown. Pushed yourself. And at great emotional cost. I used to think you were a lazy man. And maybe you were. But you're not anymore." She sniffed, patted her perfect hair, and finally, finally made eye contact with him. "I don't hold grudges. It's immature. And you've proven yourself just fine."

Matty banged through the back door, smashing through the moment and demanding Seb's full attention while he laid out the three different types of autumn leaves he'd found in the backyard with Grandpa Sullivan. And then dinner was on the table and then it was bedtime for Matty, almost immediately followed by bedtime for the Sullivans.

Just a few short hours after that mega-bomb conversation with his mother-in-law, Seb sat alone in his workshop, all the lights clicked on. He leaned back on two legs of his folding chair and clicked open his phone, going immediately to his texts. There were two new messages from the women he'd had to cancel on last week. He'd made the dates impulsively. They were both his age. Now they both wanted to reschedule. He clicked his phone closed and tossed it onto one of his workbenches.

He didn't need to text right now. Texting was another man's game. Strangely, it was with Muriel's words in his mind that Sebastian rose, selecting one raw slab of wood from his shelves and then another and another. He was going to do what he did best.

He worked until midnight. With no drawings, no plans, he let the wood surprise him. Just the way he liked it.

SEB SPOTTED VIA from afar a few times that week. But he didn't like what he saw. She looked slow and sad, and she was constantly alone. Usually he'd spot her with Sadie or Shelly or Grace, sometimes Cat. They'd be sitting next to one another in the teacher's lounge or laughing over the Xerox machine. But she was chronically alone now. And the one time he went to her office, she'd been on the phone, offered him no more than a polite wave. He'd been certain her eyes were red like she'd been crying.

Something was up. He resolved on Saturday morning that, if she wasn't at softball that afternoon, he would call Serafine to check and see if everything was all right. Ever since he and Serafine had figured things out via text, that they weren't a love match, he'd become much less stressed at the idea of hanging out with her. In fact, he'd been toying with the idea of inviting her over again, sometime when Tyler was supposed to come over as well. He liked the idea of seeing his friend as off-kilter and schoolboyish as he'd been a few weeks ago. It made Seb feel a little less like a twerp for nursing this crush on Via. *See? Grown men can act like fools over pretty women; it happens every day.*

Seb, Matty and Crabby, the whole motley crew, pulled into the parking lot next to the softball fields. Two seconds later, the Sullivans pulled their Benz smoothly into the spot next to Seb's truck. He tried hard not to sigh. They'd wanted to come to his softball game, of all things.

Seb was fairly sure that they decided to come only *after* Matty had spilled the beans that no one specifically watched over him while Seb was playing. But it wasn't like he was running wild! Seb could see him the whole time. Still, no matter what the reasoning was, Sebastian found himself both looking forward to and dreading the thought of seeing Via for the first time in a week and a half under the watchful eye of his mother-in-law.

He'd had exactly zero more heart-to-hearts with Muriel, if you could even call it that. But still, he was very well aware of just how sharp her vision was.

"Remember what we talked about, Matty?" Seb asked

his son as he hauled him out of the booster seat in the back of his truck. Crabby hopped down with leonine grace. The effect was immediately squashed by the tongue lolling out one side of his mouth.

"Right. Don't give Grandma and Grandpa a heart attack while they're playing with me outside, and don't make it seem like you let me run wild like a lost boy," he recited, almost verbatim.

"Right. And there's a stop at Ample Hills ice cream in it for you if you can manage to pull the whole thing off, capisce?"

"Capisce." Matty nodded extremely solemnly. He took his artisanal ice cream very seriously.

"Well. This is quaint," Muriel said, her utilitarian pumps clicking on the parking lot pavement.

"What's the difference between a softball field and a baseball field?" Art asked, pushing his thick lenses farther up his nose and buttoning the middle button on his tweed blazer.

Knowing his in-laws enough to realize that neither of them actually expected an answer, Seb hiked his bag over his shoulder, took Crabby's leash in one hand and Matty's hand in the other.

He was halfway past the bleachers when he saw her. Hair dusting her shoulders as she leaned forward to tie one shoe and then the other. Those mid-length sweatpants hugged her in some very interesting places, and her team T-shirt was a size too large, which for some reason, Sebastian found adorable. She straightened up and was pulling her hair into a bun when she looked around and saw him staring at her.

He looked like a dope, he was sure, standing there with his arms overflowing with bags and kids and dogs and that look on his face like he thought she was just about the cutest thing to ever walk the Earth. But there was nothing he could do about that. Not really. It was just who he was. This was what he had going for him.

She waved a little, and Seb realized that he'd stopped walking in his tracks. He attempted a little wave back and ended up tangling Crabby's leash with his softball bag. When he'd finally sat Matty down on the lowest bleacher, tied Crabby to one of the crossbars and re-slung his bag over his back, Muriel's eyebrow was raised so far up her forehead her plastic surgeon would have fainted on the spot.

Seb chose not to acknowledge it and instead nodded to his in-laws. "See you after the game."

"Ice cream!" Matty flashed him a double thumbs-up and then turned to his grandparents with an expression so contrived it was almost comical. "Shall I show you where I play?"

Seb was laughing to himself as he stepped down into the dugout.

"What's so funny?" Sadie asked him from where she stood next to Via and Rachel.

He made a feeble attempt at not immediately drinking Via in like a glass of ice water on a hot day.

"I told Matty to put on a good show for his grandparents in exchange for Ample Hills and I'm pretty sure he just used the word *shall*."

The three women burst out laughing, and Seb took the unguarded moment to study Via's face. Looking at her hurt. Or it felt so good it hurt. Either way. His chest clamped down like a dog's mouth on a hand trying to take its food away. She looked like she'd been crying again, but she was also here, in her softball stuff, laughing and talking. So that was a good sign. He wondered, for the millionth time that week, what the heck was going on with her.

"Ample Hills ice cream is definitely worth pulling out a *shall*," Sadie agreed. "Are those your parents? They don't look anything like you."

"No, those are his grandparents on his mother's side." He was well out of earshot so he allowed himself a single sigh. "They've been here a week."

"A week!" Sadie screeched and then threw a hand over her mouth when her voice carried. "Sorry."

Seb laughed. "It's okay. It's not as bad as it sounds, really. They're super helpful people."

He couldn't help but notice that Via was inching away from the conversation and that Rachel was inching in.

"How is that big project you've been working on?" Rachel asked, blinking those sweet blue eyes at him. Seb wondered how she planned on playing softball in clothes that tight.

"Project?"

"You mentioned last week that you were thinking of starting a new furniture project."

"Right." Seb's gaze shot over toward Via before glancing away. She was practically standing behind Rachel now, facing out toward the field. "Yeah, I've started it. It's turning out really well. A coffee table and two matching side tables. My typical copper and oak. I'm thinking I might work on a dining table to go with it as well."

"Wow," Rachel breathed, and it was then that Seb realized just how close she was standing to him.

Okay. *So.* That had apparently become a thing while he'd been too busy crushing on Via to notice. He liked Rachel. She was cute, too. Young thirties, sweet face, always had a nice manicure. But he didn't think about her when she wasn't around. She didn't make him want to tuck an afghan around her feet. Maybe he couldn't explain it that well. Either way, he took a decent-size step to one side and caught Rae up in conversation until the game started.

Halfway through the fifth inning, Seb determined that Via truly was avoiding talking to him. He sidled up to one side of her as she leaned against the chain-link fence, watching Sadie steal second base. He left a healthy two feet between them.

"Hi."

She jolted and gave him the fastest glance of all times. Her cheeks were pink. "Hi."

"Uh, are you wanting me to leave you alone? I'm wondering if I should apologize for the way I acted that night last week. I know we've just started becoming friends, and maybe I pushed the limits too fast."

"No! Seb!" She turned then, one shoulder on the fence and her cap pushed high off her forehead. "Of course you don't have to apologize for that. That was an incredible moment. I was grateful to be there with you through that."

He mirrored her pose and the movement brought them closer. He looked down at her, a solid foot between their heights. He noticed, for the first time, that he'd always just thought of her eyes as *dark*, but they were almost amber around her pupil. She'd taken off her gold studs to play softball, but there was a light purple stone on a silver chain around her neck.

"All right," he conceded. "Are you okay, then? You've been MIA."

"Yeah. Yes." She flicked her eyes out toward the field again and her hand came up to absently brush against the purple stone. "I took a few days off to go upstate."

"Vacation?"

She shook her head and her eyes filled. "There was

just something I had to do. And once I got back, well, I've been spending a lot of time with Fin."

He was deeply relieved to hear she'd been spending time with her best friend. Maybe it was because he didn't know anyone else who resembled her—the slightness of her physicality, gold skin, dark eyes, that squished nose—but looking down at her now, she just looked very solitary. It worried him. Because of Matty, Seb's mini-me, Sebastian never had to worry about being completely alone. But Via on the other hand, she had no family. Not even a Muriel to criticize her in her kitchen. It made Sebastian want to invite himself over to her house, bring his kid and dog and make sure that there was enough noise in her life.

She used her wrist to push at the tears that swelled in her eyes and looked away from him, out toward the field. He wasn't made uncomfortable by other people's tears, but he knew when it wasn't the time to push. "What's the purple for?" He nodded at her necklace.

Her fingers brushed it again. "Amethyst. Apparently, it's kind of a cure-all. Or so Fin says."

"So you're not okay." He crossed his arms over his chest and searched her face for an answer. She looked so small right now, her delicate collarbone peeking out of her shirt like a piece of elegant jewelry. The only things big about her were those baleful eyes, and they were filled to the brim with unshed tears. He had the insane urge to make her soup, turn on a Disney movie or soft music. Damn it. He kind of wanted to rub her feet. He inwardly grimaced. Now was not the time to perv out.

She laughed at herself, the sound tight with tears as she swept her cap off her head and rubbed at her eyes with her wrist. "I don't know what I am. Don't mind me. I'm just a crazy lady who came to play softball."

"Man, I've been there before. Well, except for the lady part. Trust me, I was a crazy man for just about all of Matty's year four on this Earth." He nudged her gently with an elbow. "You were there."

"Oh, Seb, you were just fine. And don't worry, this isn't that kind of crazy. I think I'm just having a midlife crisis."

Sebastian threw his head back and laughed at that one. Really laughed. His cap came a little loose at the movement, and he jammed it back on his head. "Via, I hope to God you live longer than fifty-four years old. There's no way this is a midlife crisis."

She gave him a watery smile. "Fine, an identity crisis, then."

He cocked his head to one side. He'd always thought of Via as someone who was very certain in who she was, but he supposed everybody put up a bit of a front in that regard, particularly at work.

"Hi, Sebastian."

Seb turned and spotted Giles. He attempted not to wince at the interruption.

"Hey, man." He held out his hand.

Giles shook his hand and kept a straight face for only a second before he melted into bubbling, effusive praise. "We are over the moon about the mirror we commissioned from you. Seriously. It is gorgeous. And exactly what we wanted. And hand delivery, my, my, *my*! Expect a positive review on your website."

"You're the client he was building the mirror for?" Via's eyes were wide, but she was, thankfully, holding in the smile that teased at the corners of her mouth.

"You saw it?"

"I saw it in an intermediary stage. He does good work. It was very cool."

She hadn't liked it any better than Seb had, he knew, but she was sweet.

"It's more than cool—it's revolutionizing our living room. Seriously, if I could turn my eyes into heart emojis, I would."

The mirror had been a real bitch to make and boring as hell. But Seb couldn't argue with that kind of customer satisfaction. It was always nice to feel appreciated. And Giles looked like he was about two steps from wearing a shirt with Seb's face on it.

"Well, I'm glad you like it, man. I truly appreciate your business."

The inning ended and it was time to shuffle back to the outfield. Via winked at him, a little pink in the cheeks, as soon as Giles turned away. Seb swallowed back his laugh and tried not to watch her jog out to shortstop.

Instead, he turned and looked into the bleachers. Art and Matty were playing some card game, facing one another, Crabby was sniffing around underneath, and Muriel was looking right at him.

CHAPTER FOURTEEN

SEBASTIAN WAS JUST chatting with one of the lunch ladies when he heard the shouting from down the hall.

Becca, the lunch lady, scrunched her wrinkly face up. "What the hell is that?"

Seb was already skirting around the lunch tables and jogging down the hall. *That* was a man screaming his royal head off. Not the kind of sound anyone wanted to hear in an elementary school.

Lunch wasn't scheduled to start for another fifteen minutes, so Sebastian wasn't worried about kids flooding the hall immediately.

Following the echoing, reverberating voice, Sebastian found himself half a hallway down from Via's office.

"If this bitch thinks she can tell me shit about how to raise my daughter—"

Sebastian left his stomach behind as he ran even faster.

One of the third-grade teachers poked her head out of her classroom door; clearly the man's voice was carrying.

Sebastian was ten feet away from Via's open office door when he heard the firm, dulcet tones of Principal Grim's voice. Well, thank God Via wasn't in there alone.

Sebastian skidded to a stop in the open doorway, one hand on either side of the frame. His breath caught at what he saw.

A humongous man, maybe six feet tall and a doughy two hundred and fifty pounds, was leaning across Via's desk, viciously pointing a finger at Via and Principal Grim, who stood side by side. Via's cheeks were pink, but she looked calm. Shit, even her hands were tucked into the pockets of her trousers. Fin's purple necklace glinted against the golden skin of her chest.

Principal Grim looked just as calm, if not a little less patient. Her wild dyed hair was starting to come a little loose from her barrette. She raised a hand to quiet the man shouting obscenities, and when that didn't work, she raised her voice herself.

"Mr. Tate. I'm going to ask you one more time to *sit down*. And you are obviously being extremely inappropriate if even Mr. Dorner could hear you all the way in the cafeteria." She gestured toward the doorway.

Sebastian intentionally pulled up to his full height of six foot four. He wasn't as big around as this guy, but he wasn't as squishy either. He crossed his arms over his chest and let his biceps flex a little.

The man, a sheen of sweat shining on his forehead and his brown hair sticking up in a few places, sneered at Sebastian. But he sat his ass down in the chair.

Principal Grim gave Seb a meaningful look, and he stayed right where he was in the doorway.

"Mr. Tate, I understand that you have taken offense to some of the things that Miss DeRosa has written in this report. And that you resent being asked to come in to go over them. But I will have you know that I familiarized myself with your situation and reviewed this report before she was authorized to show it to you. I stand by everything she says. I have complete confidence in her."

"She doesn't know shit about my family life."

"She's a licensed and qualified professional who knows a great deal more than you think she does. And honestly, the fact that you view this kind of aid as a personal attack reveals quite a bit, Mr. Tate."

He puffed up. "She can't tell me I can't see my own fucking kid."

Via took a small step forward. "Mr. Tate, I'm going to repeat myself here. I'm not the one who said that you couldn't see Sarah. The courts did. I had to get special clearance to even allow you to come in for this meeting, seeing as it isn't during your previously appointed visiting hours. Your case administrator and I thought it would be a good idea to go over some strategies—"

"I don't need strategies to hang out with my own fucking kid."

"I'm telling you that, based on my conversations with Sarah, you *do* need strategies. Some of them aren't as bad as you think. Here."

Seb watched as she opened up a folder and selected a few papers to hand across the desk.

The man leaned forward and, in the blink of an eye, smacked the papers out of Via's hand with a full swing of his arm. Via gasped and jumped backward, cradling her hand against her stomach.

"Hey!" Principal Grim and Sebastian yelled at the same time.

"It's okay!" Via shouted.

"Out." Sebastian's voice was deadly low, on a register that was only ever used for fighting. Lithe as a cat, he'd inserted himself between the desk and Mr. Tate and that put him pretty close to nose-to-nose with this guy.

Seb's adrenaline pumped through his veins, making everything stand out in high definition. The bead of sweat on Mr. Tate's brow, the chip on one of the teeth he was currently baring, the spiraling, rainbow glitter of the crystals catching the light in the window of Via's office.

"Out. Now."

"Fuck this," Tate growled as he stalked to the doorway, Sebastian not more than two inches behind him.

Principal Grim was there too, the ballsy little lady. She put two fingers in her mouth and whistled to the security guard who was running down the hall, belatedly on the way to see what all the ruckus was. The guard radioed for some assistance, and it wasn't more than three minutes before Mr. Tate was escorted out of the building with three guards and Principal Grim. Sebastian didn't follow.

The lunch bell rang; they'd need him in the cafeteria, wading through an ocean of tiny people, opening juice boxes and settling swapped sandwich disputes. But he didn't go. Instead he turned back into Via's office and quietly shut the door behind him.

"It's okay," she repeated. She was standing with her back against the far wall of the office with one hand cradled in the other.

"It sure as hell is not okay," Seb said, a little more forcefully than he might have liked. He closed the distance between them in two long strides, dragging her desk chair along behind him. She lowered herself into it steadily, taking a long breath in and then out.

"Look at you," he muttered, resisting the urge to brush the hair out of her face. "Your color's all high. Your eyes are blown out."

She looked like she'd just gotten off a roller coaster. But in a bad way.

"Let me see." He reached for her hand and she let him take it. She used the other hand to tug at the neckline of her shirt. Sweat was turning the hair at her temples an even darker brown. Seb reached over and lifted the small window with one hand, and she let out a little choked sound as the cool air washed over her.

He bent over her hand, kneeling beside her. Dang,

she was so small. If he'd laid her little golden hand on top of his, her fingers wouldn't even have made it to his second knuckles. She wore no rings or polish, just clean fingernails.

He would have found that very sexy if it weren't for the sour pit in his stomach. She winced when he pressed gently on the back of her hand. It was pink and a little puffy.

"I can make a fist," she told him. "And wiggle them."

"Show me."

She did and he was satisfied that nothing was broken. "It's just gonna be a bruise, Seb. And on my left hand, too. Not even that big a deal."

Her voice was steady and her breathing was returning to normal. Her cheeks were still pink, and her eyes were still wide, though.

Seb rose and, suddenly painfully aware of his size, backed up to lean against her desk. He planted his hands beside him and tried to think small thoughts. Last thing he wanted to do was intimidate her right now.

"I mean, you get to say what's a big deal or not, when it happens to you. But that seemed like a big deal. He was screaming obscenities at you."

"This is Brooklyn, Seb. I hear worse than that practically every time I ride the train."

He grimaced. "I'm not talking wackos on the subway, Via. This is your place of work. That man—"

He cut himself off.

"We were handling it up until then."

"Well, I can't argue with that. You two looked like you were ready to put him on the witness stand or something. I swear. Remind me never to get on the wrong side of you and Grim."

She smiled a little at that and straightened out her blouse. He noticed that she didn't use her left hand, and her right was shaking just a little. "This whole thing is gonna be such a mess. Oh God. There's gonna be so much paperwork to do."

"Paperwork," he repeated blankly. "Violetta, a WWE contestant just tried to smack your hand into the next dimension and you're worried about paperwork."

She glanced up at him in surprise. "You called me by my full name."

He resisted the urge to pinch between his eyes. "I'm attempting to make a point here."

"Sebastian, we all deal with scary shit in our own way. Yours, apparently is to puff yourself up like a grizzly bear and then talk it to death immediately after it happens. Me? I just need a second. Okay? I need to think for a second."

He deflated a little. She was right. He was demanding all kinds of crap right now. And for what reason? He didn't even know. Just to reassure himself that she was okay. Maybe he was fishing for some sort of verbal contract that she'd never get into a situation like that again as long as she lived.

"You're right. Just about took a decade off my life, but you're right."

"I can already see your new gray hairs," she said, with just a touch of dry in her tone.

He grimaced at her. "Trust me, they're not new." He glanced at the clock on the wall. He'd been missing from lunch for five minutes. It was probably *Lord of the Flies* in there. He glanced back at Via, who was shoving her chair back behind her desk and taking a deep swig of water. She was trembling. "Damn it. I don't want to go."

He hadn't meant to say it out loud.

"I'm fine, Seb. Really." She waved a hand through the air and it was meant to be casual, but the darkening red on the back hit Seb like a punch to the eye. "I'm gonna take a second, cry, fix my makeup and get on with my day.

Which is now probably going to include a multipage incident report. Asshole," she murmured under her breath.

Seb grinned. One well timed *asshole* had restored way more confidence in her well-being than all the hand waving in the world. "Well, do you at least have any lunch?"

"I do. I brought a salad from home. I'll be fine."

Her office door flung open and Principal Grim strode back in, bushy hair flying. "Via, darling, that was quite the show, now, wasn't it? How's the hand?"

"I'm fine," she said to Seb, a steely look in her eye. "It's fine," she said to Principal Grim.

Seb nodded, took one last look at her and ducked out to do his job.

IF THE BASKET of fries he'd dropped off at her office without a word right after lunch had been considered hovering, then Seb was straight-up helicoptering as he waited outside her office after the final bell.

The thing with Via, though, was that he was pretty sure she'd tell him if he was overstepping.

The point ended up being moot because the second she stepped out of her office and saw what waited for her, she cracked into an eye-rolling smile. Matty stood there on one side of Seb, sucking on a juice box and crunching on some peanut butter crackers. Crabby stood on the other side, wagwagwagging, that pink tongue lolling every which way.

"Well, if it isn't the brute squad." She laughed.

"You're getting an armed escort home whether you want one or not, my dear."

"Armed?" She raised an eyebrow.

"Yeah. Matty's packing."

She burst out laughing and Matty looked back and

forth between the grown-ups. "Packing what, Daddy? Are we going somewhere?"

"Just to Via's house."

"Why do I need a bag for that?"

"You don't, twerp. I'm just being annoying on purpose."

"Why?"

"Because it makes Miss DeRosa smile."

The smile wobbled off her face, and he could have kicked himself. Was he *flirting* with her right now? His off-limits friend who'd been accosted earlier in the day? Could he be any denser?

"Well," she recovered quickly. "I suppose I wouldn't mind the company."

They walked home, three people and one happy dog, Matty filling the silence with school chatter and snack crunching. Seb was kind of shocked at how close their houses were, not more than a ten-minute walk. That was practically living together by New York standards.

She lived in a boxy apartment building on Eighty-sixth Street, next to the aboveground trains and so close to the drink you could smell the salt on the air.

"Sometimes I think Brooklyn has microclimates like San Francisco," Seb remarked as they strolled up to the front of her building.

"Oh?"

"Yeah, here you are only ten blocks from me but you can smell the ocean from your spot."

"I know. And the *chebureki*." She nodded to where two stooped Russian men sat across from one another at a makeshift chessboard. One of them had a little steaming cart next to him, selling the savory Russian pastries for a dollar apiece.

"Oh yeah, I guess this is almost Bath Beach. I heard the Russian population was moving out this way."

She nodded. "Another Italian neighborhood with no more Italians."

"I guess we're all just Brooklynites in Brooklyn."

She nodded and he wondered if she was thinking about her parents. "Want to come up and see the place?"

She's nervous to go up alone. The thought struck him like a jolt from a toaster, and he felt warm and weird all at once. God, he didn't like thinking about her being scared. He sort of hated her boyfriend right about now, this Evan guy. Why hadn't she called him? He surely had a key. Shouldn't he be waiting up there with a glass of wine and a fresh-baked lasagna? Bubble bath and a foot rub? *Something* to soothe her after the horrible day she'd had.

The other half of Seb, the half that he wasn't as proud of, was glad that he got to be the one to go up there with her. Some ancient, testosterone-pumping part of his chemical makeup pictured himself peeking in her closets with a Maglite, kicking at a misshapen lump in her curtains, making sure the place was safe for her.

"Sure." He rocked back on his heels, answering immediately. "You don't mind the dog?"

She looked at him like he'd gone crackers. "Crabby? No. I don't mind Crabby."

Via took Matty by the hand and led him through the front lobby of her building. It was one of those old, decrepit buildings that had gotten a bad facelift sometime in the last decade. There were sheets of frosted green glass dividing the entryway in two and a skinny purple carpet leading toward the elevator. But the granite floors were spiderwebbed with cracks, and the pleather armchairs that sat next to a fake fern in the corner were layered over with dust. Such typical Brooklyn.

She walked straight past the row of little metal cubbies and didn't check her mail. He wondered if that was because she didn't usually get any or if those mailboxes didn't open, a problem he'd had at an old place.

The elevator was brass and reflective, old-world. There was even a gate that had to be yanked to one side to get it to start. Matty did the honors, delighting in the smudgy fingerprints he left on the shiny brass handle.

Via led them to the dark wood door of her apartment. All the other doors had crooked, rusty numbers, but hers had a perfectly shiny, aligned number 5C. He knew, without a doubt, that she'd done that herself and it made him want to bury his nose behind her ear. Kiss both eyelids.

He was such a goner. Such a dumbass for doing this to himself.

Her hand shook, just a touch, as she scrabbled the key into the lock.

"Violetta." He stilled her with just his fingertips to her wrist. "I'm just coming up to see your apartment; you know that there is nothing wrong in there. There's no way that…" *He could be in there.*

"I know." She nodded resolutely. Her lips were white from pressing them together. But then she tossed her hair back and attempted a smile. "But what's the point in being friends with Thor if you don't get to watch him throw a little muscle around?"

That caught him off guard. He laughed. And then laughed harder at the expression on Matty's face.

"Did Miss DeRosa just call you Thor?"

"You'd have to ask her."

Seb put one hand in between Matty's shoulder blades, a silent reminder to *be good in our friend's house.* He tightened his grip on Crabby's leash.

She swung the door open and led them inside. Sebastian immediately realized that he was holding his breath and shook his head at himself.

"Don't worry about your shoes," she called, though she kicked her own small heels into a basket.

Seb looked meaningfully down at Matty and they followed suit, no matter what she said. She dumped her bag onto her couch and sidled into her kitchen. "Matty, you want a snack?"

His little boy padding after Via and Crabby behaving for once, Seb took the opportunity to really look around. It was spick-and-span. Not obnoxiously so, but still, she obviously was a cleaner. Her furniture all matched, though it was as horrible as she'd warned him. Cheap particleboard crap that you couldn't even have the satisfaction of burning due to all the chemicals. But her space was nice. Maybe a little plain, with a pop of color here and there.

He liked it. But it was…lonely.

He couldn't exactly explain why, but the loneliness was palpable in this house, like a scent on the air or a reflection in a distant mirror.

Seb hated himself for doing it, but he looked around for evidence of the boyfriend. A baseball cap was slung crooked on her coatrack, but he recognized that as hers from softball. Beyond that, everything looked decidedly girly. Even the books on her very packed shelves were organized in a rainbow based on the color of their spines. He didn't know any guy who would do that.

"Matty's having pretzels and hummus. Do you want some?" She appeared in the doorway of her kitchen, one foot balancing on the top of the other.

"Sure." He paused. "Are we overstaying our welcome? Your radar for that goes completely out of whack once you have a kid."

"Let me rephrase. I'm inviting you to come have pretzels and hummus."

He nodded and walked with Crabby into the kitchen. He stopped in his tracks. The living room had been lonely. But this room right here? This was downright crowded. There was a riot of color in two different fruit baskets, with plenty of vegetables thrown in as well. She'd taken the door off her pantry and every can on her shelves was again arranged by rainbow color. And she had a lot of cans. There was a lumpy, lopsided bouquet of every color on her windowsill, currently backlit by the afternoon sun. Her dishes on the drying rack were mismatched and bright, and she had a wall lined with hooks where every kitchen utensil imaginable dangled.

He was no expert, but he could recognize the good stuff when he saw it. Copper ladles and sharp, heavy knives with pearl inlaid in the handles. There was something mouthwatering percolating in a slow cooker, and when she opened the fridge to get the hummus, Seb's jaw dropped straight open.

"Good Lord!" His hand landed on hers as she started closing the fridge door. He yanked it back open. "What, are you running your own farmers market or something?" There was every green thing imaginable, roots curling akimbo, three different shades of every vegetable. "You have two different kinds of beets. Who in God's name needs two different kinds of beets?"

She laughed, but there was a very healthy blush working its way up her cheeks. "I like cooking, okay?"

"Apparently." He knew his eyes were as big as pancakes, but he seriously had never seen this much produce outside of a grocery store. "You really cook with all this?"

"Of course. I'm usually cooking for two."

He felt some of his rising giddiness pinprick away into

the air. Of course. She cooked for Evan the Supermodel. *Ponytail-having bastard.*

"Fin comes over most nights to eat with me. And most mornings, now that I think about it."

Hmm. What the hell did that mean? That she didn't cook for her boyfriend? It was a stupid mystery to try to be solving when he could just be enjoying her company.

"This doesn't look like our hummus," Matty said dubiously as he eyed the Tupperware she'd just cracked open. He'd slid up onto one of the chairs at the small breakfast table and was drumming skeptical fingers on the linoleum top.

"It's homemade," she replied absently as she fished in one cabinet for pretzels.

Seb's heart sank. This was where his picky-ass kid was going to turn up his nose at a beautiful woman's homemade food and make Seb feel like an inept father who stuffed his kid full of mac and cheese.

But then Via did something amazing. At the same second she was selecting a pear from her fruit basket, Via dipped a pretzel in the hummus and just jammed it right in Matty's mouth. His eyes widened in surprise as much as Seb's did. And then Matty's eyes widened even more.

"It's good."

"I know," Via replied from the kitchen sink where she was washing the pear.

Seb slid down next to Matty and tried it. Damn. It was better than good. This Evan asshole better marry Via DeRosa, or he deserved a punch straight in the dick.

Via brought a plate of sliced pears and slid down across from Matty and Seb. Crabby's tail thumped under the table and she reached down to give him some pets.

Seb watched her while he crunched his pretzels. He saw the toll the day had taken on her. Her wrinkled silk shirt, her lipstick chewed off, the eye makeup slightly smudged over one eye. And that hand, already tipping from dark pink into purple. He wanted to speak to her but didn't want Matty to overhear. Seb pulled out his phone.

I'm so sorry for what happened today, Via.

She jolted just a little as the text vibrated in her pocket but she ignored it, obviously too polite to answer a text while she had company.

Seb made eyes at her until she got his message and opened her phone. He asked Matty questions about his day at school while she pecked out a one-handed response.

I'm okay, Sebastian. It wasn't your fault. It wasn't anyone's fault but his.

He took a deep breath. She was right of course. But still…

I wish I would have intervened sooner. And then you wouldn't be hurt. Don't console me. You're not supposed to console me when you're the one who left that room with a bruise.

She smirked at him as she read his text.

Then what do you want? Tough love?

God. He wanted any type of love that she would throw his way. If he were a different man, maybe he would have typed that out. But he had a kid chomping pretzels next to him and a dog sleeping on his foot. And she had a boyfriend. And was twenty-seven years old, for fuck's sake. How many times had he been through this with himself?

Anything to make you feel better.

She frowned down at his text. She sighed and took a big bite of pretzel and hummus, looking out the window. She was tweaking her nose one way and then the other when she finally responded.

Yeah. Worst birthday ever.

"It's your *birthday*?" He hadn't meant to speak it out loud but there it was. His stomach gave an almighty flop, like a sea lion on a wet dock. In all his musings over Via DeRosa's age, it simply hadn't occurred to him that the woman had birthdays. Dumb but true.

Just because she's older doesn't mean she's old enough, he reminded himself. He'd been clinging so tightly to the number twenty-seven that twenty-eight felt strangely slippery in his mind, like he couldn't quite pin it to the same bulletin board that her former age had been fastened to.

"Really?" Matty straightened like he'd been electrocuted. At six years old, birthdays were far from routine. In fact, they were pretty much as special as dinosaur sightings.

"Really," she admitted, pursing her lips together.

"Oh God." Sebastian face-palmed. "Matty, finish up. We've gotta get out of here. I'm sure Miss DeRosa has a fancy dinner or a party or something to go to."

Via shrugged. "You can stay for a bit. Fin is coming over for dinner, but beyond that, nothing too special. You're not crashing."

Matty was doing his best electric-shock-part-two impression. "Dad, can we stay for dinner?" He leaned in very close to Seb's face, all hummus breath and bits of pretzel flying everywhere. "There's usually cake on a birthday," he whispered loud enough to make Via burst out laughing.

Seb was glad that someone was laughing. Because to him? This was mortifying. "We're having dinner with Tyler and Mary, remember? To celebrate your grandparents leav—because we haven't gotten to see them in a while."

"They can come," Via said, in that quiet, calm, easy way that just *slayed* Seb. "I obviously have plenty of food."

"Oh. Are you sure? You're going to cook for all of us on your birthday?"

She leaned forward, her voice low and conspiratorial. "Don't you kind of want to see Fin and Tyler in the same room again?"

Seb grinned. Well, she made a good point.

She turned and let Matty capture her attention as they chatted about the hummus and the potential for birthday cake. Seb just watched her. Her color was back and the dullness in her eyes had faded almost completely. Maybe they were overstaying their welcome, he wasn't sure. He was just glad they got to stay.

Fin arrived at 5:30 with a backpack full of cheap wine and fancy grape juice for Matty. She'd kissed both Seb and Matty full on the mouth, smelling like sage and lavender, and whisked through the house in a skirt that went to the floor.

She was blindingly beautiful, but Seb found himself completely comfortable around her now that she was simply his friend.

Mary and Tyler arrived together at six, when they would have arrived at Seb's. Mary had a small gift in tow, and Tyler had delighted Via with a handful of pink carnations. Seb wished he had something to give to Via that would make her whole face go long and open and lit up like that.

He'd settled for being her sous chef while she cooked for everyone. Though he had to admit that it was probably more of a gift for himself than it was for her, standing hip-to-hip at the counter, his elbow brushing hers every so often. Seb held his breath and butchered some tomatoes he was supposed to be dicing when she laid one hand on his shoulder to boost herself up to an overhead cabinet.

He studied his handiwork. "I really can't tell if I'm making this easier or harder on you by offering my cooking skills."

She gave up on reaching the spice she'd been grappling for and bit her smile back as she peered at his gelatinous mess of tomato on the cutting board. She looked up at Seb, her eyebrows raised and her bottom lip between her teeth.

"Well, it'll still taste the same, won't it?" he asked anxiously.

Via burst out laughing. Seb couldn't help but drop his eyes to her mouth. "You're doing fine, Seb."

He laughed with her but a truth had just come crashing down around his ears. He liked her so much he was *willing* to torture himself by being around her. His mother-in-law's advice echoed in his head. Her voice was spooky and ominous, and he knew Muriel would have rolled her eyes at how melodramatic he was being. But he wondered if she was right. He wondered if maybe, just maybe, the adult thing to do here would be to respectfully tell Via of his feelings. No pressure, just information.

He nearly jolted at that treacherous line of thought. So what if she dumped Evan? Would that matter, really? Even if she fell into Seb's arms, his arms would still be forty-two years old. With a kid and a baggage claim full of issues. He tersely reminded himself Evan wasn't in the way of him and Via. Everything was in the way of him and Via.

She tapped his shoulder and he turned, looking down at her.

Didn't mean he wouldn't mind her kicking her boyfriend to the curb, though.

"Mind grabbing that lemon pepper?"

He easily reached up into the cabinet and handed it down to her.

"Thanks." She grinned up at him, all golden skin and amber-brown eyes and crooked teeth and damn. Just. Damn.

He cleared his throat. "Can't believe you got Matty to eat that hummus earlier today."

"Sometimes kids just need you to make the choice for them."

He nodded, in total agreement on that front. "You're really good with kids. Did you always know that you wanted to work with them?"

"Mmm, since I was twenty or so. At that point, I'd had two years of college under my belt and I was far enough away from the system to feel a little less…haunted by it. And that was around the time that Jetty passed. Fin and I had to go through her house, her belongings, and I saw physical evidence of all the ways she'd supported me through the years. Trophies, photos, letters from me to her.

It made me realize how much she'd done for me. Made me want to do the same for other kids."

"Made you want to foster?"

"Maybe someday," she said as she weighed her head from side to side. "I think I'd be a good mom. But I'll need a lot more money for that." She grinned at him. "And a much larger apartment."

He turned away from her quickly, momentarily stunned by that easy smile of hers. She wanted to be a mom but wasn't ready...for circumstantial reasons. Did that mean that if she suddenly had more money and a bigger place, she was emotionally ready to be a mom?

His stomach churned as she moved around next to him, sliding his tomato mush into a pot and then placing some onions to dice on his cutting board.

"Mostly, I was thinking of ways to reach the most kids at once. Do as much good as I could, you know? I considered being a social worker, but that ended up hitting a little too close to home for me. I've seen so many of them over the years. I ended up going into education and the further I went into the program, the more clear it became that I needed to focus on counseling as well. So I went back for my master's and here we are."

He chuckled at her nonchalant delivery. "Voilà."

She smiled at his wry tone. "Easy as pie."

"Yeah. Getting a master's is just like pulling a rabbit out of a hat."

She opened her mouth to reply but just then Mary bustled in from the other room, a joke in her eyes. "Oh my God. I think Fin is telling Tyler's fortune right now, and the poor guy looks like he's about to pass out."

"She's not!" Via looked horrified, like her friend had decided to put the punch bowl on her head after one too many jungle juices. She hustled immediately out of the kitchen, seemingly to intervene. Seb took a deep breath and was grateful for the momentary reprieve from her little, golden presence. The kids conversation had been a step too far for him. He didn't need to torture himself with information like that unless he was going to actually *do* something with it.

The second she was gone, Mary's midnight blue eyes slid over to Seb, a sly little look on her face. "And what's going on in here?" The last word was punctuated by her rolling up on her toes.

Seb leaned forward and really gave Mary the once-over. She'd pulled her hair back in a tight, matronly bun, and she wore an extremely unflattering sweater. "Why do you look like that?" he asked, in lieu of answering her pointed question. "That's the ugliest sweater I've ever seen."

He expected her to be outraged. Mary was a very fashionable woman and had often found herself in the position of defending her sophisticated fashion choices to Tyler or Seb. But today she just grinned. "I changed after work. I just didn't want to seem threatening at all."

"Threatening? To who?"

"Don't be dense, Seb." She raised an arched eyebrow and looked pointedly at Via as the shorter woman scuttled back over to the stove.

"It wasn't a full-on reading, but she was definitely trying to spook the hell out of him."

"Miss Via?" Matty asked as he strolled into the kitchen like he owned the place.

Seb turned quickly, and Via laid a hand on his arm. "I told him he could call me Via when we're doing friend stuff and not school stuff. He actually insisted on keeping the Miss."

Seb loosened and nodded at his son, impressed with his politeness.

"What's up?" she asked him.

"When's dinner? I'm really hungry. Plus, I finished that coloring book."

Seb winced. There was no way he'd finished that coloring book in twenty minutes. He knew exactly what he'd find when he went to look at it. A two-color scribble on each page and a declaration that it wasn't fun if the page wasn't perfectly pristine.

"Oh, well, that's great that you finished it," Via said. "Because nobody has made me my birthday fort yet."

"Your birthday fort?"

"Yeah." Via cocked her head at him, spoon in the air. "Every birthday, someone makes me a big fort that I can eat my birthday dinner in. But nobody has done it yet. You wouldn't happen to be good at making forts, would you?"

"I'm the best at forts. The BEST."

He really was. So good, in fact, that Seb wondered if his son might be as interested in architecture as he'd been at one point.

"Great. I have to finish dinner, but I'll get you started."

"I'll help," Mary chirped, her eyes on Via, obviously just about as charmed by her as Seb was.

Who am I kidding? No one is as charmed by her as I am.

It was half an hour later that everyone sat on the floor of Via's living room with plates of homemade pasta in their laps and a pillow fort precariously towering over them. Crabby hovered, semi-obediently, at the edge of the fort, licking the air at the scent of the sauce and wind-milling his tail at anyone who glanced his way. Fin had lit some candles and dimmed the lights. The room twinkled a golden orange, and all of them had instinctively lowered their voices to match the mood.

The conversation flowed much more casually than the other time the group had spent together. Tyler still sat as far from Fin as he possibly could have and alternated between looking anywhere but at her and staring her down.

Seb could only hope he looked a little more casual. But he probably blew that when he choked on his wine when Mary opened her big mouth.

"Where's Evan tonight, Via?" Mary asked.

"Oh." Via looked up quickly, wiping her pretty mouth with a napkin. "He's still upstate with his family."

Upstate.

She'd said she had stuff to do upstate and then had spent the next week crying. Seb forced the traitorous wine down his throat and crammed a bite of pasta in his mouth, avoiding everyone's eyes. He could swear that both Mary and Fin were looking at him.

His mind raced as his stomach tightened down like a tank preparing for battle. Seb figured there were a few different things that could have happened here. Either she'd gone upstate to visit her boyfriend and then cried her eyes out because she had to come back to Brooklyn and just missed him so badly. Or maybe going upstate had nothing to do with Evan and it was all a coincidence? Or. Or. Or. She'd gone upstate, and things had gone badly. *I mean, he's not here on her birthday,* a little, asshole-ish voice whispered in Seb's ear. What if they'd broken up?

When he finally looked up again, the conversation had flowed on, and it was past 7:30. Matty pushed his bowl of pasta aside and laid his head on Seb's crossed knee. Seb absently pushed his son's hair from one side to the other. The candlelight flickered as Fin rose to clear everyone's plates and Seb's eyes lifted to Via's naturally. She was looking at him. At his hand on Matty's head. But then she was looking directly in Sebastian's eyes. Unwavering. Her eyes were a dizzying color, somewhere between gold and brown. And for a minute, all they did was just look at one another.

Seb felt drunk and disoriented when Fin came back in with a lit birthday cake, and Via broke their staring game to laugh and clap her hands.

He had only had one glass of wine, but he felt like he was currently floating in a lazy ocean the temperature of a Jacuzzi.

He shook his head and joined in with everyone as they sang for her birthday. Matty perked up at the prospect of chocolate cake, and Mary brought out her present for Via.

"Ugh." Seb groaned as Via carefully peeled back each layer of tape and wrapping paper. "You're one of those people? Just rip it!"

"Sebastian, you have so much to learn about our Violetta," Fin told him, a little smile on her face. "She's gonna save that paper, and later, she's gonna iron it."

"Serafine!" Via admonished as a healthy blush bloomed on her cheeks. "There's no reason to waste it! It's reusable!"

Seb's stupid, wasted heart thumped hard. An idiotic, clumsy ka-bump. He hoped his smile wasn't as dopey as he thought it probably was. Look at him. So far gone, he was crushing on her wrapping paper habits.

"The coasters I wanted! Oh, Mary!" Via flung herself across the pillow fort and grabbed Mary up in a hug. They both laughed.

"I take that to mean that you like them."

"Give them here, sister," Fin requested in that slow, curling drawl. She inspected the coasters. "That's nice frosting."

"Frosting?" Tyler asked.

"Jetty, the woman who raised us," Via explained, "used to say that a good, steady life was like cake. And that every once in a while, you deserved a little frosting. Just little things, little gifts to yourself. Things that don't make sense to spend your money on unless you've paid your bills and have a job and all that. Frosting."

"Via's always liked her frosting extra shiny," Fin said, a loving smile on her face.

Seb thought of the copper utensils and pearl-inlaid knives in her kitchen. He looked around at her decor, little bursts of prettiness all over. Colored glass that caught the light, a pillow with little mirrors embroidered around the edges. He thought of those little gold studs she wore, understated and still, somehow, princess-like.

Seb felt like he could have stayed in the soft, comfortable cave of the candlelit pillow fort with his friends for the next couple of weeks. He didn't want the world to make him leave. But his lonely dog was whining at the edge of the fort, and his son's head had lowered to his knee again. The sun had long since set, and it was a school night, after all.

Via was one of those people who cleaned up the kitchen as she cooked—*Muriel's wet dream*, although he tried not to think about that for all sorts of reasons—so there wasn't much cleanup to do, besides the pillow fort.

"Sorry to bail," Seb said as he rose up with Matty in his arms. The kid was already spider-monkeying himself around his dad's hips and neck, one hot cheek on his shoulder and cake breath wafting up into Seb's face. Seb tightened his arms around his boy, filled with love for him.

"No, no." Via waved away his apology. "It's almost bedtime. I'm just so glad you stayed. Fin and I probably would have eaten at the regular old dinner table instead of a pillow fort."

"You liked the fort?" Matty asked sleepily, tilting his head to see Via.

She stepped over to Matty and Seb, absently stroking a hand over Matty's back. Her hand briefly brushed over one of Seb's, and he refused to clench it into a fist, even if it felt like he'd been sunburned in a good way.

"I *love* the fort."

"It was my birthday present to you."

Seb knew he was biased, but damn, his kid was sweet sometimes. Apparently Via thought so, too, because she leaned forward, puckering her lips, and gave Matty a kiss. The top of her head brushed against Sebastian's chin, and he shifted a little. He was extremely conscious of their nosy-ass friends all watching him.

"All right." Was that his voice? All gravelly and gruff as hell? "Thank you for having us. Sorry we're leaving you with a mess."

"I'll stay and help clean it up," Mary insisted.

"I'll help you get your dog and kid and all the rest of your crap home, Seb." Tyler was already gathering Matty's schoolbag.

The goodbyes were quick and nondramatic, and it wasn't until Seb and Tyler were walking home, side by side down the dark sidewalk, that they looked at one another and shook their heads.

"Jesus Christ, man," Tyler murmured, checking to make sure Matty was asleep on Seb's shoulder. He was.

"Yeah. I mean. Damn it."

They both knew what they were talking about.

Tyler sighed. "I won't give you shit about how dopey you were with yours, if you don't give me shit about how dopey I was with mine."

Seb laughed and shook his head, at himself and his friend. "Deal. God. We're like a couple of teenagers."

"Middle schoolers, I'd say. We had girlfriends in high school, remember? It was middle school that we were blushing at parties, too scared to tell the pretty girls that we wanted to make out in the back of a movie theater."

"That's what you want to do with Fin?" Seb asked dryly.

"I probably wouldn't kick her spooky ass out of the back of a movie theater."

They laughed and chatted, making fun of themselves for the rest of the walk back to Seb's.

CHAPTER FIFTEEN

OVER THE NEXT WEEK, Sebastian watched Via very carefully for signs of trauma. He was deeply grateful that the incident with the man in her office hadn't been worse. In fact, the bruise was already completely gone from her hand.

He only saw her at softball and school, there being no particular reason to see one another extracurricularly.

November waltzed in in that stiff-wind, fall-downpour, golden-leaves-at-every-turn sort of way. And then dumped eleven inches of snow on the city.

Welcome to winter, mofos.

Just when you thought New York would let you dip a toe into anything. Nope.

Seb was embarrassed at how cute he found Via's winter coat. Especially the fact that she was wearing it in the middle of a staff meeting. She was so put together and stylish, he'd figured her for a peacoat kind of gal. But there she was, zipped to the chin in a puffy REI coat he was pretty sure was only used for subzero winter sports.

"Don't say a word," she growled as she plunked down into the chair next to him. "Hi, Shell. Hi, Grace." She accepted the gum he automatically handed around and lifted an eyebrow.

"You said not to say a word." He grinned and lifted his hands in an *I'm unarmed* type of gesture. "It's not my business if you have to wear a polar bear parka when it's forty-two degrees outside."

"First of all, that's saying a word. Second of all, the temp dropped to thirty-nine and there's a foot and a half of snow on the ground!"

Seb swallowed his smile down. "There was a whopping seven inches that's been reduced to a measly four in the sun. Matty didn't even wear mittens today!"

"That child is insane. And this school is insane. Can't the city of New York afford heating in its public schools?"

"Oh, we've got heat," Grace assured her as she turned around in her chair. "It's just not evenly distributed. Trust me. Come on down to my classroom and bring your Hawaiian shirt and a piña colada."

"It's true," Shelly admitted. "But the woman who had your office used to complain, too, Via. Maybe your heating is broken."

"I'll come take a look after the meeting," Seb said.

Via furrowed her brow. "You think you can fix the heating in a ninety-year-old building?"

He shrugged. "Not sure until I see it. But I'm pretty handy."

Seb turned to her, and his breath caught in his throat. *Was she...?* Yeah. Yup. Yes. She was side-eyeing his hands and blushing. Straight-up blushing.

Via quickly turned away and shuffled through her messenger bag. But when she straightened up a minute later, not having removed a dang thing, Seb was fairly certain she was just attempting to look busy while she got her blush under control. Interesting. Very interesting.

Grim chimed the staff meeting to order, and Sebastian struggled to pay attention to a single word that was said.

It was either his imagination, or Via was especially wiggly today. Usually, she sat completely still, the picture of stoicism. But today she crossed one leg over the other and then switched back. Every time her weight shifted, her shoulder knocked into Seb's. Frankly, he wasn't even positive that she could feel it under all that coat, but every touch was kicking his heart into his ribs like the smash of a piñata at a children's birthday party. Her hands were jumpy, too. She touched her hair, the back of her neck, her fingers dancing over the knee of one leg, tracing the herringbone pattern.

He had no idea what was going on with her, but frankly, wiggly Via was apparently a turn-on for Seb, and he didn't need to be popping wood in the middle of a staff meeting.

"Are you hot?" he leaned over and whispered. He'd miscalculated the distance and he felt the light, fragrant brush of her hair over his lips. Whoops.

"What?" she asked him, her mouth dropping open and a half-scandalized expression blooming on her face. Half-scandalized and half…something else. The reality of the situation hit Sebastian like a sack full of baseballs to the face. *Oh.* She thought he meant a different kind of hot. An inappropriate kind of hot. To Seb's thinking, there was only one reason that her mind would have taken her there so quickly.

Because she *was* hot. The inappropriate kind.

Extremely, painfully aware of their surroundings, Seb attempted to defuse the situation. "Your coat. You're acting like you're overheating."

"Oh." A flush crept up her cheeks and her eyes were just a little unfocused.

Hold the phone. Had she just looked at his mouth?

"Right. Yeah. You're right," she muttered.

She quickly unzipped her coat and let it loll off the back of her chair. Seb immediately, deeply, regretted prompting her to remove it because her warmed scent lifted off her skin and into the air. She smelled herby and sweet at the same time. Had he ever really noticed that before? Like rosemary mixed with almond. And maybe, yeah, just the sexiest little touch of girl-sweat in there, too.

Christ. He needed to scream into a pillow. Preferably Via's pillow. That smelled exactly like her. Did he say scream? He meant huff into it while he dreamed of every dirty-sexy sex position on the planet.

Was this the longest staff meeting in the history of all time or was it just him? He shifted his hips in his chair and glared at the clock on the wall. Good God, they were only fifteen minutes in. He didn't know what the hell was going on with Via, but he didn't know how much more of this superheated charge he could endure.

She seemed horny.

Fuck. He realized what it was. Evan, the dumbass-shiniest-hair-having, luckiest-SOB-in-all-of-history, was probably still upstate with his family. She probably *was* horny.

And Seb had to endure the sweet torture of her wiggly nearness, and then whenever she saw her boyfriend next, Evan got to reap every single benefit of a hot little Via DeRosa. Great. Just great.

He couldn't think of a single other reason why she would be damn near combustion in the middle of a staff meeting.

Her knee started to toggle up and down, jostling his chair slightly, and Seb prayed for sanity. His hand sliced out and pressed her knee into stillness. He felt her eyes snap to the side of his face, but he didn't look at her as he took that hand back and jammed it into his pocket.

He pretended to be riveted to whatever the hell Principal Grim was yammering on about.

Finally, finally, the meeting was over, and Sebastian stood up so fast his seat scooted back a few inches. "I'm gonna run and check your heating real quick before I grab Matty from aftercare."

"Sure," she said faintly, looking as dazed as Seb felt. "I'll come with."

Seb said a few goodbyes and then they strode together toward her office. They were walking fast and far apart from one another. It felt weird. She held her coat in front of her like a Roman Catholic nun with her hands in her sleeves. That was weird, too. Seb felt very much like he was playing a game and no one had bothered to explain the rules, or even to tell him that the starting gun had gone off.

They turned in to her office, and Seb immediately got to his knees in front of her heating unit. Luckily, the ornate iron gate lifted neatly off. He started inspecting it, trying very hard to ignore her heated, glowing presence behind him.

"You, uh, got a haircut," she said quietly.

"Oh. Yeah. Yesterday. It was time."

"It makes your hair look darker."

"Yeah. Both Matty and I have hair that can't make up its mind. Dark when it's short and blonder when it's long or in the sun." He attempted to twist a few knobs on the piping and realized he needed a better angle.

"It looks nice."

"Thanks," he grunted, lying on his back and trying like hell to twist the rust off a handle that wouldn't budge.

"And you're wearing a new shirt."

She sounded nervous as hell. He glanced up at her and realized that she was standing just about as far away as the room allowed. She'd also put her coat back on and zipped it clear to her throat. "Nah. It's an oldie. I just bring it out when the weather gets cold."

"Well." She cleared her throat. "Regardless, you look handsome."

"Thanks," he repeated, his brow furrowing. Some puzzle pieces started to click down into place, and Seb was immediately terrified that he was going to break this foggy, warm haze that had fallen over her. He moved slowly as he messed around with the pipes, unwilling to startle her.

"I thought for sure that you must have a date tonight, because you look so nice."

Was she fishing?

"Nope." He finally got the knob to twist and he heard the telltale hiss of hot water, unblocked and starting to fill the pipes of the heating register. He dusted off his hands and rolled up to his knees. "No date."

Free as a bird, something inside him wanted to add. But Seb clamped down on that. He wasn't free as a bird. He had a kid and a dog, and she was in her twenties with a boyfriend—as far as he knew. Even if she was biting her lip and looking at him like she wanted to go behind the jungle gym and kiss at recess, that still didn't make Seb free as a bird.

"That oughta do it," he told her, setting the iron gating back into place and putting his hands on his hips, mostly so he didn't reach out and test the puffiness of that coat.

"Wow!" She looked surprised, like she'd barely remembered what he'd come into her office to do in the first place. "Thanks!"

"You got it. I'm gonna jet and grab Matty. I'll see you tomorrow?"

She nodded absently and moved over to her desk to gather up a few papers.

Sebastian gave her a quick wave and melted out the door of her office. He was both intensely relieved and wildly disappointed to be free of her.

SOFTBALL GOT RAINED OUT, so it wasn't until the next staff meeting that Seb really got to see Via again. He was painfully curious if it would be back to normal, or if it would be anything like last week. Sexy, tense last week.

"I see you left your sleeping bag at home today," Seb said, grinning at her as he slid into the seat next to her. He greeted Grace and Shelly and passed out gum.

"If you're referring to my *very fashionable* winter coat—" she shot him a look "—yes, I left it at home. Some guy fixed the heating in my office."

"Sounds like a great guy."

"Meh, he's fine. A little full of himself."

They both laughed and only stopped when they found a hot pink envelope being wagged in each of their faces.

Seb saw his name scrawled carefully across the front. "What's this?" he asked Sadie, who was the person doing the wagging.

"Open it and see!" she squealed, practically bouncing on the spot.

"You set the date!" Via said, her voice delighted. "Oh, Sade, I'm so happy for you guys."

"It's the weekend after next," Sebastian said, frowning down at the invite, assuming it was a typo.

"Yup. We wanted to give people as little notice as possible. Rae's family is huge, but they won't all be able to make it on such a tight time frame." She whispered the last part out of the side of her mouth.

"Wow." Via stared down at the invite. "Okay. Cool."

"So, please fill them out during the meeting and then hand them back to me by the end, because I don't have the time for tardy RSVPs, 'kay?" She air-kissed and then moved on to pass the next row their invites.

Via pulled a pen from her bag and neatly wrote her name on the line. She checked *fish* instead of *chicken* and then put a *1* in the box for number of guests attending.

Seb felt the light scratch of her pen rattle him like Godzilla's footsteps. He could almost hear the echoing reverberation of that number one rolling around his thick skull.

"Evan still upstate?" he asked, not even caring that she'd know he'd been peeking at her response card.

"Hmm?" she asked, handing the pen to him.

Seb nodded at her invitation. "Your boyfriend will still be out of town next week?"

"Oh." She dropped her gaze immediately to the invitation, flipping the incriminating information over. "Ah. No, he's back in Brooklyn. I heard."

She heard. SHE HEARD.

That had to mean one thing. That could only mean one thing. Was he breathing? He commanded himself to breathe. It would be the geekiest move of all time if he passed out right now. Seb forced himself to write his name down on his invite.

"But he's not my boyfriend anymore," she said softly, her eyes looking everywhere but at him.

Seb felt like spiking the save-the-date in the end zone. Like tap dancing down the hallway of the school. Like tipping her back in her chair and kissing the hell out of her.

But then the look on her face at that softball game flashed through his eyes. The way she'd wiped tears with her wrist, looking so small and lonely.

He found he didn't have to lie when he replied with, "I'm sorry, Via. Breakups are hell."

"Yeah." She nodded.

"How long ago?" he asked, sort of hating himself for fishing.

"Um, when I took that trip upstate last month? You remember, right after...you were sick."

Right after he'd spilled his guts out to her. After she'd taken care of his sick ass. After she'd put Matty to bed and sat with Seb on the couch. Did the timing of it mean anything? Was it all coincidence?

He had no idea what to ask next. How to ask what he so desperately wanted to know. *Was I in your heart when you left your boyfriend?* "Was it messy?"

She nodded, something that looked like guilt in those brown eyes she still wouldn't turn in his direction. "He was pretty blindsided. It took a while to convince him that I meant it."

Seb tried to imagine what it would feel like to have Via DeRosa leave you. Suddenly, months of pent-up resentment toward this Evan kid just kind of dried up. He felt sympathy. Seb was sure she'd been sweet as pie during the breakup. And fuck if that wouldn't have made it even worse.

"Damn."

"Yeah. I'd never broken up with someone before," she said, almost thoughtfully.

"Never? You're twenty-eight years old. You must have had lots of boyfriends."

She smiled a little. "I've had a few."

Seb wanted to punch a wall, and then himself in the face for bringing up this line of conversation. He didn't want to hear this shit.

"But they all broke up with me."

"Not possible." The words were out of his mouth before he could even consider not saying them. They were sharp and high resolution. The kind of words that said a million other words. He was practically telling her *I wouldn't break up with you*.

She started at his tight tone, but otherwise didn't indicate that he was being a total psycho. "No, seriously. Like clockwork. Bing, bang, boom. It was sort of weird to be the one ending it this time. But…" She shrugged. "It wasn't fair to stay with him when—" Suddenly her eyes were on his, brown and clear and making the air crackle with static all around them. "When I wasn't being honest with myself."

What the fuck does that mean?

Principal Grim started the staff meeting and Sebastian swallowed down his growl of frustration. His mind was in about eight different places all at once, and he'd never in his life felt more aware of another person as he was of Via DeRosa. She crossed one leg over the other, and Seb held his breath. When she tapped her capped pen on the back of the hot pink invitation, Seb felt insane, like she was trying to tap out a message to him. And when she leaned forward to whisper something in Shelly's ear, he caught that scent again. Almond and rosemary.

So many things hit him at once. He hadn't realized quite how constrained he'd felt that she'd had a boyfriend. He'd convinced himself that it didn't matter either way. But here he was, considering the fact that he could now flirt with her, guilt-free, and the idea was swelling up like a piece of ripening fruit.

She was single. She was available. She was free.

He held back a groan.

She was single and free. Which meant she was probably going to get on Tinder like everyone else her age. She was going to date and hook up and party. She was free, but that didn't mean she was available to Seb and all the baggage that came with him.

She was in her twenties. Just like yesterday and just like tomorrow. She was single, and it changed so much.

But it didn't change everything.

Fuck.

CHAPTER SIXTEEN

"So," GRACE SAID matter-of-factly as she heated up left-overs in the microwave. "You broke up with your man?"

The penny finally dropped. Via had been utterly be-mused after the staff meeting to find Grace and Shelly practically zipping her into her coat and dragging her back to Grace's house. Grace only lived a few blocks away from Via, so it wasn't a huge imposition. But Via had had no idea why she'd been ushered into an unexpected dinner of leftovers in Grace's snug little one-bedroom on Eighty-first Street.

"We couldn't help overhearing at the meeting," Shelly said with just the slightest bit of pink on her cheeks.

Via wondered with chagrin exactly what else they'd overheard over the last few weeks. She knew that her feelings for Sebastian couldn't exactly have been considered covert.

"Oh. Yes. Evan and I broke up."

"What a shame," Grace said as she took out the container of chicken stew from the microwave, stirred it and put it back in. "Shell, would you mind slicing that bread? Via, are you the kind of girl that requires a salad at every meal?"

"Um." She wasn't sure how to respond to that.

"If you are, go ahead and fix yourself one."

Via laughed at the judgment in Grace's tone, as if eating salad at dinner was something she wanted very little to do with. "I'll be fine with whatever we're having. Uh, thank you for inviting me for dinner."

She was really stretching the meaning of the word *invite*, considering they'd basically frog-marched her to the house.

"Whenever we hear that one of our colleagues is going through a hard time, we try to have a sit-down with them," Shelly explained, putting the bread on the table and coming back to sit next to Via.

Was that what was happening to Via? Was she going through a hard time? Via thought of the way breakups were depicted in movies. Pints of Häagen-Dazs and tears over rom-coms. She was sad over ending things with Evan, sure, but she had to admit, she hadn't had that drafty feeling since she'd come back from upstate and packed up all his things from her apartment. She chewed her bottom lip.

"Actually, this is how we became such good friends with Sebastian," Grace said, groaning a little as she lowered herself into the chair across from Shelly and Via. The stew steamed on the table and Via did the honors of serving up a bowl for each person. She was glad for the task because she could feel each woman's eyes on her face and she knew that they were looking for a reaction to Sebastian's name. "When we found out he was a widower, we had him over for dinner, told him about our husbands, and we all just sort of bonded from there."

"He mentioned that you'd both lost your husbands. I'm so sorry about that. Was it recent?"

To Via's dismay, Shelly's eyes filled with tears. "Richard passed about five years ago, but it feels recent for me."

Grace leaned across the table and squeezed Shelly's hand, and then she pointed to a picture hanging on her kitchen wall. It was of a very young Grace and an equally young Latino man who stood behind her with his arms crossed over her chest. "Esteban died about thirty years ago. My kids are starting to get after me to date."

Via hid her surprise. It had never occurred to her that Grace had been in an interracial marriage. But that was probably because Grace was an older white lady and Via had just made assumptions. She suddenly thought back to her lunch with Sadie when Sadie had been so surprised to hear that Via was a foster kid. It made sense in a new way now. You never could tell who someone really was unless you broke bread with them, actually stopped to listen to what they were trying to tell you.

"Thirty years is a long time," Via mused. Unbidden, a question popped up and out of her. She didn't mean to ask it, but maybe her conversation with Sebastian about grief had greased some internal wheels because Via didn't feel uncomfortable asking. "Do you ever get over it?" She cleared her throat. "I lost my parents when I was twelve. And some days it feels just as hard as it was back then."

Grace raised her eyebrows in a knowing way. "Get over it? No. Not if what you actually mean is forget about it."

"In my experience," Shelly chimed in, "the way I feel has changed a lot, but I can't imagine ever getting over it. My sister wants me to date, too, just like Grace's kids." In an uncharacteristic show of temper, Shelly let her spoon clatter back to her bowl of stew. "What is it with people's fascination with other people's dating lives?"

"Shell," Grace said in a dry tone, "what do you think we're doing with Via right this very moment? Sticking our noses where they don't belong."

Via laughed. Now that Grace had actually said it out loud, any suspicions Via had had about their motives just sort of evaporated away. These were two well-meaning new friends, who were trying to support her. Could she really blame them if they wanted a little gossip as a side dish?

For some reason, she got the impression that whatever she said tonight was not going to be repeated. Her confessions were protected by these two women who'd been through plenty in their own lives. Even so, she resolved not to let on anything about how she was feeling for Sebastian.

"You don't seem so nosy," Via assured them.

"So…" Shelly started, laying a hand on Via's forearm. "You're all right, then? Not too torn up about the breakup?"

Via thought back on her last month, wanting to give an honest answer. "The first few days were really hard. You know, picking up your phone and realizing that you don't have anyone to call."

And realizing that you invested two years in someone who did not fit into your life. Who didn't even want to fit into your life.

She gulped. "But I had my foster sister there with me for most of it, force-feeding me popcorn and tea and making me talk about my feelings."

Grace and Shelly both laughed, exchanging eye contact. Via instantly understood that their bond was one of friendship and sisterhood just like hers and Fin's.

"Why did you break up?" Grace asked.

Via gulped again.

Because you can't date one man and have a burning grain of sand in your heart for another. "It was time. We…wanted different things. I guess I realized that I'd been staying with him for the wrong reasons."

"Sex?" Grace asked candidly, making Shelly sputter

into her stew and Via laugh at the unexpectedness of the comment. "What? I'm old, I'm not oblivious."

"Sex didn't factor into the breakup," Via said as diplomatically as possible. She tried to gather her thoughts. Normally, in this situation, she would try to think of a generic answer. But something in her told her that Grace and Shelly might actually understand if she tried to explain the real reasoning. "People who grow up with family, I think they don't even realize how much of a tether that is. If you have your family to anchor you to Earth, then you can kind of…take some chances flying your kite. But when I lost my parents, that tether went away and I had to find other things to anchor me down. Like work and my reputation and—"

"A nice, steady boyfriend."

"Exactly," Via said, pointing her spoon at Grace. She was thrilled that Grace seemed to understand. "And after a while, I realized that it's not fair to stay with someone for that reason. Or at least in my case, I started to feel like I was using Evan for what he could provide for me instead of staying with him because of what we had together."

"So, the breakup was easy then?" Shelly asked.

Via laughed in a pained way. "No. No, it was not. It took about three days up at his parents' house in New Paltz and it was a dramatic cry-fest the entire time. And then when it was over, even though I was relieved, I came home and the cry-fest started all over again."

Grace frowned at her. "Just so you know, you've got a perfectly good kitchen table to cry at right here." She pointed at her kitchen. "You need to cry, call me and Shell and we'll throw you a whole cry-party. A cry-parade. We'll all cry together. It'll be a bonanza. Your foster sister can bring the popcorn."

Via laughed and to her surprise, actually felt tears rise

in her throat. How sweet was that? How sweet was all of this? She let herself relax even further.

The evening ended up being quite nice, though it wasn't until Via locked the door to her house behind her that she finally allowed herself a long, soothing breath. She let the gravity of what had happened in the staff meeting wash over her.

Well, it was done. It was over. Sebastian finally knew that she'd broken up with Evan. God, Via had been stressing out over how to tell him for weeks. Or if she even should tell him. No matter how she'd sliced that particular piece of pie, every single way she'd tried to tell him ended up seeming desperate and obvious. *The subtext is strong with this one.*

Seb, just so you know, Evan and I broke up. *Because I have feelings for you.*

Hey, Seb, I'm fine, just going through a breakup. *That you caused because you're handsome and sweet and such a m.a.n.*

Just so you know, I'm single now.

Yeah. That one was EXCLUSIVELY subtext.

She'd been too scared to tell Seb because then he'd know about the dense little grain of sand between her lungs that she'd been carrying around for him ever since that night on his couch.

And if she was honest, it wasn't a grain of sand anymore. It was growing, ravenous, devouring the world. She felt like her feelings for Seb were the size of a soccer ball, lodged between her lungs and trying to suck everything right in. She could barely believe she'd been able to hide those feelings from Grace and Shelly tonight.

Her feelings for Seb were made of gravity; nothing was safe. She watched a movie on TV after work, cried, thought of Seb, and just like that, *Maid in Manhattan* was sucked into the ball in her chest. She made lasagna that she thought Matty would like: *bam!* Sucked into her feelings for Seb. She saw a dog on the street that walked the way Crabby did: *bang!* The hungry ball of feeling was fed, always demanding more.

She'd greedily absorbed every moment with him over the last month. She'd even stopped by the lunchroom every now and then to watch him with all the kids. Laughing with one group over a joke inside a fortune cookie. Helping one kid heat up his leftovers in the microwave. Splitting up a scuffle between fifth graders. He waded through the kids like a papa bear surrounded by cubs. It made the breath catch in her throat and her hand press over her heart.

And of course, it made that dense ball of feeling grow even denser, even hungrier.

Spending her birthday with him had been a dream come true. She couldn't remember a time when she'd been happier than that night in the pillow fort. And when those gray-green eyes of his had found hers across the room? Well. God. She'd been about two moves away from curling into his lap like a kitten. Friends be damned.

Fin had pushed her to tell him how she felt, but Via was very, very unsure. What would the point of telling Sebastian really *be*? This whole thing with Evan only proved to Via how much of a mess she really was. She tried to be so orderly and prepared for everything but there she went, clinging to her relationship with Evan for an embarrassingly long time. That was not the behavior of the person she wanted to be. It just showed her exactly how little she'd be suitable for someone like Seb, who needed someone reliable in his life. Not a woman who couldn't even figure out her feelings about her own boyfriend until they nearly smashed down the door.

She'd freaked herself out with this Evan thing. She'd thought she was so grown-up, and then she'd gone and lashed herself to someone like him. It just proved she didn't know shit about shit.

Except that she did know one thing. That she couldn't stop thinking about Seb. She was pretty certain he was attracted to her. But she had no clue if he wanted anything more than that. Actually, the only evidence she had was to the contrary. He'd said that Fin was too young for him. And Via was roughly three years younger than Fin.

She'd done the math. It wasn't encouraging.

She had to admit that he did seem a lot older than she did. His demeanor, the grays at his temples, his ability to keep a cool head under all circumstances. The way he listened with patience and full attention. He was never distracted by his phone or by the television. Something about him seemed old school.

She only hoped that she didn't seem correspondingly young to him. Empirically, she knew she wasn't completely immature. She'd worked to have a stable, steady life. But up until a month ago, she'd had an extremely immature boyfriend, and that was points against her. She should have seen that Evan wasn't the real McCoy. There'd been sign after sign. And she hadn't been able to see any of them until Seb had walked into her life and shown her what grown-up really looked like.

Her ultimate fear was that he'd see her as a girl with a crush.

Well, she did totally have a crush on him, but that was just the topmost layer of her feelings. Her feelings were dense and strong. And, God help her, growing roots.

Via tossed her school things on the couch and strode into her bedroom. She carefully placed her work clothes into the dry-cleaning bag and pulled on workout clothes. She'd take a jog to Fin's. That would help clear her head.

This wasn't a disaster. Sebastian knew she was single now. But he hadn't exactly seemed like he'd understood everything ELSE. That she was single because of this soccer ball of pulsing romance that just wouldn't stop growing. So, her cover wasn't blown. She didn't have to deal with it all quite yet.

Via tied one sneaker, then the next. If anything had almost blown her cover, it was the staff meeting last week. Jeez Louise, she'd been out of control!

Well, it wasn't her fault that he'd shown up with a new haircut, all fresh and tight, and a dark brown shirt that completely set off his eyes. She'd felt like a middle schooler about to kiss the poster of a rock star when she'd caught her first glimpse of him that day. That had been around lunch, and she'd fully prepared herself to sit next to this handsome, dapper man-of-her-dreams at the staff meeting, no big deal. But then she'd sat down, and he'd looked even better close up.

What followed had been the most embarrassing hour of her life. Via had been so turned on just from *sitting next to him* that she hadn't even been able to sit still. He was just so much arms and long legs and those big old boots, untied at the top. She'd wanted, irrationally, to dip her foot in one of those boots, watch herself get swallowed up in something that was his.

And then, horror of all horrors, he'd called her out on it! Sort of. She'd thought he was asking if she were turned on—which she was. She'd been mortified when he'd just been commenting on how hot her coat must have been.

But the torture hadn't ended there. Nope. Instead of putting herself out of her misery and just going home, she'd watched him fix something for her. And then she'd

jabbered on about how good he looked until he got uncomfortable and left.

He hadn't seemed particularly turned off by it, but he
definitely hadn't stuck his head into her office to say hi
that week. She'd hoped he might. But no, he'd kept a very
respectful distance. The way he always did.

Now he knew she was single. Would he act differently?
Would he put up distance between them? The way she'd
seen him do with some of the other young and single
teachers? She'd noticed that he was politely distant from
Rachel these days, even though Rachel didn't seem to
get the drift. Would he do that to her too? Firmly friend-
zone the single girl?

Or, she gulped as she locked up her house and zipped
the key into the pocket of her running leggings, would
he try to close the distance between them?

She wasn't sure she could handle either option.

She made it to Fin's in record time. Apparently, all this
zinging uncertainty was good for something.

Fin opened her apartment door with a cold glass of
water already in hand for Via.

"But I didn't even call to tell you I was coming."

"Sister, I felt your vibes coming from two blocks
away."

Via laughed and followed her into the house. It smelled
like microwave popcorn and incense inside. Like Fin. Via
instantly felt calmer being in her circle. Fin had always
been able to do that. Pretty much since the day they'd
met one another.

"You wanna guess what happened? Or you want me
to tell you?" Via asked as she sat her sweaty body down
in the porch chair on Fin's balcony. Fin did the same, lifting her wool socks up to the balcony rail and reclining
like she was poolside.

"I'm tired tonight, fill me in."

"He found out I broke up with Evan."

Fin's eyes snapped open. She didn't have to ask who the *he* was in this scenario. Via figured that Fin had known about her feelings for Seb even longer than Via had.

"How?"

"It was at the staff meeting today. He saw me filling out a wedding invitation and RSVPing as just me."

"And…"

"And he asked a few questions and then went to pick up his son."

"Were there more sexy vibes? Like last week?"

"I think so. But I can never quite tell with him."

Fin shook her head. "You must be stuffing cotton in your ears, eyes and nose not to pick up on what that man is putting out for you."

"What's he putting out for me?"

Fin rolled her head to one side, her hair falling into her face for a moment. "Passion."

Via sighed and stood up, leaning forward on the balcony and looking out toward Prospect Park. The trees were stark, and in mid-November, the sun was already fully set at 6:00. A man rode by on the street six stories down, a boom box lashed to the back of his bike. A Beyoncé song.

"This is bad news for you?" Fin asked from behind Via. "That a man like Sebastian Dorner has passion for you?"

"No, it's not bad news. But, I don't know, it's not quite what I'm hoping for."

Fin laughed and nudged the back of Via's knee with her socked foot. "I know you crave stability above all else, love. But what woman doesn't want passion?"

Via turned around once more and wiped the sweat from her eyes. "He thinks I'm too young for him, Fin. I can tell he finds me attractive. But I want more than that. I want him to…consider me."

"Consider you for what?"

"As a person he could really love."

"Is that how you're considering him?"

Via dropped her slender body back into the porch chair and huffed. "Yeah. So what? He's incredible. And I have this, this, this—" *soccer ball of hot feeling. A gravity-based, world-sucking black hole of want* "—really big feeling for him. And I'm scared he'll just look at me and think, *child.*"

"Violetta, you're the most mature twenty-eight-year-old on the planet. You put yourself through college, paid off your debt in two years flat, live on your own, pay your taxes, recycle, read the news. Christ, you even get your clothes dry-cleaned. What more could the guy want?"

"That's exactly it. I have no idea what he wants! What if he just wants to hook up? And then what if people at school find out! Fin—" Via cut herself off, gulping down an acid feeling in her throat. The idea of becoming a source of gossip at her place of work was so abhorrent to Via that she felt momentarily sick. She'd learned at age twelve never to rock the boat again. Drama got kids switched to new foster homes. Drama equaled instability. And Via needed a rock-solid foundation for her life to even feel *remotely* comfortable.

"So, you don't want to start anything with him because you don't know whether or not it'll end up being casual?"

"I guess?" Now Via was even confusing herself. "But I also don't know if it makes sense to hope for something serious, considering how badly I botched this whole Evan thing. I mean, how could I ever, in good conscience, insert myself into Seb's and Matty's lives knowing exactly how mixed up and torn up and screwed up I am?"

"Via."

Via barely heard her. "Fin, you and Jetty are the only two relationships in my life that I've been able to keep. I—you know that I always end up isolating myself from people in some way or another. I'm too sad, by nature, you know? Or maybe not nature, but by circumstance. When my parents died, it changed me. Loneliness, sadness, it's just a part of who I am. How can I put that on somebody like Sebastian, when he's got a kid and a life and…"

Via dropped her face into her hands. "The whole thing is a nonstarter. It's a bad idea to be casual, it's a bad idea to be serious. God, I should have just worked things out with Evan." She lifted her face from her palms. "I can't believe I did this to my fucking life. Just tossed everything up in the air like a bowl of confetti. I spent so much time building things with Evan, and then in just a few months, everything goes up in smoke. I mean, God, how could I have let this get this far?" Via dropped her face back into her hands. "If I had just realized what was happening, I could have pulled back from Sebastian, and I never would have gotten feelings for him, and then I could just still be with Evan. Instead, I'm out here in no man's land, adrift as fuck."

"Via! Good God!" Fin jumped up, laughing her ass off. She strode back into the house and came back out a minute later with a cup of rosy tea in one hand and huge, honking amethyst in the other. "Good God. Here. Drink this and put this over your heart chakra."

Via had been patched up by Fin's unorthodox methods way too many times to scoff. So she took a deep breath, trying to calm her racing heart, and chugged the tea. "Oh. It actually tastes good."

Fin raised an eyebrow. "You were expecting...?"

"I was expecting it to taste like old fish like that last poison you had me drink."

"That poison cured your allergies if I recall correctly, sister."

Via nodded. Fair enough. Under Fin's watchful eye, she leaned back in the chair and laid the rough-hewn amethyst crystal over her heart. She closed her eyes and breathed deep, willing the stone to take some of her anxieties away. Whether it was the crystal or simply her friend's loving presence, Via couldn't say, but her racing heart gave way into a softer tempo. A tear leaked out of one side of her eye.

"No matter how many knots you tie, this problem is still just made from one rope, Violetta."

Via cracked an eye and looked at Fin. "What do you mean?"

"You want to be with this man, and you're telling yourself you can't. And, good God, do you have a lot of reasons."

"Those reasons stand," Via insisted.

Fin shrugged. "Only if you prop them up."

Via huffed a little bit. "Won't you just leave me alone and let me be mean to myself?"

Fin laughed. "Via, either you're brave enough to try or you're not." She paused. "I'll love you even if you want to keep being a little coward."

Via laughed and groaned and slurped more tea. "Things were easier with Evan. Even if they weren't perfect."

Fin rolled her lovely, dark eyes. "They weren't easier, they were just more predictable. Why do you keep telling yourself these lies about Evan? I don't get it."

The answer floated up like ice in a glass being filled with water. Via clamped down on it, tested the strength of it. "There was very little danger of ever truly wounding Evan. And I really liked that. Depended on it, actually. Because I knew I was never in danger of dragging Evan down with me. He never cared enough to get dragged down."

"Well," Fin said, taking a small green crystal out of her pocket and laying it on her own forehead. "We're just catching all the fish today." She slid her eyes over to Via. "Don't you see that the same thing that kept you with Evan is the same thing that's gonna keep you from Seb?" She snatched the crystal off her forehead and sat up, her eyes blazing. "But let's forget about the men for a second here, sister. The real issue is that you treat your whole life like a play you're staging. You're trying to get every set piece positioned just perfectly so that when the actors show up, everything goes according to plan."

Via grimaced at how true that was. "But life's not a play."

"Nope. And there's no script. And besides, a good actor doesn't need a stage."

"Ugh," Via groaned, scrubbing at her eyes with the heel of her hand. "Why is it so hard to ask for what you want?"

"What *do* you want?"

Via took a deep breath. "I just want a steady life. No more surprises. I want to be able to rely on someone besides myself. And you, of course. I don't want to date a twerp who can't keep a job or remember to pay his electricity bill. I don't want to take care of everyone around me. I just want to feel safe. And secure. And somehow, I'm single again, crushing on a man who may or may not be crushing back. And even if he is crushing, who knows if he wants to date? And if he wants to date, who knows if he's stable? I had everything nice and level, and then my idiot heart went and stomped on the other end of the seesaw."

"Yes, that all makes perfect sense. Because Evan was such a *steady* part of your life. That twenty-seven-year-old man-child sure was *reliable*. He wasn't flighty or forgetful. He knew exactly what he wanted out of life. He didn't make you pay for shit all the time. And he sure was good at remembering your birthday."

Via laughed at the list, even though it hurt a little bit to hear it, and then rolled to face her friend. "Sarcasm doesn't suit you, Fin."

"Via, when you're this gorgeous, everything suits you."

They both laughed then, and it was loud and unlady-like and deeply cathartic. Via took the crystal off her chest and handed it to her friend. "I'm nuts, Fin. Don't mind me. I'm just coming loose at all the edges." Via put a hand over her eyes and then propped her feet up on the railing with a deep breath. "All the edges I thought I'd already tucked in."

"Yes, well, c'est la vie." *That's life.* "It has a way of untucking the blanket."

They sat in silence for a minute, Fin studying the mud-dying blue of the night sky and Via studying Fin. "Everything all right? You seem tense, Finny."

Fin looked affronted, like the idea of tension offended her. She sniffed, her dark eyes flashing obsidian in the dark. "I am not tense."

Via swallowed her smile. Serafine St. Romain might have been mysterious and hard to read for many people. But Via wasn't one of them "You sure are."

Fin let out a long breath. The murky sky reflected in her big, light eyes. When she spoke, it was the flatness in her tone that immediately told Via just how hurt she really was. "My application got rejected again."

"No!" Via immediately reached out and squeezed Fin's hand.

"I don't know what to do. Maybe get an office job?"

"Fin, no. You'd wither away in a corporate atmosphere."

"But they keep saying that they don't take applicants who make their money in cash. I guess they've been burned too many times by hustlers who are trying to make some extra money by taking in a foster kid." Fin laughed humorlessly. "Can't make enough money slinging on a street corner? Take in a stray child! The state pays your grocery bill."

"If that," Via muttered, remembering all the ways Jetty had had to make ends meet to raise two children at once. Via made a rare noise of frustration. "It's just so backward. You're the exact type of person they want fostering kids. You're responsible and kind and intelligent and compassionate. Just because you tell fortunes for a living, they reject your application. Meanwhile, they're just gonna keep on siphoning kids into overcrowded homes with overworked foster parents."

"They don't trust me. I go in for the interview with all this hair and all this jewelry and my spooky accent and they think, *She must be on drugs.*"

Except for this last time. It had been heartbreaking. Via had come over and dressed Fin in the most sedate outfit she had. Slacks and a blazer. She'd braided her wild hair back and limited her to three pieces of jewelry. And still, somehow, application rejected.

"It drives me nuts because I feel like the people in charge of the system have absolutely no idea what it feels like to be a foster kid."

"Exactly." Fin stood and paced from one side of the

porch to the other. Fin had been in and out of the foster system in Louisiana before her mother finally got her shit together enough to sign over custody to her sister, Jetty. Fin and Via both knew exactly what it was to have nothing to hold onto but yourself. To store every other bite of food in your pocket because you didn't know where your next meal might come from. To fall asleep with strange sheets on your cheek and strange smells in your nose. To be told that this new stranger was your brother now, or your sister. Or your mother.

Fin brushed tears from her eyes and rounded on Via. "I've seen too many kids run afoul of the system. Took me too many years to end up here. With you and Jetty. I've seen every kind of neglect under the sun. And now I just have to sit on my porch with you and know there are children out there who need me. Right this second."

Via held out her arms, like she used to when they were skinny preteens, them against the world. Fin went immediately into the sweaty hug her sister offered and they snuggled together on the small porch chair. "Can you see what will happen to you, Fin? The way you do for other people?"

Via had asked this question before, and she knew the answer. Maybe it was her gentle way of reminding Fin what was what.

"Yes, I can see some of it, maybe one-eighth of the picture. Just like everyone else."

"And what do you see? Do you see a kid in your future?"

"No." Her voice was rigid and brittle. "I see a man. And I love him and hate him at the same time."

"Who is he?"

"I don't know. If I knew, I'd be running in the opposite direction."

CHAPTER SEVENTEEN

THAT FRIDAY, VIA rushed into Cider for happy hour. She was ten minutes behind everyone else and she looked like it. Her messenger bag was overflowing with paperwork she had to do this weekend. *Fuck you very much, Mr. Tate.* That particular incident just wouldn't die. Also, her hair was flying in nine different directions, she could just feel it, and she'd lost a button on her favorite peacoat. Not to mention she was pretty sure her scarf was only over one of her shoulders right now. With her luck, the other end was trailing on the ground.

She spotted the teachers' crew in their usual corner and bypassed them straight for the bar instead.

"Hi, Christian," she called. She and the silver fox of a bartender had become pretty friendly over the last few weeks. She hadn't bothered to tell him that she and Evan had broken up, mostly because she never wanted to get his number on a receipt again. She liked him, though. He was a casual flirt, pretty funny and very easy on the eyes.

"Gorgeous," he said as he coasted a hand down the bar counter. "You look…a little disheveled, to be honest."

She barked out a laugh. "I believe it. Hell of a day."

"Apparently." He grinned at her. "Your usual?"

"Please." She waited obediently by the bar, attempting to dig out her wallet without upending everything else. She could only imagine the show she was putting on for all her teacher friends across the room. She was sure she was in for some healthy ribbing from Sadie the second she sat down.

"Darlin', go sit your cute ass down at the table. I'll bring it to you."

"Are you sure? You don't have to serve me, Christian."

He rolled his eyes. "It's either that or help you pick up all those papers that are about to come tumbling out of your bag when you try to carry your beer."

She laughed again, shaking her hair back. "Fair enough."

She tossed him a friendly wave and then made her way over to the teachers' table.

"Good Lord, Via, did you encounter a tornado out there?" Sure enough, Sadie was the first person to say something.

Via hung her messenger bag over the back of the only free chair, whipped off her coat and scarf, and smoothed her hair as she plunked down into the seat. She let out a deep breath as she looked around at her friends. "So predictable, Sade, that you'd be the first person to make a joke."

Via's eyes stalled halfway around the table when her gaze landed on Sebastian. He never came to happy hours. Like, ever. But there he was, not four feet away. Via blinked at him. He took a swallow of beer and then raised his eyebrows, taking the corners of his lips with them.

She couldn't help but give him a surprised little smile back. Via scanned the rest of the table. Of course, Rachel was sitting on Sebastian's left, already pawing at his arm and trying to get his attention back.

Grace was on his other side. Sadie, Cat and Shelly were in the other spots. And on Via's right was a substitute teacher Via had seen around but never been introduced to before. He was cute, in a totally geeky kind of way. Severely parted blond hair and thick rimmed glasses. He looked like he could probably have fit into Via's size two trousers without having to suck in very much at all.

"Hi, we haven't met." He held out one hand. "Greg Hauser."

"Hi, Greg, Via DeRosa."

"You're the school counselor, right?"

"That's right, for third through—"

"Gorgeous." Christian leaned across her, setting her dark beer in front of her.

"You're a godsend." She flashed him a quick smile, not too flirty, and tried to hand him the cash she'd tucked into her hand just a moment ago.

He waved her off. "On the house."

She frowned after him. That had been a little presumptuous. He'd basically just bought her a drink. She hoped none of her teacher friends had let it slip that she was single.

"Friend of yours?" Greg asked.

"What? Oh. Sort of. I just know him from these happy hours. So, you're a sub?"

Via felt a buzz in the pocket of her trousers. And she knew, she just *knew*, that it wasn't from Fin. There were a few other people who texted her on a regular basis. But some sexy, haughty, spine-dancing sixth sense told her exactly who'd just texted her. And she could feel his eyes on the side of her face as she made small talk with Greg.

She kept her eyes on Greg's face while he answered her question, but she couldn't for the life of her have repeated a single thing he'd said. In fact, it was as if Greg had started speaking French. She waited a few more seconds, nodding politely before she pulled the phone out of her pocket, taking a sip of her beer at the same time.

She kept her face completely neutral as she opened the text from Seb. Not only did she not want him to see her giggling like a schoolgirl at any text he sent her way, the rest of these ladies at the table had such a nose for gossip, they'd be on her in a second about what cute guy she was texting with.

Got yourself quite the fan club, Miss DeRosa.

She looked up at Seb, who was grinning at her across the table. Could say the same for you, she texted back, noticing that if Rachel leaned any closer to Seb, her breasts would actually be resting on his arm.

"Hey, Sade, how's the wedding planning going?" Via asked, leaning back so as not to cut Greg out of the conversation completely.

"Oh, a whirlwind. Romantic. Stressful. The whole nine."

"Did you invite everyone from school?" Cat asked Sadie.

"Sure did."

"Jesus. That's a lot of people."

"Well, certain family excluded, we wanted a big, honking celebration. The gaudier the better." Sadie shrugged. "Wasn't that long ago it wasn't even legal. We're ready to sing it from the mountaintops."

"I love it," Via said, grinning at Sadie. "Is it gonna be traditional? Wacky? Whimsical? Hippy dippy?"

"Yes," Sadie answered, making Via tip her head back and laugh. Her phone had buzzed a few seconds ago, but she could show a little restraint, couldn't she?

She let the conversation flow on around her, like she was a rock and it was a stream. She finally looked down at her phone. And then she laughed out loud.

You mean Grace and Shelly?

She rolled her eyes again, before her gaze fell on a very interesting sight. Geeky Greg was leaning back in his chair, talking to Rachel. And she was talking back. She was still sitting way too close to Seb, in Via's humble opinion. But she was tilted away from him.

I think I spoke too soon. Greg just stole your girl.

She caught his eye and looked pointedly at the two people sitting between them, Rachel and Greg.

I've gotta say, Seb texted back almost immediately. Greg's kind of blowing my mind right now.

Via bit her lip to keep from grinning like a giddy, flirty fool. Greg's got game.

Then they were both laughing. Looking down at their phones, sure, but laughing together, even from across the table.

Seconds later, Via got another text, but it wasn't from Seb. It was from Cat. Via raised her eyes to her colleague sitting on the other side of Sadie and opened the message.

I think he came here tonight for you.

Via's breath caught in her throat and suddenly she felt a little ill. Flirting with Sebastian was one thing. Having her coworkers knowing and discussing it was a whole other bowl of soup. Via scooted her chair back and squeezed Sadie's shoulder. "Just hitting the bathroom real quick."

And then she was gone down the back hall and into the bathroom. She looked at herself in the mirror over the sink and almost groaned. She was pink-cheeked and messy-haired. Her lipstick was long gone, and her eye makeup was just a touch clumpier than she liked. She looked like a teenager who'd just gotten free tickets to a band she was dying to see. She looked like she'd just been kissed for the first time. She looked like—

The bathroom door swung open, and Cat strode in, chagrin in her eyes and both hands extended toward Via. "Oh, honey, I didn't mean to embarrass you."

Via held her hands out for Cat and let herself get swallowed up in a hug. "It's okay."

"No," Cat said vehemently, pulling back from Via and squeezing her shoulders. "It's not okay, I should have kept my big trap shut. None of that is my business."

"No." Via waved her hand. "There's nothing there that could even be your business. There's nothing."

Cat paused. "What do you mean?"

"I mean that it's nothing. There's nothing there."

Cat bit her lip and stepped back, crossing her arms and making her knee-length poncho sweater tuck in the middle. "I'm gonna say one thing, and then I'm gonna shut up forever, okay?"

"Okay."

"It really seems like there's something there."

"Oh God." Via turned to the sink and let cold water run out onto her hand. She touched her frigid fingers to the back of her neck. "I don't want to be the object of gossip, Cat. I can't do that. I don't have the luxury. I have my apartment, my one friend, and this job. That's it. No family, barely enough money to keep me afloat for a few months if I got fired. And that's all. I already look like I'm about seventeen years old, everybody tells me. And I just can't have a rumor destroy everything I've worked for."

"Via, darlin', I think you're getting ahead of yourself. First of all, you're young and hot, and so is he, and I'm sorry, but that's the stuff that rumors are made of. All right? Gossip is *not* a sophisticated bitch. It takes the lowest hanging, most obvious fruit and waits for it to make a baby or divorce its wife, all right?"

Via laughed, despite the panic and nausea coursing through her system.

"And second of all, *fired*? Grim is basically in love with you after the way you handled that whole thing with that angry dad. You're not in danger of getting fired, even if there are salacious rumors buzzing around about you. I'm serious," she added, her face following Via's as she lolled it to one despairing side. "You're single, he's single, and as long as y'all don't do it in the hallway, I'm pretty sure no one is gonna give two shits."

Via somehow went completely tight with humiliation and still managed to laugh. "Let's not put the cart before the horse, Cat. He and I have never even insinuated that we might…"

"Wanna put a baby in each other?"

"Oh my God."

Both women were laughing now.

Cat stepped forward again, and this time she had a steely glint in her eye, her arms still crossed. "Via, I want you to leave this bathroom knowing, in your gut, two things, okay?"

"Okay…"

She held up one finger and then the other, her long brown hair tossing back over her shoulder. "One. Fuck the haters. And two. That man came here tonight to be close to you. No bones about it. And I'm pretty sure he wore a new shirt."

CAT WENT OUT FIRST, and Via followed a few minutes later. She was still scattered and trepidatious, but she took what

Cat said to heart. There were already too many obstacles in the way for her and Seb. She didn't need to be out here creating new ones.

Fuck the haters. He came here for me.

Via pulled up short as she realized that Rachel and Greg had vacated the table and were now standing at the bar, hip to hip. The seat next to Seb was open. She ignored every nervous, whiny impulse that was rearing up inside of her and instead she plunked herself down in the seat formerly known as Rachel's.

"Hi," he said, obviously a little taken aback by the look in her eyes, which Via could only guess said *crazy woman*.

"Hi."

"Everything all right? Cat ran after you pretty fast."

"Oh. Yeah, totally fine. Just a misunderstanding."

Seb's eyes searched hers. Those gray-green beauties, like seagrass turning belly-up in the wind. Via was holding her breath because of course she was. The man was big as a house and smelled like laundry detergent. Of course she was attempting to keep that scent inside her as long as possible.

"A misunderstanding that I should know about?" he asked slowly, quietly.

A little petal opened up in Via, a bloom of surprise. He wasn't playing coy. He wasn't coming right out and saying anything explicitly, but he was kind of, sort of, acknowledging that she and he might be mixed up in a misunderstanding together. That wasn't saying nothing...*right?*

"Well..." Via chose her words very carefully. She was alternately terrified of slamming the door closed or flinging it way too wide open. "I guess I'm not sure."

Seb's eyes continued to search hers for a minute. "Fair enough. You want another?"

"Oh." Via looked down at her empty beer glass. "Sure. I'll buy, though. I didn't exactly pay for my last one."

She was rising up in her chair when he laid one of those gigantic, rough-palmed hands against her forearm. "Sit. Please. Let me buy you a drink."

His eyes were right on hers, not bouncing around the way Evan's always had. It was disconcerting almost, to have a man be so sure of himself. It wasn't that he was confident in how she would react, exactly. It was more like he was holding his hand out to her and waiting patiently to see if she would take it.

"All right," she answered, and to her dismay, heard a small tremor in her voice. Via watched him stride away toward the bar. He said something that made Christian the bartender laugh. And then she watched Seb forcibly jam cash into Christian's hand. He came back, a beer in each hand, shaking his head.

"What was that all about?" she asked him, accepting the beer he was handing down.

"Son of a bitch does not want anyone but him buying you beers." Seb glowered over at the bar, and Via watched as Christian shot a cocky smile in their direction, shrugging his shoulders.

"I was afraid of that," Via muttered.

"Afraid? I thought the Golden Oldie over there was the man of your dreams."

Via laughed, rolling her eyes. "You're never going to let me live that down, are you?"

He shrugged, grinning into his beer.

"I never said that *that* guy—" she nodded her head dismissively in the direction of the bar. Was she really doing this? She was doing this. Fuck it, she was just going to say it "—was the man of my dreams. I just said that I'm attracted to older men."

Seb shifted in his seat, his stance widening just a bit. He didn't exactly lean toward her, but he might as well have. His eyes fell to the bottom half of her face, and it was strangely as if somebody had hit Mute on the music. There was a rising buzz in her ears that seemed to correspond with the tingle in her fingertips.

She waited, but he said nothing. Had she struck him speechless?

A whippy, charged feeling suddenly zipped through Via. Nothing about their circumstances had changed in the last ten seconds. But suddenly, Via didn't feel significantly younger. She didn't feel younger at all. Suddenly, she felt like there was a chance that she might, sort of, be in charge.

To test it, Via let her eyes drop to the condensation on the outside of her beer. She drew a little squiggle through the fog. She lifted her finger to the rim of the glass and touched every inch of it. When she looked up, Seb's eyes shot to hers on a delayed reaction. He'd been watching her hand.

Keeping her eyes on his, she cocked her head to one side. She let that same hand inch forward and carefully, carefully, touch the cuff of his navy shirt, rolled to his elbow. "Is this a new shirt, Seb?"

He looked a little dazed, his eyes a little fuzzy, as he shifted his hips against the seat. Via swore she could see his heartbeat in his neck. "Ah, yeah, actually."

He scraped a hand over the back of his neck and around to his stubble.

"When you mentioned my other shirt last week, it got me thinking that I hadn't bought any clothes for myself in a long time. Maybe a couple years."

Since his wife?

"It's easy to just roll out of bed and slap on my dad uniform. And I guess I just wanted to…look a little nicer."

For me?

"Well, you do look very nice. I like it. But I also like your dad uniform. It's very lumberjack."

He snorted, set his beer aside and wiped his chin with a napkin as he laughed. "Christ. That is not the look I've been going for."

She laughed, too. "That's my problem, too. I go for a certain look, and everyone thinks it's something else completely."

"What look do you go for with all this?" he asked, leaning away from her and squinting at her outfit, like he was trying to get the whole picture.

"I pretty much desperately try to wear anything that will make me look thirty." They both laughed, but as soon as she'd said it, Via knew she'd said the wrong thing. Reminding him that she was still in her twenties right now was so stupid. They'd just stepped into this new, hot little rhythm. They'd been flirting. She was positive. And now his face was sobering, and he was thoughtfully looking into the golden effervescence of his beer with a look so sad she just wanted to nuzzle his neck like a puppy. Great. Just great.

Seb jolted a little and pulled his phone out of his pocket. He'd gotten a text.

"Sorry," he muttered distractedly. She couldn't help but notice he'd tipped the screen away from her a little. Was he texting someone he didn't want her to know about? Another woman maybe?

Of course, he probably was, Via tersely reminded herself. She needed to stop acting like a lovesick kitten. This was a single, virile, incredibly attractive man who dated people. It was common knowledge. Dating often included texting. There was nothing wrong with him texting some other woman right now.

Seb chuckled and handed the phone over to her.

Oh. He was showing her whatever had been texted to him. It was a picture of Matty and Crabby leaping toward one another in the air. They were obviously in the middle of some sort of wrestlepalooza. They were on a dark green mat of some kind.

Via laughed delightedly, her mood significantly warming as she looked down at this kid she liked so much. He looked delirious with delight, and a little hysterical.

"Mary's babysitting," Seb explained. "And things always get a little out of hand when Mary babysits."

"He looks like he'll be a perfect angel when it's time to put him to bed," Via joked and Seb snorted again. "Where are they, though? You guys have a playroom I don't know about?"

She thought of the second floor she'd never seen.

Seb leaned over her shoulder to look at the picture, he must have zoomed in before he handed it over because his arm snaked around her and he zoomed out now. She realized the green mat wasn't a mat at all; it was a comforter on a huge, wooden bed frame. "Nah, they're in my room."

So, that was his room. She was staring at Sebastian Dorner's huge, handsome bed. Cool cool cool. No big. No big at all. Her hand started sweating.

She took one last look at the picture and was just handing it back when a banner slid down from the top of the screen. He was getting a text. She didn't see what it said, but she didn't miss the name. Marisa Simmons. "You got a text."

Her hands empty, Via filled them with the beer she suddenly didn't want. She rolled the glass between her palms and scanned the bar, hoping she looked casual. It really looked like Greg was making time with Rachel up at the bar. She was sitting on a stool, tilted toward him, and he had one hand on the bar top, boxing her in. Via sighed a little as she looked at them. Rachel was pretty and sweet. Her top was, in her usual way, a little too tight for school, but whatever. They were definitely in the same age range. Via imagined they'd go home together and see what happened.

She was so jealous she was suddenly exhausted. She felt like she could sleep for a week. She wanted to find a cave and a double-wide sleeping bag. She'd stuff the other half of the sleeping bag with queen-size pillows and pull the blankets over her head. When she woke up, she'd still be single but maybe she wouldn't be pining over the sweet giant sitting next to her.

"Another one bites the dust."

"They look like they're hitting it off."

Seb and Via spoke at the same time. And then again, when they both identically said, "What?"

"Oh," Seb said, shaking his phone a little. "I was just saying that I've had another strikeout from a woman."

"She rejected you, you mean?" Via was very confused. She felt like she was on one of those wobbly chain bridges they had on playgrounds. He was talking to her about the woman he was texting? Was that a buddy-buddy type of thing to do or something else altogether?

Seb laughed. "Thanks for the vote of confidence. No, well, I guess she sort of did. She kept wanting to meet up at times that I was busy with Matty. She got frustrated. Bid me good night and good luck."

"You weren't busy with Matty tonight," Via said quietly, her heart doing its best imitation of a hummingbird.

"I'm busy with you tonight." Seb shrugged. Almost like it was no big deal. "What were you saying before?"

Via commanded her mind to start working more clearly. She was being ridiculous right now. She just needed to get herself together. Live in the moment. She could analyze everything later. "Oh, just that Greg and Rachel look like they're hitting it off."

"Yeah," Seb mused, cocking his head to one side to study them. "Greg's got way more game than the geeky hair initially implies. Like that, for instance. Solid move, Greg."

"What move?" Via asked, confused. She must have missed something.

"See the way he stepped to the side just then? Well, he did it so that she'd turn to face him. Which she did. And now that she's facing away from the bar, your Golden Oldie will be less likely to flirt with her. And he just boxed out that other guy. AND best of all for good old Greg, her knees are touching his leg now."

"Wow." Via was bemused. She looked for a second longer and then dismissed the idea, shaking her head. "I think you're giving him too much credit. The guy just moved over a few inches. There's no way he had that master plan cooking."

Seb gave her a pitying look. "Via, if you're a guy talking to a pretty woman at a bar, there's *always* a master plan."

It wasn't lost on her that Seb was a guy, and she was a pretty woman, and they were, in fact, in a bar right now. If she were Fin, she would have immediately pointed that out, watched while Seb squirmed. But she was Via. So she kept things moving instead.

"Maybe," she conceded. "But that move was so subtle. I really don't think that was part of the Greg school of romance."

"Trust me. As a man who used to do that," he pointed

toward the lovebirds, "fairly successfully, it's the *little* moves that count. The big ones are far less successful."

Sebastian leaned back just a touch in his chair, and Via shifted to hear him better. She both thrilled and despaired at the idea of Sebastian picking up women in bars. It was sexy and deflating at the same time. "What do you mean?"

"I mean that Greg wants Rachel to only pay attention to him right now. And he wants to touch her, just a little bit. Now, he could have achieved all of that by just reaching out and grabbing her chin, tilting her face toward him."

Via wrinkled her nose, and Seb pointed at the expression she was making.

"Exactly. Most women would hate that. Not all, and maybe if Greg had done that, Rachel wouldn't have minded. But probably, she would have smacked his hand away, slid off the barstool and come back over here. So, instead, Greg just sort of moved over an inch or two and got what he wanted in a much more respectful way. And Rachel doesn't feel pushed around or manhandled. Win-win."

"Huh." Via felt terribly naive. She'd gone home from a bar with two men in her life. One of them had been Evan. She wondered now how many of these subtle moves those men had employed on her. "I don't know. I think a woman knows exactly what's going on in a situation like that. Men aren't slick. If he's putting the moves on her, she'll know. And that?" She pointed back toward the bar. "Wasn't a move."

"Some men are slick."

"You?" She raised her eyebrows at him. Her look said skeptical, but her brain said, *Flirt with me more, you gigantic, gorgeous man!*

Seb shrugged. "I mean, you're pretty much sitting in my chair right now, aren't you?"

Via looked down in surprise and realized that… yeah. Somehow while they were talking, he had shifted enough, and so had she, that she'd leaned all the way toward him. She was sitting on approximately one eighth of one corner of her own chair and the toe of one of her heels was about half an inch from the toe of that unlaced boot of his.

She straightened up immediately, her eyes going wide and her cheeks going pink.

He chuckled, but his eyes searched her face, checking to make sure it was okay that he'd just done that.

She dipped her chin to him. She was flustered, but not exactly put out. "Hats off."

He studied her face for another second. "Now, if I wasn't subtle, I could have done the same thing by crowding you." He demonstrated by flinging an arm over the back of her chair and pushing his wide-stanced legs into her space. Via felt the blank circles of other people's faces turn to look at them, but she almost, *almost* didn't care.

He leaned back and stopped crowding her. As soon as the heat from his body was gone, mild embarrassment rushed into its place. He was more than flirting with her. He was showing her exactly how he'd seduce her. Except without actually seducing her. It was confusing. And hot. Via wished like hell that their colleagues would all simultaneously decide to go home and watch *Jeopardy!*

"Or I could have dragged your chair over or slid an arm around your waist and put you in my lap." He was compiling this list casually, apparently unaware that Via was sort of melting into a pile of vibrating honey in the chair next to him. "But all of that is way too aggressive in my opinion. I'm not trying to intimidate you into feeling me. I want you to want it, you know?"

The proverbial you. He's using the PROVERBIAL YOU. She bullied herself into believing it. Because otherwise, he'd just point-blank told her that he wanted her to want him, and that didn't happen in real life, in this bar, on happy hour Friday with a bunch of their colleagues talking shop three feet away.

Via surreptitiously let out a long, slow breath and took a sip of her beer. She tried to look casual. "Right. I guess that makes sense."

"Maybe I'm rusty," he told her, his eyes like bright lights on the side of her face.

"You're not," she answered too quickly. If he hadn't heard the mild tremor in her voice, he was as thick as a brick wall.

When she looked over, she knew a different man would be smugly grinning at her, knowing he'd gotten under her skin, given her a thrill. But not Seb Dorner. Nope. He was just looking at her, serious as could be. That plain-handsome face, all wide and open and blunt. All of it set off by his dark haircut and…she noticed, a clean shave. He really did look nice tonight. Like he was dressed up for a date. She wondered when exactly he'd decided to come to happy hour. Was it while he was getting dressed that morning?

"I wish I could stay," Seb told her and those honest eyes of his told the whole story. No subtext. No lines. Just the truth. "But I got a kid needs tucking in at home."

Can I come?

She sucked her lips into her mouth along with the words. "Understandable. It was nice that you came out, though."

"Yeah," he agreed. "Maybe I'll try to do it more often."

Seb tipped his glass, one swallow left, toward Via's and they cheers-ed. Her breath caught and her eyes snapped away because was that…? Did he…? Yes, she was almost positive that he'd laid his pinky over hers for just the hottest little second when they'd clinked glasses.

But he was up and pulling his coat on, saying his good-byes all around. He'd been gone from the bar all of three minutes when she felt that familiar buzz in her pocket.

He wasn't around to see her nerd out over his texts so she didn't bother stopping herself from whipping her phone out of her pocket in a flash.

Should have asked at the bar, but you're gonna take a cab home, right?

Now that her body wasn't tense and spotlighted and tingling like hell from his mere presence, Via could once again pay attention to the gravity-hungry dense cloud of feeling in her chest. It grew another inch and sucked the whole bar into its ravenous force field. She loved *every-thing* right now.

He was concerned about how she'd get home. What a flipping gentleman.

Grace always walks me home. We're only a few blocks from each other.

The text reply came almost instantly. Grace is lucky.

Another buzzed through a few seconds later. Have a good night, Miss DeRosa. You made mine.

She thought of about thirty different ways to reply but all of them, all of them, said way too much. Put every single one of her cards on the table. In the end, she just went with the ever solid You, too. He could go ahead and interpret it in whatever way he wanted.

She saw the let's-get-the-hell-out-of-here eyes that Grace was throwing her way across the table, and Via was grateful. She needed to get home, get in the bath and squee her face off.

She said her goodbyes around the table, kissing Sadie and Shelly on the cheek and squeezing Cat's hand. She slid her coat on, arranged her scarf and bag and stepped up to the bar to say goodbye to Christian. She gave Rachel and Greg a wide berth, not wanting to mess up whatever flow they had going on; apparently it was much more subtle and complicated than she'd ever thought and she didn't want to risk anything.

"Bye." She waved over at Christian.

"Hold up a minute," he called, mixing a drink and flashing her the one-minute symbol.

Via looked over her shoulder, saw Grace talking with Shelly still and figured she had a minute to spare.

A second later, Christian was in front of her, wiping his hands on his bar towel and leaning toward her. His salt-and-pepper fade was crisp, his shirt ironed and his tattoos tantalizing. He really was handsome. But Via felt no flutters. No swelling of feeling. Not a single tingle.

"So, what's the deal, Via? Are you single or what? You're breaking my heart over here."

Her eyes widened at his sudden honesty. She'd figured he was the kind of guy who flirted with everyone. He was a bartender; there were big tips in it for him after all.

"Oh, ah." She stumbled over her words before she looked back up at this man. She didn't really know him, and he didn't really know her. What did she have to lose here? Without even really consciously deciding, the words were tumbling out of her mouth. "I'm single. But I'm not free. I'm really, really into someone."

Christian hung his head in mock defeat. He looked back up at her. "That old guy who bought you a beer? Really?"

Via couldn't help but laugh. "He called you old, too."

Christian snorted. "Figures. He's as threatened by me as I am by him."

She smiled at his candor.

Christian peered at her from squinted eyes. "I'd tell you he's too old for you, but I think I'd be cutting off my nose to spite my face."

Via laughed again. "Have a good night, Christian."

"Yeah." He sighed. "You, too. See you next Friday." He took a step away from the bar and then leaned forward again, pointing at her. "You're paying for your beer next time."

Still laughing, she nodded her head. "Fair enough."

CHAPTER EIGHTEEN

SEBASTIAN FELT LIMBER, energized and off-kilter as hell as he, Matty and Crabby pulled up to the softball field the next day. This was their last game of the season. He was wildly disappointed that he wasn't going to have an excuse anymore to see Via dancing around the bases, diving for line drives and knocking the ball back to Queens.

He'd been supercharged when he'd gotten home from the bar last night. Matty had subconsciously picked up on his dad's energy and had been a little hellion for an extra hour past his bedtime. But Seb hadn't cared.

He'd just blatantly flirted with Via DeRosa. And she'd flirted back.

I'm attracted to older men, she'd said.

There weren't a ton of other ways to interpret that statement.

Seb let out a long, slow breath and hauled Matty out of the car and hooked Crabby up to a leash.

He knew that if he looked for an issue to worry over right now, he'd find it. Their age difference was ridiculous; she was too young for a real commitment. And he had so much baggage, a real commitment was pretty much the only thing he was looking for.

But it wasn't those thoughts that swirled in his head as he led kid and dog to the bleachers. No. It was that sly smile she'd given him across the table when they'd been texting. It was the V of exposed, golden skin above her trim little blouse. It was the way she'd so naturally leaned into him. He'd been praying last night that she didn't look down at his lap. He was pretty sure her eyes would have bugged out of her head had she known he'd popped wood just from watching her drag a finger through the condensation on her beer glass.

Seb wasn't ashamed. He was heated and loose; he felt like he could play four games of softball back-to-back. Something pumped through his veins, hard and fast, and Seb liked it.

Seb spotted Via in the dugout, stretching and chatting with Sadie, and it was enough just to see her, for the time being. She was here. He was about to go over there. He felt like there was a wolf in his chest, sniffing the air for a mate.

He finally understood why they howled at the moon.

Because flirting was so fucking fun.

Seb parked Matty on the second row of the bleachers and tied Crabby's leash there as well. He leaned forward and fussed with his son's new winter coat. It wasn't that cold out today, but he was gonna be sitting still for a while. He pulled the hood up around Matty's ears and zipped it to his chin.

"Too tight, Dad," Matty groused and zipped it back down.

"You're gonna get cold."

"You made me wear two pairs of pants! I'm so hot I'm gonna puke." Matty was one step away from a full-on pout-fest, and Seb knew when to fold 'em.

"You're right. Are you gonna read or do your puzzle?"

"Read. I like the book."

"Cool," Seb said, inching away from his son like he was a wild animal he didn't want to spook. "Snacks are in the bag. You can have whatever you want. And we're gonna grab pizza afterward with the team. Just so you know."

"Why?" Matty looked up from digging through the bag for the snacks and the book.

"Because it's the last game of the season."

Matty shrugged. "Okay. Sounds boring, but I like pizza."

Seb leaned forward quick and kissed his son on the top of the head. No muss, no fuss. He was growing up and didn't want as much PDA from his dad anymore. But Matty was already opening his book and blocking out the world.

"Matty."

He looked up.

"It's cool that you're reading."

Matty nodded. "I know." He held up his fist. "Knuckles, Daddy."

Seb knocked fists with Matty and jogged over to the dugout and grinned down at Sadie and Via, who were sitting down, stretching their hamstrings. He held a hand out to both of them and hauled them upright. He couldn't help but trace a thumb over the back of Via's hand.

"Hi."

"'Sup," Sadie said back, stretching her arms over her head.

"Hi," Via said, almost shyly, her eyes just barely meeting his.

"Holy shit!" Sadie whispered in excitement, squinting over toward the stands. "Is Matty reading on his own, for pleasure?"

"Yes," Sebastian said in bemused delight. "I mean, I always keep books on his bookshelf and today, for some reason, he just picked one off the shelf and started reading it after breakfast. He *asked* if he could bring it along.

I swear, my eyes must have exploded like when Bugs Bunny sees a pretty girl."

"Well, as his former first-grade teacher, please don't mind if I take a little bow." She did just that, making Seb and Via grin.

"It's very cool," Via agreed. "It shows a ton of different skills all at once, to sit by himself and read in a sustained fashion."

"Right?" Sadie agreed. "Reading comprehension, focused attention, willingness to—"

"You two are such teachers," Seb cut in, a smile on his face. "My reaction was like, cool, you mean I don't have to pack toys?"

"Well," Via said as Sadie started calling the team together for her traditional pregame pep talk. "It's a teacher victory for sure, but it's definitely a dad victory, too."

She grinned up at him and knocked her shoulder against his. When she straightened, facing Sadie, Seb closed the distance between them, just a touch. He stood with his shoulder slanted just behind hers. The sleeve of his shirt brushing over her hair.

She reached back to put her hair in a bun, and her elbow knocked him gently. He could smell that rosemary scent of hers and realized it was probably her shampoo. He wanted to bury his face in her hair. But he settled for poking lightly at her bun. She looked back over her shoulder at him, one eyebrow raised and a flush in her cheeks.

He shrugged, offering no explanation for poking at her. He knew it made him seem like an elementary schooler, poking the girl he had a crush on. But he didn't care. She was cute and so was her bun. And he couldn't drag her down in the dugout and press his face into that hair like he wanted to, so he settled for a bun poke. He did it again, and this time she knocked his side with her elbow.

He nudged her back.

She made a little tsking sound and pretended to listen to Sadie talking as she nudged him a little harder, bumping him to one side with her shoulder.

Seb was glad they were standing in the back of the crowd because this was ridiculous, and probably would have been mortifying if anyone was looking.

Via gave him one last little shove that had enough of her soft hip involved to have Seb clearing his throat, and then she was jogging out to shortstop, screwing her hat on her head.

THEY WON THE game and went for pizza. Sebastian felt like he could lift a bus as he tied up Crabby to a bike rack outside the pizzeria. He pulled a rawhide from his back pocket and had the pup's tail thumping a mile a minute.

When he ducked back inside, it was to see Matty in Via's arms. She'd picked him up to choose which type of pizza he wanted from the glass case and apparently it was very serious business because they were speaking to each other very solemnly.

Honestly, Matty wasn't all that much smaller than Via. He was a big kid and she was a small lady, but her strong arms held him with no trouble. Matty easily hitched his legs around her waist and his arm over her shoulders.

Seb walked toward them, like he was in a dream. But a supercharged high-def one. He felt like he was outlined in bright color, high speed and flinging through the air. He felt like there should be a beam of light coming out of his chest right now, spotlighting his son in Via's arms. Because there were so many reasons to slow down where she was concerned. But then…this. His gigantic son in her tiny arms. Come on. If there'd been bowling pins in his way as he crossed the restaurant toward them, he would have scattered them to the winds.

"You smell good," Matty was telling Via as Seb stepped up to them. He was lifting up her crystal necklace, clear pink today, and inspecting it as he spoke.

"Considering I just played a full game of softball, I'd say that would be very surprising."

Seb made eye contact with Via. He pointedly leaned forward and sniffed her. "Nope, he's right. You smell very, very good."

"I smell sweaty," she corrected, her cheeks flushing.

"No, you smell like muffins. And a *little* sweaty," Matty corrected.

"Plus, girl sweat smells good," Seb chimed in.

Via blushed even further, but to Seb's ultimate delight, she leaned forward into his space and sniffed. "Apparently, so does boy sweat."

"Are you guys flirting?" Matty asked out of the blue, still gently tracking the crystal on her necklace from one end of the chain to the next.

Seb's heart stuttered to a screeching halt. He thought about the fairly blatant tightrope that he and Via had started walking. Matty had just twanged the hell out of it. And now he and Via were going to fall off of that tightrope, one side or the other. He just hoped they ended up on the same side.

"Subtlety is a luxury only the childless enjoy," he said to Via, making her crack a smile even through the shocked nerves that had bloomed over her face.

Seb turned to his son. "What do you know about flirting?"

Matty shrugged, his eyes still on Via's necklace, as if he were a little embarrassed about the topic. Well, that made three. "Just that Brian Addison was teasing me and Joy for playing together and said that we must be flirting because I'm a boy and she's a girl and we were teasing each other. But I don't think we were flirting."

"Brian Addison sounds like a twerp," Seb replied, reaching out for his son. Matty went from her arms to Seb's without a peep. "Or he probably has a crush on Joy. Or on you," he added, realizing that he didn't want to instill something ignorant in his son.

Matty shrugged. "I don't get it."

Seb nodded. "Trust me, it doesn't get less confusing. But we can talk about it more at home if you want." And then he looked up at Via, straight into those brown eyes of hers that made him want to press his nose to hers. "But just to be clear, yes, we were flirting."

She sucked in a little breath, and Seb couldn't tell if she was thrilled or put off by his forwardness.

"Why?" Matty asked.

Again, Seb went with the truth. No point in lying and confusing everyone. "Because she's fun to flirt with. And sometimes it just happens. Because she's so pretty."

Her hand went nervously to her necklace and she toyed with it, just like Matty had. The gesture snapped a twig somewhere inside Seb. There was no more sneaking up on this feeling. It was there and in his face and in hers. Whatever this feeling was, it had jumped the fence. It was out now, in between them, living and breathing.

Now they had to decide if they were going to walk toward it together or turn tail and run.

"Yeah," Matty agreed. "Plus, she smells like sweaty muffins."

Seb and Via both barked out surprised, delighted laughter, tinged with equal parts hysteria and relief. Matty had tossed them in the soup, but also, it kind of seemed like they'd both been too scared to jump in the first place.

THAT WEEK'S STAFF meeting was just as charged as softball practice had been. She'd sat with her shoulder pressing against his damn near the whole time. Her legs looked slim and long in her work-fancy trousers that ended in heels of some kind or the other. And, to Seb's surprise, she wore a little gold ring on her left thumb.

He'd reached out and touched it halfway through the meeting. The metal was warm and almost soft under his finger. She'd glanced up at him, her bottom lip between her teeth.

"Frosting," he'd whispered.

She'd grinned at him in such a way that he'd practically wobbled out of the meeting half an hour later. He didn't get to see her much that week at all, but he ducked his head into her office right after work on Friday afternoon. She looked up from where she was packing files into her messenger bag beside her desk.

"Hey!" she squeaked, and then cleared her throat. "Wow. My voice. Sorry for the Minnie Mouse impression."

"Quite all right." He tucked his hands in his pockets so he wouldn't do anything dumb, like stroke those sharp little cheekbones in her place of work. "I just wanted to say bye."

"You're not coming to happy hour?" she asked, sounding disappointed enough that Seb had to keep from puffing out his chest.

"Nah, I don't wanna stand Matty up two Fridays in a row."

"Understandable. You two have a hot date?"

"Yup. Microwave hotdogs and the Nets on TV."

"Sounds like heaven."

"You like the Nets?"

She looked at him like he was an idiot for even asking and he had to forcibly fight the urge to propose to her right then and there.

"So," she started, rocking back on her heels.

She was nervous and he found it impossibly cute. Like so cute he took a little memory snapshot of her standing there, trying to work up the courage to ask what he thought she was going to ask. He decided to help her out.

"So, I'll see you at the wedding tomorrow?"

"Yes," she answered resolutely. "I can't wait."

She held his eyes, and Seb could have sworn they were making some sort of promise to one another.

He'd deeply enjoyed the time since he'd found out she was single. Flirting with reckless abandon, nurturing silly little daydreams about her, allowing himself just the barest, lightest of tastes of what it might be like to be her man. But he also knew it wasn't sustainable. Somewhere, in the back of his mind, he'd known that the wedding would be punctuation of some sort, for this stage of their game.

And from the nervous, giddy, wanna-kiss expression on her face, she knew it, too.

CHAPTER NINETEEN

"Ho-ly Mother Mary," Cat groaned from beside Via.

Grace was the next one to chime in. "Good GAWD, that man can wear the hell out of a suit."

A midsize knot of PS 128 faculty huddled together outside the entrance to the Brooklyn Botanic Garden. Sadie's wedding ceremony was going to take place in one of the gardens there, and then the reception would be in their beautiful, glassed-in event space.

Via had never gone to a wedding before, but as she stood in between Shelly and Cat, already laughing, she found she was very excited to go wherever the night took her. Very excited indeed. It was an unseasonably warm mid-November day; the air had a slight bite to it that was offset by bright sun. The yellow leaves that still clung to the trees had the same effect on the blue sky as makeup on an eye. Everyone lifted their faces to the perfumed fall breeze.

Via turned to see what Cat and Grace were commenting on, and every single thought in her head was wiped clean.

As long as Violetta DeRosa lived—be it another hundred years—she would never forget the way Sebastian Dorner looked crossing Flatbush Avenue in a charcoal gray tailored suit. He waved a car across in front of him and strolled over toward the group of educators. God, she'd always had a thing for mirrored aviators. And week-old haircuts. And was that…? Yes, he was wearing a vest underneath the coat. She'd always had a thing for vests. And midnight blue ties and crisp white shirts. And damn. She couldn't breathe.

He looked so unbelievably hot walking up to the group, sliding his sunglasses into the pocket of his coat, smiling around at everyone, that Via *almost* missed the way his eyes doubled back, immediately, to her. Almost.

Via knew her dress was a stunner. Fin had bought it for her at a sample sale a year ago but she'd never had a real reason to wear it. The jade green silk fit her like a glove from breast to knee and was seamless, wrinkle-less perfection. The neckline scooped modestly over her breasts and was held up by two gaspingly thin straps that fell far down her back, showing her almost to the base of her spine. The color did things for her eyes, she could admit.

"Well, don't you look dapper," Shelly said to Sebastian, her eyes shining with unshed tears.

"You look beautiful, too, Shelly," Seb said as he studied Shelly's face. "Is everything all right?"

"Oh, don't mind me. This is just the first wedding I've been to without Richard and—"

Shelly cut off in surprise as Seb gathered her in close for a hug that had that force field in Via's chest swallowing Brooklyn whole. This man was making feelings grow inside of her so fast and so hard that she didn't even know what to direct them toward. She watched him from across the group—and she wasn't the only one. He was like some rare form of wild beast that had somehow been convinced into a three-piece suit. Via couldn't help but feel, for one painful second, like his presence in her life had to be temporary. Nothing this beautiful and rare could possibly last.

"I'll be your wedding date, Shelly," he told her, a firm hand on each of his friend's shoulders.

"Oh, Sebastian." Shelly blushed all the way to the roots of her hair. "You don't have—"

"I'm sad my husband's dead, too," Grace cut in blandly. "Be my date."

Seb laughed at her irreverence. "I'd never turn down two dates."

He held an arm out to both ladies just as the gates opened and the guests were allowed to find their seats at the outdoor wedding.

Via followed the group, a little at odds now that Sebastian was here but hadn't even said hi. She watched from a row back as he got the two ladies settled in.

"Via, you really look stunning," Cat said from beside her. "I couldn't even staple myself into a dress that looked like that."

Via laughed. "Oh, Cat, you look beautiful, too. I love that style."

"But seriously, the color and everything, Via, it's breathtaking."

"She's right," Grace said, turning around and eyeing Via's dress.

Via blushed and fussed with the program in her hands. She could feel the bright lights of Seb's gray-greens on her, but still he didn't say anything.

"Oh, here we go!" Cat squealed as music started and people rushed to find seats.

Via cried the whole dang wedding and was extremely proud of herself for remembering to bring spare makeup. Because, girl, she needed a fix up.

Sadie looked gorgeous and radiant with her short red hair braided back and her romantic, trumpet-style dress. But it was Rae who really brought the waterworks on for

Via. The short, black-haired woman wore a handsome tailored suit and the biggest smile Via had ever seen. She didn't think she'd ever seen someone look prouder than Rae did when Sadie walked down the aisle. Maybe she was getting caught up in the moment, but Via felt like she was watching Rae come to terms with the fact that Sadie was picking her, forever.

Their ceremony was fast and emotional and barely intelligible through all the tears. It wasn't more than a few minutes before Sadie was bending Rae backward for the kiss of a lifetime. The two of them straightened up, threw their joined hands in the air and completely cheesed for the wildly cheering crowd.

It was getting chilly with the sun going down, so the caterers bustled the wedding guests inside the venue. Cocktail hour was scheduled to last for a while, so the first chance she got, Via excused herself to the bathroom and fixed her makeup.

She felt wrung out after the high emotional intensity of the wedding, like a sponge after a really great bout with a saucepan. A good cry always did that to her. But as Via eyed herself in the mirror, she realized that it was more than that. She felt like she was filling up with air and leaking it at the same time. Like her insides were somehow producing glitter and glue simultaneously. She was a glittery, sparkly, sticky mess inside her chest.

God, had she ever felt this way before? Like, ever? About anyone?

After all the attention she was used to getting from Sebastian, it was strange to feel the loss of it. Almost like a vacuum. She shrugged to herself in the mirror. Either she could address it head-on with him or she could let it go. But she refused to allow herself to brood. She was here to party down for Sadie and Rae. Glitter glue be damned.

Deeming herself presentable again, she stepped out of the bathroom and into the back hallway that led to the reception area. She stopped in her tracks.

Sebastian was leaning against the wall, apparently waiting for her, his hands in his pants pockets and his feet crossed at the ankle. The second he saw her, he pushed forward. Closer than normal, but he wasn't touching. Her high heels brought her up to a solid five-foot-eight, but she still had to drop her head all the way back to be able to look him in the eye.

"You're so gorgeous it hurts," he told her, point-blank.

She jolted like he'd zapped her with a little kiss of electricity. She opened her mouth but couldn't think of anything to say. His words were still absorbing into her, like beads of wine over cloth.

"I wanted to tell you immediately, but I worried it might embarrass you in front of everyone. And I didn't want to say, 'you look nice' or 'very beautiful' or something lame like that. Because the truth is, I can barely look at you right now. That's how unbelievably gorgeous you are."

Thank you. That's the nicest compliment anyone has ever given me. Sebastian, I have feelings for you. I want to treat this wedding like a date. And then I want to go on a real date.

Any of that would have been acceptable in Via's eyes. They were all words that were tripping to fall out of her mouth. Maybe it was his nearness, his size, the warm pine man-scent that was emanating from him, but Via found herself with a terrible case of brain scramble and she ended up simply blurting, "You look really hot."

She would have face-palmed herself right into a coma if it weren't for the sun-shaming, earthquaking, heart-stuttering grin that exploded over his face.

"Thanks," he said, his earlier intensity melting into a much warmer expression. His eyes skated lazily over her face, and he reached up to touch one of the gold studs in her ear. Her breath caught at the intimate feel of his rough fingertips at her earlobe. He wasn't being seductive, he was just toggling the earring around, almost the same way that Matty had been absently playing with her necklace the other day. "You wanna get drunk and dance and celebrate our friend?"

"Yes," she answered immediately. It was the perfect invitation.

SEBASTIAN SIPPED CHAMPAGNE and laughed his ass off with Grace and Shelly and Cat and felt like part of him was walking around outside his body. Via was chatting with some people he didn't know on the other side of the room. She was accepting an appetizer on a toothpick from a caterer who nearly swallowed his tongue when she smiled at him. And then she was swiping a glass of champagne from the bar and settling herself in the free seat at their table, grinning over at Rachel, a dozy, loose, electric expression on her face.

The whole time, Sebastian felt as if he were split in two. Half of him was sitting here, in this chair, chuckling as Grace and Cat narrated voices for each of Rae's gawky cousins in the corner. And the other half? Well, the other half was over there with that little, warm, golden, wavy-haired sex perfection charming everyone she came in contact with.

He'd felt a variation on this feeling before, with Matty. Fatherhood had a way of making a man feel like his heart had grown two stubby legs and chubby little forearms and a tiny, blunt face alternately scowling and laughing. Even though he'd had a lot of room for improvement as a father in the first three years of Matty's life, it didn't mean he hadn't loved his son to distraction.

He'd always felt better when he and Matty didn't have much distance between them. He didn't like the world getting in the way of his heart. In a way, that's how he felt right now. Like he and Via were a unit, two parts to one whole and he just wanted to be *next* to her.

Actually, he wanted to be a hell of a lot closer than next to her. Inside of her was pretty much what he had in mind. He wanted to slip his hand up that green dress and watch his paw disrupt the fabric. He bet he could span her entire stomach if he spread his fingers wide enough. He also bet she had a light little touch. He wanted her to torture him with it while he took that dress in two handfuls and just smelled it. Honestly, he kind of wanted to do disgusting things to that dress. Destroy it. Just to take the edge off before he turned around and did all those same things to her.

When they'd come out of the bathroom area together, a woman Seb didn't know had called over to Via. Her face had lit with recognition. And as much as Seb wanted to completely dominate her entire night, keep her all to himself like a child with a Blow Pop, he nodded her off to greet her friend. She'd taken one step and turned back, looking over her shoulder in a way that had damn near brought him to his knees. If he'd had a pencil in his mouth, he would have chattered it down to a toothpick. That look she gave him, it was a little *see you later* promise.

She'd gone and mingled, and so had he. And now she was sitting much too far away.

Her eyes glanced over at his and ricocheted away immediately, her cheeks going a deeper pink than he'd ever seen before. He realized that his heart must be in his eyes. He must look like he was thinking very dirty thoughts.

Seb attempted to be a little more discreet. He tried to fix his face and look generically out at the crowd of people who were dancing to the cocktail hour DJ's Motown mix. But his eyes went back to her. He dragged them away. They went back to her. Again and again.

This went on for about fifteen minutes before Cat leaned over and nudged him hard in the shoulder.

"You better put a condom on those eyes, Sebastian."

"Excuse me?" He jolted at her words.

"Either you wear a rubber on those eyes of yours, or you're about to get Miss DeRosa pregnant from twenty paces."

Sebastian, extremely aware that he was talking to his son's second-grade teacher right now, had the humility to look pretty chagrined. He dragged a hand over his face and tried to wipe the dirty sex thoughts off of it. "That obvious, huh?"

Cat raised an eyebrow and her glass of champagne to her lips. "About as subtle as a jackhammer."

"She looks really, really beautiful. I'm, ah, having trouble keeping my eyes to myself."

Cat clapped her mouth closed, like she was stopping herself from saying something.

Sebastian rolled his hand through the air like, *spit it out*.

Cat leaned forward. "Seb, she's making that same face right back at you. Ah! There's my husband. He couldn't make it in time for the ceremony, but now that he's here, I'm going to get horribly drunk and do illegal things to him."

She slapped Seb hard on the shoulder and rose. He wondered vaguely if other parents had this kind of relationship with their children's educators. Probably not.

Seb felt a light heat on the side of his face and looked

up fast enough to catch Via unawares. Sure enough, she was watching him. And the look on her face was…very inappropriate. In fact, she was looking at him like she was trying to get *him* pregnant at twenty paces. He cleared his throat, took a deep breath and lifted his chin up once, as if to say, *Come over here.*

Her eyes on his, she rose from her seat with all the effortless grace of a bird. God, she was beautiful. A second later, she plunked down in the seat that Cat had just vacated and leaned across Seb to say something to Grace and Shelly that Seb didn't even hear.

He was too busy suffocating in the nearness of her. Her bare shoulder firmly pushed into his as she leaned across him. A laugh tremored through her and shook something loose in Seb's chest. He looked down and her fingers were in a pyramid on the seat of her chair as she held herself in a lean. He wished she'd put her hand on his leg instead.

Seb let out a long, low breath and laid his arm along the back of her chair. *Good enough for now.* When she leaned back, the ends of her hair danced over his arm.

She looked up at him, an expression on her face that he couldn't quite interpret.

"What?"

"Nothing," she replied way too quickly. She glanced at his armpit and looked away.

"Seriously." He nudged her warm, soft side with his free hand. "What is it?"

She sighed, like she didn't want to say what she was about to say. "You just smell really good is all."

He grinned, smug and so damn happy. "Glad you like it."

She grumbled something into her champagne that he

didn't quite catch, but this time, she staunchly refused to reveal it.

The reception went into full swing after that. The happy couple was announced by the DJ, and Seb grinned when Via jumped to her feet to cheer.

"Look at them!" Via teared up. "God, can you imagine being that happy?"

Uh. Yeah.

He was pretty much that happy right this very second.

Then everybody filed back to be seated for dinner. Seb's eyebrows rose in surprise as he glanced around the table. Rachel had brought a date to the wedding, he hadn't noticed before.

"Apparently, Geeky Greg has *major* game," he whispered in Via's ear, causing her to snort into her water.

"Good for him," Via replied, and then her eyes went thoughtful. "And good for her, too. They've been looking at each other like they're the luckiest two people on the planet."

Via was just so sweet, always seeing the best in—

"But frankly, I wouldn't care either way as long as it means Rachel stops jamming your biceps between her boobs."

Now it was Seb's turn to choke on his water. He coughed it out and turned to her with a little smile that he attempted to smother. "You noticed that, huh?"

"Sebastian, the astronauts in the Space Station noticed that. She's not exactly subtle, is she?"

He thought about making a joke but instead erred on the side of complete and utter transparency. He didn't want her worrying. He'd had a taste of that watching Christian the bartender fawn all over her and he wasn't a fan. "Then you probably noticed me removing my biceps from said boobs over and over."

She raised an eyebrow. "I noticed."

"And since you're such a careful observer, you may have noticed that I'm not a flirt." One of his fingers, still on the back of her chair, lightly, breathlessly, played in the ends of her hair for just a moment.

Her eyes cut to that side and then back at him. "I have quite a bit of evidence to the contrary, Seb," she said dryly.

He laughed. "Well, let me be clear then. I'm not a flirt with anyone I'm not completely swept away by."

Her face went from dry and amused to pliant and soft. Soft like warm pillows and wet lips and down comforters and snow outside and *come here, let's do that again*.

They let out twin breaths and then simultaneously turned away to gulp champagne. This was getting out of hand.

A light tinkling of metal on a glass rang out through the hall, and all the teachers at the PS 128 table straightened up.

"Does anyone else feel like a staff meeting is getting called to order?" Grace hissed across the table and made them all burst out laughing.

Sadie, sitting at the head table, grinned over at her teacher buddies like she knew exactly what they were all laughing about.

The speeches commenced, and the caterers set out food on the tables in large bowls. It was family style with about thirty dishes to choose from.

"Jesus, this is like Thanksgiving," Seb muttered to Via.

A solemn look passed over her face, and he wondered what her Thanksgivings were like usually. His were rooted in Sullivan family tradition, because he and Matty always made the trek up to White Plains for the holiday. It wasn't the most raucous day of the year, but the predictability of the traditions had come to be a sort of familial comfort over the years. And Matty loved it.

Soon, the speeches were over, the music was back on, and everyone was simultaneously grinning and groaning at the humongous slices of cake being passed around.

Sebastian couldn't eat another bite. He also couldn't possibly simmer in this seat for another second. He could have sworn that the air around him was shimmering with heat and lust. He wanted to collapse on the woman beside him, drag her under the table. The tablecloth could be their bedroom walls. Fuck it, he'd pay rent for that.

He made a last-second attempt at saving his sanity in front of people he respected.

"Wanna dance, Shell?"

His sweet older friend blushed, took a healthy slug of champagne and daintily wiped her mouth off. "Sure!"

Seb was a big guy, but he'd always been light on his feet. And so, apparently, was Shelly. The two of them danced their way from one side of the dance floor to the other. He two-stepped and boogied with her through an upbeat song and then twirled and guided her through a slow song. He had Shelly's arm looped through his as they strolled back toward their table. He thought maybe he'd take Grace for a spin and then, hopefully, spend the rest of his night with Via in his arms.

"Hold it right there!" Grace shouted as they walked up to the table. She had a chunky, retro Polaroid camera in one hand that apparently the guests were allowed to use. Seb and Shelly dutifully posed, and then Shelly rushed forward for the photo, shaking it.

"Now, you two," Grace demanded, hauling Via up from her chair and launching her toward Seb.

Apparently, Grace had quite the arm because Via stumbled forward on her spiky heels, and Seb just had time to catch her. One of his hands gripped her elbow, and the other splayed across her waist. He pinned her against him to steady her.

"Smile!" Grace called and Seb was dimly aware of a camera flash. He was sharply aware of the warm woman simultaneously slipping and settling against him. Via looked up at him, straightening, and Seb had the strangest feeling that his life had just become an abstract painting. The light and lines blurred and pixelated around him; everything was fuzzy and bright at the same time. The world was made of strokes of concentrated color. Everything was a gift tonight. The music, the scent of flowers, the sheer, contagious joy of the brides. All the energy of it funneled and tornadoed around Seb and Via.

And then Grace shoved the Polaroid into Seb's hand. "It's a beaut," she crowed.

"Oh," Via whispered, looking down at the picture that was just developing.

Seb stared at it as well, horror trickling through him like a drop of poison in an IV. He felt like the clothes on his back were slowly freezing, starting at his shoes and working all the way up to the collar of his shirt. He couldn't believe what he was looking at. He felt sick. And so fucking angry at himself.

Realizing that his hand was still on Via's hip, he slid away from her, taking the picture with him. He shoved it into the pocket of his slacks. He didn't want her to look at it anymore.

"Seb?" she asked.

Both she and Grace were looking at him like he'd just broken out in hives. Maybe he had. He felt hot and scratchy. Either his clothes were shrinking, or he'd just made a complete and utter fool out of himself. Via was looking at him, confused as hell, and she was so gorgeous there in her green dress that he was almost tugged back into their cloud of yum. But the picture pulsed in his pocket, and he was reminded of reality.

A familiar buzzing ring had Seb jolting. He pulled his phone from his pocket. "Sorry, that's Matty calling from Tyler's phone."

He flashed the phone toward the women and strode out of the hall. He took one back hallway and then another, striding up a set of back stairs that led toward the Botanical Garden gift shop. Everything was dark and quiet. Huge windows lined the hall, and the gardens were stark and spooky outside. There were no lights on in the hall, so Sebastian could just barely see his reflection in the glass.

Seb fell into a crouch and grabbed the back of his head for a second. He sighed and answered the phone. "Hey, buddy."

"Hey, it's Ty."

"Everything all right?"

"Yeah, Matty's just finishing up in the bath, and I wanted to see how the wedding was going before he got on the phone to say good night."

"Great. It's great."

There was a pause on the other end of the line that let Seb know he wasn't fooling anyone. "Then why do you sound like you're about to go play in traffic? Did something happen with Via? I thought tonight was gonna be the night."

Seb considered not answering. The Polaroid pulsed in his pocket again, and he pulled it out. "Things were good at the beginning. Like pretty clear that something was gonna happen, you know? We were all flirty and shit." Seb sighed.

"Yeah? And then what?"

"And then my colleague took a fucking Polaroid picture of us."

"Pervy."

"Shut up," Seb said, laughing despite himself. "They leave Polaroid cameras around for the guests so you can add your picture to the guestbook, I guess."

"So what's wrong with that?"

Seb looked at the picture in his hand. The sight of it made his stomach curl. He could see now that he'd been totally swept away since that happy hour last week. He'd been surfing a wave of adrenaline and desire for her. The only things that had existed were the ideas of *more* and *closer*. Reality had fallen by the wayside. But now he had evidential proof of reality in the form of a Polaroid and it was bitter as hell.

"I look old enough to be her father in this picture." The truth fell out of him like a dead fish onto a dock. "I've never really seen us together before, side by side like that. But she looks all young and fresh. She's laughing and leaning on me. And I look like Hugh fucking Hefner."

For months, he'd been slowly circling around the reason the age difference bothered him so much. And here was the answer, in convenient photograph form. He looked at this picture and he saw his own age. How much further down the walk of life he was than she. He knew exactly how it felt to bury a spouse. He'd lived through that excruciating hell. How could he ever allow himself to dump that possibility on someone else? He knew he was majorly getting ahead of himself, but if things worked out between them, he was pretty much guaranteeing that she'd be the one to put him in the ground someday. How could he ever do that to her? Especially knowing what she'd been through with her parents. It was reprehensible. Inexcusable.

"Seb, I'm sure that's not true. Your age difference isn't that extreme, and you're not that old."

"Well, I look decrepit in this photo. Old as shit. Half my fucking head is gray hairs? How come you didn't think to mention that to me? Hey, Sebastian, just so you know, you look like it's time to get your AARP card."

"Seb, you're being ridiculous. Maybe it's just a bad photo. Because you don't look that old in real life, and once again, forty-two is NOT OLD."

"What was I thinking, Ty? I knew it from the beginning. I'm way too old for her. But then she broke up with her boyfriend, and I just started thinking *what if*? You know? And I got carried away. But the truth remains. There's no way this is what she really wants. A boyfriend a decade and a half older than she is."

"You don't know what the hell she wants!" Ty yelled. "You're at a wedding with a beautiful woman who obviously has the feels for you, and you're spiraling out like a little bitch!"

"Ouch."

"I'm sorry, but it's true. Seb, you've been putting up obstacles for women for the last few years because you were still healing. And that's fine. But now you're putting up an obstacle for this woman, and it's gonna hurt you *more*. I can't take more Hurt Seb, okay? I reached the lifetime allotment. It kills me to see you sad, man."

"Tyler."

"But this time, happiness is an *option*, Sebastian. It's an option, and you're shitting on it. Why? Because you've done what everyone in this fucking world does and aged? Fuck you, man. Buy some hair dye if you have to, but don't fuck this up. Don't you dare trip at the finish line, you puss."

"Wow."

"The truth hurts."

"Apparently. Jesus, Ty." Seb scraped a hand over his face. His old-ass face. "Seems like you've been keeping that little speech on tap."

"You can thank me later after you wet your whistle."

"You're disgusting. I can't believe I let you babysit my kid."

"Speaking of, you wanna talk to your dad?" He said the last part away from the phone.

Seb heard scrabbling as the cell was passed over, and he let his racing mind rest for just a second. The picture burned him. It was horrifying and embarrassing. He looked like a creepy uncle lusting over a high schooler. But maybe Ty was right. Maybe he was focusing too much on all the things that could go wrong instead of the things that could go right.

"Daddy?"

Seb smiled. Matty was breathing too hard into the phone as usual. "Hey, buddy."

"Guess what Uncle Tyler let me watch on TV tonight?"

"What?" Seb leaned on the wall behind him, taking some of the pressure off his knees from the crouch he was still in. And he let his kid's voice siphon some worry right off of him.

VIA STOOD AT the end of the hallway. Sebastian was twenty feet away talking into his cell and crouching. From the soft look on his face, he was talking to Matty.

Something had been wrong when he'd strode out of the main hall, and Via had no idea what it was. He'd been spooked, like a bear scenting a forest fire on the air. She'd lingered for a few minutes before she'd followed him.

She figured she could hang back and say nothing and potentially watch this thing with him shrivel up and smoke away, or she could follow him and figure out what the hell was going on.

Via stood at the end of the hallway to give him a little privacy. She'd come up here intending to talk. But talking was the very last thing on her mind as she watched him smile into his phone, saying something soft and re-assuring to his son.

An image of him dancing with Shelly traced through her mind. Shelly had been so pleased, so happy to be dancing. Seb had towered over her, confident and sure in his dance moves. And now he was talking to his son on the phone. Wishing him good night.

"I love you, too, little man. I'll see you when you wake up, okay? Good night."

Seb ended the call and needled the corner of his phone into his eyebrow for a second before he shoved it in the pocket of his suit pants. He rose up slowly and sighed, still leaning against the wall.

He had no idea that Via was down the hallway, burning for him. Her heart galloped in her chest as she realized what she was about to do.

Her heels clicked on the tile floor as she stepped forward.

Seb's head flicked over and he looked surprised to see her. "Via," he started.

But then he apparently took in the expression on her face, because he didn't say another word as she rapidly closed the distance between them.

He looked torn. She couldn't tell if she was about to make a humongous fool out of herself. But maybe that made it all that much better. Because who cared about being a fool? Fear of being foolish had kept her in a me-diocre relationship with a man-child for two years. Fear of being foolish had kept her lonely for far longer than that. She didn't care if he rejected her or rebuffed her. She didn't care that when she was just five steps away his hands came up between them. She didn't care that she couldn't tell if he was going to grab her close or push her away.

There was just one pulsing word in Via's head as she closed the distance between them, laced her fingers in his short hair and yanked his head down: *this*.

This was what she wanted.

The quick inhale that said he was holding his breath, too. The almost vulgar heat of his calloused hands as he—thank Christ—firmly slid them over her bare back. The demolition of space between them as she clamped herself to him. This. This. This.

She might have marched down the hallway to grab him, but he was the one who started the kiss. He dropped his head and pressed his mouth to hers. His lips were a firm, experienced slide, and there was no describing a flavor like that. Man and chocolate cake and dark hallway where the autumn gardens leaned in on every side. Everything was bathed in deep blue light, and Via knew they'd somehow found their way to the bottom of the ocean.

One of Seb's hands lightninged up her back and tangled in her hair; he tipped her head back, and she realized again just how large he was. He surrounded her on almost every side. The new angle had her mouth slipping open, and Seb made a noise, tore his face to one side to breathe and came back to her. He dropped a gruff kiss to her bottom lip, pulled back and did it again. When he slouched, lifted her and landed his lips on hers, his tongue swept into her mouth.

Basically, Via attempted to climb the mountain of his body. She wanted the mountaintop. She wanted the crisp, terrifying summit. She thanked God that her dress had a slit up the side because it allowed her to hitch one of her flexible legs over his hip.

She was dizzy and could only think about tracing her tongue along his, which was why she was startled when her back was firmly pressed into a brick wall.

Her eyes fluttered open and she realized that he was caging her in, pressing her back and… *This*. Yes, one of his hands had reached back and touched at the strap of her high heel that was currently pressed into his ass. His hand traced up her calf and to her thigh then doubled back to the soft skin at the back of her knee.

Via gasped into his mouth as his fingers pressed into the hollow of her knee. He made a sound in response, and his hand slid higher up her thigh.

Then, suddenly, Seb was unhanding her and taking four quick steps away from her. Via sagged back against the wall.

"Fuck," he muttered, pacing past her once, twice.

And then he was back. One hand in her hair and the other reaching down to toss her leg over his hip again. She was breathing his air, swallowing his low, frustrated noises.

She stroked her tongue against his and straight-up moaned when his hand pushed a few inches farther and stroked over the smooth, naked curve of her ass. His hand kept going until he hit her hip and apparently found what he was looking for. The delicate line of her G-string. He was saying something directly into her mouth, but either it wasn't English or Via's brain had better things to do. His fingers spread across her hip, tangling in her underwear.

Her fingers ached and she realized it was because she was white-knuckling the fabric of his coat.

This.

His mouth was hot and endless and everything she'd never known existed. It struck her like a slap in the face; she'd been surviving on Easy Mac when all along there'd been filet mignon. She sucked at his bottom lip, bruised it with her tongue. She could feel the rough scrape of his stubble just at the border of his lips, and it enflamed her. It was like he was scraping her clean with his roughness.

She clamped teeth down, and he made the noise a lion makes in the night when he spots prey. That hand of his was farther up her dress, and he pinned her to the wall with his hips.

Via felt the shocking hardness of him press into her stomach, and she wiggled against it.

"Gah, fuck, goddammit," he growled against her lips. His hand slid out of her dress and clasped her over top of the heated silk. He pressed his forehead into hers. "We gotta slow down, baby."

"I—" She stopped trying to speak and just forcibly dragged him back into the kiss. Even with the heels, she was still up on the tiptoes of the one foot she had on the ground, trembling and reaching for that motherfucking mountaintop. He cradled the back of her head, nipped her lips and dropped his mouth to her ear.

"We gotta slow down," he repeated, his voice like chocolate gravel, a glass of red wine drip-drip-dropped from one lover's mouth to another.

"Why?" was the only word that made its way to the surface of Via's electrified, squirming ocean.

"Because you're about to get yourself fucked in a coat closet, and that is *not* how I pictured this going."

No one had ever said something like that to her before. She tightened and clung to him, her body stiff while her insides melted into the hottest honey. She was very aware of the fact that she'd soaked through her underwear.

"You've pictured this?" she asked with basically the very last bit of air in her lungs.

He laughed, kissing her lips, one eye, the skin just under her ear. "Jesus, yes. God. Haven't you?"

"Yes," she whispered, and their eyes clashed for the first time since she'd marched up to him. His eyes were storm gray in the dark hallway. There must have been a window open somewhere because she could smell the fresh earth of the gardens, the sharp, dying tang of autumn leaves. And Sebastian. She could smell Sebastian.

"We have to slow down," he asserted, for the third time. But Via couldn't help noticing that he hadn't unhanded her. His hands were on the outside of her dress now, sure, but he still had one hand on her ass as he pressed her into a brick wall.

She tested him, attempting to lower her leg, but he held her still, kept her wrapped around him.

"We don't have to," she said in a low voice, making sure to keep her eyes on him. "Slow down, I mean. We don't have to. I won't break."

He sighed, equal parts pained and joyful. Leaning down, he planted one openmouthed kiss on her neck. "You're right, we don't have to. But we're going to."

"Why?" she asked again, dizzy with heat for him, like she'd been dozing in a hot car. This time the word was much more desperate than the first time she'd asked it.

Slowly, he lowered her leg from around his waist and straightened her dress. He bent toward her, about to kiss her again, but instead he raked his hand over his face. The sound of stubble against his rough hand was loud in the quiet hallway. He pulled back and paced away.

Seb pulled something from his pocket and handed it to her. "What do you see when you look at that?"

Via felt shocked and soft, as she had the first time

she'd looked at the Polaroid. She glanced up at him and saw that he was legitimately waiting for her to answer the question. She cleared her throat and was pretty surprised when her voice didn't shake. "I see you, looking so handsome I can barely breathe. And you're holding me. And I see me." Unbidden, her eyes tightened with tears. She blinked them immediately back. "I look so happy that it makes me sad."

"Makes you sad?"

She didn't look up at him, instead kept her gaze on the Polaroid. "Because I haven't seen myself look this happy in a really long time. And more than happy. I look like I belong. Look at that! I look like I got invited to this party and I'm exactly where I'm supposed to be." She held the photo far away and then close again. "I haven't looked this happy since I was a child."

Since before my parents died.

The words were unspoken as she handed the precious Polaroid back to him. He studied her face for a second and then looked back at the picture. "That's really what you see?"

"Yes." She cocked her head to one side, wondering what he was trying to get at.

He shucked the Polaroid against the fingers of the opposite hand. "Via, I'm forty-two years old."

"Okay." What was he getting at?

"That doesn't give you any sort of reaction?" His eyes were shadowed and inscrutable across the hallway.

She wanted to cross over to him. But she had the feeling that a lot hung in the balance of her answer. She did the only thing she could. She told the truth. "It gives me a little thrill, I suppose. The same way any new information about you does. But I'd figured that's about how old you were." She took a tentative step forward. "I love learning new things about you, Seb. I'm hungry for it all. I wanna know everything."

He made a sound, almost like she'd punched him. Seb crouched down, onto the balls of his feet and gripped his silver-brown hair with both hands for a moment. She took another step toward him. When he rose up again, his eyes were blazing. He was bright with so many emotions she couldn't have begun to separate one from the other.

"All right," he said, almost to himself. "All right."

He stepped toward her and met her in the middle of the hallway. He reached for her face, took her in his hands, swallowed her up in that warm grip.

"All right," he said one more time and let his hands fall to her shoulders. "Okay, here's what we're gonna do. We're gonna stick to the original plan. We're gonna go downstairs and drink a little and dance a little and celebrate Sadie and Rae."

She squinted up at him, her blood humming and her heart turning cartwheels in her chest. "Okay...but I gotta say, I'm kind of partial to the coat closet plan."

He laughed and groaned and dragged her to his chest all at once. "Yeah. Me, too. But we're going slow, remember?"

Via sighed and traced her hands up the lapel of his coat. When she got to his neck, she tucked her fingertips into the collar of his shirt, making him squirm. "At the risk of sounding repetitive here, why the hell are we going slow?"

He quirked a little indulgent smile at her. "Let me think of a way to explain it." His eyes got distant as he thought, and his hands traced over her back. Via briefly let herself dream of a world where Sebastian Dorner absently touched her with freedom. It made her shiver. He brought those green-gray lasers back to her face. "You like dark chocolate?"

"Of course."

He smiled at her almost affronted tone.

"Well, you know, a Hershey's Kiss you can just unwrap and eat any old time, right? Circumstances don't matter, it's always—" he shrugged "—pretty good. But dark chocolate? A really nice slice of dark chocolate?" He brushed the waves of hair back from her neck and landed another one of those endless, searching kisses on her throat. "Well, that's not the way you eat the dark chocolate you've been saving."

He took a second and exhaled against her. "You ever tried to eat dark chocolate when it's cold? It's still delicious, better than any other chocolate by far. But if you let it warm up, in your mouth, it melts. And there are fifty—a hundred—times the flavors there. You can taste things you never knew existed."

She was pretty sure she'd never breathe again, but whatever, it had been a good life. "So that's what we're gonna do?" she asked, sounding like she'd just run a mile.

"Yeah." He kissed her neck again. "I'm gonna warm you up, Via. Until I can lick you off my fingers."

"Fuh-uck." She dropped her forehead to his chest and was utterly delighted when he burst out laughing. She lifted her face to his. "I guess I'm not gonna argue with that."

He slid his hands to hers, their palms meeting for the first time. She gave a deep sigh. She tugged herself away from him and yanked his hand. He loomed over her, barely budging.

"Well, let's go do the Electric Slide," she said, making him laugh and follow after her.

They held hands until they made it down the stairs and then she turned to him.

"You don't have to explain, baby," he said, reading her mind and making her pulse skitter at the endearment. There was just really something about that word in his deep voice that made her feel like she was lifting off from Earth. He took her fingers and rubbed them over the stubble on his face. "You're not quite ready for holding hands in front of everybody."

He kissed her fingers and let them drop.

She was both wildly disappointed and intensely relieved. Tonight, they didn't have to make public declarations. They could just dance the night away, laughing and shouting with their friends. And that's exactly what they did.

CHAPTER TWENTY

THE NEXT MORNING, Sebastian lay in bed and stared at his ceiling. He could swear the helium in his heart lifted him straight off the bed, covers and all. He scraped hands over his face and stretched, cracking nearly every joint in his body.

Lord, the woman could kiss.

He let himself drift in memory, eyes half closed, body heating as he remembered the feel of her in that hallway. Slight and hot, she'd been like a slim, electric feather in his arms. He'd wanted to lay her down right there.

She didn't care about the age difference. Seb still had to get over it. But he wasn't going to let it keep him from kissing her. It didn't bother her and that was just about all he needed to know. For now.

He rolled and picked up his phone off the nightstand. 8:00 a.m. He'd only slept for five hours after walking Via home and kissing the lights out in her front lobby. He hadn't dared follow her upstairs. He stood by his dark chocolate theory.

Seb could hear Matty talking to himself in the living room, playing some imagination game with his toys. Used to be, the second Matty woke up, he was feetfirst into Seb's bed. But these days, he often occupied himself for an hour or two. It made Seb both sad and happy that that was true. Kid was growing up.

He unlocked his cell phone and sent a text without thinking too hard on it.

Come over for breakfast.

He stared at it for a second. And then sent another.

Or invite me and Matty over for breakfast at your place.

He didn't care if he sounded bossy or overanxious. He needed to see her. In her normal clothes, no makeup. Just plain Via. He needed to kiss plain Via. The person he'd been crushing on for so long.

Right now, she was an emerald-golden-peacock-princess in his memory. That green dress. The glinting of her tan skin in the dark hallway. Shit. It was like a dream. Might as well not have even happened. He needed some good old-fashioned Sunday morning kisses. Messy hair and T-shirts.

When she didn't text back right away, he wondered if he'd texted too early. Hell, they'd been out all night, maybe she wasn't even awake yet.

But when he came back to his phone a minute later, toothbrush in his mouth, he saw a text waiting for him. Like a little present from the gods of crushes.

I'll be over in twenty. Should I bring anything?

He thought for a second. I've got pancake stuff and orange juice. And if picking anything up is going to delay you, then skip it. I just want you.

He rinsed off in the shower, slid some sweatpants on along with a soft gray T-shirt, slathered on a little deodorant and called it a good job. Another text.

You're making me blush, Mr. Dorner.

He opened his bedroom door and lingered in the door-way for a second. Gimme proof.

A minute later he got a picture of her. A selfie.

God. She was young.

And so fucking pretty.

Her hair was up in a bun, there was no makeup on her face and the hood of a sweatshirt was pressed up against her neck. Sure enough, there was a very healthy blush on her cheeks.

Seb traced a thumb over the picture. He completely understood what she meant last night, about being hungry for any little detail. Feeling thrilled about any morsel you might pick up. This picture was like finding a gold coin on the beach. He closed out of it, took two steps down the hall and then opened it up again. Just looked.

God, you're pretty.

He closed the phone, shoved it in his pocket and went to spend some time with his son.

MATTY ANSWERED THE door for Via; he had a bored look on his face, his pajamas still on. "Do penguins live in the Antarctic?"

But he pronounced it "Antarquick."

"Let her in before you make her a *Jeopardy!* contestant!" Via heard Seb's deep voice calling from one end of the house.

Matty stepped aside but his eyes were on her, still obviously waiting for the answer to his question. She stepped into the house and toed off her boots. It was chilly this morning, and she'd worn winter boots, thick wool socks, slim jeans and a dark blue T-shirt underneath her bulky ivory wool sweater.

"Some do," she told him. "But not all of them. Have you learned about hemispheres at school yet?"

He nodded.

"Well, penguins only live in the southern hemisphere."

"I told you she would know!" Matty hollered back through the house at his dad.

Seb appeared in the doorway of the kitchen, a dish-towel over his shoulder and a cup of coffee in his hands. "I should have known she would know." His eyes darted to his son. "Remember what we talked about?"

Matty half scowled, half smiled. His eyes darted between Via and Seb. "Yeah. That you're gonna kiss and that I'm allowed to ask whatever questions I have."

Well. That was pretty much the moment that the force field inside her chest pulsed once and absolutely exploded. The world didn't stand a chance. Planet Earth was swallowed whole into the feeling in Via's chest. Nothing was safe. She was in love with the entire world. The freckles on Matty's nose. Crabby padding in from the other room. The Armenian couple loudly chatting in their front yard two houses down. She loved it all. Seb's barely cut grass in his postage-stamp yard. The damn dishtowel. She loved everything.

He'd told his son that they were gonna kiss. Questions welcome.

Well, just. GOD.

The ache in Via's cheeks told her exactly how hard she was smiling. Seb crossed the hallway, gently kneeing Crabby to one side. He put the cup of coffee in one of her hands and framed her face.

"You look cute," he told her and kissed her.

It was quick and sweet and left Via utterly dizzy. She stepped forward when he stepped back. Bracing one hand on the wall, she took a quick, necessary sip of coffee. "So," she said, her voice just a touch unsteady. "Pancakes?"

"Pancakes," Matty agreed, reaching up to toggle around one of the knobbier parts of her sweater. He led all three of them into the kitchen.

VIA JUST MADE things better. He couldn't explain it exactly. And he didn't think the mystery needed to be unraveled anyway. But just having her there made everything a little brighter, tastier, sweeter. Seb watched as she and Matty chatted over the kitchen counter. She sniffed at the pancake batter and then proceeded to raid his spice cabinet.

It was nothing compared to hers, but, apparently, she found what she needed. She sprinkled this and that into the batter and then remixed it. She handed it to him to put on the griddle and casually searched through his fridge.

"Well, that doesn't sound fair," she was saying to Matty as she quickly diced up some bananas and put them in a little bowl with just a touch of brown sugar sprinkled over them. Next was the broccoli. Seb had no clue what she was going to do with that. But she did some magic something with potatoes, peppers, onions and garlic and had some sort of hashy side dish percolating within minutes. He watched her slide the broccoli into the pan as well.

"That's what I said!" Matty agreed. "But Brian said that it didn't matter how I felt. That he was the one who'd gotten it from the top of the play structure, so he was the one who got to keep it."

"But he was the one who threw it up there in the first place!" The *it* was a very cool mossy stick that Matty had found in the woods next to school. It had a bend in it that looked just like an elbow and had apparently been quite the hot ticket item at PS 128, grade two.

"I know," Matty agreed vehemently, mutiny in every line of his face. Seb, spotting the crayon that Matty had absently picked up, slid a fresh sheet of computer paper under his son's hand, wanting to spare his countertops.

Matty started drawing. Seb stepped around Via to put the first round of pancakes on a plate. He tried to ignore how good it felt to dance around a kitchen with her. Effortless and exciting at the same time. She piled the hash into a steaming bowl and set everything on the counter in front of Matty.

Seb poured orange juices and tried to transmit, via Dorner brainwaves, good manners toward his son.

As predicted, Matty wrinkled his nose at the suspiciously vegetable-looking side dish. "Do I have to eat that?"

"You should try it," Seb said.

"Matty, what spices do you like?" Via asked.

"I don't know. Salt. And cheese."

Seb's cheeks flamed. "God. I swear we don't eat like cavemen here. He also likes oregano. The green stuff in pasta sauce," he reminded his son. He snapped his fingers. "Oh! And rosemary. You like rosemary potatoes."

"Well, rosemary would taste really good on this." Via turned to the spice cabinet and hunted some down. She served herself some of the hash and then sprinkled some rosemary over top of her portion. She gave it a little flourish, like a witch over top of a brew.

Matty watched her, not entirely convinced. But when Seb scooped a little of the hash on his plate, Matty did exactly the same thing as Via and sprinkled rosemary on.

"Sweet baby Jesus," Seb groaned when he tasted the pancakes. "What did you add to these?"

She just winked at him. "They taste even better with the bananas and sugar."

They sure did.

They ate slowly, chatting and laughing. Matty carefully picked around the broccoli in the hash, but he ate everything else from it.

Sometime during breakfast, a mid-November gray drizzle had started, and Matty used the development to leverage himself into a movie. Turned out, he wanted to watch a movie that Via had wanted to see, too. Seb had already seen it twice, thanks to Matty's cajoling. It was some dumb sports movie. But he didn't complain. Because Matty and Crabby lay in a pile on the floor, happy and full. And Seb and Via sat on the couch.

First she sat squarely on one cushion, him on the other. It wasn't long, though, before he reached out for her hand, lacing their fingers and giving her a slight tug so that she was leaning against him. He tucked her into his side and was delighted when she curled into him, her knees pressing into his thigh.

By the end of the movie, Seb had an arm thrown around her shoulders and was driving them both insane by tracing pictures over the slice of skin at her hip where her sweater had ridden up.

"Okay," Seb said when the credits rolled. Good God, his voice sounded like he'd run it through a cheese grater. "Time for day clothes. It's not raining anymore. We're gonna hit the playground."

Matty rolled away from the TV and spotted their position for the first time. His blunt face pulled into a question mark. "Why are you sitting like that?"

"All snuggled up?" Seb asked, remembering that he'd

resolved not to hide things from his son. He didn't want to confuse Matty.

"Yeah."

"Because it feels good, and we both wanted to." That was the best he could come up with.

"Warm and sweet on a rainy day," Via added. "Wanna come see?"

She held out one arm to Matty, and to Seb's surprise, he automatically rose right up and skirted around the coffee table to come over to her. He crawled up on the couch and snuggled into her side, tossing his legs over her lap and wiggling his toes at his dad. "Yeah. I guess it's nice."

Seb tweaked one of Matty's toes and made him giggle.

"Do I still smell like sweaty muffins?" Via asked with a smile on her face.

"Nah. Just regular muffins," Matty said as he took a hearty sniff. "And the breakfast you cooked." He slid away from the grown-ups. "I'm gonna get dressed."

Matty ran full speed into the kitchen first, Crabby nipping at his heels. Seb knew exactly what he was doing. Checking the kitchen thermometer.

"It's thirty-eight degrees, Dad!"

"All right," Seb called back. "So that means pants and a long sleeve and good socks!"

"Yeah, yeah," Matty muttered and Seb watched him plod down the hall toward his bedroom to change.

"He hates winter clothes. Actually, he hates anything that'll keep him warm. The kid would live in the freezer if he could."

Via smiled, looking down the hallway where Matty had just disappeared. She squeaked when Sebastian looped her waist and tugged her to him, chest-to-chest. He was slouching back against the couch, and they were somewhere between sitting up and lying down.

"We've got about five minutes until he's back out here," Seb whispered into the hollow below her jaw. Via made a noise, something that reminded Seb of a nervous kitten.

He kissed her right there, where he could feel her wild little pulse under his lips. And he did it again. She tried to turn her head but he nudged her back with his nose, exposing that long, gorgeous neck. He trailed a hot line with his tongue up to her ear and allowed himself the distinct pleasure of finally laying lips to those little gold studs that had driven him nuts for months.

Then, one finger on the bottom of her chin, he guided her mouth to his. Maybe it was the time limit looming over them, or every little brush and touch in the kitchen and on the couch, or maybe they were just still that heated from last night. But they both immediately melted into the kiss. It was all tongues and stuttered breath. She was a hot slide against him, and he couldn't help but press his teeth into that pouty bottom lip.

They heard Matty's footsteps slapping down the hall, and he gave Via one more kiss, straightening them up. Seb rose and quickly rearranged himself in his underwear, not wanting to give his son an eyeful. When he looked down, though, he'd apparently given Via an eyeful. She stared at his pants, her eyes wide and unfocused, one hand over her mouth like she was trying to keep the kiss trapped inside.

Seb chuckled, because his son was home and there was nothing to do besides laugh. He touched her bun, high and a little crooked now. "I'm gonna put some jeans on."

He heard Via and Matty packing snacks for the outing and attempting to track down Crabby's leash. When Seb came back out, he blinked. Kid, dog and woman were all completely ready and *smiling* at him. He couldn't remember if that had ever happened before. When Muriel helped get things ready, she was efficient, but Matty always ended up in a foul mood.

Right now, though, he was holding Via's hand and grinning ear-to-ear.

Right. Okay. Wow.

The walk to the park only took about fifteen minutes. The sidewalks were dyed a dark gray from the rain, and the sodden trees drooped against the steely sky. Seb was just getting ready to warn Matty that Joy might not be there today because it was still drizzling, but sure enough, Joy was building some sort of fairy house on one side of the structure, and her parents sat side by side on the bench as always, matching ponchos covering both of their heads.

"Are those Joy's parents?"

Seb nodded, waving at them. Via walked over and sat right next to them. "Hello."

They nodded at her, smiling politely. Seb had been through this same thing with them before. They were always friendly, but it was like they really, really didn't want to speak out loud. Via reached into her pocket and pulled out her phone. She typed something into it and held it out.

"Vee-yah," Mrs. Choi attempted and had Seb's chin dropping down. He'd literally never heard the woman speak before.

Via handed the phone to Mrs. Choi, and Seb watched while the women typed things into Google Translate, trying things out in one another's languages. Matty and Joy played for an hour and a half before the Chois decided to head home.

Matty held both their hands on the walk through the park, Crabby sniffing along beside them.

"How did you know to do that?" Seb asked. "With the phone translator thing?"

She shrugged. "My dad was fluent in English when they came over from Italy, but it took my mom years and years. When I was a kid, she was really embarrassed of her thick accent. She always kept a pen and paper with her so she could write things out instead of speaking out loud. I thought it might be the same for them. Sometimes having it written takes the pressure off."

"I want you to come back to the house with us," Seb said, overwhelmed by her and starting to feel anxious at the thought of her going home.

"All right," Via said quietly, her eyes on Matty.

They cooked again, an early dinner. After dinner, Seb knew that she was preparing to leave. "You could stay, you know," he whispered against her lips while he kissed her in the kitchen. Matty was playing with Crabby in the other room.

"I know, but Matty will need some time alone with you. Today was a lot of new stuff for him to process. He needs some normal bedtime with his dad."

"I always forget that you went to college for this. Child psychology stuff."

"I went to graduate school for this, too," she reminded him, one eyebrow raised.

Seb growled a little, pulling her a touch closer. "Your master's turns me on."

She laughed. "If you say so."

Via slipped out of his arms and went to say goodbye to Matty. Seb followed after her.

"We're coming with you," Seb told her.

"What?" She knelt next to Matty and Crabby.

"We're gonna walk you home," Matty replied, already

well aware of the drill. Seb felt a swell of pride in his son. Look at him, being all gentlemanly.

"You guys don't have to walk me home. It's only 6:00 and a ten-minute walk, if that."

"Violetta, don't argue. Dorners walk people home."

"He's right," Matty said. "We even walk Mary home. And she lives really far away. And Daddy doesn't even kiss her."

Via laughed and threw her hands up. "If you say so," she repeated again, but Seb didn't miss the joy in her eye.

CHAPTER TWENTY-ONE

IT WAS STRANGE that Matty and Seb were the only people who existed anymore. She couldn't quite explain it. She went to work, joked with Sadie, kept up on appointments and ate dinner with Fin. But then she'd see Matty and/or Seb, and every image got sharper, brighter, that much more real.

Which was why Via was at loose ends when the boys went to White Plains for Thanksgiving break. The Department of Education had made the Monday and Tuesday of the holiday week professional development days. So, with the free Wednesday off as well, the kids had a full week off starting the Friday before Thanksgiving.

Via skipped that happy hour—gratefully, considering she still wasn't quite ready to face all the questions about her relationship with Seb—and headed straight home with Matty and Seb. She wasn't trying to be nosy, but her organized little heart nearly seized up when she saw the manner in which Seb and Matty were packing for their trip.

Perhaps that's how she wound up on Matty's floor, teaching him how to lay out outfits for the week. Next on the agenda was how to properly fold a T-shirt. But when he asked her how to choose which books to pack? She threw up her hands.

"That's like trying to tell an artist which colors to paint with," she told him.

Seb laughed from the door and hauled her to her feet. "You've helped my kid enough. Now it's time to help me."

Via followed him back to his bedroom, Crabby winding through her feet and hopping up on Sebastian's bed like he owned the place.

She paused at his doorway, like she still wasn't sure if she was invited inside. Seb came to stand right behind her, one hand up on the door frame next to her head. He brushed the hair from her neck and placed a kiss, a perfect kiss, on the back of her neck.

Via leaned backward an inch and let her eyes wander around his room. The walls were a dark, masculine blue that was still a little romantic somehow. He had a big wooden dresser on one side, a floor-length mirror on the open back of a closet door, and she could see an en suite bathroom, mostly white, on her right. There were two big windows over top of the bed.

Via let her eyes rest on the matching copper bedside lamps, the half-drunk glass of water, the dog-eared book and the—gulp—reading glasses. Everything in Via's body pulled tight when she pictured Sebastian lying in bed—shirtless, because hey, this was her fantasy—with those black-rimmed glasses on, reading.

Finally, finally, she let her eyes fall to the bed. That same green comforter she'd seen in a picture once was smooth over top of the queen-size frame. The bed was made nicely, but not obsessively so, a little rumpled in one corner. And the headboard was a raw slab of wood, obviously something that Sebastian had made on his own. The whole effect was gorgeous and sexy…and completely intimidating.

She felt his warm hand at her lower back, and Via realized he'd threaded his fingers through the belt loop at the back of her trousers. He gave her a gentle tug forward and backward, his mouth dropping to her neck again.

"You know," he whispered hotly over skin he'd just dampened, "every time I've pictured you in my bedroom, it was never for that reason." He pointed into one corner that she hadn't looked at yet.

A sound of total horror exploded out of her. She winced and covered her eyes with her hands.

"Oh my God, Seb. How can you possibly stand that?"

Her trepidation about his intimidating bedroom completely forgotten, Via pulled away from him, striding in and planting herself on the floor next to the open suitcase. She grimaced at the pile of unfolded clothes, the half-full travel bottles strewn about, the mismatched socks.

He chuckled. "I'm hoping you find this charming and not grounds to break up with me."

Via tried not to startle at his words. She hadn't realized that they were in a place where they *could* break up yet. Did that mean that he considered them to be together? Did that mean that they were exclusive? The idea utterly thrilled Via, but not as much as it shocked her.

Sure, they'd texted the entire week. Made out in his living room three times. And talked on the phone, just because, twice. But in Via's world, that could mean anything. Shit, she'd been sleeping with Evan for six months before he'd even admitted that they were dating.

Via yanked the suitcase toward her and fiddled with it, hoping to cover her reaction.

"Charming or not," she told him in a totally normal voice that she thanked the heavens for, "I'm about to have a coronary. Go fill these up while I start folding."

She shoved the travel bottles into his hands and turned to the pile of clothes. He set the bottles aside.

"I just totally freaked you out, didn't I?"

"What?" She didn't look up at him as she started pairing socks, tucking them into one zippered pocket as she went.

"Fuck," Seb swore suddenly. He sat abruptly on the ground and leaned his back against the bed. When she looked up at him, his head was down, and he was roughly scraping a hand over the back of his neck.

"Seb, what's wrong?" Alarmed, she dropped the socks she was working on and leaned toward him, one hand on the ground.

"Nothing. I just...feel so fucking old."

"Why?" she asked incredulously.

"Because I'm fucking this up. I don't know how to date a woman in her twenties."

"Seb."

"I'm making you pack for me, for fuck's sake. Like what the hell is that? And then I say the words *break up* and you look totally freaked out. Which is fine. Because I've obviously committed some sort of dating faux pas. But the problem is, I haven't dated since my twenties, honestly. Cora and I weren't even really dating when she got pregnant." He lowered his voice, aware that Matty was awake and playing in his room down the hall. "We were just kind of regularly messing around. And then we were getting married. Nothing in between. And before that, there hadn't been anyone serious in—God—years. So yeah. Basically, I haven't done something like this," he gestured between them, "in fifteen years, and—"

She cut him off when she crawled between his legs. He looked down at her. He was so big and she was so small that his bent legs pretty much surrounded her, and when he rested his elbows on his knees, well, she was completely inside Sebastian world.

"Seb," she said as she leaned forward and messed with

the buttons on his old blue work shirt. "I think we just freaked *each other* out."

"So I did mess up with the breakup thing?"

"No." She shook her head. "You didn't mess up."

His hands looped behind her as she gathered her thoughts.

"I was just surprised was all. I think because you have to be, you know, together to break up. And Evan didn't consider us together for, I don't know, half a year. I didn't even know if he liked me for months after we started sleeping together and—"

The look in Seb's eye had the words dying in Via's mouth. He looked like he could set paper on fire with his mind.

"Seriously, if I see that kid again, I'm punching him straight in the dick."

Via's mouth dropped open and she threw her head back to laugh. "I don't think that's necessary. Cosmically, you kind of already did."

"What?"

"I mean, I broke up with him because…" She paused. Wow. Sitting here in this warm little Sebastian cave was making her all kinds of comfortable and she was apparently just spilling all the tea. The words were tumbling right out of her.

"Because…"

The look in Seb's eye told her he'd already guessed exactly what the *because* was. Via took a deep breath. She wasn't going to skitter away from this moment. She wanted stability in her life? That meant leaning her weight against something that was strong. Things with Evan had been predictable toward the end, sure, but there'd been no substance. No strength.

"Because I realized I had feelings for you. And it wasn't fair to him or to me to pretend like I didn't."

The cave of Seb's arms and legs got noticeably smaller as he pressed her into his chest. She tilted her head to one side, and he mirrored her, following the nervous path. "I have feelings for you, too," he told her in that low, low voice of his that reminded her of thunder in the distance. "In case you haven't noticed."

He leaned in to kiss her but paused. "Just to be clear, I'm not dating anyone else right now. I have absolutely no desire to do that."

"Me either," she replied immediately, and made him smile. He tucked her in a little closer.

And then he did kiss her. His hands linked behind her back, and her hands stayed on his shoulders. But somehow, it was still the dirtiest kiss they'd ever shared. Maybe it was the scent of fabric softener on the sheets at Seb's back. Or the blue walls that made Via want to blink her eyes lazily closed. Or the fact that he'd just made that confession so much easier than it had ever been before. But Via was starving for him.

Her mouth was open before the kiss even started, her tongue lining his lips and then pressing viciously against his. Their teeth clacked, and she made a little sound into him. She changed the angle of the kiss, and he followed her. She was pressed so firmly against him that she could feel the hard length of him growing against her, and she couldn't help but press harder.

"Mmph." He tore his mouth away from hers and looked at the clock on the wall. "I've gotta—we've gotta—ah. Bath time. For Matty. Not for you and me. I mean. I wouldn't say no, but—"

He stopped rambling and came back to her mouth. She sucked his bottom lip into her mouth and needled it with her teeth. Pressing her forehead to his, she attempted to catch her breath. "Go put your son to bed. I'll deal with this mess."

Twenty minutes later, when Sebastian trekked back into the room with a damp and pajamas-clad Matty, Via was almost finished packing. His clothes were neatly folded in the suitcase. All she had left to do was refill the travel bottles.

"G'night, Miss Via," Matty said, crossing to her, his arms extended. She was already sitting on the ground, so he slid right into her lap, his arms around her neck.

"Good night, you sweet, perfect, little person." Via couldn't help the swelling of affection for the sweet kid in her lap.

"I'll miss you when I'm in White Plains."

She blinked at him. He'd said it with so much fact in his voice, so little trepidation. "I'll miss you, too. Eat some green stuff for me, okay?"

He made a face but sighed. "Okay."

And then he leaned forward, a pucker on his lips. Via gave him a light peck, her heart nearly exploding, before she set him on his feet and he padded out, Crabby following behind.

A few minutes later, she was zipping the bag closed.

"I didn't actually mean for you to do all the packing," Seb said from the doorway. "I thought it would be an excuse to get you used to being in my bedroom."

Via turned and rose up. "I don't think I could ever get used to being in here, Seb. It's so…sexy. So intense."

"Really?" He looked around in confusion at his room. "I think it's really calming."

She cocked her head to one side. "Of course you would. You're sexy and intense, too."

"Is that so?" he asked, stepping into the room and gently kicking the door closed.

Her eyes widened. This was a turn she hadn't been expecting.

"Matty's asleep already," he said, seeming to read her thoughts. "But I'm not going to ravish you. I just wanna see something."

Two steps forward and he lifted her up into his arms. He turned and tossed her through the air. Via yelped as she landed on his bed, bouncing and laughing.

"Yup. I was right."

"About what?" she asked, gasping, perfectly flustered.

"That you look absolutely stunning all mussed up and lying across my bed."

She straightened her blouse and smoothed her hair. "I'm not mussed."

"You're mussed." He prowled toward her and crooked her blouse again, tangled his hands in her hair. "And I like that I'm the one who made you that way."

Seb kissed her again. He stood; she kneeled at the edge of the bed. His hand smoothed around to the top of her ass and she had the suspicion he was lacing his fingers into her belt loop again.

Via's arms went around the barrel of his chest and up to press against his shoulders. "God, you're big," she whispered. "I can barely touch my own fingers behind you. How much do you weigh?"

"Excuse me?" he chuckled against her lips, and the hand at her ass deftly untucked her blouse. His thumb traced a circle on her bare skin, electrifying and melting her all at once.

"You're just, I don't know, built like an animal. So big. So sturdy. I feel like if I could unzip you from here—" she pressed on the bottom of his throat "—to here—"

and down to his navel "—I could probably fit all the way inside you."

"That is very weird. And really sexy somehow." He chuckled again; this time his other hand got in on the un-tucked shirt action as well.

Suddenly, Seb used his considerable weight and leaned her backward, her back hitting the bed. He crouched over her, one hand at her back, one holding himself up and one knee on the bed.

"We won't have sex," he gasped, practically into her mouth. "I just have to touch you a little bit."

"Yes," she whispered, incapable of more than that small amount of speech at the moment.

Seb's mouth fell to her neck and the hand at her back circled forward. He tugged her shirt all the way from her belt and let his hand trace over the hot skin of her belly, up to her ribs. He wasn't letting his weight down onto her and Via was pretty sure that was because if he did, there'd be no telling where all this led. He held himself just a few inches away from her.

She gasped when his thumb made a firm line at the underside of her breast. She wore a silk bra, but even that liquid fabric felt too coarse against her nipples; they were tall and begging to meet Sebastian. His hand was so big that she felt like he was touching her everywhere at once, and she shivered when his mouth fell to the hollow between her collarbones.

Seb slid backward, planting both knees on the floor. His hands rested on her hips as he eyed her, spread across his bed, her shins pressing into his chest. With his eyes on hers, he slowly lifted her shirt, an inch, another inch, until the golden expanse of her stomach was exposed, her hip bones jutting out above the waist of her pants.

Finally, Seb let his eyes drop.

"MotherFUCKER," he groaned as his eyes fell to the tattoo at her hip. A stylized line drawing of a rosebud. One of his rough fingers outlined it. "DeRosa," he whispered, tracing the rose.

She nodded. He'd understood immediately. Even though it was perhaps an overdone thing to get tattooed on one's body, Via had done it for personal reasons. It was her family's name in that tattoo. Her heritage. An image to remind her who she was and where she came from.

His lips were the next thing to touch the tattoo, followed by his tongue along her hip bone.

"This was here the entire time," he muttered, almost to himself. "Your trim little pantsuits. Classy gold studs. Perfect hair, polite little face. And the whole time a tattoo on this fuckable little hip. Jesus."

He kissed his way across her stomach to her other hip, pressing his stubble into her softness. Via tried to open her legs; she wanted to wrap herself around him. But he firmly kept her knees together.

"Dark chocolate, Via," he reminded her, biting her hip bone and making her jolt.

She let out a long breath. "Right. Yeah. Okay. Dark chocolate."

She gasped when he planted his hands at her hips and flipped her over onto her stomach. "I can't look at that tattoo anymore or I'm going to have us both naked in about six seconds."

But he didn't stop either. Seb kissed his way up her spine, pushing her shirt out of the way as he went. She couldn't stop tightening and flexing as his stubble scraped her everywhere. She made a breathy, desperate sound when she felt his teeth close over the clasp of her bra. He lifted it up off her back and pressed it back down. She could swear he was smelling her, rubbing his face into the smooth skin of her back.

And then—there was a God—he laid his weight down over her. Via tipped her head to one side, her cheek flat on the mattress as she felt his hardness press into her ass. She was completely covered by him, pressed down flat on the bed. Her lungs struggled to get in air, and she loved it. She completely loved it.

Seb rolled off of her and breathed hard, scraping his hands over his face. Via let her eyes wander down his gorgeous body, long and wide. She could practically see the heat squigglies rising up off of him like in the cartoons. Her eyes stuttered to a stop when she saw the ridge in his jeans.

The view was impeded by the jeans and the shadowy lighting. But Lord. She forgot about breathing. Who cared about it? It was a waste of time anyway. She watched her own hand creep across the bedspread. She marveled at her own boldness, and at how tiny she felt next to his big body.

Seb, his hands still pressing into his eyes, had no idea she was coming for him. She passed her hand over the ridge in his pants, and he hissed, like he was in pain, immediately leaning up onto his elbows. His eyes were on her, bright and wide. She didn't look up from what she was doing.

She outlined him through his pants. Up one side, pausing at the head and making him curse again, and then back down the other side. She laid the heat of her palm flat against him and then, finally, met his gaze.

"Violetta," he said, and she wasn't sure if it was a warning or a plea.

She let her hand drift to his hip as she lifted herself, crawling over him.

It was an hour before they tore themselves away from

one another. They were both unbuttoned and hot. Messy and breathing very hard. Via felt like a high schooler, all fired up and nowhere to go. Touching and kissing Seb was pretty much the hottest thing to ever happen to her, but they both seemed to tacitly agree that it wasn't the time to get naked together yet. Their sweaty makeout on top of Seb's covers was enough.

"I have to put you in a cab," Seb growled into the palm of his hand, his eyes, lionlike, on hers.

"Okay," Via agreed shakily. Matty was down the hall. This was getting out of hand. "I have Uber on my phone."

Seb shook his head, pulled out his own phone and dialed a number. "Hi, Rico, it's Sebastian Dorner. I need a cab at my house. All right. Just around the corner—she's in Bensonhurst, too." Seb's eyes shot up to Via's. "Yes, she's a she. Five minutes? Great. Just charge it to the card I have on file."

He was paying for her cab home. And he knew his car service dispatcher by name. Ugh. She really did have to get out of here before she did something insane like take a nap in his dirty laundry like the lunatic she was beginning to suspect she was.

Seb dragged her up from the bed and bustled her down the hall, like having her in the bedroom was too dang dangerous. When he got her to the front door, he sat her down on the stairs that led to the second floor of his house. He grabbed one boot and then the other, shoved her feet inside them. Next came her coat. He paused halfway through zipping it and pressed a kiss, over her shirt, to the plumpest part of her breast. He'd never done that before, and it had her jumping, her legs spreading at the knee. He pushed her knees back together and zipped her the rest of the way. Next, he found her hat and mittens in the pockets of her coat and put those on, too. Her messenger bag from school was slung across one of her shoulders before he brought her to standing and dragged her forward.

"I'll miss you when I'm in White Plains," he told her, leaning down.

"I'll miss you, too. Eat something green for me."

He smiled against her mouth. "I really will miss you, Via. I wish we weren't going for the whole week."

"It'll be good for Matty to be with his grandparents. And you and I can talk on the phone. And when you get back, it'll just be the best."

And she would try very, very hard, not to make her loneliness his problem while he was gone. A week did seem like a very long time when it stretched out, imminent and ominous.

He kissed her again and walked her out to the cab that was idling in his driveway. Seb leaned down, sized up the driver and apparently deemed him acceptable. One more kiss and then she was in the cab, waving bye and trying not to be a baby.

"IF YOU SIGH one more time, I'm going to send you out in the backyard with your son."

Muriel's voice snapped Seb out of his reverie.

"And you've promised that you'd stop moping."

"Right. Sorry, Muriel."

Sebastian was on his back on her kitchen floor, fixing the garbage disposal on Sunday morning. He and Matty had been in White Plains for a day, and Seb thought he was going out of his mind. He couldn't stop wondering how Via was spending her time. He knew that she and Fin had their own Thanksgiving traditions together, but there were a long few days rolling out before Thursday. He thought of her lonely apartment. How alone she'd looked at the softball field after her breakup. Over the week leading up to the holiday, there were bound to be lengthy, silent stretches of solitude for Via. Not that solitude was a bad thing, but he couldn't help but think that she needed more noise in her life. Noise that he and Matty and Crabby were more than happy to provide.

He really wanted to be in Brooklyn. He wanted to spend this week with Via. But he wasn't going to deprive Matty of time with his grandparents, and he damn sure wasn't going to subject Via to time with Matty's grandparents. Everything in him wanted to hit the gas, but he didn't want anyone he cared about to get trampled in the process. So here he was, lying on the kitchen floor, sighing.

"Don't be sorry." *Just do better.* The subtext had all the subtlety of the broad side of a bus.

Sebastian could see Muriel's neat white tennis shoes standing next to him. At first, he'd thought she was just overseeing his work, but he was pretty sure she was taking notes up there, trying to learn how to do it on her own if she had to.

"Right."

Things were quiet for a while, and he was impressed when she passed down a wrench without him having to ask.

"So, things aren't better with your woman?"

Involuntarily, Friday night passed through Seb's mind like a high-speed movie. He coughed. "Ah."

He wasn't sure what to say. He was talking with his late wife's mother about his new woman. He cleared his throat.

"Oh, come on, Sebastian. I deserve to know about things that affect my grandson."

"That logic is a little wonky, Muriel. If you're in the market for gossip, just ask."

She made a little outraged noise from above him that made Seb laugh.

"No, things are good, I think," he divulged, to soothe her. "I'm just in my own way."

She was quiet and he could hear her organizing tools. "In your own way how?"

He considered her question. "Do you think I'm too old to be doing this? Trying to start something new with a woman?"

"Old?" She scoffed. "Don't be idiotic, it doesn't suit you."

"I'm forty-two, Muriel."

"Yes, and…?"

"She's twenty-eight."

She was quiet for a second. "That's hardly a scandal. As long as she's presentable. Oh Lord on high, tell me she doesn't wear those horrid midriff shirts."

Seb laughed. "Cora wore those midriff shirts."

"And I thought they were horrid then, too."

He could have sworn she laughed.

"Well, no. She's very professional. And put together. She's sweet. You actually know her or might remember her. She was Matty's pre-K teacher."

"Oh. Yes, I vaguely remember her. She was good with Matty, if I recall correctly?"

"She was good with him then, and she's great with him now. It comes naturally to her, I think. But they also have a genuine connection. They're…friends." There wasn't really a better word for it, but it felt strangely inadequate.

"His pre-K teacher," Muriel repeated, and seemed to be racking her memory. "She was very small? Dark hair? I can't quite picture her. That year is…foggy for me." She sounded like admitting it was a real weakness.

Seb scooted out from under the sink and leaned forward on his knees. "Yeah, me, too." He slanted a quick look up at her. "She was at that softball game, too. I wasn't sure if you'd recognize her."

"I knew it!" Muriel crowed before quickly regaining her composure. "I thought for sure you were attracted to that woman. Though, I didn't realize who she was. Or that we'd already met."

"Did you interact with her much when Matty was in her class?"

Muriel lifted one shoulder. "A bit. I remember thinking she was good for Matty."

"Yeah. She actually did this one thing that really helped me after Cora passed. Do you remember that checklist I used to keep up on the fridge?"

"Yes."

"Yeah, she made that for me. And that was really helpful, in a logistical way. But the real thing she did for me was to kindly, gently, tell me that I was neglecting my son."

Muriel made a sound that Seb would never be able to interpret if he lived a hundred years. She sounded outraged and in agreement at the same time.

"She was right." Seb wiped his forearm against his eyes. "I was lost and spinning and a bad father. And she just firmly told me to do better. I clung to that for months. The idea that I could do better. And all I had to do was follow that little roadmap she gave me. And every day, I got a little bit better at it."

"It simplifies it to say it was all because of her."

"I know. It was a little thing that she did, in the long run. Compared to everyone else. Tyler moved back from Cali. Mary was over at the house every other day. You and Arthur have been Matty's other parents. No question. And there's no way I could thank you all for what you've done."

"And you shouldn't. We're family."

"Yeah. Well, Via wasn't. And there was something about what she said and the way she said it, it just woke something up inside me. Something that wasn't even awake before Cora died. She woke up this thing that had me wanting to try. No, not even wanting. Needing. I knew that I needed to try. And that there was no room to be scared. Or for disintegrating. All I could do was try to make things work for Matty."

He stood and washed his hands at the sink. Muriel handed him a clean dishtowel.

"And you found your way back to her?"

He nodded. "She works at PS 128 now." He paused. "I know she's young. But I've gone on a few other dates and they…weren't right. I just felt bad after them. I felt like I was better off alone than trying to make something like that work."

Muriel turned away from Seb, and he was shocked when her shoulders wilted once and then rocked. She was crying.

"Muriel." He put a hand on her shoulder. He was utterly aghast. God, had he told her too much? He hadn't seen her cry since that horrible night in the hospital. She'd been waiting for Seb when he'd come out of the morgue. He'd identified Cora. And the two of them had utterly broken in two separate chairs. Unable to even look at one another.

"I'm sorry," Muriel said, and Seb handed the dishtowel right back to her. She brushed tears from her face in a businesslike way. "I just got overwhelmed for a second. I was thinking about how Cora would feel if she knew you were dating. And at first it made me laugh and then I just…" She gestured at her teary eyes.

Seb teared up a little more, laughing through it. "She

was very territorial. Even with someone she wasn't all that jazzed about being married to."

Muriel didn't deny that he and her daughter hadn't been the perfect match. And he was glad she didn't. He could always count on her for her honesty. "Regardless. She wanted the best for Matty. Think about that, Sebastian. That was truly what she wanted. The best for Matty."

"Of course."

"Don't you realize that she would have divorced you if she didn't think you had it in you to be a good father?"

He whipped back, his shoulders contracting like a snail into its shell. The thought had never occurred to him before. "I—"

"A woman like Cora. So definite. So sure. Everything black and white and loud. She married you like that." She snapped her fingers. "Don't you think she would have left you in exactly the same manner if she hadn't known you'd be good for Matty?"

"What are you saying?"

"I'm saying that if this woman is right for you, then you owe it to Cora, to Matty, to make it work. Get out of your own way, Seb."

It was the first time she'd ever shortened his name and it hit him almost as hard as her earlier proclamation had. "Muriel."

"You are going to give that boy a good life. You had one woman who gave you a son, and now, apparently, you have another who's going to help you raise him. Figure it out."

With that, she was marching out of the kitchen and Seb was left behind, his mouth open like a fish.

VIA SET HER dishes to dry in the rack and sighed. Friday evening had been on constant replay in her head the entire weekend. She'd thought she would toss and turn with Sebastian gone, heated and uncomfortable. But she'd fallen into a deep sleep when she'd gotten home and woken up starving. She was attempting to distract herself with work.

And even now, Sunday late afternoon, the weak sun rolling sideways in the sky, she had files spread out on the breakfast table in her kitchen.

She'd just eaten a light dinner and was going to settle down to some paperwork. She had work tomorrow, but it wasn't a full day. Just professional development from twelve to four. It wasn't so bad.

But she couldn't stop the sigh as she sat down at the table. She was lonely. It wasn't a new feeling; it was something she'd lived with ever since her parents had died. The second she was alone, she got incredibly lonely. Time with Fin made it subside, time with Evan used to. And time with Seb and Matty damn near demolished it. But they were in White Plains for the week, and Via was here, with nothing to do but work and make a menu for her and Fin's annual Thanksgiving.

Her phone gave a buzz and skittered sideways on the table. Via leaped forward and nearly threw it on the floor in her haste to answer it. She tried not to feel guilty at the little bursting bubble of disappointment in her gut when she saw that it wasn't Sebastian.

"Hi, Fin."

"I'm gonna pretend you're actually happy to be talking to me."

Via couldn't help but laugh at her friend's intuition and candor. "I'm not unhappy. I was just…"

"Hoping to flirt with your man?" Fin's smile was very clear in her tone. "I don't blame you. How'd this week go?"

Via knew, without having to ask, what Fin was referring to. The Sunday night after the wedding, when Via was staring down the barrel of a week with her nosy colleagues, she and Fin had come up with a game plan for how she was going to deal with any of the possibly impending gossip: she was going to tell the damn truth.

We like each other, we're seeing what happens. What's new with you? That was Via's line. To anyone who asked. Via had practiced it in her head forty times on the walk to school and had still had to change into her backup shirt when she'd gotten to her office. She'd been a sweaty, nervous mess the whole day.

"Well," Via replied to Fin's question, "Sadie texted me from her honeymoon to tease me about me and Seb flirting on the dance floor. And Grace and Cat pumped me for information at the staff meeting."

"Did you give them the line?"

Via smiled. "Yes. And neither of them tolerated it. They basically threatened to give me a swirly unless I told them some details."

Fin laughed. "So…did you?"

"I told them a few things." Via thought back to the conversation with her two feisty friends. "It wasn't as hard as I thought it would be. They weren't gossipy, really. They were…happy for me. Thrilled, actually."

"Did you talk to the principal yet?"

"Yes. Seb and I had a meeting with her after work on Wednesday to disclose our relationship, so that she'd know we were dating, in case we were breaking any rules. But she just laughed and clapped her hands and claimed that she'd known all along."

Fin paused. "You don't sound as relieved as I'd thought you'd be."

"I guess I'm still waiting for the other shoe to drop? I mean, my friends have all been nice to me about it. But

I still feel like everyone is whispering about me and, I don't know, it makes me nervous."

"Cost of doing business."

"Hmm?"

"Sister, part of leaving the shadows is people realizing you're there. You've been so desperate to blend in as Via Nothing-to-see-here DeRosa, that you have no idea what to do with the reality of people actually seeing you. Odds are, they aren't gossiping. They're probably just processing. Even with as hot as the two of you are, two people steadily dating isn't going to be a topic of conversation for too long, you know?"

"Steadily dating." Via laughed out the words. "You make it sound so appetizing."

"Isn't that pretty much your dream come true?"

They laughed and talked for a few more minutes before Fin had an appointment with a client to get to. The second the phone clicked off, the quiet of her home seemed to fold in around Via. And not in a good way. Alone again. Blue aura. Defined by loneliness. She could handle it, the same way she always had. By filling up on love when she got the chance and one foot in front of the other for the rest of the time. It unnerved her that the few days she'd spent with Seb and Matty this week had been *so* special that her lonely moments were starting to seem even lonelier. It was like trying to get reacclimated to a cold shower after she'd been introduced to hot bubble baths.

She was starting to get worried that there was no going back to the old way.

It wasn't terrible, she told herself, this loneliness. But she curled her feet under her as she sat at the table. She tried to press herself tight and small, an attempt to ease the ache of emptiness inside her.

Via threw herself into her homework and was ten minutes into making notes when someone knocked on her front door.

"Who is it?" she called as she crossed her living room, pausing on one side.

"Seb."

Her heart kicked as she flung the door open. And sure enough, there he was. One hand on either side of the doorjamb, larger than life. His winter coat was open at the zipper and his boots were mostly untied. His hair was covered in a stocking cap. He pinned her in place with his gray-green eyes.

"Seb! Oh my God. Come in!" She stepped aside and he came in, kicked off his boots and hung his winter wear on her coatrack. "Why are you here?"

"Matty's grandma sent me back to Brooklyn."

She closed the door and followed him into her living room. "Why?"

"Because I was moping about you." Via's heart skipped. "She said not to come back until I've figured a few things out with you."

"What things?"

Seb didn't answer. He was too busy trailing his eyes over her, devouring her. "You're wearing your yoga clothes."

"I went to a class earlier."

He closed the distance between them in two steps and lifted her clean off her feet. He had two rough paws at her ass as she linked her feet behind his waist. "You drove me crazy that day you led the staff meeting through yoga. I've never wanted to bite someone's ass more than I did yours."

Via laughed as he stomped over to the couch and collapsed down on it with her straddled over his waist.

"As I recall, your ass looked pretty bite-able as well."

He grunted, barely acknowledging her comment as he traced his hands down her sides and back up. He tangled his fingers in the straps of her sports bra. His eyes fell to her chest. "Hey, where'd your boobs go?"

"Seb!" She laughed, outraged and charmed at the same time. "Shut up. I have the kind of boobs that squish all the way down in a sports bra."

"They don't have that problem in other bras."

"No, they're very respectable in a push-up bra."

He grunted again and this time his hips jutted upward just a little bit. He leaned forward and bit her exposed collarbone, his tongue tracing where his teeth just were.

"I should shower," she whispered, trying to rise up off him. But he clamped an arm over her waist and held fast. "I'm sweaty."

"Sweaty muffins."

They both laughed, and Via rocked forward on him. "What things are we supposed to be discussing?"

"I don't know," he growled into her neck. "Can't think."

She laughed and rolled her neck to one side. "Try."

He growled again; this time it was just pure, guttural noise. "She says I need to show you something."

"Show me what?"

"It's at my place."

"What is it?"

"I'll tell you when I show you." He bit the neckline of her tank top and peeled it down her chest just a little. She gasped when he buried his nose between her breasts and inhaled hard.

"Should we go to your place then?" she asked, her hips moving of their own accord over him.

"Yeah," he grunted. "After."

After what? She almost asked out loud, but then he

tightened his hold on her hips and rolled up to meet her. Sebastian's hands were everywhere. He was simultaneously holding her in place and rolling her against him. He had one hand tracing over the back of her neck, one gripping her ass. He was up under the back of her sports bra and tracing a circle on her hip bone.

His mouth covered hers and Via was pinned in place, vibrating and rolling and climbing. She was grinding herself against him to the same rhythm of her tongue over his. His jeans were rough against her inner thighs as she shamelessly press-press-pressed against the pipe between his legs.

She was rising, climbing, racing, and abruptly, she stopped, embarrassment a quick bite at the back of her neck. Oh God, she'd been humping him like a teenager. But he growled and grabbed her by the hips and started her rhythm all over again. This time it felt so good that her embarrassment burned up in the passion like thin atmosphere in the thrusters of a space shuttle.

"That's right," he said, directly into her ear. "That's right."

He was soothing her and stoking her at once, guiding her to where they both desperately wanted her to go. She was tensing, her fingers opening and closing on his shoulders. Her head fell back on her shoulders like she was looking for God in the ceiling of her apartment in Brooklyn. The couch creaked with their movements, and she felt a bead of sweat trace down between her breasts.

She spread her legs even wider as she rocked against him. One of his hands slicked up her back and held her weight as she leaned back and rode him. She felt it coming. Heard the warning shots. Knew it was coming for her and wouldn't leave until she was wrung out. Via barely had time to raise her head. But somehow her mouth found his, latched on just in time for her to snap the tether of her pleasure and curl her toes into the next life.

Her eyes were closed so hard she saw stars. She was delightfully sick with a wild dizziness. There was a well of pleasure within her that Seb was wringing out of her like water from a wet ponytail. She was aware that she was gasping into Sebastian's mouth. Saying things, probably his name. She may have begged for mercy. She'd never know. All she knew was that when the passion subsided, when she collapsed forward, melting against him, his arms came fully around her.

He hugged every inch of her, cradling her to his body like she was the most precious thing in his life. Many, many seconds later, she sucked in a breath and realized that she was still alive. Seb kissed her ear, her hair, her eyebrow.

"Je-zuss."

When she pulled back from him, he looked like he'd gone through the dryer. Rumpled and flushed and completely bemused. Embarrassment, stubborn asshole that it was, started to creep back into her.

He grabbed her chin, one arm still around her. "I feel like I just went to church," he whispered against her lips, kissing her, warm and openmouthed.

She laughed, surprised. "What the hell does that mean?"

"I mean I feel like I just got absolved or prayed or saw heaven or something."

"Seb." She glowed with both pleasure and embarrassment. Until he leaned up and kissed away the rest of her sheepish feeling.

"So pretty. That was so fucking pretty."

He slid his hands from her cheeks and then down to her sides. He gave her ass a little spank that made her squeak. "All right. If you have to, go take a shower and then we'll go to my place so I can show you the thing."

"But," she sputtered, looking down between her legs at his ridiculously apparent erection. "But you didn't…"

He pressed a kiss to her lips. "We've got plenty of time for that."

"But—"

"No buts. Just take a shower if you want, and then we'll get out of here."

CHAPTER TWENTY-TWO

SEB HAD VIA'S hand in his when he jogged up his front steps. They'd driven over from his house, and his leg had jangled the whole way. He couldn't help but feel that everything was up in the air with her. He wanted it good and settled, and, in his mind, the keys to all of it were at his place.

"Actually." He turned to her as they stepped in through his front door. "Leave your boots on. I have two things to show you. The first one's fun, and the second one's intense. Let's start fun."

He led a mystified Via through his house and out his back door. "I can't pin down this mood of yours."

"What do you mean?" He pushed open his back door and danced backward through it, leading her toward his workshop.

"I mean that you get to my house, intense as hell, seduce me in about three seconds. Then you pile me into your truck, and now you're two-stepping me into your workshop."

"You think that was me seducing you?" he asked, stopping so fast she clunked into him. He steadied her with two hands on her shoulders. "That was nothing. Trust me."

He kissed her fallen-open mouth and unlocked the padlocked garage door. He led her inside, closed the door against the cold and flicked on lights here and there.

"What did you—oh, wow! Seb, oh my gosh, this set is gorgeous. And it's so perfect for you guys. It'll look beautiful in your living room."

He followed her gaze to the oak slab coffee table and matching side tables in the middle of the room. They had gorgeous copper legs and tons of small accents up and down one side. He'd thought about doing the intricate copper decoration on all sides but decided instead that he liked it on just one side, liked the imbalance of it. It felt realistic to him.

He felt something open up inside him, the kind of swooping pit that the first plunge of a roller coaster makes inside of a person. His muscles tightened in anticipation. "What makes you think these are for my house?"

"Oh." She looked stumped for a second before stepping forward and slicking one of those perfect little hands of hers over the finished top. "Well, I guess it was just a feeling. But also because they remind me of the two-sided dining table that you said you're keeping for you and Matty. I guess they seem like a set."

He turned, eyed the table in the far corner of the workshop. He traced his palm over his stubble. He hadn't consciously done that, but now that she mentioned it, she was dead right. He'd gone and made a set. Except...

"I made the coffee table and the side tables for you."

She took a step back from him. And then another. Her eyes widened. "No."

"Yes. All the way down to the copper embellishments. I know you like shiny things."

"Seb." She turned a complete circle, like she was lost, like she was looking desperately for answers in any corner of his workshop. "I can't accept this."

"They're your belated birthday present. And of course you can."

"Sebastian, people pay thousands of dollars for these, I can't—"

"You're not *people*, Via. You're Via. You're Violetta. Miss DeRosa."

He was closing the distance between them and she was stock-still, her hands in her hair in the most harried gesture he'd ever seen her make.

"They're so beautiful. They need a real home, Seb. Not my crappy apartment on Eighty-sixth."

"You have a nice apartment. And it feels like a home. A little lonely, maybe. But these will help with that. And me and Matty and Crabby will be over all the time and that will help, too."

"What did you say?"

"Which part?"

"Lonely."

Her expression cracked and to Seb's horror, she went from amazed at the gift to utterly broken all in the span of one word.

"Via." She was in his arms and shaking.

"I am. I'm lonely. I'm so lonely. My aura is blue. Fin told me. It's blue for lonely." Her arms were between them. She was hugging herself and Seb was hugging her. He wished she'd put those arms around him.

"Via."

"Seb, I was lonely even when I was with Evan. I can't—oh God. I can't do this. I can't bring this into your lovely happy house where you sing Prince with your son and your happy-ass dog. And I can't accept the gift."

She was jogging toward the garage door, lifting it, and like a shot she was across the yard.

Seb went after her, locking the workshop up, because this was Brooklyn after all, and then he was through the house to her.

"Stop! Via. Wait." He tossed himself in front of the front door, his arms outstretched. "Please wait."

She had two stubborn streams of tears on her cheeks, and they damn near broke Seb's heart as they caught the light in his dim hallway.

"Please wait," he repeated. *Before you do something you can't undo.*

She stared at him, her big down coat halfway zipped, her hair messy from her hands. And she just put her face in her hands and cried.

She was quiet and sweet, but the sobs racked her body. Seb did the only thing he could think to do. He led her into her favorite room of the house, the kitchen, and unzipped her coat. He tossed it aside, right onto the floor, and gave his own the same treatment. Seb hiked her up onto the counter and shucked off her boots, chucking them down the hall, like that would keep her from leaving. He left her just long enough to put a pot of water on to boil. And then he was back at her knees, spreading them and inserting himself into her space. His arms went around her and his hands worked up and down her spine, one and then the other, a hot constant band of reassurance. He enveloped her and soon her sobs subsided.

He could hear the water heating behind him. He wrenched open his pantry, pulled out chamomile tea, and then, on second thought, his emergency bottle of bourbon. He made a cup of tea and filled a shot glass with whiskey.

He set both beside Via. Looked at them. Took a swig of her tea, took the shot and refilled it. She laughed a little through her tears.

"Here." He held up the tea. "And if you want it." He held up the fresh shot.

She took it.

"Please, baby. Tell me. Tell me what's happening." His hands went all the way down her arms. She swallowed down some of the tea and took a deep breath.

"I'm scared." Her voice was a whisper.

"Of what?" He paused. "I mean, me, too. God, me, too. But what is it that you're scared of?"

"What if…" she sniffled "…what if I'm bad for you?"

A fresh bout of tears blossomed and Seb wiped them away with his rough thumbs.

"Jesus. There's a whole cloud of fear in this kitchen right now. From both sides. Okay." He paced away. "For the record," he said, pointing out back toward the woodshop, "that is not how I thought that was going to go."

She laughed again.

"Okay." Seb was hitting a stride. Weirdly, it was Muriel's words that were fortifying him. "Here's what we're gonna do. We gotta get the fears out into the open. We've gotta just say them."

"What do you mean?"

"I mean, fuck our fears. Let's just air them out so we can realize how freaking stupid they are. Yeah? You said one. You're scared you're bad for me. Utterly ridiculous, by the way. You're so good for me that I pretty much could only see you and Matty for the rest of my life and be straight-up thrilled. But yeah, you said one. So now it's my turn." He took a deep breath. "I'm scared that I'm too old for you."

"What? The age difference doesn't mean anything to me. I think we fit on so many levels."

"Don't. Just rapid-fire here, say your next fear."

"Okay." She needled her lip. "I'm scared that I've been lonely for so long that I won't be able to shake it. I'll infect you and Matty with it."

"Good. Okay, I'm scared that when I'm fifty-eight and

settling nicely into my beer gut, you'll want someone your age. Hip and hot." This rising feeling was somehow fierce and soft at the same time. He was basically telling her that in some fairly prominent corner of his mind, he was considering an extremely long-term future with her.

Her eyes grew and she opened her mouth to reply but clapped it back closed. She shook her head at him. "I'm scared you think of me as a child."

"That's ridiculous. You're more competent than I am." He pursed his lips at the look she quirked at him. "Right. Fears. Okay. Here's a doozy. My biggest one. I'm scared that I'll die before you do. And you'll go through what I did when Cora died."

She reeled back from him.

Well, any hope he may have had at playing this thing cool went right out the window with the birds. His heart pistoned in his chest, and his hands went clammy. He couldn't tell if that look on her face was because he was basically handing her an invitation to be the person who laid him in the ground one day, or because he was saying he wanted to be with her until he died.

Her hand clapped over her mouth. But then her legs snaked out and wrapped around his waist, drawing him close. "I'm scared of that, too. Of you dying. I'm scared of me dying. Of Matty. Crabby. Fin. Shit, meeting Tyler and Mary made me so sad because I knew they were going to die someday. How fucked up is that?"

Finally, finally, her arms went around his waist. She was hugging him back. And still the words tripped off her tongue. "I'm scared that I'm too sad for you. I'm an orphan, Seb. I'm defined by grief. Sadness. Loss. Death. I've never been the same, it hit me at such a young age. You deserve happiness. You deserve to move on. I don't want to drag you down."

He landed his forehead against hers. "Via, you are not dragging me down. You're elevating me. You push me toward the light. God, you've been doing that even when you don't mean to."

He stepped away from her.

"Wait here. Don't move." Seb ran to his bedroom, opened the nightstand beside his bed and jogged back to her, still on the counter, shakily sipping her tea. He slipped the paper into her hand.

She was confused as she peered down at the creased, stained paper. Then her eyes widened when she recognized it. The checklist she'd made for him two years ago.

"You kept it."

"Via, I staked my life on it. You dragged me out of the muck. You took my hand. You were so kind." He couldn't help but kiss her. "So firm." Another kiss. "So fucking painfully honest. You told me the truth and I saw it. I understood it. Through your eyes. And I decided I wanted to live. I was dying and taking my son down with me. You made me live, Violetta. And you didn't even love me then. Now?" He cupped her face and kissed her again. "Now that we're here, all fucked up over each other? Can you only imagine how good we'll be for the other? Via, I'll *be here*." He pointed one finger down at the ground, as if to say this house, this earth, this life. "I don't wear suspenders. I'm not hip. But I'm here. Every day. This house. Matty. I do my job, and I show up. That's me. No matter if we're together—if you're lonely, you come to me. You come to me."

She nodded her head, her eyes blurry with tears. "I haven't had that in a really long time," she whispered. "A place to go no matter what."

"Well, now you have it. You've got me. And Matty. We're not flashy or exciting, but—"

"You're perfect," she gasped out the words. "Exactly what I want."

There were more words to say. Of course there were more words to say. But the air had gone all bright around them. His kitchen was no longer his kitchen; it melted away into one amorphous blob. In Seb's mind, there were now three things: Matty, Via and everything else.

And it was Via here in front of him that kept his feet on Earth. Her legs were clamped around him, and her fingers were somewhere, everywhere, they were suddenly hugging so hard it hurt. There were the tears and gasps of two people who'd seen the worst there was and were now seconds away from the best.

He was vaguely aware of lifting her. "Kitchen or bed."

The words were gruff and he barely recognized his voice as his own. Colors were blurring and sound was moving slow and fast, in great arcing waves.

The only thing that was in bright focus was Via's face. She cocked her head to one side. "Both?"

A gasping bark of a laugh burst out of Seb as he tumbled backward onto the kitchen floor, holding her tight and shielding her from the impact. They ended up with her on top, and Seb rolled them. He was shocked and thrilled when she continued the roll and pinned him backward again. He saw himself reflected in her eyes. They were both wrecked messes. There were so many emotions on her face, but there was one that was shining through the most.

He'd inadvertently named it before. And now he came face-to-face with it.

Love.

Miss Via DeRosa in love and on top of him. Her body slim and heated in that tight long-sleeved shirt and straight-legged jeans. Oooh Lord. He felt like he'd been holding his breath for years, and she was the first breath of air he gulped down.

She was still pinning him down by the shoulders, so Seb reached his hands down and popped the button on her jeans, then made quick work of the zipper. He slid her pants down the crouched curve of her ass, and he loved the awkward tug and pull of it. This wasn't porn. This wasn't perfect. This was him trying to get as close to this woman as physically possible. It was for pleasure, yes. But it was also because there was just so fucking much to say and language could only take them so far.

She let him shimmy her out of her pants and then she reached down and yanked his shirt off of him. They both laughed when the collar caught on his chin.

What are we doing? This is crazy. We need to talk.

All of that was loud and on the air. But they ignored it. Cast it outside like a stray cat. There wasn't room for anything in this bright, warm kitchen except for the two of them. He grabbed her by the hips and dragged her forward. He needed to inspect these panties.

Yowza. They were rose pink and everything. "I could eat these with a knife and fork," he informed her, sliding his hands up her thighs.

She laughed. "And you said I was weird."

Sebastian's breath caught as he watched her eyes drop to his chest. As long as he lived he'd never forget Via looking at his chest for the first time. She looked stunned, wild.

"This," she whispered, dragging one finger over the dips and planes of his chest and stomach. "This. This can't be for me. You're too beautiful."

He let out a strained laugh and looked down at himself, almost expecting to see something different. But he was just the same. Wide and substantial, plenty of chest hair and flat nipples. He shrugged. "Just me."

"My turn," she told him and gripped the bottom of her shirt in her crossed hands. His hands chased hers as they rolled up her body, tracing over every inch of skin she exposed. When she tore the shirt off of herself and tossed it to the side, the noise that came out of Sebastian was akin to pain.

She wore a rose-colored bra, lacy and sheer, but it was all that skin that drew his eye. She was perfect to him. The tight little set of her shoulders, the flat plane of her stomach, the toasted color of her Mediterranean skin. She had two knobby little elbows and something about that had a feeling tearing through Seb, bright and tender. He could see her heartbeat banging away behind her ribs, knocking against her body.

He couldn't help but raise up and press his lips to that little bang-bang-bang in her chest. It was the most important to him. She was skittery and nervous and turned on and warm and alive. She was alive, and her body had a rhythm that it refused to let go of. All that pain she'd withstood. Twelve years old and alone in the world, terrified and young. And still, *bang bang bang*, she'd kept on living. This was a woman who knew how to be alive, and for that, he wanted to show her every sweet, pleasurable thing he knew how to give. He wanted her to realize that *this* was her gift for surviving. This. This right here.

She was straddled in his lap, and he cradled her, one hand at the small of her back and one in her hair. Slowly, carefully, he started leaning her back. She let her weight rest in his arms and a tremor shook them both—where it originated, him or her, he'd never know. Because she was laid out in his arms, and there wasn't room for anything but this.

Seb kissed her mouth. His hands clenched on her as he realized that her flavor was beginning to be familiar to him. He could pick that flavor out of a million others. Their tongues found each other and slid, almost chastely. It was like a hug. He had a flashing memory of that day in the farmers market when she'd taken his one hand in both of hers, a hand hug. And now she'd figured out how to hug him this way, too. It had him teasing her lips open farther and taking more of that taste, the slick, secret gateway to her heart.

She was starting to wiggle against him, on his lap in just her bra and underwear. He tipped her farther back, the weight of her back on his forearms, him leaning over her. He convinced himself to tear his mouth from hers and started to kiss down her neck. He was jealous of every stretch of skin that came next. He wanted to taste, to kiss all of her at once. There was always some golden smoothness that called to him. He pressed his face into her breasts, over the lace of her bra, and growled into the soft heat of her there.

Seb used his chin to press one of the cups of the bra down and she gasped at his rough stubble over her soft skin. Her legs tightened around his waist as his mouth closed over her exposed nipple. He used teeth first and then tongue. She wiggled more and more, her fingers in his hair, holding him to her as he tongued her.

Then she reached back and unhooked her bra and tossed it aside, guiding him to her other breast. He growled again, liking this side of her. She raked her hands down his neck and over his shoulders. The movement of her hips became less a hot little wiggle and more a rhythmic ride.

Sebastian pulled back and looked at her. Her eyes were hooded and fuzzy, her mouth was open and pink, all swollen. There was high color spreading over her skin.

He felt like an ancient mortal who'd somehow swindled his way into an encounter with a goddess.

He rose up with her, his hands at her ass and her legs clamped around his waist. She wasn't hard to lift, and Seb suddenly felt a swell of protectiveness for this woman in his arms. His jeans were uncomfortably tight, constraining his hardness. He reached down and flicked open the button on his jeans. It didn't help.

"Seb," she whispered as he strode down the hall.

"Yeah."

"I'm really nervous."

"Me, too," he admitted as he pushed open his bedroom door and set her on his bed. He flicked on his bedside light, the one that cast the striped pattern of shadow all across the room. She was alternate shades of yellow and blue in the funky lighting as she knelt there, naked down to her underwear. Brooklyn was shut out by the blinds. There was no one but the two of them in the world. He sucked in a breath as he looked at her. Just looked at her kneeling there, waiting for him with her knees spread apart and one hand on the bed.

"Really?" She looked surprised by his answer and relieved all at once.

"Of course, Via." He shucked his jeans down, kicking them off one foot at a time. He wondered what sex with Evan had been like for her. Not in a jealous way, really, but in a sad way. The way she was looking at him made him think that she had some very specific ideas about sex. Maybe some nonrealistic ones. "I'm about to finally touch a woman I've been crushing on for so long. That would make anyone nervous."

Her eyes were on his underwear, and, he was sure, on his very obvious arousal for her. She glanced up at him and licked her lips, her eyes wide windows.

"Via." He waited until he had her gaze, her full attention. But then he found that he didn't really have anything left to say. Anything left was for their bodies to do.

Seb knelt in front of her and reached out for her ankles. He brought them forward so her legs hung off the bed. And that's just where he started. First it was his hands over her feet. He traced her arches, her ankles, he even screwed a finger in between her toes and made her giggle.

Next, he circled her calves, traced the back of her knee. He used two hands apiece on her thighs and touched every inch of her legs. Then each hip. Her belly button. He laid her back and pressed his hot palms to her breasts, but he didn't let himself get sidetracked. He laced one arm over her head and then the other. His fingers traced over her armpits, which made her shiver, and up to her elbows. Every one of his fingers touched every one of hers. His hands slicked up her throat before he turned her on her stomach. Sebastian dragged his palms over every slice of her back, tracing the shadows from the lamp. And then down into her rosy underwear and over her ass. When he turned her back to her side and lay on his as well, he buried his fingers in her hair. He touched her entire scalp and then the shells of her ears. Next were her eyebrows, her eyelashes, her eyelids. He walked his fingers down her nose and traced her lips.

"Sebastian," she whispered, and her lips trembled.

But he ducked his head, buried his nose in her underarm, and took a hearty sniff. Nothing, literally nothing, smelled better than a slightly sweaty Via DeRosa. She was still trembling nerves, struggling against her own desires. Her thighs worked against one another and he figured it was time to get them out of their own way. Seb slid down the bed and spread her knees apart. Without preamble or discussion, he landed his mouth between her legs.

VIA'S BACK ARCHED off the bed. Her hands flung out like she was looking for some cosmic handhold to keep her tethered to Earth. Her entire body hummed from his touches. He'd warmed every inch of her, set her buzzing and owned her. She'd know that man's touch if she were blindfolded, if he wore gloves. She'd never been touched like that in all her life. Like this was the most important thing that would ever happen to either of them. Maybe it was.

And now his hot mouth was between her legs. She still wore her underwear, and he didn't seem to mind. He worked her through the fabric, one of his giant hands circling her ankle and the other spread across her stomach, pinning her to the bed.

His tongue started to work in slow circles, around her clit, and Via's hips bucked. She wasn't sure she'd survive this. But then he was sliding upward and it was her nipple in his mouth instead. The hand at her leg started an inexorable slide up her calf and then her thigh as he suckled her. He was rougher there than she'd ever experienced, like he was trying to swallow some ungettable part of her soul. She couldn't think. Couldn't do anything much more than grab at his hair.

He took long pulls at her breast and then moved to the other. She felt each suck from somewhere deep inside. Apparently, all her good parts were connected by some internal, slippery, glossy chain that he was tugging at. His tongue was at her breast but she felt it between her legs. By the time his finger hooked her underwear to one side, Via was swirling with sensation and literally begging for more. She could feel the individual threads of the comforter beneath her, the tickle of his leg hair, the delicious scrape of his stubble.

And then—yes, God, yes—she felt one of his wide,

rough fingers at her entrance. He didn't press in. Instead he stroked her, playing in her wetness and groaning against her breast. His mouth slicked up to her neck, her ear.

"I want inside you, baby. I've touched you almost everywhere, and now I want inside."

She let her knee fall even wider to the side. "Yes. Seb. Please."

He pushed that thick digit inside her quickly, and he turned his face into the comforter and said her name into the bed. He was still, but she was electric, riding an internal beat and pushing herself against the heel of his hand.

A moment passed and he lifted his head, a little smile on his face. "That's my job," he told her. He reared back, onto his knees, and tossed that loose leg over his shoulder. One of his hands stilled her hips and the other worked itself even farther inside her. He didn't tease her. He circled her clit with his thumb insistently, watching her face and increasing the pressure when she could take it.

"That's right, baby," he murmured when she started to gasp, when her eyes started rolling back. "Don't fight it. Just give it up. Give it to me."

It hit her in a long, rolling wave that had no clear beginning and no clear end. Her body was tight and arching as she tried to tame the pleasure that wanted no leash, no master. The pleasure he gave her fully owned her body. Her leg pressed so hard into his shoulder, she couldn't tell whose skin was whose. She shook with the rolling perfection of it. The tips of her breasts seemed to spark and ache. The best orgasm of her life, and somehow, she needed more.

Seb, seeming to sense that she needed closeness, stripped off her underwear and fell over her. His mouth came to hers and both thumbs to her breasts. He was gentle on her tender, glittering body, but even his small little teases against her nipples were waking her again. She wrapped her legs around his waist, smashing her heat against his hardness.

"You're so pretty when you come. Seriously, I hope it's the last thing I see before I die."

She laughed, surprised, but it ended on a moan when he kicked his hips forward and pressed them together. The only thing that separated them was his underwear. She was ready. She needed him. It was time. Now.

"Seb," she said, her hands falling to his hips and pushing at the waistband of his underwear. But he slithered away from her, back down her body until he was face-to-face with her womanhood.

Via's heartbeat kicked up another notch, and some of the nerves he'd fully dispelled when he'd first laid her down started to pick their dizzy heads up from the floor. His gaze was penetrating and heated, and she resisted the urge to wiggle.

She gasped when he grabbed her firmly by the hips and rolled her. Somehow, Via ended up on her hands and knees on the bed straddled over his head. She looked down at him, self-consciousness rising in her until he gripped her ass and dragged her down to his mouth.

Any protesting she might have done immediately dried up at his first, hot contact. He didn't go in for the kill. At first, he simply tasted her. Via's legs tensed and trembled on either side of his face as he slammed his eyes shut and slipped his tongue inside her. His hands tightened on her ass as he groaned, a helpless, captive noise.

"I knew it," he groaned against her. "I knew it."

Were she capable of words, she might have asked what it was that he knew. But all she could do was grip the sheets and hang on for dear life. His tongue was dangerous, deadly, insistent. He sucked and pulled, swirled and circled. He was by far the most skilled lover she'd ever been with and she knew why—he was creative. He was practically playing in her. Gripping and paying attention and enjoying himself. She dropped her head to watch him and saw his eyes were trailing their way up her body, immensely appreciating the view. His feet were planted and his hips were working upward in the air. He was so hard, he was pulling the waistband of his underwear up and away from his body. It was that sight that had Via rearing back so that she sat up tall over him. He didn't stop eating at her, but his hands went instantly to her breasts.

She trembled, spread even wider and laced her fingers through his as he worked her nipples. This orgasm caught her by surprise. He almost tricked it out of her with some fancy dance step of his tongue that he did over and over once he realized that she'd pulled tight, that her eyes had gone wide and unseeing, that she was somewhere off in the stratosphere, tasting stars and shivering in the cold heat left behind by an asteroid.

She collapsed to the side, halfway on top of him. She was breathing hard and sweaty, her vision covered by the comforter. She was trembling, laughing, slicking her hair back from her face.

"What's so funny?" he asked, out of breath himself. He patted down the covers so that they could see one another.

"Nothing." She looked at him. "Everything. Dark chocolate."

He grinned and reached for her. But with a surprising burst of energy, she was rearing up and reaching for his underwear. She pulled them, quick as a flash, down to his knees and halted, full stop. She couldn't help but gape.

Because, Mamma mia.

She reflexively looked down at his feet. Yup, those were ginormous, too.

He kicked off his underwear all the way. "You look worried."

"No, I'm..." She didn't know what she was. "Really turned on. That is the most beautiful thing I've ever seen."

"Come on."

She was utterly delighted when he blushed and the body part in question grew another half inch. Acting on impulse, and because every part of her was dying to, she leaned down and licked all the way up his shaft, circling the head.

"Holy—" He lunged upward and gripped her by the shoulders.

"No?"

"Yes. A fucking million percent yes."

She smiled and knelt over him again. He leaned back on his palms and she felt his eyes on the side of her face as she pursed her lips and took him through the soft barrier of her mouth. She worked her tongue and swallowed him down as far as she could. Her eyes fluttered closed and she felt the light feather of his fingers pushing her hair off her face.

He threaded his fingers into her hair, and Via was thrilled and turned on when his breath washed over her in violent gasps. When his hips began to lift an inch or two off the bed, he gently pulled her off of him and dragged her into his lap, where he dropped his forehead to her shoulder and just hugged her. He held her tight and breathed so hard, the skin on one side of her body went alternately hot and cold with his inhales and exhales.

When he pulled back, she got a good look at his eyes. Dilated and desirous. "Via..."

"Yes. Yesyesyes. Right now."

He smiled, came back to himself just a touch. His hand struck out to his nightstand and fished around for a condom. He came up with an unopened box and the sight of it warmed something in her. Instinctively, somehow, she just knew that he'd bought these for her.

She tipped his head back and kissed the hell out of him. Even though the distraction slowed his hands down, she didn't care. She heard him open the condom, felt him reach around behind her back and sheathe himself. His hands came to her back and he did that one-after-the-other endless rub that simultaneously soothed and just about destroyed her.

Via made sure his eyes were on hers when she rose up on her knees. She reached between them but didn't look away from him. She guided the wide head between her legs. Via lowered herself down as Seb held himself perfectly still. His eyes were dilating and retracting, his mouth slung open, his face tight and loose at the same time. She took him in an inch and breathed. Goddamn, the man was big. She swiveled her hips and took another inch. Little by little, she worked herself down on him until there was a final two inches to go and apparently, Seb had hit his limit. When she pushed down the final time, he thrust his hips upward and they both gasped, frozen, said each other's names.

"Oh God," Via whispered. Her fingers were on his shoulders as her head fell backward. But then his hand was at the base of her head and tipping her back forward so that he could see her face.

She lifted up and then back down. They gasped and reached out for one another. There was so, so, so much friction as they clutched each other. She felt like she was touching damn near all of him. He hugged her so tight and she'd never felt safer or more desired in her entire life. She'd never in her life been made love to like this. Like it truly mattered. Like she mattered. There was no vanity here. No self-consciousness. This was about connection. Delicious, unending connection.

Suddenly, Seb gripped her around the waist and scooted them backward so that his back rested against the headboard. His hand fell between them and worked at her clit.

"I want you to come again," he growled, his head falling back onto the wall behind him.

"I came so much already." She figured it was probably his turn.

"Again."

She faltered in her movements, taking him all the way in and pausing. "I can't usually...during...never, actually." She really hadn't intended on divulging that piece of information, but it seemed to light some fire inside him.

"Try," he said. "Just try." He spread his arms out along the headboard and her mouth watered at all that muscle, those long arms, the chest hair on display for her. "I'm not going anywhere. Just try."

She knew what he was telling her. That he was a grown man who could control himself. That he wasn't going to go off like a rocket after three strokes. That she could work herself against him and really see what was what. The thought simultaneously thrilled and terrified her. But this was Seb. All handsome and plain and gray-green seagrass eyes. She trusted him. And that's what it all came down to.

Via lifted herself and slid back down. *Feels good but not quite it.* She swiveled on him. *Closer.* She jutted forward, took him all the way to the hilt and circled. *Yeah. There it is.* She found a rhythm, and judging from the pained/blissed-out expression on his face, it was working just fine for Seb as well.

She gasped and planted her hands on the wall behind him as she rode and rode. At first, he seemed content to just watch, but as she built, his hands came to her hips, up her back, her breasts and neck, her hair.

When she broke, her eyes wide and amazed, her body trembling like he'd hooked her up to a live wire, he let her shake herself out and then bowled her over and onto her back.

"Thank fuck," he growled, half laughing as he braced his feet against the headboard and pushed forward. "You were killing me."

He arranged her legs around his waist and braced himself on either side of her head. He was restrained gorgeousness, wild pleasure, an animal, a god. The lamplight lit him from the side as he pumped into her, the bed shaking on its legs and his noises of blurred ecstasy filling the room.

"Everything," he said into the skin of her neck. "Everything."

He tightened and pulled back to look in her face. Via had the distinct pleasure of watching Seb spiral out, unravel and come apart at e.v.e.r.y. fucking seam.

CHAPTER TWENTY-THREE

"WE'RE NOT GOING to sleep yet, old man."

Seb cracked an eye at her, blocking out the light with his biceps. "Just a catnap."

"Nuh-uh." She sat up, pulling at his arms. "No sleep. It's only 8:45 at night. I'm feeding you instead."

That had him pulling his arm away. "What are you making?"

"Come and see."

She slid all the way down his body to slither out of bed, and it was that more than the promise of food that had him lumbering to his feet. She walked, buck naked, out of his bedroom. He had to follow the woman who'd just destroyed him. Destroyed him and remade him. Seb sat up on the edge of the bed and realized that for the first time in three years, he didn't feel like an imposter in his own romantic life. He wasn't acting or faking it. He was exactly where he was supposed to be.

He grabbed his briefs off the floor and joined her in the kitchen, squinting against the bright kitchen lights. He watched as she grabbed his T-shirt off the ground and slipped it on, fishing around in the fridge for food. Seb simply couldn't believe that he got to touch her. He'd been waiting for her for so long that it still almost didn't seem real.

Seb took a seat at the barstool and watched while she started making pancakes. He could watch her clean a toilet, and he'd still be amazed at her grace. It felt strange to be anywhere but the bedroom. But especially in the kitchen, after their conversation there. The intensity of it still rang in the air.

"How are you feeling?" she asked him, apparently sensing the same thing. "After all, you know, that?"

"All what? The sex?"

"Uh, sure. But I also meant after my total and complete freak-out."

He rose and went to her, standing behind her while she flipped pancakes at the griddle. His hands slid under the T-shirt she wore and he hugged her back against him. "You weren't the only one that freaked out. And I feel... like I just ran a race. You know that loose feeling in your chest? Relieved and tired and healthy."

She turned to him, her eyes cautious. "It's not going to be the last time that happens, Seb. I'm not always happy. And I've been lonely for so long that it's changed me. Made a real impact on who I am. It won't always be as fun to be with me as it might feel right now."

Seb reached out and flipped off the stove. He picked her up by the hips and walked her into the living room. He sat her down on the couch and crouched in front of her. "Via, I can't help but feel like you're stating the obvious here. Let me just be really clear, okay? I understand that you are a complete human being, with a lifetime of complications going on inside you. I'm not looking to carve away the hard parts. I'm not looking for three-quarters of a person to be with. I want the whole thing. All of you. I want a real relationship. Where sometimes your shit gets in the way and sometimes mine does, and we're patient and we talk about it. I don't expect you to be issue-free. And I definitely don't expect our love for each other to just magically dissolve our respective hang-ups.

All I want is to keep growing. To keep growing alongside someone I can lean on and who leans on me. And to argue and hold each other accountable and celebrate the good stuff with and make love to and come home to."

He was breathing hard and gripping her knees. She reached forward and just like that, she was the one comforting him.

She slid forward so that she was wrapped around him, mostly in his arms and mostly off the couch. "You said love."

He leaned back and took her with him so that she sat on him and he sat on the floor. He made sure to hold her eyes with his. "I don't know what else it could be."

"You love me." It was half question, half disbelief. "You're sure?"

He tightened his hands around her; he wanted to laugh but could sense the seriousness of the moment. He cast around for a way to explain it. "Via, I'm positive. I'd suspected it for a while, but I knew it the second I walked up to the Botanic Gardens before the wedding. I'll never forget seeing you in that green dress for the first time. It was like being hit with a hatchet. A clean hit. Right down my center. I got changed from one person into two."

"What do you mean?"

Well, she was really gonna make him spell it out.

"I mean that before that, everything about me was easy to keep track of. All in one place. And then you happened, and now half of me is walking around in here." He tapped a heavy finger over her sternum. Like she wouldn't break. And he knew she wouldn't.

"Oh, Seb." She was looking at him now, with such tenderness it almost alarmed him. He was hit with the sudden urge to make sure she understood. Everything.

"I wasn't a good husband to Cora," Seb whispered, the

words like bitter poison on his tongue. Via was simultaneously the last person he wanted to say this to and the only one he ever could. "But I'm stronger now. Better now. I understand so much more about the world. We'll figure it out, Violetta. We just have to try together."

"Seb, I'm in. I'm really, really in for this."

"Me, too," he replied hurriedly, the words tripping off his tongue in relief and rising giddiness. "I mean, obviously I am." He laughed and exhaled and slammed his eyes shut. *I'm in.* Her words repeated themselves in his head. He held them tight, like gemstones in a fist. He was never letting them go.

VIA'S WETNESS WAS pressed against his underwear and she ached for him. They'd just had each other, and somehow she needed him again, so badly. It was the complicated expression in his eyes that did it. She'd watched him reassure her and awaken a fear of his own all in the same speech. They were two complicated people who were marked by the losses in their lives. But she hadn't lost Seb. And he hadn't lost her. They were here together and she wanted to, needed to, show him that.

Via leaned her forehead against his and trailed her hand down his chest. She danced her fingers at the waist of his underwear, and his breathing became jagged. His hips, under hers, pushed up into her and she felt him waking up.

Emboldened by the desire she saw in his eyes, Via slipped her hand into his underwear. He was very large and getting larger. Her breath caught as she pumped him in her hand. But the dang underwear was in the way and she rose up a few irritated inches and jerked them down to the middle of his thighs. He chuckled at the frustrated look on her face, but the laugh died when she sat back on his lap and pumped him again.

He was spearing up between them and Via needed something to lubricate him. She spit onto him and he swore a blue streak, covering his eyes for a second like the sight was too hot for him to even watch. But he was huge, and it wasn't enough. So, in a move she'd never even considered executing before, she dipped her free hand through her own wetness and used it to slick his erection. She smiled when his hands went into fists where he leaned back on them.

"Fuck, Via. You gorgeous—gah—just like that. I can't—oh fuck."

He was huge and practically vibrating, speaking gibberish, and she was making him like that. She was the one doing this to him. She felt a whippy power curl out inside of her. She understood, in that second, what he'd been describing. That this was what sharing the wheel felt like. Sometimes he drove and sometimes she did. And right now, she was driving.

She rose up on her knees and guided the head through her wetness, swirling it in a tight circle around her clit.

Seb's breath washed over her and she felt his knees rise up behind her. "Condom," he bit out.

"Where?"

"Bedroom."

"Fuck."

He smiled a helpless, tortured smile at her curse. "Are you on birth control?"

"IUD," she responded immediately. She understood what he was really asking, and boy howdy, was she on board.

"I'm clean," he gritted out. "I got tested a few weeks ago after—"

She slapped a hand over his mouth, suspecting he might be about to reveal something about someone else he'd slept with. Yeah. She was not a jealous person, but now was not the time.

"Me, too," she told him and sank down onto him, taking him in one long, hip-circling downward press that sunk him to the hilt and brought them face-to-face.

Seb groaned, making a noise like he'd been shot. Via loved it. The ravenous look on his face. His hair messy. She flexed on him, made him make the noise again.

"You look wrecked," she told him, rising up and taking him in all the way again.

"Ah—damn—I am wrecked. You're wrecking me."

She got in one more stroke of her own before he gripped her hips, fell onto his back and started pumping up into her from below.

Via was no virgin, and she'd watched a little porn here and there. But she had never seen something like this before. Sebastian Dorner, big bones and chest hair and flexing muscles, the tendons in his neck standing out as he grimaced against the pleasure. His stomach wasn't extremely defined, it was more a solid wall of muscle, but as he flexed himself up and into her, she saw a hundred different ridges and shadows she hadn't noticed before. His hips were taking them a good six inches off the ground with every stroke.

Via hinged forward, her mouth falling to his chest, and took everything he was giving to her. Seb braced a hand on her tailbone and growled when she bared her teeth and bit his chest. She'd meant it to be a sweet little bite. A kiss of pain to remind him who he was with. But he swiveled his hips, and the new angle he was hitting had her entire body clenching. Her jaw closed hard on his pec and she screamed her pleasure.

She pushed herself back, one hand on either side of his head, and saw the bite mark that she'd left. It was small but deep, feral and territorial. This was her man who was fucking her brains out on his living room floor.

"No one else," she told him. She was shocked at the words that she would never have said to anyone else in a million years. But if he was shocked, he didn't show it.

He merely locked eyes with her and nodded, his lips pulled back to show his teeth. Via pressed her palm to the bite mark, and Seb pressed his hand over hers. Together they sealed in her claim on him.

His other hand dropped to her clit, and Seb made sweet, lazy, little circles that completely belied the possessive, vicious strokes of him inside of her.

She said it again. "This is it for me. No one else."

With that, he was rearing up and pulling out of her. Via gasped at the loss of him but it didn't last long. He set her on her hands and knees and was suddenly behind her. She'd never loved this position before, but with Sebastian, she was leaning back into him, spreading herself as wide as she could. She wanted him to have everything.

He stroked into her, solid and confident, before he fell over her, bracing his hands over hers and placing his mouth at her ear. "Ever," he told her. "No one else, ever."

A sound left her, wild and weak and as bright as the light of a sparkler. "Yes."

He humped into her from behind, every stroke sending them a few inches forward. The carpet burned her knees and the heels of her hands, but she loved it. Everything, even the air against her breasts, was filled with charge. Hot and delicious. When his fingers found her clit again, Via flexed every muscle. She didn't care about what looked cute or being ladylike. She simply made her hands into fists, threw her head back and bore down on him fully. She was dimly aware of his teeth at her neck for just a second.

But then the entire world was ash white and full sensation, there was nothing but bright, high-speed cloud rushing into her from every angle. She was disintegrating and shrinking at the same second. Her body wanted to contract into nothing but was stopped by the heavy, pulsing intruder between her legs. All she could do was contract around him, so hard she felt dizzy.

She could hear Sebastian's voice in her ear but couldn't tell one word from the next. All she could feel was the pounding of his heart at her back, the relentless pump of him inside her. The orgasm finally released its delicious claws from her, and her elbows wobbled, her vision going fuzzy as he pulled out of her. She heard him grunt, felt him at the small of her back. She felt his hand press his wet hardness against her, and he gave one, two more pumps before hot silk spread over her back. She clenched once more, this time around nothing, and let his weight push both of them to the ground.

His stickiness was between them, his chest to her back and suddenly, they were both laughing their fool heads off.

"Sorry. Probably should have asked before I did that. You all right?"

"Are you kidding?" she asked, her cheek against the carpet and the whole of her body just sandwiched under his weight. "That was the hottest moment of my life. But now I need a shower, and I definitely need those pancakes."

Seb pulled them up off the ground. "I manhandle you a lot," he noted as he tugged her toward the bathroom.

"I wish I could return the favor. Pick you up and toss you around and show you how fun it is."

"Maybe in a pool or the ocean."

"Coney Island this summer."

He stopped halfway through turning the shower on. "Yeah. Wow. We're gonna do summer stuff together. The three of us."

"Hell yeah." She stepped into the spray and winced when it was too hot; she leaned down to adjust the handles. "We're gonna do all the stuff."

THEY ATE PANCAKES that night, smelling like Sebastian's soap and sitting on the kitchen floor. The next morning, they woke up in a tight knot of each other's limbs and stayed in bed until they absolutely had to get up. He drove her home, watched from her bed while she changed her clothes, and then took her to school for professional development.

He picked her up from work, too. They spent the night at her house, and Seb was so wildly taken with her bedroom. He just loved it. Her full-size bed that was way too small for him, her delicate white comforter and the fussy, colorful lamps. He loved the artwork she'd chosen—bright watercolor portraits—and the scent of her everywhere.

He took her to school and back the next day, too. When they woke up in his bed on Thanksgiving, it was with just the slightest air of melancholy. He'd go back to White Plains that day. Sebastian couldn't wait until he got Matty and Via in the same place again. Because even now, with Via laid across his chest, his heart was in two places at once. Even with all the FaceTime calls, it had been too many days since he'd seen his son. But that didn't make leaving Via any easier.

"We'll be back tomorrow," he decided on the spot, cruising a hand up and down her smooth back.

"But you're supposed to stay until Sunday!"

"Doesn't matter. Matty and Crabby and I will be back tomorrow. I wish you could come with me today."

They'd talked about it, spending Thanksgiving together. But in the end, decided that Matty and Cora's parents probably needed a bit more time to adjust to a new reality with Via in it. A holiday was too high pressure. And besides, she had traditions with Fin to uphold.

"Me, too. But this way is good, too." A sudden shyness crept into her expression. "Do you wanna get together tomorrow?"

He laughed at her question. "Violetta, yes. Why do you think I'm coming home early?" A thought occurred to him. "Can we come see you right when we get home? I think I'll explain everything to Matty on the way home and then he's probably gonna wanna talk to you about it."

"Of course." She snuggled into him. "I'll be free all day. And I'll have Thanksgiving leftovers."

She played with his chest hair for a minute. Enough to make him squirm a little. Gathering her courage, she finally asked, "Maybe this weekend you could bring my furniture over?"

"Your furniture?" he asked, leaning back to look in her eyes. "I thought you weren't accepting it?"

"Well, if you're still offering it, I really want it."

"I'm still offering."

SEBASTIAN CALLED TYLER from the road on his way back to White Plains.

"Lemme guess," Ty said, without even the courtesy of a salutation. "You're calling from some tacky chapel in Vegas."

Seb rolled his eyes and laughed as he merged onto the highway, talking through speakerphone. "And rob you of the joy of wearing a tux and making a best man speech? Never."

There was a weighted pause. "Wait. You didn't actually propose, did you?"

Seb laughed harder. "Jesus, Tyler, we've only been dating for like two weeks. No. I haven't proposed."

"I mean, don't get me wrong. I like Via, a lot. But damn, you almost stopped my heart."

"I rushed things my first time around," Seb said carefully. "And I'm not beating myself up over it or anything. But yeah. No. Slow and steady, that's more my and Via's style. Gotta make sure Via has her feet under her before we move forward too much. Gotta make sure Matty has his footing, too, you know?"

"You sound different, dude," Tyler said. "Younger. Kinda like the old you."

"Hmm." It would be ironic, he supposed, if after all that worrying about their age difference, actually being in a relationship with Via was what helped strip away some of the worn-out weariness from Seb's shoulders. "I feel good."

"A sex marathon with a pretty girl will do that for ya."

"Apparently."

Seb waited for another joke from his friend. But there was just a long pause, heavy with some emotion he couldn't quite put his finger on. "I'm happy for you, Sebastian. This whole thing, you deserve it. You really do."

"Ty—"

"Yeah, yeah. I know. Gimme a call when you're back in town. I'll come over. Your girlfriend can make us brunch."

When they hung up a few moments later, Sebastian couldn't quite decide exactly which aspect of his life was filling his gut with champagne, making him want to laugh like a maniac, put the windows down in the flurrying snow. He also decided it didn't matter.

This was his life. *His.* He wasn't acting a part. He wasn't pretending. He wasn't watching the world move on all around him. He was living.

The next day, Via opened her door to Seb, Matty and Crabby. Matty's fingers were a brilliant red from his refusal to wear mittens, and she couldn't help but kneel down and squash them between her warm hands. "You look like a popsicle," she told him.

Matty laughed. "There's snow outside!"

"I saw. It's been snowing all morning. I was worried about you guys driving in it."

"It wasn't that bad," Seb said, kicking his shoes off and making eyes at Matty to do the same. "How was your Thanksgiving?"

"Excellent. And yours?"

Via rose up, and he bent down and gave her a perfect kiss. Fresh from the cold weather and warm with affection. After helping towel the snow off of Crabby's feet, she led the Dorners into her kitchen, where she had some snacks laid out. It was a few minutes later that Matty leaned across the table and started playing with the gold thumb ring she wore.

"Via," Matty asked, twirling the ring, "Dad says that you're in love with each other."

Her eyes snapped up to Seb's. He froze for a second. He'd referred to love between them a few times. But the phrase *in love* fell between them like a sack of potatoes.

Seb broke the tension by shrugging his shoulders like, *duh.* Via couldn't help but smile.

"Yup," she told Matty, but her eyes were on Seb. She watched him absorb the impact of her words. *I love you.*

"Okay."

He was quiet for a minute, still fiddling with her ring. "Matty, do you have more questions? Seems like you do?"

"Well…" He shrugged. "Are you in love with me, too?"

Her breath caught as her entire world zoomed in on the little person in front of her, a blush on his cheeks and that mercurial brown hair looking almost blond in the sunlight. She could feel his legs kicking under the table like he was super nervous. There was nothing else except for Matty in that moment. Even Seb was blurred away. "Matty, I love you very much. You're very easy to love."

His eyes slipped up to hers for a second and then drifted away. "Okay." Then he turned to his dad, a small smile on his face and his little fist in the air. "Knuckles, Daddy."

IT WAS A few weeks before he said it back to her. The three of them were watching a movie a few days before Christmas. Matty was stretched out across them, his cheek on Via's leg. Almost asleep toward the end of the boring Christmas movie, Matty rolled over and reached up to touch the ends of Via's hair.

"Love you," he mumbled right before he buried his face in her stomach and fluttered off to sleep.

Seb had tears in his eyes when she turned to him, joy rising within her like a geyser. It was a feeling she'd become very familiar with in the weeks since Thanksgiving. Maybe she wasn't the most thrilling twenty-eight-year-old in the world, but her preferred lifestyle fit with Seb and Matty's almost flawlessly. Lots of home-cooking and chilly afternoons at the playground. She'd introduced them to the rustic joys of the Cobble Hill theater over the big movieplex down the street and the three of them had been back to see three movies together, Matty and Via hogging all the popcorn between them.

There'd been strangenesses as well. The first night that Via had slept over had felt odd for all three of them and had required quite a bit of conversation between every person involved. Although, in the end, Matty seemed to have adapted to Via's presence in their lives even faster than Sebastian had. For a while, it seemed he couldn't help asking her if she wanted him to get a babysitter so that they could go to the bar or—gulp—a club. She'd laughed at that last suggestion and firmly persuaded him out of the first. When she wanted to go to happy hours with their school friends, she did. When she wanted to see Fin, she did. She'd even started spending more time with Mary, which was a very happy side effect to becoming part of the Dorners' lives.

That night, still over the moon about Matty's confession to Via, they put him to bed and went to Seb's bedroom themselves. They snuggled in close, only using up approximately a quarter of the bed, the way they always did.

Via pulled the covers up over Sebastian's shoulder, because he refused to sleep in anything more than underwear but he always ended up a little cold in the middle of the night. She rolled onto her back and closed her eyes as he absently drew patterns on her belly.

"Are you all right?" he whispered, apparently sensing her tension.

"Yeah," she said. "I guess I'm keyed up from Matty. But, also, there's something that's tugging at me. It's like something is missing, but I don't know what?"

"Missing…" Seb asked, drifting toward sleep himself but at least making an attempt at being helpful.

Via cocked her head up and looked around the room. She hadn't moved in, but there were marks of her everywhere. A picture of the three of them on the nightstand. A small jar of multicolored flowers. Her clothes spilling from one of the drawers.

It hit her, all at once, what was missing.

"Seb," she whispered to him excitedly, her face pressing close enough to touch noses.

"Hmm?"

"I figured out what's missing."

His eyes came open. Realizing how close she was, he rubbed his nose on hers. "What's that?"

She kissed him, snuggling even closer. "I'm not lonely. There's no loneliness here."

He stared at her for a moment, coming completely awake. His hand slicked up her back and he drew her mouth to his. "I know, baby. I know."

* * * * *

If you loved the charm and romance of
Just a Heartbeat Away,
don't miss Tyler and Fin's story,
Can't Help Falling.

Read on for a sneak peek...

WHEN TYLER EMERGED from the bathroom, he walked up to the nearest concession stand. Taller than most of the other patrons at the game, he had a bird's-eye view of the crowd. The first thing he noticed was that every single male head—and some of the female heads—within twenty feet were all surreptitiously glancing in one direction. He sighed, already knowing the reason for it, and looked around until he spotted Serafine.

"What's up?" he asked as he sidled up next to her.

She immediately stopped turning in a circle, peering through the crowd. "I was looking for you."

"Why?"

"Three beers and a popcorn is a lot to carry. Besides, Joy decided she wanted a water and I started feeling hungry myself."

He cleared his throat. "Okay."

They filed into the concession line and stood side by side, a good sixteen inches of distance between them. He was conscious of the looks he was receiving simply for daring to stand next to this exquisite creature.

In a different world, he would have already dated and broken up with Serafine St. Romain. If she'd been just a skosh less attractive, or less spooky. If she'd made his palms sweat just a bit less. If there had been just a tiny bit less smoke in her voice, he'd have had no problem asking her on a date, texting her, sexting her, charming her, hopping into bed if and when she was into it.

The problem was, he happened to live in *this* particular world, where she was simply a perfectly beautiful, spooky, smoky-voiced vixen who gave him heart palpitations and made him feel like a preteen who'd never even check-yes-or-no-ed a girl before.

He shifted on his feet as they shuffled up the line, trying to ignore her and also memorize every second of standing next to her. He frowned at himself, wishing he could pour a gallon of ice water over his head. *Snap out of it, Ty!*

Tyler Leshuski was no inexperienced lad when it came to women, he reminded himself. When he wanted company, thanks to his extensive contacts list and the internet, it was the rare occasion that he couldn't find it. He was good-looking and smart and funny.

He watched a man bobble his beers as he double-taked on Serafine, almost breaking his own neck like a chicken.

Tyler shook his head at the poor fool, knowing exactly how he felt. There was just something about Serafine St. Romain that made Tyler feel like his heart was wearing clown shoes.

They finally made it to the front of the line.

"What'll you have?" asked the bored sixteen-year-old girl with a hairnet on. She was the only person in a twenty-foot radius who didn't look entranced by Serafine or mystified by Tyler's place in her life.

"Ah, three Buds, two bottles of water, a large popcorn, a hot pretzel, no salt. And whatever she wants." He pointed one thumb at Serafine and didn't chance a glance over at her.

"Mmm, chili cheese fries, please, and is there any hot sauce back there?"

The girl pointed listlessly at the condiments stand and

plugged the rest of the order into the register. She held her hand out for cash. Tyler wordlessly handed over a fifty, knowing he'd be lucky to get more than pennies back in change.

They went to stand at the side and wait for their food.

"What?" Serafine eventually asked him, turning to him with her arms crossed over her chest and those bright eyes burning a hole in the side of his head.

"What *what*?" he asked back, his eyes stubbornly on the kid slapping their order together behind the counter.

"I can feel your question for me. Just ask it."

He resisted the urge to roll his eyes, but just barely. He really hated all this psychic bullshit. "You got chili cheese fries."

"So?"

"So, I assumed you were, like, a vegan or something." He'd eaten with her before at Sebastian's house but had been too distracted by her presence to pay attention to what she ate.

She lifted an eyebrow. "Why?"

He couldn't help but laugh as he finally turned to look at her. He took her in, from her complicated dark braid over one shoulder to her makeup-less face, the silver and gem rings on her fingers and bangles on her wrists. He looked her over, from her loose embroidered top to her equally loose embroidered pants and all the way down to what looked like a pair of velvet slippers. She carried with her the scent of sage and something else earthy. As painfully gorgeous as she was, her look screamed earth-child.

"Because you're all…" He rolled a hand in the air, searching for the right word. "Organic-looking."

To his immense surprise, she actually burst out laughing. He was used to making people laugh. It was one of his favorite things on this Earth. But he'd yet to make *her* laugh like that. He'd thought she was most likely one of those

people who never laughed—they merely smirked instead.
Or chuckled behind closed lips. But here he was, blinking
down at a row of white teeth, her lips, so full in repose, almost disappearing in the stretch of her smile. He got that
solar eclipse feeling again and when he tore his eyes away
from her, a faded echo of her smile followed his vision for a
moment, like he'd burned his retinas on her laughter.

"I also happened to grow up in Louisiana," she reminded him. "They run vegans out of town down there."

So, she was a meat eater. He couldn't say why that pleased
him. He couldn't say much of anything, really, befuddled
as he was by her smile, her laughter. Why did he let this
woman throw him off his game so much? It was annoying. She wasn't *actually* magical, regardless of what she
told people. There was no reason at all for him to treat her
any differently than he would any attractive woman he happened to be attracted to.

His heart banged hollowly in his chest like a rock
clanging against the side of a bucket. *Holy crap.* He was
gonna do it. He was gonna finally do something about
the hairs that, even now, were rising on the back of his
neck. He'd been an athlete his entire life, and Tyler instantly recognized this feeling. This at-bat, at-the-free-
throw-line, let-the-muscles-do-their-thing sort of feeling.

"Let's go out," he suddenly blurted to Serafine, his voice
a little too loud, his eyes on the ground instead of her face.

Shit. Unfortunately, he'd forgotten to factor in the whole
clown-shoes effect she had over him. Could that have been
any more clumsy? He wasn't even facing her. He couldn't
seem to be able to tear his eyes away from the girl in plastic gloves brushing salt off his pretzel. *Stop watching that,
dumbass!*

Serafine turned to him and, unfortunately, so did the

woman next to them, obviously extremely curious to hear how all of this was going to pan out.

"Uh," Serafine said, her bright eyes on the side of his face. It became immediately clear to Ty that he'd just clicked on a swinging light bulb in a dark room, tied himself to a chair and begged a concession's line worth of Cyclones fans to mock him.

Tyler made himself meet her eyes. He was an eye-contact sort of person, dammit! He believed in introducing oneself with his full name, in firm handshakes, in looking a person full in the face when talking with them. He'd been doing it his entire life! Why was this so hard with her?

"If you want to," he added on lamely. Clearing his throat, he tried again. "Because I want to. Go out with you, I mean."

She just sort of stared at him for a moment.

"I mean that I want to take you out," he tried one more time. "I mean that if you're into it, I'd love to take you out sometime."

"Order's up," the kid with the food called. Ten seconds later, Tyler found himself with two arms full of food and drinks and no answer yet from Serafine. He looked down at the hot pretzel and popcorn, the beers balancing in a tray, and felt like he was tumbling through the air with his arms too full to catch himself as he fell. He wanted to toss the food in the trash and bike home. Why had he thought this was somehow a good idea?

She stood there, the water bottles under one arm and her fries in the other hand. "Tyler…"

Yikes. He could practically *see* the dot dot dot lingering in the air after his name. She'd dot dot dotted him. *Not a good sign, my friend.*

Copyright © 2020 by Cara Bastone

ACKNOWLEDGMENTS

I'd like to thank my husband, who is just as proud of my imagination and accomplishments as I am. Who walks our dog by himself when there is no pulling me out of whatever scene I'm currently cannon-balling into. Who did an *actual* happy dance when we found out this book was going to be published. If there's a scene in this book that particularly rang true for you, reader, chances are my husband was in my heart when I wrote it.

I'd also like to thank all the readers of the romance genre. Without your voracious appetite for the written word, I wouldn't have my dream job. What a positive, hopeful, hilarious community of people we are.

Lastly, to all of the people who have lent their brilliance and expertise to this book in order to get it where it needed to go: thank you. Tara Gelsomino, my unbelievably talented and hardworking agent, thank you for believing in this manuscript and fighting hard to get it published. Thank you, Jess Verdi, the very first person to take a chance on me in this industry! Thank you to Allison Carroll, my genius editor. I'm grateful for your vision and ideas every single day. Thank you to Chris Wolfgang and all the copyeditors at HQN who painstakingly strive for perfection. You're my heroes! And finally, to the entire team at HQN, I'm so humbled, honored and grateful to be a part of your Harlequin family.

Get 4 FREE REWARDS!

We'll send you 2 FREE Books plus 2 FREE Mystery Gifts.

FREE Value Over **$20**

Both the **Romance** and **Suspense** collections feature compelling novels written by many of today's bestselling authors.

YES! Please send me 2 FREE novels from the Essential Romance or Essential Suspense Collection and my 2 FREE gifts (gifts are worth about $10 retail). After receiving them, if I don't wish to receive any more books, I can return the shipping statement marked "cancel." If I don't cancel, I will receive 4 brand-new novels every month and be billed just $7.24 each in the U.S. or $7.49 each in Canada. That's a savings of up to 28% off the cover price. It's quite a bargain! Shipping and handling is just 50¢ per book in the U.S. and $1.25 per book in Canada.* I understand that accepting the 2 free books and gifts places me under no obligation to buy anything. I can always return a shipment and cancel at any time. The free books and gifts are mine to keep no matter what I decide.

Choose one: ☐ **Essential Romance** ☐ **Essential Suspense**
                       (194/394 MDN GQ6M)   (191/391 MDN GQ6M)

Name (please print)

Address   Apt. #

City   State/Province   Zip/Postal Code

Email: Please check this box ☐ if you would like to receive newsletters and promotional emails from Harlequin Enterprises ULC and its affiliates. You can unsubscribe anytime.

Mail to the **Reader Service:**
IN U.S.A.: P.O. Box 1341, Buffalo, NY 14240-8531
IN CANADA: P.O. Box 603, Fort Erie, Ontario L2A 5X3

Want to try 2 free books from another series? Call 1-800-873-8635 or visit www.ReaderService.com.